THE BAMBOO AND THE HEATHER

NITA ROSEMEYER

D0033512

BALLANTINE BOOKS • NEW YORK

To my two Jeres, husband and son, on whose unfailing patience and assistance I could always depend.

ACKNOWLEDGMENTS

Grateful acknowledgments to: Alice Hutson; Dr. Robert Flynn of Trinity University; Barbara Harris of the San Antonio Public Library; Junette Woller; Barbara Giacalone; and Karla Consalvi.

A final note of thanks to the German Consul and the British Information Bureau in Hong Kong for their generous assistance.

Library of Congress Catalog Card Number: 80-80519

ISBN 0-345-28740-1

Manufactured in the United States of America

First Edition: September 1980

FROM THE MEN IN HER LIFE, MAGDA MacDOUGALL LEARNED THE DIFFERENT MEANINGS OF LOVE . . .

ANGUS MacDOUGALL—At the end of his service, the fiery Scottish sea captain expected to leave Shanghai behind him forever. He hadn't counted on growing to love his half-caste daughter more than life itself . . .

ARCHIE MONTEITH—The charming English banker. His gentle love drew Magda out of her isolated inner world and turned her into a woman. Though age-old fears tore them apart, their love would endure—in ways no one could have predicted—for the rest of their lives . . .

MAX VON ZOLLER—Magda married the mysterious German to heal the wounds left by Archie. Seeing Max's cold-blooded cousin Waldemar humiliate and blackmail him taught Magda the difference between pity and love—but not before she was plunged into a dark world of corruption and espionage . . .

CHAPIN DESMOND—The elegant British Intelligence officer was Magda's partner in an international adventure that would alter her destiny forever. He gave Magda the love she'd always dreamed of, a love that set her free . . .

Contents

>>>>>>>>>>>>>>>>>>>>>>>>>>>>>>>>>

PART ONE

Shanghai

1915–1931

>>>>>>>>>>>>>>>>>>>>>>>>>>>>>>>>>

CHAPTER ONE

◄◄◄◄◄◄◄◄◄◄◄◄◄◄◄◄

CAPTAIN ANGUS MACDOUGALL was returning to Shanghai ahead of schedule. The weather had been fair, and the holds had been full of cargo from port to port. There had been no sicknesses or deaths to report from the steerage passengers. In all, it had been a good and profitable trip. The company had reason to be pleased, and he had done very well for himself.

Captain MacDougall was a massive, well-built man, nicknamed Big Red by his crew. His face was ruddy and his hair scarlet—like a brilliant sunset: deep, dark, and lustrous. The mark of a Red MacDougall, it appeared in every generation in his family. Fiercely proud, a descendant of chieftains and kings, he wore the striking red hair proudly, as if it were the crown of his ancestors. It made a curly thatch on his head and grew low in the sideburns to meet his full square-cut beard. His moustache was long and thick and curled up ferociously. Through all that red hair and windburned, sunburned face shone two bright blue eyes—peering keenly from under heavy eyebrows bleached several shades lighter from jutting out to challenge the sun.

The Captain left some last-minute instructions with his first mate and hurriedly left his ship. He couldn't wait to surprise Mei-ling with his early arrival and he jumped, like a young man, into the waiting hansom cab. He was off to Mei-ling with no thought of a stop at the "Mates and Masters Club" for a quick one.

MacDougall patted his pockets, smiling in anticipation of Mei-ling's childlike delight when she saw the treasures he had brought for her. How she would climb all over him to discover each exotic prize. How the little minx would purr over the jade earrings, the bangles, and—he'd wager anything on it—she'd not wait to

2

wear the fur tippet from Tientsin, even though it was already June!

Oh, she was like a child, he thought, with a child's mischievous ways—but, by thunderation, what a woman! She knew how to make a man feel like a king. Aye! It had been a lucky day for him when he was persuaded by McFee to set himself up with a Chinese woman. Now, when a voyage ended, it was a real homecoming—instead of staying at a boarding-house, drinking at the saloons, and buying a woman in a whorehouse.

Mei-ling, he chuckled to himself, remembering the first time he had seen her. Bewitching lass she was, so tiny and fine-boned that he'd had a moment of doubt. He remembered well the way she stared at him—no modest maiden of downcast mien, as he had been led to expect of a Chinese girl. No, indeed! She stared at him boldly, her eyes like two black pools, shining with admiration. She walked over and stood on tiptoe, and she reached up, tweaked his moustache hard and looked astonished that it didn't come off. After his outrage over the sudden sharp pain, he'd laughed at her astonishment.

MacDougall smiled, remembering how Mei-ling continued to check him out. She had looked him over very carefully, measuring him up and down, when suddenly she reached forward and touched the bulge in his pants—and be damned if it hadn't swelled up and nearly popped the buttons off!

Her mother had tried to pull her away, but it was all she could do to hide her own smile. Mei-ling just laughed and clapped her hands in glee. Half-angry, half-amused, and wholly aroused, he had picked her up and carried her to the bedroom. She struggled, the little minx, but it was a teasing struggle that only made him want her more. Thus, they had sealed their bargain.

MacDougall fixed his cap at a jauntier angle and urged the driver to speed the horses. His memories of Mei-ling were making him impatient.

In a bedroom on Boone Road, deep in the city, the sun filtered through drawn bamboo blinds and settled on the huge four poster which was covered by a mosquito net. The net was tied in a big knot and festooned down like a frilly cotton chandelier, casting its shadow on the

3

young woman who lay there in the last stages of labor.

Her mother anxiously tottered around her on bound feet, flicking away flies with her palmleaf fan, wiping away the beads of perspiration from the pale wan face, and constantly whispering little sounds of encouragement.

The midwife was experienced and very old. Her black eyes, set like tiny beads in a crumpled piece of yellowed parchment, watched the young woman who lay there exhausted. Her scolding voice uttered staccato commands as she placed clawlike hands on her patient's belly to check the contractions.

Finally Mei-ling's body arched in a last spasm of tearing pain and a piercing scream shattered the air.

Downstairs in the living room, a group of Chinese wives of British seafaring men sat and waited, sipping tea and gossiping.

Their chatter stopped at the sound of the scream. For a moment, the house was unnaturally quiet—and then came the awaited, thin cry of a newborn babe.

The houseboy entered the living room with fresh pots of tea, candied ginger, and bowls of sunflower seeds, and he placed them in front of the guests. He looked harried and unkempt, his sparse chin-whiskers unshaven, and he wore a loose jacket instead of the traditional serving-gown.

The women stopped their talking and looked expectantly as the boy—Uni, by name—poured their tea. Tersely, he told them the news they had been waiting for, "Baby girl," and left the room.

"Aie-yah! Aie-yah!" the women lamented, shaking their heads in deep concern.

"She is young and he cares much for her. See all the gifts he gives her," said Chen-si McFee, wife of the ship's chandler.

"Perhaps it would be better if she gave the child to another to raise," replied Fien-tu Norton.

"She could say the baby was born dead," suggested one woman.

"I have heard that he does not know that Mei-ling is with child. She was still small and didn't show when he left," said another.

Sheilah Chancellor, who had been raised by mis-

4

sionaries and knew the most English, said, "They are strange, these foreigners. When I had my little Jade, Peter looked sad, and I thought it was because it was a girl. But he said, 'Poor little thing. Good she's a girl, she'll have a better chance.' He has always been partial to her, and pays little attention to our boys. Indeed, their ideas are strange."

They were still talking when the sound of horses halted at the house entrance. The bell rang loud and long. Uni ran to open the door. A strong voice bellowed: "What takes ye so long, and why the hell don't ye have your gown on? Unshaven to boot! Are ye always this slipshod when I'm not here? Keep this up and ye'll nae be here long."

There was an ominous silence.

"Mei-ling!" boomed the voice, "Where in thunderation are ye?"

Quickly, the Chinese women gathered their things and silently left the room. MacDougall looked stunned as the women appeared from nowhere, slipped by him silently, and disappeared.

"Mei-ling!" He shouted again, his voice echoing in the house. "What deviltry be ye up to?"

An old lady, carrying a basin covered with a towel, hobbled down the stairs without looking at him, and entered the servants' quarters. Angus saw heads peeking out from behind doors, heads that were quickly withdrawn after staring at him with frightened eyes.

Mme. Chen, Mei-ling's mother, came to the top of the stairs. She started to descend, thought better of it, and went up again, putting a finger to her lips, hoping to quiet him. Bravely, she tried to block him as he leaped up the steps by twos and threes. He brushed her off, pushed open the door and stopped dead in his tracks.

The familiar bedroom had changed: it was hushed now and smelled of medicinal herbs. The questions on his lips were suddenly stilled.

Mei-ling lay lost in the vast expanse of white sheets. Her thick braids made two black exclamation marks on the white coverlet that was neatly drawn over the bed. Her heavy bangs were freshly combed. Spots of rouge had been hurriedly and mistakenly applied to her cheeks, making the little face even paler. But what

5

really put a dagger to MacDougall's heart was the expression—a mixture of fear, defiance, and entreaty—in her eyes as she returned his glare.

"Mei-ling, lass," his whisper was a soft roar. "What ailment's befallen ye?"

As he approached, she withdrew even further into the bedclothes, and only then did he notice the tightly wrapped bundle lying next to her, its tiny wrinkled face peeking out at the top.

"A little bairn? Nae, 'tis nae possible." He was utterly confused and forgot to lower his voice. Mei-ling shuddered and pressed her hands over her ears.

"Lass, why did ye nae tell me? Am I the monster of Loch Ness that ye should be so afeared?"

"Mei-ling thinks maybe Cap'n no like baby. Maybe no more like Mei-ling." Two big tears rolled down her cheeks.

" 'Tis a silly bairn ye be yerself," he scolded her, and for the first time he looked at the baby closely.

"Well, I'll be damned." He started to chuckle as he gently ruffled the bright red hair on the baby's head. A huge smile appeared on his face. "I'll be double damned if I have nae spawned me a little Chinee MacDougall."

The look of dread left Mei-ling's eyes.

"You like? Can keep baby girl?" She said the last word fearfully, as though it might change his mood.

"Why, ye little heathen! What did ye think? Of course we keep."

"You come home too much early. I think baby come long before you."

MacDougall took another look at the baby in amazement. "A Red MacDougall, by thunderation!" Once again he touched the baby's hair. This time the baby twisted its tiny face, which made it even redder, and let out a mighty howl. Mei-ling tried to quiet her.

"Let her be. 'Tis the good MacDougall blood making itself heard. Now you get yerself some rest, lassie." He kissed her gently and left the room.

The word spread quickly around the household: the Cap'n is pleased—baby girl can stay.

Downstairs, a quick change had taken place. The living room had been cleaned of all traces of recent visitors,

6

and Uni had shaved himself and donned a fresh, blue serving-gown. First, he brought his master a tall drink made to his liking; then, his pipe and tobacco. Last, he pulled off the man's heavy rubber boots. Above and beyond his other duties, Uni considered himself the captain's man.

Mei-ling's mother, Mme. Chen, knocked at the door and came in timidly. She was afraid of this big red foreigner with the booming voice; however, this time she faced him bravely and recited a long speech in Chinese, of which the only words Angus understood were her repeated references to Mei-ling. He looked helplessly at Uni, who stood by, listening with great interest to what Mme. Chen had to say.

"Well, man? What's she jabbering about?"

"She say, more better for Mei-ling if you no—no—" Uni hesitated, trying to think of the right word. Then a flash of inspiration crossed his mind and he said, beaming, "She say more better you—you not make bang-bang, maybe two weeks. Baby very big, Mei-ling very small. Mama say more better you wait."

MacDougall flushed. He had learned at their first meeting how matter-of-fact the Chinese were about sex, but he had not, and never would, get used to his private life becoming a matter of public discussion. He grunted something to the effect that he wasn't an animal, and Mme. Chen bowed her thanks and left with a big sigh of relief. She had successfully conquered the wrath of the foreign devil.

On the night of June 4, 1915, Angus MacDougall, aged forty-nine, feeling a little sorry for himself because of his enforced celibacy, was stirred by two conflicting thoughts. He felt a strange and unexpected delight over his little red-headed daughter, but he also felt repugnance that he had brought a half-caste bastard into the world and sullied his own blood.

It was the thought of raising a half-caste brood which had made him hesitate when McFee first suggested that he marry a Chinese woman.

"It's all understood," McFee explained. "They know we'll be leaving them, someday—most of us, at any rate. The women and children are left with a nice sum

7

of money. They're respected by their own kind and better off than most of the others. As far as the brats are concerned: well, we do the best we can for them. But what the hell! Nobody exactly asks to be born. And they'll get a better start than most, and an education. They'll make their own way in the world—there's enough of them."

MacDougall had managed to shake off his discomfort after a few drinks, and he never let the thoughts bother him again. What McFee had said was true enough, the world was full of half-breeds wherever the white man traveled—one more or less couldn't matter. And he would enjoy his little red-headed bairn. Thinking of her, he started to chuckle again. His good Scot blood had proved stronger than the Chinese any day. She was a Red MacDougall, and deserved a true MacDougall name.

"Be damned if I don't call her Magda after me grandma and me sister. Ho ho! Now that would bleach the freckles off the old biddy's dour face if she knew she had a little Chinee niece."

And Magda, after his grandmother and hers before her, she was named—Magda MacDougall of the Red MacDougall clan.

CHAPTER TWO

‹‹‹‹‹‹‹‹‹‹‹‹‹‹‹

ON THE DAYS preceding MacDougall's return from the sea, the entire household came alive in preparation. Magda's heart would beat more rapidly, and when the day actually arrived, it seemed as though she would burst for the joy within her. She learned early to keep out of the way until her mother eagerly greeted him, fussed over him, and went through the game they both enjoyed so much: searching his pockets for presents. Then there were the games they played in their bedroom after he carried her squirming and laughing upstairs.

8

Only afterward did his rich voice bellow for his daughter. Then it was her turn to run into his arms and be lifted high in the air until she squealed in delight—and her turn to receive the little gifts he never forgot. He called her Little Red, or he called her Maggie, or lassie, or his little bairn. The man with the flame-colored hair, like hers, and the blue eyes which twinkled so merrily, became her god. Time stood still between his visits.

Even now Mei-ling was little more than a child herself in many ways. She enjoyed playing with her strange red haired doll-baby and dressing her in gaily-colored Chinese clothing. The fuss Angus made over her baby was, to her, a tribute to his love for her. But, as the child grew older, Mei-ling started to resent the amount of time Angus devoted to his little Maggie.

He found real pleasure in telling her stories about his beloved Scotland, watching her eyes grow large with wonder as he described the mist-cloaked land, the raging surfs and the sweet smell of heather in the country of his ancestors. He told her of red-bearded kings of other times, of the fierce native chiefs, who had fought and intermarried and given birth to the Red Mac-Dougalls. Angus taught her songs of the old country and was amused to hear his rich brogue echoed in her child's high-pitched voice.

Mei-ling was not amused. Her resentment of the child increased, and she began to regard her, not as her daughter, but as a rival for the Captain's affections. Once the notion was fixed in her superstitious mind, it became a certainty—and more than she could endure.

"You go away from my sight," she screamed at the child when Angus left on his tours of duty. "You are the child of evil gods, sent to punish me. You keep away from my husband or I shall beat the devil that lives in you."

Mei-ling burned many joss sticks to drive away the evil spirits, and, when angered, took a stick to Magda.

Magda learned at an early age to avoid Mei-ling and to make herself unobtrusive. She grew up a quiet, withdrawn child who showed emotion only when her father came home. With Meh-meh, her grandmother, Magda sought refuge from her mother's abuse during the long months her father was away at sea. Mme. Chen quietly took charge of her, keeping the child away from her daughter's fiery temper, which she had never been able to restrain. But she understood her daughter's fears, and only in private did she show Magda the affection the little girl craved desperately.

After one of his trips, Captain MacDougall realized suddenly that his daughter was growing up. At six, she was tall for her age and increasingly European-looking, with her hair more vibrantly the scarlet red of his clan. Once again, a feeling of fatherly responsibility stirred in him, but he pushed it away. He was due to retire in a few years and to go back to Scotland—and that would be that. In the meantime, he'd do the best he could for the lass. It was time she went to school—no one with MacDougall blood should grow up uneducated. This much was his duty. But little more.

With his conscience clear, he took the first step. Magda's pidgin English, which once amused him, he now considered a disgrace. After careful thought, he decided to ask a relative of Magda's, Chen Wen-chu, to tutor her before she entered school.

Chen Wen-chu, whose first name had been anglicized to William in British-indoctrinated Shanghai, was Mei-ling's second cousin. He was well-educated and spoke fluent and almost unaccented English. At seventeen, he was already a man, a firm and gentle man who took his family responsibilities seriously. He was the only one, besides Mme. Chen, to show any concern or affection for his little half-foreign relative, and he willingly accepted the role of tutor.

When the important day came for Magda to enter school, the Captain bought her the fanciest dress he could find, covered with lace and ruffles, and a silk straw hat with roses and long satin streamers. To accompany her, he wore his full dress uniform and donned his gold-braided cap at a jaunty angle. Though the school was only a few blocks away, he hired a carriage for the day so that they could make a fitting entrance.

They descended from the carriage, he offering her his

10

hand as though she were a princess, and they walked on the newly graveled path to the principal's office. Wide-eyed children stared and snickered with their hands over their mouths, but the two walked on unperturbed. Magda, her hand clutching her father's, kept step with him solemnly, her heart full of pride as she looked up at the tall, magnificent, imposing figure. Surely there never had been another quite like him.

Magda was seven when she entered the Shanghai Public School for Girls. It had been opened shortly after the turn of the century when Shanghai became an international center of trade. The school was sponsored and established by the Masonic Lodge, which ruled that there should be no discrimination in accepting students. The letter of the law was observed, but the spirit was sadly neglected. There was no doubt that the British staff believed in the superiority of British children, and treated them accordingly.

When the Captain registered Magda, he explained that she had been raised by Chinese servants, which accounted for her slight singsong accent. There was no glimmer of doubt in anyone's mind that Magda was anything but a proper little British girl.

The headmistress smiled at the big Scotsman and suggested he take the child to be outfitted at the Lane Crawford department store where the required school uniforms were sold.

At the department store, MacDougall instructed a salesgirl to provide his daughter with everything she might possibly need.

"Two uniforms will do for her as a start, two pairs of shoes, half a dozen of everything else," he told the salesgirl. He handed Magda a plaid coat and matching hat he had chosen off the rack. "Take this and try it on, lassie." Magda emerged from the dressing room, trim in her British schoolgirl uniform. She was glowing with excitement, her eyes sparkling, and her usually pale face flushed. Her extraordinary red hair was even more brilliant under the green-and-blue tartan tam-o'-shanter.

Seeing her thus made something in the Captain's heart turn over. There was an unfamiliar sting in his eyes.

"She's a beautiful child," said the salesgirl.

11

"Aye! That she is. That she is. A true MacDougall, there's no doubt about it."

Angus MacDougall had learned something new about himself—he had a flesh-and-blood daughter, and he loved her deeply.

Mei-ling felt the full force of her jealousy that day, and it became a constant and growing source of unhappiness. She, Mei-ling, the jewel of her husband's heart, was being replaced. Her big red man had found a new companion. This was no child of hers, Mei-ling decided—this was a changeling put in its place by vengeful demons who envied her happiness! Her loneliness and the loss of face she felt turned her against Magda, and she refused to have anything more to do with her daughter.

In Mei-ling's social circles there were many half-caste children. They played together and seemed content to accept themselves for what they were. Magda's father, however, had forbidden her to join in their play.

"Remember," MacDougall cautioned Magda from the first day she entered school. "Remember ye're half-Chinese and half-Scot. Ye must make a choice and stick with it or ye'll be stuck in the shallows with no place to go."

"I want to be just like you, Papa," she said, and her adoring look was enough to fill any man's heart.

For Magda there was really no choice. To please her father she would willingly have split herself in two and thrown away the Chinese part, which seemed to displease him so.

"Is it all right to love my grandmother and William?" she asked.

Angus took a deep breath. "Of course," he replied. The child took him so literally. And, yet, he had to admit he was pleased by her unquestioning devotion. He noticed the absence of Mei-ling's name from her list of loved ones but made no mention of it. He was well aware of the rivalry between mother and daughter for his affection, and it amused him to tease them and spark their jealousy. Mei-ling rose to his teasing every time.

At last Magda had an established place at home. Even

12

her mother dared not flout the Captain's orders. At school, Magda was a serious and dedicated student. She had a true ear for languages, and when she realized how poorly she spoke English in comparison to the other children, her natural reticence became even more pronounced—but so did her determination to overcome the handicap. It took her two years and William's patient help to speak with a perfect British accent, and this experience aroused in her a passion for languages that would serve her well all her life.

But she remained a lonely child—sitting on a bench at recess while others played around her—until, one day, the miracle happened. She and Natasha Wilkinson were both top students, but there all comparison ended. Natasha was the most popular girl in the class, the teacher's pet, even good at sports. While playing London Bridge one day, Natasha's eyes fell on Magda, who was, as usual, alone in a corner of the yard. On the spur of the moment, she called out Magda's name to be on her team.

Magda stood up hesitantly, not sure she had heard right, then joined in the game. Later, she shyly accepted Natasha's offer of friendship. As Natasha's chum, Magda was accepted by the others. She finally had a place in the class, becoming one of the circle who surrounded the vivacious, dark-haired girl with the laughing green-speckled eyes.

Sometimes Natasha became irritated by Magda's shyness and wouldn't talk to her for a day or two. Then Magda felt the pangs of rejection like a burning in her stomach—but Tasha never held a grudge for long, and their friendship was always restored.

During each of the Captain's furloughs at home, he would ask Magda all about her life at school. This time she boasted shyly, "Papa, I have a friend."

"Bring her over for tea tomorrow. Let's hae a look at her."

Magda drove the entire household crazy with her demands for cakes and sandwiches and scones. Her father, spurred by her excitement, bought a cake from Bianchi's, decorated with iced roses and violets. The servants cleaned and waxed as though they were having a royal guest. Mei-ling's lips were thin with disapproval but Magda's grandmother was pleased for her.

Magda felt very important—and a little scared—as she escorted Tasha to her house. This was the first time she had ever brought a friend home. She took Tasha directly to meet the Captain, who was standing at attention as if he were an officer reviewing his troops.

"Papa, this is my friend, Natasha Wilkinson."

Tasha looked up at the huge red-bearded man, his face as scarlet as his hair, and his little blue eyes seriously examining her from under his bushy eyebrows.

Magda watched, her heart pounding, as the two inspected each other solemnly, and then he nodded approval.

"Welcome to my house, little Natasha," he boomed, and extended his hand which she took gravely as though sealing a pact. "You be a good friend to my Maggie."

Magda sighed in relief. Her friend was accepted.

"This is my mother and grandmother," she said to Tasha, bringing her over to meet the two women.

Tasha's immediate reaction did not escape Magda's anxious eyes. She knew, once and for all, that there was something shameful in being half-and-half—that it was not only her father's prejudice as a Scot of royal blood. At that moment she made a solemn vow to herself. Never, never, she told herself, would she ever do anything to disappoint her father. Then she would be accepted as all-white. There were many half-caste children at school, and they didn't seem to mind, but her father—she glowed at the thought—her father minded for her.

Her father swelled to think how much he loved her.

The law Angus MacDougall followed was simple and severe: ask for no quarter and give no quarter. It was the way of the sea and he had embraced it since he was a boy. He was a kindly man if given his way, but cross him and he could be brutal. In his fifties, he could still whip any man in his crew if he had to. He never did. His men, from the top man on down, respected him, but some were afraid of him.

His ship was his first love. The far-away Hebrides off the west coast of Scotland came second. Mei-ling and the child were a distant third. He planned to enjoy the latter two for the length of his sea duty—until he retired and returned to the Highlands from whence he had come.

Angus was a careful man with his money, and his friends considered him wise. He was thought to have a goodly pile put away, but he never put his money in the bank to gather a meager 4 percent in interest. Instead, his hobby was to study the stockmarket and, after much deliberation, to invest in shares. So far, his investments had paid off well, and he looked with satisfaction upon his bank balance and growing wealth.

By the fall of 1925, Captain Angus MacDougall had put in the thirty years of service required by the China Coastal Shipping Company and was due for retirement. He was in full, lusty health, eager to return to his homeland and settle down to the life his dreams had made more vivid with each passing year. With his retirement pay and the income from his stocks and bonds, he would be able to live very comfortably.

When the time came for him to leave, he was generous to Mei-ling. She had given him twelve good years and, in return, he gave her considerably more than the marriage broker had arranged for.

MacDougall paid off in full the two-year lease on his house. He also gave Mei-ling a gift of all the heavy mahogany furniture and other furnishings he had purchased from the previous tenant. Finally, he established a trust fund which would pay her fifty taels a month for life (this was more than many educated Chinese clerks who supported families were paid). And he gave her, as a parting gift, five hundred dollars in cash.

Mei-ling cried a little, as was expected, but otherwise she accepted the situation with equanimity. It was a customary end to setting up housekeeping with a foreigner, and she was considered fortunate.

Magda did not understand what was happening but Mei-ling had no intention of letting her daughter remain ignorant.

"Your father thinks nothing of leaving you," she taunted the child. "That's how much he loves you."

"It's not true. He's just making a longer trip than usual. He's going on a furlough." Magda had heard the

15

phrase somewhere, though she was not sure what it meant.

"Ask him then, you little fool. Go ahead and ask him. Your father is returning to his own country and leaving his ugly half-caste daughter behind. That shows you how much you mean to him." Mei-ling sneered. But her taunts did not bring tears to Magda's eyes—she was used to her mother's jealous outbursts, and they could no longer hurt her.

Soon after this, Magda gathered her courage and decided to confront her father when they were alone.

"Papa, my mother says you are leaving us. I told her that it wasn't true, that you'd never leave me. Papa, am I right?"

"Of course you're right," MacDougall answered heartily. He had not the stomach to tell her the truth. "Don't you worry yourself, lassie. I'll see you're always looked after. I'll be away for a long time. Maybe I'll send for ye. How would that be, eh? Now give me a big kiss and a smile."

She hugged him so hard that he finally had to pry her off. Then she ran to her room and, for some reason she could not explain, she wept rare tears. She was ashamed of herself—her father had told her frequently that a MacDougall did not cry.

"I'm getting soft," Angus told himself, as the thought crossed his mind to take her with him. "What would I do in Scotland with a little half-caste on my hands? She's only a child, she'll get used to it. They all do. It's best for her to stay here."

But he found he could not easily dismiss her from his thoughts. And he was disturbed and annoyed with himself for feeling so. A few days before his departure he called William Chen to his house.

"William," he said. "I have left a substantial sum of money to be spent on Magda's education, and I'll be sending more from time to time. I'd take it kindly if you would check now and then to see that all is well with the lass."

"It will not be good for Magda when you leave. You have truly shown her great affection," William stated carefully.

"I'm very fond of the lass, but now I must go back to my own kind and my own country. It was understood and arranged to be so from the beginning."

"I understand, sir. This is the way of your people. But there are two manners of people: those who feel deeply, and those whose feelings are like shallow waters. Magda is one of the former."

MacDougall ignored William's remark. "Mei-ling will be well off, and I have provided for Magda's future."

"Yes. I understand you have been very generous with your money, Uncle."

Angus flinched at being called Uncle by this young Chinaman. Just because he lived with a Chinese woman, he thought irritably, did not make him uncle to the entire Chen family. However, he had a favor to ask, and William had influence in his family, despite his youth. He was the oldest son of the deceased oldest son of Chen Hsu-ming, Elder Brother of the Chen clan, and would himself become Elder Brother next. His family was very well-to-do—not Mandarins as they once were, but still important.

Mme. Chen's husband had died after squandering away his inheritance, leaving his wife and daughter in poor straits, with no dowry for Mei-ling. Angus was well aware of the family's status, and wanted to provide an influential ally for Magda after he left.

"Mei-ling and Magda are not good together," William repeated.

"Nonsense! They'll get over it. When I'm gone, the bone of contention between them will disappear." Angus smiled at William in a spirit of mutual understanding, but William did not respond.

"You may be sure I shall see to it, as much as it is possible to do so," he replied, shaking Angus' hand. "I hope my young cousin will not suffer, but there is little I can do between the mother and her child."

On the final day, with all his luggage stowed in the back of a carriage, Angus kissed Mei-ling goodbye and bowed his formal farewell to Mme. Chen. He gave each servant a gift of money and gave a handsome sum to Uni, the Number One.

"Look after them well," he said gruffly. "Where's the

lass?" he then asked, looking around for her. But she was nowhere to be found.

"Magda!" he shouted. "Don't ye be a foolish lass. Come down and kiss yer father goodbye. 'Tis not like ye to act so. Come down here immediately. I'm leaving right now!"

He waited another five minutes, fuming at the delay, then got into the carriage, almost pleased to have anger for company, rather than the feeling of guilt which had been dogging him all week.

Angus MacDougall prided himself on being his own man and was not usually subject to regretting what he did. The strange weight he had felt lately, his reluctance to leave China, he dismissed in annoyance. Going home to Scotland was what he had worked for—thirty years of hard work and strong competition, of long hours and danger. This was his lifelong goal, and no snip of a girl was going to take it away from him. But his misgivings still troubled him, and he forced himself to submerge his doubts in anger at Magda's last minute disappearance.

Angus settled himself in the cab and nursed his resentment. The ungrateful girl—after all he'd done for her. To think how he'd worried about the lass. Well, he was well free of her, he thought. She was like all those mixed bloods—never satisfied, always wanting more than a man was ready to give. His angry thoughts continued, adding grievance to grievance, giving full sway to his disgruntlement, until he suddenly saw that the blanket in the corner had moved. He grabbed at the bundle underneath the blanket and found Magda cowering there.

"How now, me girl, what do ye think ye're doing here? Have ye nae given me enough trouble today?"

She shivered under the storm of his wrath.

"Well, speak up, lass. What are ye doing here? I'll have to turn the carriage around now and I'll be late. I've more than half a mind to let ye off and make ye walk home."

He took her shoulders and shook her. It was the first time he had ever laid a hand on her, but, instead of quailing, she fell into his arms and held him as tightly as her own thin arms could.

"Papa, Papa! Don't leave me. Take me with you,

please." She stammered as she spoke, her head smothered in his coat collar.

"Nay, lass!" He held her close. "Nay, lass! Ye mustn't carry on so. 'Tis the way it is in life, my Maggie. Ye must be strong. A true MacDougall holds his chin up. Come on, now. Gie your papa a smile. Lass, dinna cry so. 'Tis not like ye."

Her anguish could be heard though her voice was muffled. "Is it true what my mother says? Is it true that I'll never see you again."

"Nay. 'Tis not the truth." At that moment he meant it. "I'll write as soon as I have an address and ye'll write to me. Maybe I'll be sendin' for ye. Take courage, lass. Now wipe your eyes—I've never seen ye weep before—'tis no becoming." He smiled gently and lifted her chin with his finger. "Maggie, ye must always be bonny. Have faith in me, Little Red, I'll not let ye down. Have patience and 'twill come out all right."

"Oh, yes, Papa. I will."

Angus had the driver turn the carriage around. He delivered Magda back to the house, and drove away without a backward glance. He did not want to see the swift punishment Magda would surely receive from her angry mother. The young must learn to take their lickings, he thought; it was part of growing up. He forced his mind to the future; China was already a closed book.

It took Angus six weeks to reach his birthplace, a little village on the Island of Islay in the Hebrides, on the Atlantic coast of Scotland. Whatever glory the Mac-Dougalls had known was in their history, not in their wealth. He had decided not to let anyone know of his return, preferring to see and feel the place by himself. His family—the few who were left of the clan—were not the kind to make a fuss over a long-gone sailor.

It was good to breathe the bracing air again, and to feel the chill winds bite his face. Angus walked through the wild and bleak countryside and climbed the rocky hills. He looked down at the white-capped waves that scrambled to reach the shore. They smashed against the rocks, splattered salty drops, and broke sharply against the cliffs.

How different these clear waters were from the muddy

shores of the China coast that he knew so well. How exhilarating was the air! Angus gulped it down as if it were a heady drink. And instead of the clatter and clamor of the harbors of China, the only sound he heard was the thunder of the waves and wind which drowned out all else. Instead of the stench of Shanghai, sweet-smelling yellow gorse, which grew wild everywhere, spiced the air.

The strong, constant winds of the Highlands bore his spirit higher and higher. Soon, he hoped, they would blow the past away, and those years in China would seem like another man's life. Here, only here, would he end his days.

Angus was still a lusty man at fifty-nine, and he planned to find some buxom Scotswoman to marry. He had dreamed of this for over forty years as he sailed the world, as he captained, at last, his own ship, and sometimes, even in the arms of Mei-ling. Then, when he compared himself to the hard-working farmers and sheep-herders of the sparsely-peopled island, he considered himself wealthy and was well content. Now, just one thing was lacking.

In the weeks after he returned, MacDougall visited a few relatives and went to see his sister Magda and her husband in Inverness, where they lived meagerly on his teacher's pay. Word spread rapidly that he was a "comfortable man," a bachelor, and mothers of unwed girls made him welcome. Angus laughed out loud to find that there were some likenesses to the Chinese marriage broker, and that the Scots were almost as obvious. A man was searching for a woman, and a lass had to be found to suit him.

In any case, he found himself with a spread of women to pick from.

But an unexpected thing happened to him. Angus found that the bonny girls he had dreamed of meeting were too brawny, too angular, or too full-bodied; too tall, too harsh in their speech, or too independent in manner. They smelled of the fields they worked in, or the sheep they tended, or of dogs or horses—and he found himself making comparisons to delicate Mei-ling, who barely weighed seven stone. He remembered the sweet, clean smell of her, her giggles and teasing ways, even her tantrums. But most of all, he remembered her way of making him feel like the most important man in the world. He remembered too, her natural delight in the pleasures of the bed—or her ingenuity in thinking of new pleasures—and her efforts to please him and to cater to his every want.

Perhaps, he thought, it was the Chinese way, but between them there had been no reserve: not so much a lack of modesty but an acceptance of nature—sensual and voluptuous desires were indulged and savored to the fullest. After twelve years of openness between Mei-ling and himself, it was difficult for Angus to accept the hypocrisy of polite society, and he found himself more and more frequently longing for his life in Shanghai.

He moved out of the village and went to Inverness, where there was more to occupy him and it was easier to find a woman when he needed one. But he found the bawdy-houses no longer satisfied his appetites; twelve years of a settled life had given him a taste for his own home—and his own woman. But even more than that, Angus found himself bedeviled with thoughts of Magda. He saw her serious little face in front of him at odd moments, her eyes beseeching him from the eyes of strangers. Whenever he saw children in their school uniforms, he imagined he saw Magda's face on each one of them.

"I'm going crazy," he muttered to himself one day when he stopped a little girl with red hair and saw a stranger's face instead of Magda's. He was shocked at himself. "Could it be something is wrong and she's calling me? My grandma had the gift—oh, by thunderation, I'm going daft."

He thrust Magda's image away from him, but it kept coming back. Finally he admitted to himself that the love he felt for her was not a passing thing, nor just a fond memory.

Angus had written to Magda a few times and then stopped, thinking it was best to make a clean break of it. In his imagination, he saw her going daily to the mailbox to look for a letter from him. Not only could he imagine her, he could actually feel the anguish of her disappointment.

"She'll forget," he told himself. "It's better, this way. There's no place for a child in my life. She'll have to find her own way." And then he felt her small hand tugging at his.

"Maggie, lass," he groaned. "Ye've made of my dreams a nightmare. Begone with ye!"

CHAPTER THREE

‹‹‹‹‹‹‹‹‹‹‹‹‹‹‹‹‹‹‹

MAGDA HEARD SHOUTING from the front of the house but paid it no heed. At least she had that satisfaction, she thought, in living in the back; she didn't have to see anyone, except, of course, her grandmother—her dear, gentle, loving, and ineffectual Meh-meh. Magda sighed and tried to concentrate on the lessons William had brought, so that she would not fall too far behind in school, assuming she was ever permitted to return. Six months earlier, in one of her frequent and unpredictable rages, Mei-ling had forbidden Magda to continue going to school.

Magda let her thoughts stray to the one constant in her life, her hatred for her mother. She found solace in that hatred—it was the thing that kept her going, gave her something to feel other than overwhelming despair. Only in the direst circumstances did she permit herself to think about her father's return.

Though Mei-ling was the undisputed mistress of the house, her hostility against her daughter grew without explanation, without reason. The very sight of Magda put her in a state of rage, yet she found no satisfaction in her anger because Magda never gave in to tears. Even when Magda was sent to live in the old pantry, she said nothing. Her stubbornness only fueled her mother's dislike of her.

"If you like it so much there," she mocked, "you should be a servant and dress like one." She took away all of Magda's clothes and gave her a coolie amah's faded gown to wear.

Magda looked on stoically, refusing to give her mother the satisfaction of knowing the hurt she felt. The slaps, the whippings, the insults, meant little. She was determined not to let her mother break her spirit.

She would always remember that she was a Red MacDougall. Unless—and Magda bowed her head in shame—unless her mother carried out her threat to sell her. Then, indeed, she would be lost. Her staunch faith, the pure flame of hope that her father would return, would be useless. It would be too late. It would be the end of her. But, first, she would kill her mother and then herself. About that she was determined.

Magda shuddered at the memory of that day, still so recent that every moment kept playing in her mind. Once again, she remembered hearing that terrible man of her mother's follow her into the servants' quarters; she had thought nothing of it until she heard his steps quicken and felt the prickling of a strange new fear, a premonition of trouble. She could smell the sickeningly sweet oil he wore on his slick hair, even as she hurried to her room, panting as though she had raced a mile.

She shut the door, relieved, and leaned against it; but her strength was no match for his as he pushed the door open and grabbed her. She wanted to squirm away from him, but in the small room there was no place to go. He clutched at her and tried to kiss her, his lips wet and open; he ran his hands over her body. She struggled frantically but he put his hand over her mouth to prevent her screaming, and with one foot, he pushed the door shut. His bulging eyes were bloodshot, his mouth pressed to hers, choking her with fumes of stale alcohol as he forced her nearer the bed.

It was then that her mother appeared, followed closely by Uni, who was holding her grandmother's arm. The man looked at them sullenly and slunk out of the room. Oh, thank you, thank you, Uni, for warning them—but the words were only in her mind. She was too shaken to speak. For the first time in her life, Magda felt happy to see her mother.

Her relief was short-lived. The nightmare had only begun. Mei-ling grabbed a ruler from Magda's desk and began hitting her wildly—on her arms, her head, her legs, her back—wherever Magda twisted, her mother found another place to strike. She beat her until, mercifully, the ruler broke. Then she screamed: "Is it not enough that you tried to steal my first husband with your lies and trickery? Now you do the same with my second husband. He is not to blame—you are! You have enticed him into your room with your sluttish ways—"

Meh-meh tried to stop her but Mei-ling was beyond all reason. Finally, exhausted, she left the little room, but only after promising to sell Magda to the highest bidder.

"Not that anyone will pay a good price for a witch as ugly as you—thin and graceless, with the hair of a devil and the soul of a snake." And Magda knew that she meant to carry out her threat.

She lay half on the floor, half on the bed, bleeding, almost unconscious, but her mouth was sealed by a will stronger than her body. Not a whimper, even now, passed her lips. Only the thought that somewhere her father loved her—might yet come back to her—gave her a flicker of hope, a reason to go on living.

Magda sighed heavily. She had to drive the memory away—it only served to weaken her resolution to be brave. It was all right now. Meh-meh had somehow sent word to William and he had straightened it out. What would she have done without William? What *could* she have done without him? But one day William might not be around.

Her heart cried, "Papa, Papa, Papa . . . ," before she had a chance to still the cry within her. She must not do that—it was bad luck. He would come in his own good time, as he had promised. Magda forced herself to empty her mind of all thoughts of him.

She sighed heavily once again and started to practice the Chinese writing which had become a regular part of her lessons. She enjoyed it because the calligraphy was so precise, so beautiful in its flowing lines that she had to concentrate hard and not think of anything else.

Again, she heard the sound of loud voices from the

front of the house. Perhaps it was that disgusting man again, drunk as usual. She took out the knife she had hidden under her mattress and went to place a chair under the doorknob—but first opened the door a little to hear what was going on. The voice was too strong; it wasn't him after all.

Then she heard the voice clearly—and for an instant she could not breathe. No! It couldn't be. She had wanted it so much she must have imagined it! She felt faint. Then, again, she heard it, booming impatiently.

"MAGDA! WHERE ARE YE, LASS? 'TIS YOUR PAPA BACK HOME!"

No! It couldn't be. She couldn't bear the disappointment. She had never stopped believing, even as one year passed into two. He had told her to have faith, and she had, but it was only a prayer, a hope to cling to for the future.

Then she heard Uni's voice, pleading, and once again the thundering response. Magda went to the door that separated the servants' quarters from the rest of the house. She opened the door, just a little bit—and there he stood.

"Papa!" Her voice was so small, barely a whisper, and her feet were frozen to the floor.

Uni was trying to dissuade her father from entering. Stop it, Uni! Don't you dare! she thought, but no sound came out. She started to run toward her father. It seemed like endless miles, but finally she was caught up in his arms—such strong arms, such warm, familiar arms. He held her close. Then, and only then, did all the tears that Mei-ling never had managed to force from her—the sobs she had held under control for so long— burst from her heart.

His hands, such great big hands to be so gentle, squeezed her, and his hairy face pressed against hers.

"My lass! My own wee lassie! Hush, now. My lass, weep no more, ye'll break ye self in two. I'll nae leave ye again."

He stroked her hair and kissed her wet cheeks. Her heart throbbed so hard he could feel it beating against his. Were his own cheeks wet from her tears? Her arms held him around the neck so tightly that he could hardly pry her loose.

"Now, then. Let's have a look at ye."

She stood in front of him—tall, spindly and very pale. Her head was bowed in shame for the way she appeared to him. She felt, rather than saw, his eyes narrowing into slits as he inspected her. Her hair, lacking it's old luster, was rusty now, and pulled back tightly to be braided and tied with a shoelace. Her eyes were deeply sunken, with dark circles under them. Her arms as much as she tried to hide them, were covered with fresh bruises, and where her gown split on the sides, black-and-blue marks covered her legs.

A terrible rage swept over MacDougall, almost choking him with its intensity. The blood drained from his face, leaving a network of broken capillaries like a crazy map of thin red lines drawn on muddy white. Then the blood gushed back, suffusing his face until the blood vessels seemed likely to explode.

Magda stared at him, afraid. "Papa, it doesn't matter. It's all over. Don't do anything," she whispered. "I never cried, Papa."

He nodded grimly and approvingly. Not his child, daughter of kings and chieftains, descendant of the Lords of the Isles. But he still remained in a state of seething fury. It was more than the beating, brutal though it was. It was the whole look of the girl, the frail and sickly look of her: a look of neglect and persistent cruelty. And he knew who was responsible.

"We'll make her sorry, lass. Very, very sorry," he said softly—softly for *him,* and dangerous. Magda shivered at the sound of that tone. His old crew would have remembered it.

Uni stood in front of him, a shaky barrier, fearful of what was to come.

"No can go upstairs, Masta Cap'n," he beseeched. "No can go. Have new masta."

Angus brushed the trembling servant aside and walked up the stairs with great deliberation, each footstep ominous in the breathless silence of the house.

Mme. Chen stood in front of the door to the bedroom —a valiant, if fragile, warrior, defending her family. He lifted her up easily, set her aside, and opened the door.

Mei-ling stood in the center of the room, her face a

mask of terror. She wore a loose jacket, opened at one breast, and held a mewling baby in one arm as though frozen in the act of nursing. Behind a large overstuffed chair, crouched a man who was trying to look as if he weren't there.

Mme. Chen tiptoed in, grabbed the baby from his mother's nerveless arms, and took him to safety. All the servants had gathered downstairs and locked themselves in their quarters. Magda followed her father up the stairs and watched the scene from the landing.

MacDougall's glance slid off Mei-ling and focused on the man whose eyes had never left his, as though mesmerized by the sight of him. Angus MacDougall would never know what he looked like at that moment: a ray of sunlight lit his hair which curled thickly over his face and head like plumes of raging flame. His teeth were bared in a snarl, his nostrils flared, his eyes icy blue.

With a deafening bellow as wordless as a war cry, he lurched forward, his huge clenched fist lifted as if he were some Viking ancestor with a hatchet raised to kill.

Magda's eyes gleamed with triumph when she saw her father advance against the man who had caused her such agony, and she tasted the sweetness of revenge. She heard his high screech and her heart swelled; then she saw him twisting toward her, clutching his trousers in one hand. The other hand was raised to ward off the blow he expected from MacDougall. As he stumbled by, Magda put her foot out deliberately and coldly. He tripped and his eyes opened wide as he fell heavily. Windless, witless, he focused on her, and, as if for the first time, noticed her red hair—red like her father's! Into the vacant stare of fear there came a look of horrified understanding. He scrambled up, and, half-stumbling and half-falling, ran down the stairs and out of the house.

Magda laughed, a clear merry chirp. She looked surprised at herself—it had been so long. She turned to her father who stood with arms outstretched, his temper dispelled as he grinned at her.

"He's not of our mettle, now, is he? Lass, go ye down and put on something nice. We'll go shopping later, but first I must have a word or two with your mother."

"I have nothing else to wear," she replied, ashamed.

"That, too? You will tell me everything later, but go ye now. Here be the keys to my trunks. Tell Uni to open the wardrobe trunk, and in the top drawer ye'll find a bonny suit in the tartan of our clan. Put it on—I'll be downstairs shortly."

He turned to Mei-ling.

"And you will get out of my house while I am in such good humor. And take your bastard son with ye. Take him to his father, if you know who he be. How many men hae ye had in here since I left, ye dirty heathen whore? My bed was barely cold before ye warmed it with yer lust. Take everything that's yours and get out—now!" he thundered, his anger coming back full force. The servants shivered as his voice reverberated throughout the house.

But not Mei-ling. Her initial fear was gone, and she stood defiantly before him. Tiny though she was, she dominated the room full of massive furniture.

"I not go. You go. This my house. This my furniture. You go."

Their eyes blazed at each other. But deep inside, MacDougall felt a spark of admiration. She was a feisty woman, not easily cowed, not even by him. In the past, he had chuckled when this little female, who barely reached to his shoulders and was as slight as one of his mighty thighs, stood in front of him like a little bantam cock facing an eagle, ready to dart at his eyes. But none of this showed as he spoke to her again.

"I'm going to take the lass shopping for some clothes. I canna look into your black heart and know your reasons for condemning her to a living hell, but when I come back I expect to see ye moved out, bag and baggage. If not, I shall take delight in tossing out on the street everything you own—including you."

There was a sedan chair parked outside the house when father and daughter returned—plus a large number of curious and noisy onlookers. In 1927, sedan chairs were almost an anachronism.

"It must be Elder Brother," Magda murmured, descending from the rickshaw, clutching her packages.

How bonny the child looks in the good tartan, Angus thought with pride. It becomes her, and she becomes it.

The first thing he had done was have a barber cut off that damnable braid, which shamed her like a badge of servitude. She looked like a different girl—her face animated, her black eyes sparkling, and her hair a golden-bronze halo.

"What's that you say?"

"They must have sent for Elder Brother," Magda repeated, some of the lightness disappearing from her face.

"And what can old Chen do to me?" He smiled at her reassuringly, and she looked up at him with such adoration that his own heart skipped a beat.

Uni opened the door for them as soon as they appeared on the doorstep. His face was expressionless, as befitted a good servant, but there was excitement in his demeanor as he ushered them into the living room, bowing low as if presenting them to royalty.

Chen Hsu-ming, Elder Brother of the Chen clan, was very old. He lived by, and carried out, the old traditions, even as far as the use of a sedan chair for official or formal occasions. To his door went any of the Chens who needed advice and mediation in times of trouble. His grandson, Chen Wen-chu, or William, would one day perform the same duties. William, although a modern and educated young Chinaman, had been steeped in all the old ways of family duty, and Elder Brother was satisfied that, when his time came, Wen-chu would carry on as expected.

These days Chen Hsu-ming seldom left his house, but William had persuaded him that this was an emergency. Besides, his interest was piqued by the evident liking William had for his little cousin, and by the odd situation which faced the members of his family.

Like an ancestral portrait, Chen Hsu-ming sat enthroned in a carved teakwood chair, resting his slippered feet on a footstool. He wore the old-fashioned costume of brocaded sleeveless vest fastened in front with jeweled studs, over a long-sleeved undergown of rich silk. One hand rested on the carved dragon armrest and showed a long curved fingernail on his little finger—the sign of a man who did not have to labor with his hands. The other hand stroked his wispy beard. Aged though he was, he still looked formidable and was one to inspire respect and fear. Mei-ling and her mother sat on the edges of their seats on his right, while William stood beside him on the left.

MacDougall strode into the room, holding Magda by the hand. The old Mandarin peered at this strange man who appeared to be wearing the red wig and beard of the devil in a Chinese play, and he studied the red-headed child. It was difficult to see any trace of the Chinese in her. He nodded thoughtfully. Life would not be easy for this one, with neither side prepared to accept her fully. His grandson thought well of her, and had harsh words for both parents, who had used her as a weapon against each other. Odd as she looked, this unfortunate child needed her same-looking father. She would indeed be lost otherwise.

"What is going on here? A family meeting?" demanded MacDougall.

Magda stepped forward to bow before this powerful member of the family, but her father held her back.

"You bow before no man, lassie."

"But he is Elder Brother," she whispered.

At this improper behavior, Mei-ling arose angrily and came toward Magda.

"You place one hand on my daughter, now or ever, and I shall not hesitate to break every bone in your body," Angus said coldy. Mei-ling stood still, undecided, her face distorted by anger.

Elder Brother's eyes darted quickly from the man to the woman. He said a few words to Mei-ling; she paused, then returned to her chair. He then spoke at length to William.

"My revered grandfather says he is sad that a child should not be permitted to pay her respects to the elderly," William translated drily.

Angus flushed with wrath, but his instincts warned him to be careful. The Chinese are wily, he thought, they'll start by putting you on the defensive. Better to hold yourself in control and think twice before saying anything. Temper had never won a battle.

As a sea captain he had had to act, at times, as a sea-lawyer. So, with a determined effort he restrained his ire at being put on trial in his own house, over his own affairs. There was something very suspicious going on, and he refused to be gulled.

Elder Brother spoke at length, and William interpreted for him.

"Captain MacDougall, I speak for my grandfather, who, in all serious matters, is the arbiter for the family. I do not address you as Uncle, for at this moment I am speaking as legal representative for my second cousin Mei-ling."

"I have met many lawyers in my time, William, and they can twist the truth in a dozen ways."

"I shall try to be straightforward. In 1914, you entered into a marriage contract with Chen Mei-ling. Chen Mei-ling comes from a good family, but on the death of her father, the money they had went for the sons' careers, leaving her with no suitable dowry. For this reason it was permitted that she enter into a marriage with you, who were prepared to give her the dowry she lacked."

"This is double talk. I paid a price for her," MacDougall interrupted bluntly, but William continued without a pause.

"The contract stipulated that you could annul the marriage at your pleasure, but that in so doing she would be given a sum of money to support her in her separated state."

"Aye! And I settled far more on her than the contract stipulated. At that time I cared much for Mei-ling and wanted to be sure that neither she nor Magda would ever be in want." Angus could, when he wished, speak precise and exact English. This was such an occasion.

William translated Angus' words for his grandfather, and with a slight smile he interpreted the response. "Elder Brother says he is gratified that a member of his family has pleased you well. To continue: late in 1925 you left China, leaving behind Mei-ling and her daughter Magda. The contract was considered completed. Was this not so, Captain MacDougall? Did you at any time mention returning to China?"

"No man has the right to question me or my activities, what I intended to do or not to do."

Magda looked scared. One did not speak thus to Elder Brother, but MacDougall reassured her with a squeeze of her hand, which did not escape the eye of Chen Hsu-ming.

"Your intentions are very important to Mei-ling's state of mind and account for her actions. However, let us proceed with a matter of documents. You made a deed of gift to her of all the furniture and other furnishings of this house, and also paid up the rent on the lease which then had two years more to run, and has now still half a year to go. You did this in her name. Mei-ling therefore claims that this is her house, and that you are the intruder.

"Now, from the moral point of view: Mei-ling was a young and attractive woman not quite twenty-seven years old when you left. Is it your contention that she should live alone for the rest of her life? She says that the house is hers; that since you left her, she is independent of your wishes. She says that you have no right to decide the way she should live her life, and that your entering it now and interfering with her is a violation."

"Your point is well taken, young William, and should I ever need a lawyer I should have no doubts about calling on you. But I do not concede that I have no rights." MacDougall's voice was calm and he took his time, lighting his pipe and taking a few puffs. "This is not a court of law, and you are ignoring the human factor. First of all, Mei-ling is the mother of my child and therefore I demand that she live decently. Secondly, I am a man of pride and not ashamed of my reactions. I find Mei-ling living with a man in a bedroom I paid for, nursing a baby who is not mine. She is a harlot to turn so quickly to another man—shameless, to do so in front of her daughter, my daughter. And she is dishonorable, in misusing the substantial sum of money I had left separately for Magda's education and welfare—enough to ensure that she would be brought up in a manner fitting the traditions of two great clans, the MacDougalls and the Chens."

At this last statement William gave him an oblique glance.

"But what do I find? Not only is Mei-ling openly living with a man, a baby at her breast, but my daughter is a servant in her mother's house. She is withdrawn from the school I paid for; degraded and forced to wear the cast-off rags of a servant; beaten to the point of unbelievable brutality, and subject to God knows what other humiliations. She has told me nothing, but I have my suspicions.

"I assure you that it is only by the greatest exercise of my will power that I have not done to Mei-ling what she has done to my daughter. I had previously considered the Chinese a people of honor who treasured their word. It seems I was wrong. The promise has not been kept. This is not a violation of who owns the house, it is a violation of honor; a disgrace not to me, but to you. As for the house and its contents, I did, indeed, give them to Mei-ling and she is welcome to them. I shall take my daughter away from here, and we shall make a home together."

William translated as Angus spoke. The old man barked a few questions at the women. Mme. Chen answered timidly, and Mei-ling went into an angry tirade which Elder Brother silenced by raising his hand. She quieted immediately. Then there was a brief consultation.

"My revered grandfather wishes to know if Magda is officially registered at your consulate as your daughter."

Sudden astonishment appeared in MacDougall's eyes, and the blood rushed to his face. He stood up abruptly. The knuckles of his clenched fists were white as he tried to curb his outrage, to restrain the blistering words which came to his lips. Gradually, his face paled to its natural ruddiness. He knew he had to speak carefully —and not insult them—or he could lose his daughter. But he could not keep the contempt out of his voice.

"So that is the way it is, then. You know well the situation, and now you want me to pay for my daughter. Well, my daughter is worth everything to me, and I refuse to bargain for her, as is *your* custom. Let me hear no more. How much do you want? I shall take her from this house immediately and adopt her as my legal daughter."

"You sound very righteous," William said tightly, his words precisely enunciated, icily controlled. "Your speech would be justified if one could ignore your own actions regarding Magda. I thought you might be able to see Mei-ling's point of view, but you prefer not to.

"Believe me," he continued. "No MacDougall has more pride than a Chen. Your people were barbarians, living in animal skins, when we were teachers and philosophers, living in a culture as yet unsurpassed. Our honor is more precious to us than life itself. It is only because Mei-ling has not acted according to our code of honor that we deign to discuss this matter with you.

"We will, however, not allow our cousin Mei-ling to be disgraced, or to lose face because of your actions and your speech calling her a loose woman. Nor will we so easily discard any person of our clan—even if she is not wholly of our race.

"The terms we demand are not for money, but for the reinstatement of Mei-ling's reputation. The only way that can happen is for you to return to this house as her husband. Since Magda is not registered in your consulate as your daughter, she is legally the daughter of Mei-ling—without whose permission you may not adopt Magda. You may never be permitted to see her again should you refuse the option we give you. The servants are the only ones aware of your actions today, and, I assure you, no word will leave this house if you accept these terms."

Captain MacDougall walked back to his chair and sat down heavily. He had no case against the ultimatum. Magda watched him anxiously. Besides William, she was the only one in the room who understood the two languages. She looked at William's face, as bleached as her father's was scarlet. It was like a piece of finely carved ivory—classic and emotionless. Her eyes were filled with hurt and bewilderment as she gazed at William—she had thought he was her friend and ally, and now he wanted to send her back to her mother. How could he? Her eyes beseeched him, but he met her look steadily.

Angus saw her pain and took her hand in his, squeezing it reassuringly. Poor little thing! He took a deep breath before answering the Chens. Magda studied him apprehensively as he seemed to waver.

"It's all right, lassie. Don't upset yourself." He patted her hand, then turned sternly to Chen Hsu-ming and William.

"You leave me with no alternative. Where my daughter is concerned, I am helpless to do anything but yield to

1980 COWBOY SCHEDULE

DATE	OPPONENT	SITE	TIME
SEPT. 13	OREGON STATE	LARAMIE	1:30 MDT
SEPT. 20	RICHMOND	LARAMIE	1:30 MDT
SEPT. 27	*HAWAII	LARAMIE	1:30 MDT
OCT. 4	*NEW MEXICO (HOMECOMING)	LARAMIE	1:30 MDT
OCT. 11	*BRIGHAM YOUNG	PROVO	1:30 MDT
OCT. 18	*UTAH	LARAMIE	1:30 MDT
OCT. 25	*SAN DIEGO STATE	LARAMIE	1:30 MDT
NOV. 1	*COLORADO STATE	FT. COLLINS	1:30 MDT
NOV. 8	*NEVADA-LAS VEGAS	LAS VEGAS	7:30 PST
NOV. 15	*AIR FORCE	ACADEMY	1:00 MST
NOV. 22	*TEXAS-EL PASO	EL PASO	7:30 MST

*—Western Athletic Conference Games

Season Tickets: $54 each for six home games.   Single Games—$9 each

For information contact Athletic Ticket Office, War Memorial Fieldhouse, P.O. Box 3414, Laramie, 82071, or call 766-2345.

Have a Coke® and a smile.   **COCA-COLA Bottlers of Cheyenne and Laramie**

1980 COWBOY SCHEDULE

DATE	OPPONENT	SITE	TIME
SEPT. 13	OREGON STATE	LARAMIE	1:30 MDT
SEPT. 20	RICHMOND	LARAMIE	1:30 MDT
SEPT. 27	*HAWAII	LARAMIE	1:30 MDT
OCT. 4	*NEW MEXICO (HOMECOMING)	LARAMIE	1:30 MDT
OCT. 11	*BRIGHAM YOUNG	PROVO	1:30 MDT
OCT. 18	*UTAH	LARAMIE	1:30 MDT
OCT. 25	*SAN DIEGO STATE	LARAMIE	1:30 MDT
NOV. 1	*COLORADO STATE	FT. COLLINS	1:30 MDT
NOV. 8	NEVADA-LAS VEGAS	LAS VEGAS	7:30 PST
NOV. 15	*AIR FORCE	ACADEMY	1:00 MST
NOV. 22	*TEXAS-EL PASO	EL PASO	7:30 MST

*—Western Athletic Conference Games

Season Tickets: $54 each for six home games. Single Games—$9 each
For information contact Athletic Ticket Office, War Memorial Fieldhouse, P.O. Box 3414,
Laramie, 82071, or call 766-2345.

Have a Coke® and a smile.

COCA-COLA Bottlers of
Cheyenne and Laramie

your terms. But I have two conditions. The first is that Mei-ling must keep her bastard son out of my sight and my hearing. The second and most important is that William draw up a legal document from which there can be no changing of minds. I know well Mei-ling's vindictiveness toward Magda.

"Make out this agreement, one that is binding in your law and on your honor, that Magda is henceforth to be considered my daughter, given to me with no reservations, so that I may begin adoption proceedings according to the laws of my country.

"Do you agree to this, William?"

William conferred with his grandfather, and they both bowed low in agreement.

"Then I am satisfied. Magda, you may go now and pay your respects to Elder Brother. He is well worthy of his position, and though I disagree with him, I respect his concern for his family."

MacDougall rang for Uni. He left no doubt that he was once again head of the household, as he ordered Uni to bring in refreshments, that they might cement the covenant in good faith.

CHAPTER FOUR

ᐊᐊᐊᐊᐊᐊᐊᐊᐊᐊᐊᐊᐊᐊᐊᐊ

ON HER SIXTEENTH birthday, Magda's father gave her a diamond pendant and a pair of matching earrings.

"A fine lady needs fine jewelry, lass. This is just the beginning. Your life will be full and complete, I promise you, Maggie lass, when I make my fortune. Remember that money talks loud. With enough ye can look any man or woman in the face and tell them to go to the devil if you want to. No one will disdain you because you are half Chinese, but keep it a secret, lass, for 'tis no man's business but your own."

"Dinna fuss yourself, Angus MacDougall, 'tis a proper

35

Scottish lass I'll be, or the devil take me." Magda teased her father fondly, mimicking his brogue.

He examined his daughter with pride. His blood had proved the stronger. She was a tall, slim European girl with a touch of the exotic. But, though she had the promise of beauty, her face lacked the animation to make it truly alive.

Her complexion was very fair, with an opaque quality like that of a magnolia blossom, and as fine. Her eyebrows made two silken curves over her eyes, which were large, dark, and brilliant, with the classical Oriental lift at the corners. Though tall, she was small-boned like her mother. That fragility and her eyes—though hers were more deeply set and fringed with thick black lashes—were her only Chinese heritage. Her features were delicate and her sensual mouth was an almost perfect oval in shape. But it was her hair that accentuated her extraordinary coloring. Even Titian could not have captured its radiance on canvas.

Quiet and withdrawn, Magda rarely smiled or laughed; but when she did, she shone. Her father was her sun and she lit up only for him. Her one friend was still Natasha Wilkinson. She seemed to need no other—except her father. They were more than father and daughter, they were dear companions.

MacDougall's fondest ambition was to share a good life with Magda, away from her Chinese past. In order to reach the financial position he wanted, he returned to his old hobby of studying the stockmarket and making cautious investments—a hobby which had worked well for him before. Now it became a full-time career. The Depression had caused many stocks to be lower than their worth, and he played the market carefully—never trusting too much to one basket.

When one of the men in his brokerage firm died, Angus bought the man's seat and his partnership in the company. His business fully launched, he introduced Magda to his bankers and his partners. No one had the remotest suspicion that she was not all she appeared to be. Magda spent most of her time after school in his office. It became a common sight in the business district to see Big Red MacDougall walking with his daughter—she in her school uniform and he in formal broker's attire—Prince Albert coat, striped trousers, and top hat.

Magda felt comfortable in the world of stocks and bonds, and her father discovered that she had an uncanny sense about investments. Her mind was methodical and analytical, and her memory for data phenomenal.

He taught her how to read the banking news and financial pages, and he taught her well: in a world marketplace like Shanghai, it was essential to know the political backgrounds of different countries: a gamble on a stock in a stable country was less risky than a conservative investment on one with a shaky government. He set problems for her and was gratified by the ease with which she solved them. He was not above taking her advice, at times, about an investment for himself, for she had not only good judgment but that indefinable something—an instinct for business and sound decision-making.

Angus glowed at his daughter's progress: she was now a far cry from the spindly, battered child he had rescued upon his return from Scotland. At first he was as surprised at his own decision to return to Shanghai as Mei-ling was shocked by his arrival. Angus grinned—that Mei-ling!—she was changed not a whit. By thunderation, she was all woman!

It had not taken long before Angus shared her bedroom once more. Oh, she rebuffed him grandly to begin with. She flirted with him, taunted him, and then enticed him. She had made him laugh with her tart humor, and she had made him angry enough to shake her. Then, once more, he carried her squirming to the bedroom as she guessed he would. She wanted him. She knew he desired her. But, just as important, she could flaunt her power over him to her daughter.

She and Magda had an unspoken truce, and they left each other strictly alone.

This was the shape of Angus MacDougall's life when he was sixty-six years old. It was not a hoary age, but as the years sped by he felt himself sinking into a comfortable pattern, his greatest dream still unaccomplished.

"There is a little place near the port of Sydney that I

37

came across on my travels many a year gone. There we'll build a house: on a little hill where the waves crash on the craggy rocks below and spray up a hundred feet high, falling like a thousand diamonds sparkling in the sun. Near the place is a hidden cove where the sands are washed white by the tides. This is where we'll live. But first, you will go to a fine school and learn all the airs and graces of a fine lady. You shall meet many a true friend and take your place in the world, for you're as bonny a lass as ever I did see!"

Magda listened raptly, as she did every time he filled her with his dreams.

"Oh, Papa!" she sighed.

"Aye, lass, there's where we'll go, to Australia, the land where the wayfarer is welcome. But first I must reach my goal, and time is running out."

"Don't you dare talk that way, Papa. I won't listen to you!" Magda clapped her hands over her ears as though in jest; but every time she heard her father talk of his age, a cold fear gripped her, and she shriveled inside. "Papa, let's not wait. Let's go right away, like you said, you and I together. Oh, Papa, let's do it. I don't care about being rich."

"But I do, lass, I do." Angus looked at his daughter. Her eyes were as bright as the jewels he had just given her. "The dream will not happen otherwise. It's time I changed my method of investing. 'Tis overly conservative I've been; the time has come to take a gamble on our future. Now give me a kiss and be off with ye. After school we'll study the market together and make a big killing. Then we'll sail the ocean blue, aye, lass?"

Magda laughed and gave him a big hug. She loved him so much that sometimes it made her feel weak.

It was Magda who first noticed and brought to Angus' attention a little-known stock that was rising incredibly fast despite the depressed times. Together they studied it, checking everything known about it. Magda decided it was undesirable, but Angus was hypnotized by it. This could well be his last opportunity to make his fortune. Then his sweet Maggie would have her chance while there was yet time to enjoy it with her.

He added up all his assets, and all he could borrow

—but no matter how he computed the results, even given the rise he expected from the stock, the final amount fell short of his goal. If he couldn't reach that, he thought, the gamble was worthless. A big profit demanded a big risk. Angus threw caution aside and bought the stock on margin.

The stock wavered for a few days and then it plunged. In a few days more he knew he would be wiped out. To cover his purchase he needed funds he didn't have. There was only the money he had set aside for Magda —but that was as inviolate as though it didn't exist. Only one way remained to save his skin.

All his life Angus had been an honest man. If he ever had private dealings while on his voyages, it was never at the expense of the shipping company he served. Every captain he knew on the high seas did the same. But using his clients' money to rescue himself was different. Angus hesitated—but not for long. He had to act immediately. The shadowy faces of his clients faded before the bright, eager face of his beloved daughter. And, without any further sense of guilt, he used the money of his customers to stem the tide of his personal disaster.

After five days, Angus knew that his financial ruin— and the discovery of his embezzlement—were inevitable. He had very little time left, and so he began to implement plan number two.

Magda's assets had not been touched and would be untouchable even upon his death. For years, he had placed half his profits in stocks, bonds, and trusts in her name and had so arranged the purchases to assure that when he died, no court could take the money from her. Angus had initially done this because of lingering doubts over Mei-ling's actions should he die while Magda was still a minor.

Deep within himself, Angus MacDougall wept for his daughter. Aye, the poor lass! Life had never been easy for her, and once again he was adding to her unhappiness. But he brushed away his reservations—there was no choice and no time for sentiment.

Everything was in order. The first thing he had done after adopting her was to make a will naming her as his only heir. Most important, her passport was up-to-date

—he had made it a priority to keep both of their passports so. Hence, Magda was secure on all counts.

The days passed relentlessly. The stock would spurt now and then, but not enough to cover his gamble. Time had almost elapsed, and Angus put his emergency plan into operation. A single passage was purchased on the H.M.S. *Queen Mary* to Genoa. Angus deposited Magda's passport and other papers with the purser, giving him full instructions. Suitable clothes and luggage were bought and sent to the ship. Although Magda was officially his daughter now—and legally entitled to his name and to British citizenship—he never overcame his suspicions that Mei-ling would find some way to stop Magda from leaving China, out of pure malevolence. So he kept the entire operation completely secret.

But Angus decided to confide in part in William Chen. He'd learned to trust and like this young Chinaman who had, by a strange sequence of events over the years, become a friend. He gave William the details of his arrangements for Mei-ling's welfare in case of his death and asked William to be the executor of her estate. Then he handed him an envelope containing $5,000 and asked William to dole it out to Mei-ling as he thought best.

"Do you expect trouble, Uncle?"

"Who knows when trouble will descend? Keep a watchful eye on my lass, William, wherever she may be. I have advised Magda that, should she ever leave China, she should cut all ties here, except for you. There must always be at least one person in the world she can turn to in case of misfortune, and I can think of no man I trust more than I do you. I would like to know, William, that if anything should happen to me, that you will never fail her."

"Rest peaceful, Uncle. Be assured I shall always see to the welfare of my cousin Magda. Not only do I have a deep and abiding affection for her, which she returns, but I am also the head of the house of Chen. It is my duty to be responsible to those who come to me for protection and guidance. Much, I think, as the 'laird' of your country."

"I can ask for no more than that. About Mei-ling—I have asked you to be her executor, but it goes deeper than the legal task. All her money will pass through your hands alone. She is still a young woman, full thirty-five years younger than I, and the chances are that she will marry again when I die. I would like to know that her money will not go astray."

"You show me great faith, Uncle. Be sure I will not fail in any of your wishes to the extent that I am able."

They shook hands warmly, MacDougall feeling a great relief, and William leaving the office with grief in his heart.

Magda was mystified by her father's instructions. Without any explanation, he told her to go directly from school to the jetty on the bund and to take the launch and board the H.M.S. *Queen Mary* which was anchored near Woosung.

"Dinna ask me any questions, but do as I say, will ye, lass? Dinna go home to change, but go on board directly from school. Everything is arranged. Wait on board. It may be a long wait, but dinna worry yourself —and dinna be alarmed if the ship leaves with ye aboard. Have faith in me, lass. Trust me to do what is best for the two of us. Have no doubts but remain on board whatever happens."

"But, Papa—"

"No questions, not now. It will all be explained to ye in time. Do ye not like a bit of mystery?"

He placed his hands on her shoulders and gazed deeply into her eyes. "I'm proud of ye, Maggie, lass, as proud as any man can be of his daughter. You have brought into my life a depth of riches I had not thought possible. You are a true daughter of the MacDougalls. More than that I cannot say. You are descended from ancient people, strong and proud people, from Celts and Picts and Vikings—fighters all. Hold ye head high in the world, lass. It does not respect those who whimper and turn tail."

He drew her close to him and kissed her. Magda felt hot tears fill her eyes and she brushed them away with a tremulous smile.

"You're making me cry, Papa, and that's not worthy of a true MacDougall, especially a Red One, is it now?" She tried to mimic him, but it didn't come off. For some unknown reason, the moment had become charged with emotion.

"You sound as though you were saying goodbye." Her voice was muffled against the rough tweed coat. "You're not up to something, Papa? Are you?"

"Now, would I fool you, Maggie MacDougall? Give me a big hug and a kiss and be off with ye. Remember, you are not to go home, nor to telephone anyone, but to go straight to the ship and wait. Will ye do this for me?"

Magda looked at him reproachfully, "Have I ever not obeyed you, Papa?"

"That's my good lass. I depend on ye to do exactly as I tell you." He gave her another kiss and she clung to him for a moment, as she used to do when she was a child, until at last he pried her off. With a pat and a little push, he sent her on her way to school.

Angus felt drained as he watched her straight, slim figure disappear. Perhaps it was the intensity of his gaze which made her turn around and hesitate, as though she wanted to return; but instead, she waved and walked on, dragging her feet just a bit.

His eyes misted until the image doubled and tripled—becoming a blur of movement fragmented with the colors of the tam-o'-shanter she always wore.

Magda wandered around the ship disconsolately. She felt a little self-conscious, still wearing her school uniform in the crowd of well-dressed men and women. Time passed very slowly. More passengers and guests arrived, and Magda watched anxiously for her father as each launch brought another load of people.

Why was she aboard? Why was her father not? Were they finally going off to Europe? Was this the departure they had planned for so long—free and unencumbered, ready to make a fresh start? Oh, Papa! You should have let me say goodbye to Meh-meh, and William, and even Tasha. Why have you been acting so strange lately, Papa? This morning I didn't want to leave you. I felt you hurting inside and it made me hurt. You could have told me, you know—I can keep a secret. Something is the matter—something . . .

A desperate knot of desolation gripped her. A sense

of foreboding chilled her, and she shivered. Papa, she called from deep within her, as though her silent voice could reach out to him, Papa, what is wrong? Don't play games with me. Are you coming aboard? Am I sailing alone? Papa . . .

The ship's whistle sounded the first warning. Passengers crowded the decks, waving to their guests who were boarding the launches back to Shanghai. Magda watched the boat with the pilot aboard. Her father knew them all. Perhaps her father had come with him. She watched hopefully. In her mind's eye, she already saw the big man: his uncovered head glinting in the sun, his hair now speckled with white but still dominated by the red as was his full beard and moustache. She saw his face lifted up, eyebrows jutting out to protect the narrowed eyes as they peered up to find her on the crowded deck, half-smiling in anticipation of surprising her. She was so sure this time. Her hand was raised partway to wave at him. But the dream did not become real. One solitary man climbed aboard.

The second and final blast sounded, and the anchor chain was hoisted. Magda felt the ship vibrate as the propeller turned in the water. Her fear turned into despair as she saw the churning of the water and watched the ship pull out slowly. Her whole body was one screaming cry: Papa, Papa, where are you?

Hypnotized, sightless, she watched the shoreline fade. The ship moved away, away from Shanghai and from all she had ever known. It seemed as though hours passed before the ship lost speed. The pilot climbed down the Jacob's ladder and jumped into the pilot boat trailing beside the ship. It was her last chance to leave. She couldn't sail, she didn't *want* to sail without her father. And she knew—she had known all the time—that he wasn't aboard. She moved forward, her hand up to signal the pilot, her mouth opened to shout. The pilot knew her: he would let her leave with him. But an iron will stopped her as though a hand had clutched her shoulder.

"Have faith in me," he had said once before, and he *had* appeared in her moment of greatest need.

Angus made such final arrangements as were necessary. He still checked the stock—it had gone up slightly again but not nearly enough to matter. The day of reckoning had come. In the eyes of the world he was bankrupt, and worse, an embezzler. The sale of his seat on the exchange, his partnership in a good brokerage firm, and his office furnishings, would in part, pay off his creditors. Possibly a scandal could be averted. Most important, no one could touch Magda's holdings. There might be some trouble over the insurance, even though it was more than seven years since he had taken it out before leaving for Scotland. It was intended to cover all contingencies, but insurance people could be tricky, he knew. Angus shrugged. Magda would be secure enough without it.

Everything was in order, as far as he could tell. He felt exhausted, drained of emotion. He checked the time. The ship should be well on its way out to sea.

With Magda safe from scandal and retribution, Angus MacDougall, with anguish in his heart for his daughter, but with confidence that he was doing the right thing, said aloud, "Maggie, lass, 'tis sorry I am to be leaving ye this way, but there's nought else to do."

He took his revolver, ready primed, carefully placed it at the right side of his temple—he demanded that this, above all things, be ship-shape and proper—and pulled the trigger.

Magda was in no mood to join the merry-makers leaning over the railings and watching the ship pass from the Whangpoo River into the Yellow Sea. She went to the purser's office. She knew her father well enough to know he'd prepared for every contingency, had made meticulous arrangements so that she would have no problems. She was not surprised to find her passport there, her passage all paid for, and a cabin on deck assigned to her. The purser was too busy to talk to her then, except to say that he'd see her later.

She followed the steward to her cabin. New luggage sat neatly placed on the slotted bench. She sat herself down beside it, unthinking, unmoving—waiting.

There was a knock on the door. The purser entered, full of good cheer and friendly apologies—he knew she would understand, he said, she was a captain's daughter. He had served with her father. After asking if there was anything he could do, he wished her a good trip and handed her a thick sealed envelope.

"Captain MacDougall asked me to give this to you when we were underway—probably a surprise gift for your vacation. Enjoy it!" He laughed cheerfully, gave her a half-salute, and left the cabin.

For several minutes, Magda held the envelope in her hands without moving to open it. "My papa is dead," she said aloud to the empty room. She was consumed with loneliness. She felt her own breath choking her. With a great effort, she slowly and carefully pried open the envelope and read the words.

Maggie, my lass: I made the big gamble and it failed. You were right, lass. You said the stock was unstable, and so it was. There were so few years left for me to share with you. I was becoming old and losing my wonderful dream, my vision. Ahead was the future, yours and mine together. We spoke of it so often, daughter: a new place where there would be no shame for you.

Your position in the world would be assured, my bonny lass, without fear of discovery, and with all the advantages your beauty, intelligence, and money could bring. My dream for you, daughter, was more and more out of reach each day. I took the chance in full knowledge of the consequences.

There should be no shame, no taint, in being what you are, but there are many who, as I did at one time, think there is. It is not a kind world, and I did not make it the way it is. But I did make you, my Highland lass, and I want you to be happy. You are all I ever wanted. I wish I could remain with you, to help you over the rough places, but it cannot be. I cannot permit you to face scandal and the humiliation when the truth of my investments is exposed, for I used money that was not mine to use. Nor can I face it myself. I never ran away from anything in my life until now.

The last act of my life was to deceive you, my poor little girl. My heart goes out to you. I know the hours were long, waiting for me—I'll be sharing them all with you now. I know the despair you must have felt, afraid

I was deserting you again when I did not appear. Aye, lass, I also felt a great despair, but this is the only way I can protect you from my sins.

I only regret not seeing you in the full bloom of your womanhood. It will be a fortunate man who makes you his wife.

Forgive me, lass, for turning you out into the world alone. I must pay the piper his dues, but you will be safely out of it.

About money: You are secure financially. When you reach your majority, the money will be yours to handle. Be careful with it. The Hong Kong and Shanghai Bank is the executor of your estate until you come of age. My good friend, Sir Alfred Wilkie-Hume, is the only person outside of your family and Natasha who knows your background. Keep it that way. I needed Sir Alfred's assistance in completing your adoption. He is a true gentleman of the old school, and your secret is safe with him. He also wrote a letter of recommendation to St. Ursula's Convent in Lucerne, Switzerland. I have made inquiries in the last few years, and this is a finishing school of the highest caliber. Young Phillips, the purser, has all your school records.

I also enclose the details of your accounts. I have asked Sir Alfred to send you periodical reports, as I know of your interest in following the market.

That is all there is, Maggie, my very dearest. Forgive me, and know I have loved you from the moment I saw your wee red head. Don't grieve for me. Until you were born, I did not know what it meant to love. Now I do not know how to say goodbye.

As I sit here, there is no goodbye, just the sight and the thought of you, my lass, my bairn, a true MacDougall, a Red MacDougall. 'Tis no light thing I do. Those who came before me would say I take the honorable way out.

Stand tall, and straight, and proud in the world, for you have good blood in you. If you learn prayers at school, say a few for your old father, who needs them badly.

Maggie, believe me that my hand is in yours, and will be there always till the end of time.

Papa

No. No! NO! A hopeless whimper grew into a silent scream which engulfed her. The world whirled around her. She was pleading, crying inside: Papa, Papa, come back! Don't leave me, Papa!

But, like a tidal wave receding beyond the horizon only to gather force for a still more powerful thrust, the truth surged back—again and again—assaulting her, tearing apart her resistance.

Forlorn, abandoned, Magda sat in the cabin, her world crushed, meaningless, empty. She was truly alone.

The sheets of paper she clutched fell from her hands.

Minutes passed. The room grew dark. She treasured the darkness; she became part of the darkness.

And then suddenly, in her despair and desolation, a strange warmth touched her. Magda felt her hand being clasped in the huge and tender grip she knew so well. The familiar feeling of reassurance swept over her.

"Papa?" she called out softly in wonderment. "Oh, Papa, you haven't really left me. Oh, my Papa, you'll always be with me, just like you said."

Only then came the healing tears of release, as she heard in her mind, as clearly as in life, his booming voice, so tender and dear, soothing her as it had in the past.

"I'll do all the things you set out to do, I promise you, Papa," she whispered to him between her sobs. "And I will be brave, no matter what happens."

PART TWO

Archie

1936

CHAPTER FIVE

◀◀◀◀◀◀◀◀◀◀◀◀◀◀◀◀◀

MAGDA STOOD BY the railing of the promenade deck of the S.S. *D'Artagnan*, the pride of the Messageries Maritimes fleet of luxury liners. Sporadically she had noticed the clear waters of the South China Sea slowly becoming muddied as the ship entered the Yellow Sea and plowed into the delta of the Yang tse Kiang. In a few hours they would be arriving in Shanghai.

A kaleidoscope of pictures flickered through her mind. She made no concerted effort to think of anything, but let the images come as they would. Without realizing it, she wiped out recollections of her mother. But she lingered over each second she had spent with her father—a jumbled montage of happy memories.

A small launch came alongside the ship. The Jacob's ladder was tossed over the side and a single figure climbed aboard—the pilot who was to guide the huge ship through the shallows of the delta and lead it to safe anchorage near Woosung.

A moment of heartsick *déjà vu* brought back the circumstances of her departure from Shanghai and reawakened the nagging disquietude that it was an error to return to the place of her birth. Shanghai had nothing left for her but an aging grandmother, whom she had not seen in five years, and her cousin William, with whom she corresponded intermittently.

She smiled when she recalled the look of consternation on the face of Mother Superior when she handed Magda the letter from William, written in Chinese, and asked for an explanation.

Magda glanced at it rapidly.

"It is a letter of condolence from the son of a Chinese friend of my father's. I studied with him and we decided to write in Chinese so that I wouldn't forget the language."

How quickly, Magda thought, she had learned to change half a truth to half a lie.

With Mother Superior's permission, the correspondence continued in Chinese. That, indeed, was William's idea. He wanted her to remember the Mandarin he loved, the language of poets and philosophers. But it was she who insisted, for privacy, that they write in code. Her father had so imbued her with the idea of secrecy that she applied it to all things.

Magda smiled to herself, remembering how she had constructed the first simple code: transposing every seventh word backward. As soon as William had mastered one variation, she developed another. It became a matter of pride with her to translate letters from him without checking her codebook. She enjoyed the mental exercise. It gave that first dreary year in the convent a little spice.

Magda indulged her natural affinity for languages and learned them with remarkable ease. She enjoyed the patterns of words, analyzing them in regard to each other; there was a rhythm, a cadence, a logic of languages, which fascinated her. She spoke French, Italian, and German as naturally as she spoke English and Chinese.

The years at St. Ursula's had passed pleasantly and slowly. But Magda made few friends at the school.

She had always been alone—but she learned to be even more seclusive. Sister George had reached out to Magda, had tried to break through the barrier which existed in the girl's mind; she noticed that Magda chose not to join in the free give-and-take of idle chatter, teasing, and the easy laughter which convulsed the other girls at the school. One day, Magda overheard Sister George say to an unseen girl, "You must be especially kind to Magda, and patient. Her background is strange—" Magda did not wait to hear the rest. She ran to the garden and hid in the lower branches of a big oak tree. Leave me alone —leave me alone—everyone please just leave me alone, she cried frantically in her mind. She wanted to die. Isolated now in body and spirit, Magda knew she would be isolated for ever.

The Sisters had been kind enough. Each in turn attempted to draw her into the Church, especially dear Sister George. How wonderful it would have been to have found such faith and tranquility as Sister George had.

Magda thought, with some nostalgia, of the Sisters and their valiant struggles to make young ladies of the girls who came to the convent from all over the world. She had written to Tasha: "They teach us how to sit and how to stand, how to dance and how to ride, eat and drink; even how to converse. We are indoctrinated with the principles of decorum, especially by my favorite Sister George and her constant reminders that a '*jeune fille bien élevée*' does not do thus and that it is not '*comme il faut*' to do the other. If I obeyed all their instructions I would never have to think for myself again. I could glide through life, smiling graciously, and say the right words on every occasion. It sounds pretty futile, but I must admit that it does give one a sense of confidence knowing that one will not make a '*faux pas*'—by social standards, at least. In the unlikely event that I should ever be presented at court, I could make a most convincing curtsy!"

The ship's blast shook Magda out of her half-world of reverie and revived more poignantly the heart-wrenching memory of her father. So vivid was the vision that, for the flash of a moment, she saw him distinctly: the tall massive man, his hair and beard blazing in the sun, his blue eyes twinkling with joy at the sight of her, his hand out to grasp hers as he had done so often and did still in her thoughts.

The anguish of her loss had dimmed, but *he* had never really died for her—not so long as she could conjure him up at will.

"You are making an idol of your father," Sister George would remonstrate in vain. "Such adoration belongs only to God."

Smoothly, the pilot brought the ship to safe harbor. Five years earlier, at almost this identical spot, only the influence of her father's iron will had prevented Magda from getting off the ship. Perhaps, she thought, it would be an act of faith not to disembark now.

"All passengers for Shanghai, this way please," the

chief steward called out. Everyone who was leaving lined up and boarded the passenger launch. Magda was among them, still feeling a chill of apprehension as the launch pulled away from the ship and headed for the ferry docks.

When she had impulsively decided to return to Shanghai Magda notified no one of her decision; but by the time the ship reached Hong Kong, she felt a desperate need to have someone meet her at the ferry dock, and she sent a cable to Sir Alfred Wilkie-Hume, her father's most trusted friend, announcing her arrival in Shanghai. Though the Hong Kong and Shanghai Bank was the executor of her estate, Sir Alfred, the bank director, had kept in touch with her during the years she had spent in Switzerland. Perhaps, just out of courtesy, he would meet her or send someone. It had become vitally important that she not be alone her first hour in Shanghai. If only I could have spent it with William, she sighed.

Shanghai's skyline came into view and Magda felt an unexpected thrill of excitement as she identified the major buildings which lined the bund. There was the imposing Hong Kong and Shanghai Bank—she was sure she could see the two marble lions recumbent in front of it. And she smiled involuntarily when she recalled the old story that the lions would roar whenever a virgin passed by—and that they had never roared yet. Shanghai humor, but she remembered believing it as a child. There was the tall British-American Tobacco Company where Tasha's cousin worked. It was quite a prestigious place to work, and Tasha had been lucky that her cousin had gotten her a job there. Magda couldn't help remembering that it was shortly after Tasha informed her of her job that their correspondence had slowed to a trickle.

The Whangpoo River teemed with traffic. Magda didn't remember the sampans being quite this cramped, nor how picturesque the junks were from a distance, with their many-hued, patched sails billowing out, their bamboo veins making them look like bats' wings. How filthy the river was, with all the floating garbage!

The bund was packed with people, rickshaws, wheelbarrows, food peddlers. It was hard to realize that she had been part of all this. Had there always been this extreme poverty? So many beggars with such horrible deformities?

The launch tied up at the jetty and everyone piled out. Magda stood alone on the dock, momentarily lost between past and present, then walked slowly, trailing behind the others to the Customs House.

Archibald Whitcombe Monteith stood by the entrance of the Shanghai Customs House, bored and impatient, waiting for the S.S. *D'Artagnan* to bring in its loads of passengers. Trust Lovejoy to hand him this errand. He was a banker, not an errand boy, he had entreated, but old Lovey told him firmly that everyone had some extraneous duties to perform—as long as the Hong Kong and Shanghai Bank was the only guardian Miss MacDougall had, it was only proper that a member of the staff should pay her the courtesy of meeting her. Archie, Mr. Lovejoy had smiled, his mouth twitching slightly at the corners, Archie was the newest member of the staff, and so the job fell to him.

Archie saw the dock attendant signal, and a motor launch appeared in view, anchored in its berth, and disgorged its passengers.

As the assistant purser made his way toward the Customs House, Archie stopped him.

"I'm here to meet a Miss MacDougall. Is she on the launch?"

The officer looked blank.

"*Mlle MacDougall. Avez-vous une Mademoiselle MacDougall ici?*" Archie repeated in his schoolboy French.

The purser looked puzzled and Archie patiently repeated the name, trying to give it a French twist, though the name did not lend itself to many variations.

At last, the Frenchman's eyes brightened. "*Ah oui! Ah oui! Ma'mselle M'Dougalle, Eh bien! Regardez; m'sieu, la mademoiselle là-bas avec les cheveaux rouges.* Zee red hair. *Elle est très jolie, n'est-ce pas?* Very beautiful. *Bonne chance, mon vieux.*" With a friendly wink, the French officer gave him a half-salute and entered the building.

"Good luck, old man," Archie repeated, grinning. "*Mais* truly."

It didn't take him long to pick her out. Under a small hat, perched jauntily on her head, her red hair blazed.

She halted, looking a little lost, and, even from a distance, a bit apprehensive. The purser was right. She was a beauty, by Jove! Archie's face lit up and he loped toward his charge with awakened interest.

As she stood poised on the dock, debating what to do next, Magda saw a young man talking to one of the ship's officers at the entrance of the Customs House. She noticed him because his hair was so blond that it looked almost white, blinding, in fact, in the midday sun. He walked toward her with the easy stride of an athlete—a boyish-looking man with the typical natty air of an Englishman, like the Prince of Wales grown tall. To her surprise, he stopped right in front of her. His candid blue eyes widened as he stared into hers.

"Oh, I say—you can't be—that is, are you Miss Magda MacDougall?"

Instead of her usual reticence, Magda found a smile trembling at the corners of her mouth.

"Yes, I can be. Yes, I am."

"By Jove! What great luck for me."

Magda's reserve rose immediately at what she presumed to be the young man's forwardness. She started to walk away, pleased nevertheless that she had worn her favorite cocoa-colored linen suit with the matching hat and her rust-and-pink silk scarf, all of which helped to bring out her vivid coloring. She turned quickly when she felt a strong hand at her elbow.

"Oh, I say! I do honestly beg your pardon. I'm Archie Montieth, from the bank. Mr. Lovejoy received your cable—he's assistant to old Humey—well, anyway, he thought you should be met, and sent me." Archie smiled his delight in the mission and solicitously took her arm and led her inside the building. "The old man didn't think a hotel would be suitable for a young lady right out of convent school, so I've been chasing around and found an apartment for you. Just booked it for a week, pending your approval. It's at the Royal Arms, opposite the racecourse on Bubbling Well. Oh, I say! I'm rattling away a mile a minute, aren't I? I'm not like this all the time. Please believe me." He appealed to her so earnestly that Magda could not help responding with a smile.

"I believe you," she replied, pleased and surprised by his frank admiration.

"Look, give me your luggage chits and I'll get you cleared out of customs. Sit here. I'll be out in a jiffy."

Archie found her a quiet corner in the bustling hall and miraculously produced a chair. He was as good as his word, emerging a few moments later with her bags. Magda, seeing other passengers who had been ahead of her, and who were still waiting, thought once again how the British had a way of expecting service on demand and getting it.

"You know, Mr. Monteith," Magda said as Archie helped her into the taxi, "I'm truly grateful to you and the bank for the trouble you've gone to, but it isn't really necessary for you to go on any further."

"Not for all the money in the world would I let you go on without me," Archie replied, following her into the car. And with exaggerated gestures and pompous tones he declared, "I'd be derelict in my duties if I did not escort you personally to your new residence."

Magda laughed at his clowning. "Well, in that case, I can't deny you that privilege."

"A privilege I intend to take full advantage of," he said cheerily and grinned at her. To his dismay he saw the smile leave her face, and a wave of uncertainty creep over it. Suddenly she looked young and vulnerable. Archie felt an urge to protect her from all harm, especially from insensitive oafs such as himself.

"Oh, I say—what I meant was—I didn't mean that the way it sounded—that is to say—I'm really quite harmless, y'know. They even called me 'Bunny' at school. I don't suppose you'd care to call me that yourself, would you?"

"No, Mr. Monteith, I'm sure I wouldn't," she answered firmly. A smile started to twitch at her lips and she couldn't resist asking, "But why did they call you Bunny?"

"I can wiggle my ears," he answered very logically, and he demonstrated. Magda laughed, long and gaily, as she considered the young man beside her.

There was something so engaging about him and his frank interest that she found herself slowly losing her reserve and feeling extraordinarily at ease with him by the time they reached their destination.

"I haven't laughed so much in years, and for the life of me, I don't know why," she said, wiping away a tear.

"But that's the whole idea. Laughter is no good if you have to find a reason. Now, I hardly ever find jokes funny and I must say that when everyone else is rolling over some story I feel like an awful ass."

"Do you feel that way also? I always thought that perhaps I didn't have a sense of humor." The taxi stopped in front of a new modern building, and Magda gathered up her things while Archie paid the driver.

"You have a reservation for Miss MacDougall?" Archie asked the Eurasian desk clerk, after they had entered the building.

"Yes, sir. Number 416 on the fourth floor. I hope you'll be satisfied, Miss MacDougall. If there is anything I can do, please let me know."

"Just a minute," Archie interjected. "Is it facing the racecourse as I requested?"

"I'm sorry, sir, we have none available at the moment, but we have Miss MacDougall down for the next one that becomes vacant."

"Well, you'd jolly well better get one now," Archie said pleasantly enough, but there was no mistaking his tone of authority.

The slight, sallow-faced clerk flushed an unbecoming red and said stiffly, "I'll see what can be done, sir."

He left his desk and went into the office behind him. They heard the sound of voices and then a large ruddy-faced man accompanied the desk clerk out of the office.

"You're Mr. Monteith from the Hong Kong and Shanghai Bank?"

"Right the first time, old boy."

"Rogers here made an error." The clerk tightened his lips in silent resentment. "Your apartment is on the floor above, number 510. Your requirements were: one bedroom, one dining/living room, temporarily furnished prior to your deciding to lease, plus bathroom and kitchen. Apartment facing the racecourse. A servant's room is available, if you want one. It's all taken care of, sir. You may call on us for a servant if you wish, Miss MacDougall. We're always happy to do business with the bank and to give them every priority, Mr. Monteith."

He bowed unctuously to Archie and Magda, scowled

57

at the clerk who stood close-mouthed and rigid, and returned to his office.

Magda's gaiety dissolved as she witnessed the little scene. It was almost as though her own dignity had been assaulted, vicariously. This is the sort of thing Papa tried to save me from, she thought, unhappily, feeling the young Eurasian's humiliation.

"I'll send the porter up with your luggage, Miss Mac-Dougall," the clerk said formally.

"Thank you so much for getting me the apartment with the view, Mr. Rogers. I really appreciate it."

If she noticed the men looking at her with some surprise at this outburst of cordiality, she paid no attention.

"Not at all, Miss MacDougall. Glad to be of some help. I hope you enjoy it. It's really great fun in the summer—you can see the races from your verandah. The porter has the key to your apartment."

She nodded agreeably to him and turned to Archie.

"Goodbye, Mr. Monteith. Thank you for taking such good care of me."

"By Jove! D'you mean you're not going to invite me up to see this exciting view?" Again he became aware of the change in her manner. "I say, I hope I didn't say or do anything to displease you."

"Not at all," she said politely but pointedly. He looked so crestfallen that she relented. He couldn't help being what he was any more than she could change what she was. "Come on up if you wish to and we'll see this much-discussed apartment together."

The porter was bringing in her luggage and the door was wide open when they reached the apartment. They walked through a tiny foyer and into an airy room where the sun streamed in through open French doors which led to a small verandah. Magda took off her hat and shook her hair free as she stepped out onto it.

A ray of the afternoon sun caught her in its glow, and her hair seemed to take on a fire of its own—forming scarlet, silver and gold lights like a flame atop her delicately formed body.

" 'Oh lovely lady, garmented in light from her own beauty,' " Archie quoted softly.

"Mr. Monteith, you are embarrassing me."

"I apologize, but neither Shelley nor I can contain ourselves at moments such as these."

"You really should go back to the bank. They'll think you've had an accident."

Archie looked at his wristwatch glumly and sighed. "I suppose I must. Will you allow me to take you to dinner tonight? I promise not to pay you a single compliment."

"Thank you, but I think not. I have to unpack."

"I'll bring you back whenever you say so," he entreated.

Magda laughed. "You really are too insistent, Mr. Monteith."

"I suppose I shouldn't try to persuade you," he said dolefully. "You must be tired."

"There isn't too much to tire one on a ship like the D'Artagnan."

Archie's face lit up. "Does that mean you accept?"

He was like an irrepressible boy asking for candy, Magda thought, amused. After all, why not? Even Sister George would approve of the propriety of a bank introduction. It would be a lonely evening, this first one in Shanghai.

"Do you always get your way, Mr. Monteith?"

"If I want something badly enough. And I want like the devil to take you out to dinner. Dress or not?"

"Oh, I imagine I can find something not too badly mussed."

"Tip-top! How about seven-thirty?"

"Better make it eight."

"Right-O! I'll be here on the dot. Cheerio 'til then."

Archie walked down the five flights of stairs. It would be too ordinary to take the elevator. He didn't want to share his elation, not even with the anonymous porter. He felt light-headed. It couldn't be possible to feel this way about a girl he'd met barely an hour ago. Love at first sight was romantic pulp, he told himself. He knew he was walking down the stairs, that he was placing one foot ahead of the other, because he reached the bottom of several floors. But he couldn't feel the impact of his feet touching solid ground. Archie grinned sheepishly at himself as he floated downward, led by the vision of Magda's face and form dancing in front of him—the huge fathomless dark pools of her eyes shining softly with mysteries untold; the brilliant hair which stole the sunlight and preserved its glow even in the dark; the cushioned oval mouth, so primly closed but promising unexplored passion and sensuality.

It had taken all his inbred self-control not to take her in his arms and crush his lips against hers, to fold his arms around that slim and fragile body—to feel his mastery of her.

Archie was shocked at himself and at the pictures forming in his mind's eye. He had never known himself to feel so passionate and intense about anyone or anything before. He shook his head violently to clear his mind. "You're suffering from a touch of the sun, old boy. Get hold of yourself! You're going off half-cocked," he admonished himself, at the same time recalling Magda's timid efforts to smile as though unaccustomed to the game. His heart contracted with sudden compassion and tenderness.

He hailed a nearby cab and returned to the bank but found it difficult to concentrate on his work.

Magda stood for a moment in a daze after Archie's departure. What had happened to her? She had laughed and chatted and joked with him as effortlessly as though she were accustomed to easy comaraderie; more than that, she had actually accepted a dinner date.

She walked shyly to the mirror and inspected herself, wondering what he saw to admire so extravagantly. Men had stared at her before but she had attributed it all to her coloring, especially her hair. She peered at her reflection. Somehow, today, it seemed as if she were looking at another person. The same undistinguished face, she thought, with the same neat, delicate features, and the eyes she had never liked because they slanted and reminded her of Mei-ling. Somehow though, she didn't look like herself. It was as though an invisible mask had been stripped off, leaving her face young and vulnerable and full of hope. It was alive with animation. Her mouth was smiling softly, beyond her control. Her eyes were dancing —they looked like enormous black diamonds against her flawless complexion which was now slightly flushed with an inner glow. Magda turned away from the mirror. Suddenly she felt naked and exposed, and she didn't want to explore further.

In her years in Europe, Magda had met several men who showed their interest. However, after her courteous and impersonal refusals to their invitations, none had persevered after a second, or at most, a third time. A man once attempted to embrace her forcibly; her indifference was an insult to him and her own best defense.

She simply never *had been* stirred emotionally, and she was content to remain that way. She preferred to be an observer in life—not a participant. Had she been granted a secret wish, it would have been to remain impervious to all emotion: it was safer that way.

Though a bit shocked at herself for breaking her own rules, Magda justified her date with Archie. He was a diversion in a day of stress, and, besides, she felt much more mature than he—in control. He amused her. She felt carefree in his company, in a way she had not experienced before. Dressing for dinner, she found herself looking forward to seeing him again.

A messenger delivered a small box shortly after Archie had left. It contained a spray of orchids—small speckled ones, unostentatious and exquisite. There was a note: "Do them a favor and wear them this evening."

The flowers simplified her choice of a gown. A muted-yellow sheath, deceptively simple, a perfect background for the jewellike flowers when she pinned them to the neckline. The little black spots intensified the contrast of her eyes to her complexion, the dulled yellow of her dress was a perfect foil to the brilliance of her hair, and a touch of pale-pink lipstick provided the right touch of sophistication.

Magda laid her wrap and evening-bag on a chair. Her heart beat rapidly as she waited. It was all too extraordinary—surely this simple boyish admiration was not turning her head. What had she in common with this young man who filled the role of privileged upperclass Englishman with such nonchalance—a breezy young man, pleasing of feature, beguiling of personality, and one who probably had never been crossed in his life except perhaps in failing to make a top score in cricket! Far better for her if she closed the door right now. What about her vow never to become involved? But Magda knew she was talking to herself without conviction.

The bell rang and she rushed to open the door. She had no idea how radiant she looked, sheathed in shades of gold from the top of her glistening head to the slippers on her feet.

She hardly recognized the man at the door.

The boyish Archie had turned into a man—a remarkably handsome man, at ease with himself and with the world, a man who behaved with supreme confidence. She felt a little discomfited: she preferred the impetuous boy. There was little doubt, however, about his admiration for her. His eyes, brilliantly blue, brightened when he saw her. He started to say something, but instead, he put his finger to his lips as though to seal them. Magda felt an enormous relief. She was not ready to cope with anything more than lightness.

She laughed gaily, "You are a fool, you know."

"I never break my word," he stated firmly. But his eyes showered her with praise.

Archie took Magda to the Cathay Hotel at the corner of Nanking Road and the bund. It was considered the most luxurious hotel in the Orient. Certainly, the dinner, the wine, and the orchestra would compare favorably with the best in Europe.

Archie was a wonderful dancer and Magda was silently thankful that her years at St. Ursula's had included ballroom dancing, for she was perfectly at home following Archie's lead. They didn't feel a need for conversation, but they were frequently interrupted by a stream of young men who came up to be introduced to Magda —on the pretext of talking to Archie.

"Why, you're so popular!" she marveled with good-natured mockery. "Is there a soul in town who doesn't know you?"

"Popular, my eye! They want to meet the prettiest girl in Shanghai and I'm the lucky bloke who met you first and have prior claim."

"But no one has a claim on me, Mr. Monteith."

"Can't you try to call me Archie?"

"I've been indoctrinated with formality—it's not easy to drop."

"Do you always do what you're supposed to?"

"I'm not easily tempted to break any rules."

"Well, I'm going to keep you so busy that you won't have time for anyone else. Oh, good, they're playing my favorite waltz. Shall we?"

They stood up and Magda was struck again by how completely Archie harmonized with his environment. It was not simply that he was wearing the right clothes. She wondered how it felt to be like him and have a sure place in the world; to know who you were, and never have to consider it.

She was drawn to him in a way that seemed quite unfamiliar to her; but more than that, she felt an almost sensuous pleasure in following his lead, in swaying and dipping to the light pressure of his hand on her waist. There was a strange fulfillment in submitting to his guidance. She flushed when he looked at her—what on earth had ever given her the idea that he was an immature boy she could control? A warning bell sounded in her head.

"How about trying out some other places?" he asked when they returned to the table.

"No, thanks. I've enjoyed the evening immensely, but it's midnight and, like Cinderella, I must go home."

"Tomorrow?"

"I can't take so much rich fare. You must remember I've lived a very sober life. At any rate, I'll be busy at the bank tomorrow, settling my affairs. I've made an appointment with your Mr. Lovejoy."

His face lit up. "The bank? That's great! How about a spot of lunch when you're through?"

"I'm sorry, I'd love to, but I have too much to do and plan."

"I guess I can't take no for an answer." He smiled at her quizzically, raising an eyebrow. "Look, d'you remember the lad with the little blonde? Well, he suggested that we make a foursome at the French Club this Saturday. How about it?"

"That would be fine. I'd love to." The words tripped out before she had a chance to stop them. Her desires were starting to rebel against her self-imposed restraints.

"Topping. I'll set it up, then."

"I don't think I've ever enjoyed an evening more,

Archie," she said as he escorted her into the Royal Arms.

He took her outstretched hand and kissed it gallantly.

"Thank you for the 'Archie.' Is it exchangeable, Magda? Magda! It suits you. There is something incorruptible about it. Magda!" He tasted it for sound. "A sense of mystery, of a locked door difficult to open. You laugh, and catch yourself being surprised by the sound of it."

He looked into her eyes—his own no longer full of mischief, but serious and probing.

She pulled her hand away.

"Perhaps we had better go back to Mr. Monteith," she said almost coolly. "Goodnight."

Magda entered the elevator, shaken by Archie's perception.

"You utter fool! You clumsy oaf!!" Archie was at a loss for words with which to castigate himself as he watched the elevator taking Magda away. Forgotten was the delightful evening—he remembered only the laughter being erased from her face, because of what he had said. Icy reserve had replaced her gay animation—a happy melody turned into a dirge.

"If you want to win her, you'd better let up, play the clown for all it's worth." And in mouthing the words to himself, Archie realized that he wanted to win her more than he'd ever wanted anything. He also knew that he would have to beguile her, find a way to put her at ease with herself, to gain her trust and confidence. Only by doing this could he help her to erase from her mind and memory whatever it was that had marred her life. For this he knew absolutely: something or someone had hurt her deeply.

Magda woke up the next morning and ordered breakfast from the restaurant downstairs. When the tray arrived, on it stood a vase of early daffodils with a card attached.

"Please forgive me for speaking out of turn. I'll eat the daffies for penance. Bunny." There was a sketch of a rabbit with big lopsided ears—his front paws raised in prayerful attitude, his eyes lifted to heaven.

"What an idiot," she thought happily. And she ate breakfast with new appetite.

CHAPTER SIX

≪≪≪≪≪≪≪≪≪≪≪≪≪

MAGDA'S GOAL IN life had always been to make her father's dreams—that she be accepted as wholly white and that she make half a million dollars—come true. The first was always on her mind, preceding every word and action. As for the other—in tribute to her father's memory, Magda decided to double the amount. That the world was in a financial slump did not discourage her. She was positive that there was still money to be made in the stockmarket if one studied it sufficiently, and she did. While at school in Switzerland, she had immersed herself in financial journals and stockmarket analyses and shunned fiction. If the good Sisters found her taste in reading material unusual, they considered it less harmful than the lurid novels the other students smuggled in. They were, however, a bit dismayed when she requested, and received, permission to take special courses in accounting, political science, and international law—all of which Magda considered essential to the making of intelligent investments.

She had given herself an imaginary twenty-five thousand dollars with which to play the market. In the years since she started, Magda had built her make-believe sum to a quarter of a million dollars, finding it just as interesting to analyze the reasons for her losses as those for her gains.

On the day Magda was to graduate from St. Ursula's, Mother Superior had called her to her office and announced that she had received a request from Sir Alfred that Magda be permitted to remain until she turned twenty-one.

"This letter was to be given to you on graduation day. I am not sure that this is a good idea." She regarded Magda with sorrow as Magda stared numbly at a letter in her father's handwriting. A wild hope raced through her head

—her father was still alive! Somehow, she took the letter from Mother Superior and made her way to her private place of refuge, the old oak tree. She climbed to the lower branches and sat there, shaking. Finally, she mustered the courage to open the letter. The words were weaving in front of her eyes.

My Maggie: It is so hard to let go of you and of our dreams. On this day, I see you graduating. I am very proud of you—I know these years have been difficult but you have great courage and will not give up. But one thing I must ask: that you not return to Shanghai until you are of age, if at all. I do not trust Mei-ling where you are concerned. Try to find some other corner of the world to make your home. You have become a fine lady, and you can take your place with the best. I love you very much, my sweet lass. Know that I will be with you forever.

Papa

"I have the bags of social tricks you wanted for me, Papa," she said sadly. She tried to shake off the spell of despondency that fell heavily on her. Instead, she drew on her father's love for her, which was stronger than death and the passage of time.

Aside from her continued study of business and finance, Magda spent the next two years at St. Ursula's, perfecting her languages and traveling all over Europe.

She devoted much time to searching for a spot where she could feel at home and settle down. But there was an insistence within her that she return to her homeland, at least once. It seemed ordained that she fulfill her father's lost hope from where it had sprung—Shanghai. At last, on her twenty-first birthday, she bought her passage back to China.

When it came time to make her farewells, Magda's eyes unexpectedly welled with tears as Sister George kissed her on both cheeks. "Open the gates of your heart to loving others, and love will enter yours," she said, her lined face full of compassion.

At ten-thirty on the day following her arrival, Magda

was shown to Mr. Lovejoy's office in the Hong Kong and Shanghai Bank. He saw a well-dressed, quiet, young woman, attractive and poised, carrying a large handbag. He greeted her courteously.

"I understand you want to go over your accounts. I have all the material here."

"Thank you." She took a folder from her bag and waited for him to start. She then checked off each item against her list of bonds, securities, and mortgages held in trust for her.

"Our figures tally," Magda said, and then proceeded to ask him several questions she had written down in advance.

Mr. Lovejoy was slightly flabbergasted. He had readied himself to play the role of kindly advisor to a naive child; instead, he faced a very knowledgeable young lady who understood a great deal about finances.

Crisply and positively, Magda outlined what she wanted him to do. "Can the bank make me a loan of fifty thousand dollars, using as collateral the securities which come due in two years?"

"That seems reasonable. I shall have to check, though."

Then she asked him to recommend a brokerage firm, preferably American, as she intended to trade heavily in American stock as well as in world currencies.

Mr. Lovejoy shook his head gravely. "I think you are making a serious error in changing good investments into mere gambles."

"I took a gamble in returning to Shanghai, and it could be the best thing I've ever done." Her eyes sparkled when she thought of Archie. Not that she took him seriously, but meeting him had been a good omen—an auspicious beginning to her life in Shanghai and her long-awaited plans.

A clerk brought in the large bundle of mail that had accumulated for Magda. "You have a great deal of reading matter here," he said.

"My homework," she said smiling radiantly. The long awaited plan had been put in motion.

Magda, her arms laden with papers and magazines, took a rickshaw home. She sat back uncomfortably. She had forgotten the smells of stale garlic and sweat which wafted back to her from the jogging coolie. The discomfort, however, seemed negligible in the glow of her anticipation. She could hardly wait to get to her apartment.

That evening, she read—developing strategies, computing, making lists—but her concentration was frequently interrupted by a pair of bright blue eyes looking up from the page in front of her. They were sometimes merry, sometimes serious. At times, she imagined a fleeting smile, a laugh, a whispering remark. Magda struggled to banish the visions.

"This is utterly ridiculous, *absolutely* ridiculous. You're acting like an infatuated fool about someone you've known only a few hours. I won't have it." She spoke aloud, the more forcibly to erase the image of Archie. She returned to her work. But, a little later, for no apparent reason, a soft smile played on her lips. It was after midnight when she went to bed, exhausted and unsettled.

She was awakened the next morning by a phone call.

"It's a lovely morning. The tennis courts in the club have been set up. How about an early game?"

That's very kind of you, Archie, but I must refuse, Magda thought very clearly. But, instead, she heard herself say jubilantly: "What a splendid idea! Give me half an hour."

Archie monopolized her every minute when he was not working, and Magda found herself helpless to reject him. Who was he—this man who absorbed her so completely, who took her dancing, horseback riding, tennis, swimming? Archie seemed able to divine her every mood. Suddenly her life was no longer her exclusive domain. Archie was everywhere—with her on long walks, sitting on the verandah talking seriously, looking at her with eyes that blazed.

What was happening to her? Who was this stranger occupying her body? What had happened to her self-discipline, her coldly analytic approach to every aspect of her life? And—who were these people who had accepted her so freely, in whose company she attended an interminable round of parties?

It was a difficult adjustment for Magda. She was drawn in two directions: when she was with Archie she was excited and happy; when she was by herself, she wanted to withdraw into her shell, to remain untouched. Touched! She felt a shiver run through her. He was constantly touching her. The first time he kissed her lightly on the cheek, she was shaken. She supposed she should be indignant—a man, almost a stranger, had taken an unprecedented liberty. But the kiss was as soft as the touch of a butterfly's wing, and as gentle. She could not make a fuss about so simple a matter.

Archie waited patiently for some signal, some kind of encouragement. He knew that if he were to win her, he must court her slowly. She was encased in a shell which would snap if he pried it open too roughly. No, not a shell—that was too hard. No, she was as though swathed in veils, and, as each veil was drawn away, he saw more of the warm, vibrant person hidden within. He knew she cared for him. She wasn't the kind of girl who just wanted attention—he'd known plenty of them. No, Magda was unique: outwardly reserved, but, like a high-strung c̶ she could be cajoled and coaxed, gently, easily. She ha̶ become accustomed to his touch or she'd shy away. ̶s it possible that she had never—with her looks and appeal? It made her all the more precious. Once in a while, he held her hand; or put his arm 'round her shoulders. At first, she had stiffened. Now, he felt she was coming to accept his caress. Softly, slowly does it, he thought.

Archie was afraid he'd lose control one day and, unable to resist temptation, would clutch her hard against him—show her all that a kiss could be—crush her to his chest, covering her with *real* kisses. Ah, yes, but not yet old chap, he warned himself.

It was all Magda could do to refrain from leaning against him and smoothing his ruffled hair. When he lay on the lawn after a game of tennis, she yearned to put his head on her lap.

Archie! she shouted inside her head. Magda! she scolded herself. She refused to be in love. But when Archie held her hand and they ran to the pool to jump in together, her hand felt a stranger's. She felt her pulse quicken whenever he looked at her, his eyes flashing blue fire. Sometimes she felt as though she had been bottled and sealed and put away in storage—to await the day the cork would pop and she, like champagne, would spill out, bubbling and sparkling, full of her newly acquired spirit.

But the old Magda refused to accept the new concept of

herself. She feared the stirrings within her. Far too long she had been safe and unencumbered, and she fought hard to remain that way—insulated from all personal involvements which only left a girl open to being hurt and abandoned. If the thought of marriage had ever occurred to her, it was as a someday thing with a distant, vague man—not the result of a breathtaking romance which completely took control and forced her to become involved in her womanhood.

For several weeks Magda followed her planned schedule. She contacted her broker, established credit, and made her long-awaited entry into the world of finance, completely on her own.

She felt an occasional twinge of conscience that she had not yet gone to see her grandmother or called William or made any effort to contact Tasha. But the reminders of her past flitted by unheeded in the face of Archie's attention to her.

Magda decided it would be a nice gesture to invite Archie to dinner at her apartment. Always practical in money matters, she had some idea of a bank trainee's salary, and she wanted to reciprocate.

"And," she said when she invited him, "I'll cook it myself."

"Do you mean you can cook, too?" Archie teased her, and she laughed. That was also new. She was learning to accept teasing without drawing into her shell.

"How else could we learn to be gracious hostesses?" she replied with mock primness. "A good mistress must learn to instruct her servants properly. I can turn a bedsheet with the best of them and could probably be a top-rate maid in a hotel, if I had to. You will have a feast, trust me."

"With my life."

For the occasion, Magda set the table herself. Everything had to be perfect. The tiny rosebuds Archie sent were arranged in a low silver container as a centerpiece, with matching pale-pink candles on a candelabra. The tableware, crystal, and dinner service she had recently purchased were placed on a dazzling white-damask cloth, while a bottle of wine, wrapped in a linen napkin, nested in an ice-filled silver bucket.

At each setting, she placed a shrimp-filled tomato, sauced with a special dressing learned from a great chef, on a bed of lettuce. Hot, crisp French rolls, specially ordered from Marcel's, were wrapped in a napkin, and a small table between the two settings held a chafing dish bubbling with the *boeuf bourguignon*.

Magda wore a simple white dress with pink rosebuds pinned at the waist. Her face was flushed by her exertions; her eyes were bright with excitement. She looked over the table with satisfaction; even Sister George would have approved.

The bell rang and the houseboy went to open the door.

"Archie!" Magda said warmly, her hands outstretched in welcome. As naturally as though it were their custom, he enfolded her in his arms, and hers went around his neck as he kissed her full on the lips, tenderly and gently at first. Then, his arms tightened and his kisses became hard and urgent. Magda responded eagerly and passionately. All conscious thought lost, feeling only the quickening of her heartbeat, she pressed against him.

"My God!" he whispered, his face buried in her hair. "I've wanted to do this since the moment I saw you."

They clung together without speaking. To Magda it was as though she had been reborn—complete, fulfilled—with her heart and Archie's beating as one, their minds flowing together.

Finally, she drew away from him. She searched his face as though she had never seen it before. She put her hand out, touched his lips with wonder, and caressed his cheeks with her fingertips.

"I never knew it would feel like this," she whispered.

"God, but I love you!" He took her hands and kissed them. For a while they just stood there, holding hands and gazing at each other.

"I've dreamed about this for so long, I can't believe it's really happening. God, but I love you," he repeated, reaching out for her. But she pulled back.

"No more, not yet—I must take this in slow doses," she laughed tremulously. "I don't think I can breathe. Come and see the feast I have prepared . . . for you."

He tore his eyes away from her, momentarily.

"By Jove! How on earth did you manage all this?

71

Everything looks delectable, though it's not exactly food I crave."

"Please, Archie. I need to . . . recover my senses."

"That's the last thing I want you to do. All right then, just one little kiss and I'll let you go."

It was enough for them to touch, with electric impulses vibrating between them. A minute, ten minutes—an eternity. And then, as though the moment were too full to endure, he poured out two drinks, and, holding Magda at arms' length, he led her in an old two-step, contemplating her ardently. He began singing in a high falsetto, "O drink to me only with thine eyes. . . ." Magda giggled helplessly as he swirled her around. Between gasps, she whistled the accompaniment and they both ended in full voice, "Or leave a kiss but in the cup and I'll not ask for wine."

"And you even whistle," he said, hugging her rapturously.

Somehow, dinner ended, and they drifted out to the little verandah—his arm around her waist, she leaning on him. Fear and insecurity, and all of the things which had troubled her so long, now ceased to exist. She rested against him and found comfort in his strength. They kissed gently, exploringly, as though they had their whole lives to share their feelings. The bud of their love was sweet; in time, it would flower miraculously.

"In all of my life, dear love," Magda whispered as though talking to herself, "there was a great emptiness in me and nothing to fill it. After my father died, I was just a shell of a person and was content to remain that way. And now—and now—the emptiness has been filled with you." She drew a deep breath of contentment. "I feel unworthy, Archie, as though it is too much for one person to have such happiness, and it will be taken from me."

"Never while I live," he promised her, and he sealed it with a lingering kiss. "Let's get married right away. If we were in England I'd hie you to Gretna Green and say all the important words tonight."

"We've only known each other such a short time. You've got to consider this rationally."

"Love is not rational, why should we presume to be?"

"Oh, Archie, we have a lifetime ahead of us. There's your mother, what would she think if you just married a girl you knew nothing about?"

"Stop worrying, dear heart. My mother is a dear old girl. She's raised us single-handedly and trusts us implicitly. If she met you she'd love you instantly and say, 'Archie, you've got the best.'"

"But Archie, you don't know the first things about me. I know you like the way I look—"

"The understatement of the year." He pulled her to him for another embrace.

"But seriously, you don't know a thing about me, what I'm like inside or—my—my—mother."

"Stop right there, my love. I don't give a hoot about your family skeletons. I only know that somewhere along the way you've been badly hurt. You don't know what it's been like all this time, not being able to take you in my arms and cover you with kisses. I was afraid I'd frighten you off. Don't think I could have been with you and remained blind, deaf, and dumb. I must tell you that I know your father took his life under questionable circumstances. I don't want or need to know more."

"It's not about my father. Until I met you he was the only person in the world I had ever loved. It's—well—it's my—my—mother—"

Archie put a finger on her lips but she struggled away. She had to speak. She couldn't live a lie with Archie—not Archie, of all people. As she pulled herself away, she imagined her father frowning at her, admonishing her not to commit this final foolishness, this act of treachery against what he had taught her. She was positive that the truth would not change Archie. But if it did—a sick feeling went through her. She felt faint at the very idea of it.

Her face was strained. Her eyes were heavy with tears and with the stress of her emotions.

"Don't you understand? I don't want to hear," Archie was saying. This time he put his hand over her mouth. He cradled her head on his chest and stopped her lips with a kiss.

"Hear me out, all right?" She nodded and he kissed her again. "Good girl! Listen to me. I'm being very serious. You are the girl I know. You are the person I will love and delight in for the rest of my life. You are the one I want. If you are in some trouble and I can help you, I'd gladly give my last breath to do so, but I don't need to hear your secrets. To me, it's a sign of our faith in each other that we accept each other as we are."

Magda looked at him, unmoving, needing to believe him.

"Let's not spoil what we have. I distrust unnecessary, misplaced confidences. That's how people learn to hate each other—one for telling some secret shame, the other for being burdened with it. Magda, my dearest darling, do you understand what I'm saying? I know I'm expounding like a professor but I have definite convictions about this matter of love. It must be taken on faith and not explored. We take each other as we know each other. I never want to hear from you, 'Why didn't you tell me that?' And believe me, I'll never say it to you. I entrust you with my life; I offer it to you. Will you trust me with yours?"

"Oh, yes, Archie! Yes! You sound so wise, so sure of yourself. You're a different person from the boy I first met."

Archie smiled and nuzzled her neck. He couldn't have enough of stroking her, hugging her, and kissing her—kissing her with a passion restrained only by self-control.

"I never believed in love at first sight, but that's how it hit me. I was so overwhelmed. I guess I acted like a bit of a fool. One does, you know—to hide. I'm rather a serious sort actually, but it makes people uncomfortable. There, you see, I'm confessing—I'm not really the silly and lovable man you've known. Do you mind?"

"You mean you're Archie, not Bunny?"

"That's right."

And Magda, who was never guilty of slouching, or crossing her legs in public, or anything undesirable in a young lady of good breeding, snuggled even more closely in Archie's arms. For the first time in her life she was completely relaxed and prepared to be dependent on another person. They both sighed in complete surrender.

"I'll send my mother a cable tomorrow," he promised.

"Let's keep it to ourselves for a week at least," she breathed. "It's too precious to share with anyone."

"To please you, all right, but don't think for a moment that I'm going to wait for an infernally long engagement. I care too dearly for you to act the honorable gentleman for long. It's all I can do to keep from ravishing you this minute."

"Archie?"

"Yes, my dearest heart."

"I love you."

They stood looking over the racecourse. On one side, the massive clubhouse and the huge park were outlined—on the other side, the sky was lit from the multicolored, dazzling, changing lights of Nanking Road.

"I never guessed that Shanghai was beautiful, but it really is," Magda sighed.

"It's the company you keep," teased Archie, squeezing her a little tighter. Lost in the enchantment of the moment, Magda knew only that she had never before been so deliriously happy.

CHAPTER SEVEN
‹‹‹‹‹‹‹‹‹‹‹‹‹‹‹‹‹‹

THE FOLLOWING MONTH, Magda saw Natasha and William Chen on the same day.

She was casually window-shopping on Nanking Road when a girl rushed by in a hurry. Magda gave her a fleeting glance and then a flash of recognition made her call out: "Natasha!"

The girl hesitated and looked back, blankly at first. Then she cried out, "Magda! I didn't know you were here. How marvelous you look."

"I was worried about you—my last two letters were returned, 'address unknown.' "

"I moved. Listen, Magda, I've got to hurry or I'll be late for work. Why not walk along with me—I'm with the British-American Tobacco Company."

"Your cousin Liz got you the job there, didn't she? It's a good place to be working. You're lucky."

"Lucky?" A derisive smirk touched Natasha's lips but not her eyes. "By all means I'm lucky."

Natasha—vivacious, beautiful Tasha—had changed. She looked grim, and, in truth, shabby. Her heavy black hair, which used to hang freely, to the middle of her back was now caught up in a tight braid and wrapped around her head. Her face looked gaunt—if a twenty-year-old face could be called so. Her changeable green eyes, formerly full of joy and mischief, were now set in dark hollows. She was thin to the point of emaciation.

"What's happened to you, Tasha Wilkinson?" Magda asked bluntly.

"Not Wilkinson. My name is Natasha Guria, and I'm proud of it." She glared haughtily at Magda and lifted her chin.

"Hello, Tasha Guria—remember me? I'm Magda, the girl you took under your wing at school. Look, Wilkinson or Guria, who cares about your name? Can't you tell me what's happened?"

"Briefly, I'm one of the impoverished White Russians who fill up every corner and cranny of Shanghai. Did you know that being a Russian puts an indelible mark on a person?"

"Look, my friend, you can't tell me anything about nationality that I don't know," Magda replied softly.

Natasha looked blank for a moment. Then, as she remembered, her expression softened.

"I'd forgotten that your mother was Chinese. I suppose you went through your own particular hell. It's pretty hard to believe it, seeing you now. You've changed a lot, you know. You look wonderful—you don't have that half-submerged droop any more. Oh, Magda, I'm glad things are good for you, I truly am. You haven't had an easy time."

"But what about you, Tasha? What of all your cousins and Aunt Olga? And your Uncle Ed? I don't think I ever met him."

"That was your good fortune. I never realized, until they were ready to leave for the United States, how much he had resented me all those years. Aunt Olga was such a dear—she always treated me like one of her own kids. But before he left, Uncle Ed let me know in no uncertain terms that he was plenty tired of supporting me. He told me I was Russian trash, unwelcome in his home, and that he was certainly not going to take me along with his family to the States even if he *could* maneuver a passport for me—which he hadn't the slightest inclination to do.

"Well, there, now you know. I certainly had no intention of blurting out all my troubles. It's a long, depressing story and I'd just as soon not talk about it. I'm a little sorry you got me started. I'd like to bury the whole thing."

"But, Tasha, how old could you have been when they left?"

"Just seventeen. That wasn't too young, Uncle Ed said. He'd supported himself long before that age, and I'd better get used to it. Anyway, he said not to worry, I'd probably go the easy way like the rest of the Russian trash. Oh, there I go all over again!" Her mouth tightened, and her eyes burned with green fire. "Look, Magda, I've got to run. I can't take any chances with my job. Let's meet soon—I want to hear all about you. You look radiant." The hard expression left her eyes and she leaned over and kissed Magda on the cheek.

"Welcome back to Shanghai, though why you ever returned to this hellhole I'll never know."

"Wait," Magda called out as Tasha rushed away, "I don't have your address."

"The office can reach me any time," Natasha flung back as she hurried into the building and was lost to Magda's sight.

Magda stood riveted for a moment, saddened by Tasha's plight. She'd have to think of something she could do for her, and soon.

But plans for Tasha were quickly obliterated by the excitement of her coming marriage to Archie, which filled her thoughts to the exclusion of all else. She twisted the ring on her finger. It was loose, and she would have to take it and have it made smaller, though she hated to take it off, even for a minute.

When Archie had put it on her finger, he'd said: "My mother told me that when I found the right girl, she wanted to be a part of it, and that she hoped I would make the girl as happy as my father had made her. He died in India in one of those skirmishes. She's a lovely lady, my mum is. She never married again, though I knew old Humey would have liked to carry her off. The old chap's been damned decent to me, if a bit overbearing."

The central stone of the ring was a deep-purple sapphire surrounded by diamonds in an old-fashioned gold setting. Archie had hesitantly suggested that if Magda wanted to change the setting it would be all right with him and with his mother. But Magda would have none of it. She treasured every bit of tradition in her otherwise rootless existence.

She looked at her watch. She was still a little early for her luncheon appointment with Sir Alfred. How very considerate of him to be interested in her still, even though her financial affairs were now in her own hands. She hardly knew him except as someone who had been a friend of her father's and who had watched after her interests in the bank. Her thoughts leaped to her father, who had wanted so much for her. "You would have liked Archie, Papa. I hope somewhere you know and are happy for me."

She entered the Cathay Hotel where she and Sir Alfred were to lunch, and she sat in the lobby. In a short time, she saw him come in. He was swinging his cane in unison with each step and was the same erect figure—she recognized him immediately—that walked with such dignity and assurance that others made way for him.

She moved toward him with her hand outstretched and a warm smile of greeting on her face. He hesitated a moment before taking her hand, and suddenly she was embarrassed that perhaps she had been over-cordial. Perhaps he did not recognize her—they had met so long ago when she was still a child.

"I'm Magda MacDougall, Sir Alfred. I doubt you can remember me after all these years."

"I could never forget that remarkable head of hair Old Mac was so proud of."

Sir Alfred hid his perturbation when he saw what a striking woman Mac's brat had grown up to be—experienced, too, he had no doubt. The situation might well be more difficult than he'd expected. She was enough to turn any man's head.

The headwaiter led them to a corner table at the back of the dining rooms. The table was almost hidden by a flowering shrub in a huge brass tub.

"Would you like a sherry?" he asked, studying a long wine list. Without waiting for a reply, he ordered a sherry for her and a whiskey and water for himself. Then he gave the dining hall a cursory glance of disapproval.

"For the tourist trade strictly—ostentatious and gaudy. At least it's big enough for some privacy. I ordered this table particularly. Well, now. Let's take a proper look at you. Switzerland has been good for you. You look extremely well."

He examined her carefully. His scrutiny made Magda uncomfortable and on display.

"I want to thank you, Sir Alfred, for being so very helpful to me all these years. I'm sure my father would have appreciated your kindness."

"Hmm! Deuced difficult, this. Don't like mixing a social meal with business. No need to beat about the bush, eh?"

"I'm sorry, but I don't have the slightest idea what you're talking about." She looked at him, puzzled and a little apprehensive.

He returned her glance, his lips tightening as he noticed the ring on her finger. "That's Hilary's ring," he said accusingly, glowering. "I suppose you imagine congratulations are in order?"

"Thank you, Sir Alfred." She cocked her head doubtfully.

"Have you introduced young Monteith to your family yet?"

Magda stiffened. At last she knew. She had been completely unprepared for Sir Alfred's belligerence. A cold shiver shot through her—a premonition of what was to come. She broke off a piece of roll and buttered it carefully; then, controlling a sharp intake of breath, she looked into the slate-blue eyes which met hers coldly. She took her cue from his attitude.

"That only concerns Archie and myself," she answered curtly.

"You are mistaken. It is very much my business when the dupe in question happens to be my godson."

"Your godson?"

"Now, now! Don't play Little Miss Innocence. Your sort know pretty well what you're doing. You appreciate my kindness, eh? You certainly show your gratitude. With all the eligible young men around, you pick on my godson. That's how you repay me, eh? Put your hooks into my godson. Thought I was soft and'd let you get away with it!"

Magda stared at him in disbelief, but, as he talked, little pieces fell into place.

"Old Humey—" she breathed.

"Old Humey, indeed!" He glared at her as though he thought she was insane.

"You're Archie's Old Humey—Sir Alfred Wilkie-Hume. Of course. How stupid of me not to have guessed."

"Hm! So perhaps you didn't know. I believe you. Now listen, girl, this is a wretched situation for both of us," Sir Alfred said, in what he considered a reasonable tone. He took a hearty swallow of his drink and beckoned for the waiter. "Have you decided what you want to eat, or shall I order for you?"

Magda pushed back her chair and started to stand up. "I don't believe we have anything further to say to one another."

"Not so fast. We have a great deal of unfinished business." He put a hand on her arm. "It's no good, you know. I shall not permit this marriage to take place. Whether you were ignorant in the beginning—of whom I was in relation to Archie—you know now and you are aware of all *I* know about you. I have no wish to be harsh. To the contrary, I have a certain sympathy for you—but there are limits. You overreached yourself with Archie. I have no intention of letting him ruin his life with a half-caste wife. Well, girl, what do you say for yourself?"

Watching her expression change, seeing the brightness leave her face and a still blankness take its place, Sir Alfred felt a shred of remorse. But the moment passed rapidly; the alternative was unthinkable. "Well, what are you going to do about it?" he repeated.

"Nothing. You must do as you wish. You must tell Archie the devastating truth of my mixed birth. I tried and he wouldn't listen."

"Very clever. Very clever, indeed. You know that Archie has a great sense of chivalry and my telling him would only lead him straight back to you. It would make you the heroine and me the villain."

"Isn't it true? You *are* evil—you wouldn't mind ruining my life, and his, too, for some outdated idea."

"Outdated, is it? Then why do you make a secret of it?

80

How many people know you're a half-caste? Well? And where there's secrecy, there's shame."

"I sit here and permit you to insult me only because I know that if I told Archie of this conversation, it would destroy the attachment he has for you. I don't want to destroy anything he loves. Won't you try to understand? He needs me and I need him. I think if I had to live without him I would prefer to die."

"Your father took that way out, miss. There's nothing stopping you."

She gaped at him, at first shocked by his callousness and then contemptuous, as she picked up her effects.

"No. Don't go. I was wrong. I didn't mean that. Can't we discuss this reasonably?"

"You have a closed mind—there's nothing to reason out." But then she permitted him to draw her back to her seat. Emotion and shock had left her—all that remained was her mechanically logical mind.

"Listen, Magda. I did not create nor conjure up the world and the inequities in it. In my world, you and your breed are tainted merchandise, contaminating all you touch." He put his hand out to stop her involuntary movement. "No. You hear me out," he said, his voice pleading as much as a man such as he could plead.

"You know the facts are as I describe them. I am merely stating the truth. You are intelligent, well-educated, attractive. You have a tidy sum of money to enhance the whole. But we both know that isn't the entire story—don't we? In my sphere and Archie's, a man who marries a Eurasian is despised. Your father knew it to be true. That is why he worked so desperately to get you out of Shanghai, so that you could have a chance where your origins were unknown."

"Men like you, and, yes, my father too, have hidebound ideas, even though you are, yourselves, the perpetrators of the crimes against us. I wouldn't be surprised if *you* had a Chinese or Japanese woman hidden somewhere in your background."

"That immediately proves my point—it is always a shameful relationship to be hidden. And that is why I can not permit my godson to be married to someone whose birth was the accident of a shameful liaison. Every Eurasian girl wants to entrap a white man for a husband, to bring herself up the ladder of social acceptance. Give Archie up and I won't stand in your way."

"That is hardly honorable of you, is it? Or are your high principles just a double standard? One set for you and one for everyone else?"

"Don't bait me. I have considerable power and authority. I'm the equal of any chit of a girl, however treacherous and devious."

"Treacherous!" Magda savored the ring of the word. "That description applies to you far more than to me. My father trusted and confided in you, and you are using his confidence to blackmail me."

"You are a silly little girl if you think that naughty words will stop me. I would go to far greater lengths than that to prevent your marrying young Monteith. You claim to love him—then how can you do this to him?"

"I don't agree with your premise."

"I warn you, I shall not permit this marriage."

"Then do me the favor of enlightening Archie, and revel in every detail of my *dreadful* secret!"

"It would suit you if I did that, eh? Send him flying into your arms to prove his love."

"You attribute such diabolical scheming to me—I should be flattered that you believe me capable of such acuity. What you ignore is the fact that I am proud of both my bloodlines. The Chens have been statesmen and scholars—their lineage traces back well beyond yours. For Archie's sake, I will attempt to clarify the situation. My father told me I had to choose one side or the other, that to linger in the middle would leave me homeless. He told me this: that going through life was like an obstacle course, and that for some there were more pitfalls than for others. He also told me that in this obstacle course I must give myself every advantage, use every faculty, or I would not survive." Magda looked into his blank face and realized it was useless to explain herself to him. His mind was closed.

"Place your obstacles, Sir Alfred Wilkie-Hume. You will not unbalance me. I only regret that I have lowered myself by listening to you this long."

Magda spoke quietly and deliberately, her face as impenetrable as her voice was sure. She picked up her gloves and handbag and left the table, her head held high and proud and her step strong and steady.

Sir Alfred found himself gazing at her departing figure with something akin to admiration. She was a fighter as well as a charmer. Too bad. He steeled himself. Everyone knew that the worst of both sides came out in a half-caste. They were wily, deceitful. This girl really looked European —if he hadn't known better, he would have been duped himself. He would never forgive himself if he did not prevent this marriage. He had looked after Hilary and her children ever since Derek Monteith died in India. His choler rose. His thin, long face became mottled and there was a white ridge on his bony, beaked nose when he thought of this residue of a man's lust and a Chinese whore's cunning—having the effrontery to wear Hilary's ring!

He beckoned angrily to the waiter, signed the check, and strode over to the club where he could lunch in more suitable surroundings, among his own kind.

Magda was shaking inwardly, with a mixture of outrage and dread, when she reached the street. She recognized Sir Alfred as an enemy now, but hearing someone insulting her as though she were beneath consideration was a monstrous shock. Her father had repeatedly warned her, and he had good reason. He knew because he felt as Sir Alfred did. Could it be possible that Archie might share their prejudice? She rejected the idea violently. He loved her. She would not dare to think of the outcome—not dare to think at all. What she wanted was blessed unconsciousness, a respite from the despair which was suffocating her.

She walked aimlessly down the bund. Without realizing it, she traced the familiar route to her old home. It was a long trek, but physical weariness made her less conscious of her emotional exhaustion. Deliberately, she allowed herself to look around. Had it all been so shabby before? The Soochow Creek was turgid with rotting garbage. The smells of food and sweat and human excrement made her gag. The noise overpowered her—sounds of dogs barking, babies crying, beggars whining, bicycle bells ringing, trams clanging, motor horns beeping, the deep rumble of heavy traffic, and, over it, the crescendo of men and women shouting at the tops of their lungs.

She walked on, turning off at Szechuen Road, past the

new post office and down North Szechuen Road. It was all so familiar—and so strange. There were hardly any Europeans left here, mostly Chinese and Japanese. She made a right turn onto Boone Road and from there, went on to her old address, again noticing that most private homes and flats were occupied by Japanese. She had been in Europe during the Japanese invasion of 1931 and had heard that the Hongkew district was becoming Little Japan. Seeing it, though, was different. If there were one people the Chinese hated more than the westerners, it was the Japanese. It was, perhaps, China's only unity—a solidarity of loathing, against a common enemy.

She passed her old house without stopping, lost in confusion, trying to come to terms with her dilemma. For an agonizing moment she tried, unsuccessfully, to wipe from her mind the very existence of Archie. If only she had told Archie about herself when she wanted to, matter-of-factly, before he'd had a chance to stop her—now it would hit him like a shameful confidence wrung from her by force.

She felt sure he would not desert her—she could not allow herself to consider the alternative—but the memory of Sir Alfred's countenance lingered, arrogant and adamant.

Did she want Archie to cling to her in pity or out of a sense of honor? Yes! Oh, yes! She wanted him in any way at all. But—No! Never! For then she would wonder the rest of her life, never quite sure of his motives.

She paced on and on, paying no attention to where she was headed—turning a corner here, crossing an alley there—and finally awoke to the fact that she was lost. It was an all-Chinese district: small, open shops without the usual English names under the Chinese characters. The street names were wholly unfamiliar. She had lost her bearings completely. She walked into a Chinese foodshop which had dried ducks and strings of sausages, barrels of rice, and the aroma of herbs. Magda asked for directions, but the reply was so complicated that she could make no sense of it.

William! As soon as she spoke the name in her mind, she knew he had been at the back of her thoughts the entire time. He was the only one she could talk to, the only one who would understand her predicament. There was no telephone in the foodshop but the owner, nodding graciously as was the custom of his people, pointed to an apothecary across the street. The Chinese were so good-natured and friendly for the most part, she reflected. What curse of the gods had made her as she was—neither one blood nor the other?

At the apothecary, she searched out William's number from among the hundreds of Chens. One person after another answered her, but finally she recognized William's voice.

"William Chen?" she asked in English, in case anyone was listening. She stifled the hysterical laughter ready to break—always so cautious, always on guard, mustn't be found out. What if someone did hear her call her Chinese cousin? Sir Alfred's spies? He didn't need any. Who was she afraid of? What difference did it make now?

"Yes. This is William Chen, Barrister at Law. Hello. Hello, who is speaking?"

"William, this is Magda." Her voice shook in spite of her efforts to control it.

"Well, well, little cousin. I was wondering when you would call."

"How did you know I was back? Are you not the least surprised?"

William laughed. "No mystery. I read the papers thoroughly and your name was on the passenger lists a few months back."

"Are you annoyed with me for not calling you sooner?"

"Magda, I am always here when you want me, and never when you don't. You have chosen a difficult path for yourself, and I would never place you in jeopardy. I knew that when the time was right you would call me."

"William, I'm lost." Lost, she thought, in more ways than one. "I'm talking from a shop. I don't recognize the street at all—I was walking on Boone Road and paying no attention."

"Don't worry, Magda. Call the shopkeeper to the phone."

After a long, involved conversation, the man returned the telephone to Magda.

"You've literally been going around in circles. It is amazing how you ever managed to reach that place. This doesn't sound like my clear-headed cousin. Are you in trouble of some kind? I could send a cab for you. Or do you want to talk to me?"

"Oh, dear William, I need your wisdom and your comfort. Please."

"Wait for me—I'll be there in about ten minutes."

William opened the rear door of the car and came toward the shop. He held his arms out in greeting and Magda ran to him. He hugged her affectionately and took her arm.

"Come," he said, helping her into the car. "We don't need an audience." A curious crowd had gathered to stare at the red-haired woman and her Chinese companion. Strangers rarely visited the little street.

Magda composed herself, holding on to William's hand and being soothed by his quiet strength.

"Is this your car?" she asked.

"Yes. It is an old one but it gives me much prestige." He scrutinized her, patted her wrist as he would a child's, and gave the chauffeur an order. They did not speak until the car pulled up in front of a small restaurant on a quiet side street.

"This is a good place. I take clients here when we don't want to be disturbed."

"I don't think I can eat anything."

"It doesn't matter."

The proprietor knew William well and led them to a private room where a waiter quickly took their order. Soon one succulent dish followed another and Magda found that she was indeed hungry. She ate with enjoyment and appetite.

"I thought I'd never want to touch a morsel of food again. It's amazing how delicious good Chinese food is —I'd forgotten. I think we know the delights of eating more than any other people."

"Do you realize that inadvertently you said 'we'?" William teased her.

"Did I?" Magda replied calmly. "There's no way I can forget it, and there are times when I wish I had chosen otherwise. I am very tired of searching for an identity. I would rather sink into complete anonymity."

"That would be impossible. The Christian Bible, I believe, has a saying that it is as impossible for a rich man to enter Heaven as it is for a camel to pass through the needle's eye. Let me paraphrase that and say it is equally difficult for a beautiful woman to go unnoticed.

"Your appearance, my dear Magda, is the basis for all your problems. Had you not had your father's red hair, would he have paid any attention to you other than a distant affection? Or disavowed anything except a financial obligation? If your father had not been bewitched by your looks, would Mei-ling, who was little more than a child herself, have known such jealousy, have treated you so badly? Beauty is both a blessing and a burden, and it provokes the extremes of hatred and love. I don't know what your present problems are, my cousin, but along the way there is a man."

"My cousin, William Confucius!" They smiled at each other affectionately. "Oh, William, you are the only person in the world I can speak frankly to. It's such a relief."

"How can I help you, Magda?"

She told her story, and William was sensitive enough to understand all the nuances. But there were moments when his nostrils flared and turned white and his expression was not so much serious as dangerous. He remained pensive for a while when she had finished. Then he sighed deeply.

"It is difficult to retain one's equanimity. There are times when I could wish the monarchy back and wish myself ruler, able to order all barbarian interlopers thrown into a sea of sharks." He scowled somewhat grimly at her shocked expression. "It pleases me that you mentioned your pride in being a Chen. There have been occasions when I, as well as Sir Alfred, suspected you were ashamed of this rich heritage."

"William, I cannot decipher it. It seems that all my life I have been taught to ignore my Chinese side as though it didn't exist. But it does. And now I know it always will. Yet it's so much easier to say nothing. What am I supposed to do? Wear a large placard around my neck informing the world at large that I am half-Chinese, half-white? Why must I offer any explanations to anyone? I am myself. Oh, help me, William, tell me what to do."

"In this, I cannot help you. It is easy to blame your

father for being so egotistical in his efforts to erase the part of you of which he himself was ashamed."

"But why, William? Why? How could he—be—intimate with a Chinese woman and yet be so intolerant of the mixing of two bloods?"

"That's easy, Magda. He used Mei-ling only to satisfy his lust, and he would never have introduced her among his own people."

"That's what Sir Alfred said. But Papa loved me."

"Yes. But first he had to make you solely his daughter."

"Oh, William, how sad that is. Poor Papa, how torn he must have been."

"I don't think Angus MacDougall was an introspective man. But, as you grew older, I think he came to realize the problems you would face, and he decided there was only one cure. That was to make you completely his and cut off the Chinese side of you which he would never have accepted."

"There was a Siamese girl at the convent, William, and another girl, half-Indian, half-English. They were open about themselves and were very popular. In fact, they were invited everywhere and accepted. Why then not me?"

"You were not a full person and they recognized it. You were afraid to make friends; you were insecure. Had you talked freely about your beautiful Chinese mother they would probably have called you exotic— I believe that is the word commonly used."

"If Mei-ling had not been so cruel—"

"It is too late to talk of 'ifs.' That belongs to yesterday. Only today exists. Tomorrow is a possibility. Would you really want to change?"

"I don't think I could, William. I am what has been made of me. I am more of the West than of the East. In fact, I blush to admit it, yet I feel the same superiority all too frequently. It's only since I met Archie that I've let the barriers down. Now I am comfortable and at ease in everyone's company. He has made me a whole person. I'm gloriously happy and I refuse to let Sir Alfred ruin my bliss. I never knew I could want anyone as I want Archie, and I am certain he loves me the same way. I know the truth would not matter one iota to him."

"And yet you did not tell him the truth."

"I would have, William. Truly I made the attempt but he stopped me."

"You spoke hesitantly, though, as if confessing—yes, I too would have taken his viewpoint on that. Had you simply said, 'I want you to meet my family—but did you really want that? I doubt it. Your reserve is too deeply instilled in you. I am happy I do not have your problem; I am proud to be Chinese. Remember one thing, Magda, should you ever decide to be one of us—we Chinese are famous for assimilating many different people into our culture. Though I must admit that being a red-headed Chinese girl would not be easy."

He sighed with understanding and affection. Impulsively, she leaned over and rubbed her cheek against his.

"I love you, William, and I honor and respect you. But I don't identify with the Chinese—except for you I feel so much more a MacDougall than a Chen."

"Life might be simplified for you if you could, though."

"Would it? To be considered a piece of merchandise to be sold or given to a husband as his property?"

"Ah, Magda, you are biased. The same things are done in white society—we are just more open about it."

"That isn't true. In other countries, women have a choice."

"And you are happier for having a choice, Magda?"

"You are a lawyer, William, and I am sure you can twist my words around. But thank you for hearing me out. It's been good medicine for me. It's clarified my feelings and, though it's not what you advise—"

"Stop right there. I have, very carefully, not given you any advice."

"Well, then, let me say that I know what I must do."

"And that is?"

"I'm going to fight for my happiness with every instinct I possess. I will not allow an opinionated and intolerant man to play God with my life. And, William, even though I shall remain part of white society, I never really felt any shame or disgrace being part Chinese. It is simply less confusing to be one or the other, not both, and I made my choice a long time ago."

"Angus MacDougall has a lot to answer for."

"Don't blame Papa. He gave his life for me."

"Even that was selfish. I'm sorry, Magda—that was cruel. I have no intention of breaking your faith in your father."

"No one could ever do that. I adore him. I still talk to him and he comforts me."

"An old Chinese custom," William said drily. "Ancestor worship."

Magda laughed and her face lit up for a moment. William realized, once again, how truly lovely she was.

"Your Archie is a very lucky man. I wish you well. And now, had you not better be going home? It has become evening. I can send you back in the car, if you like."

"Won't you take me?"

"Happily. But you may have to explain me."

"I shall say, with pride, that you are my very best friend."

But not yet cousin, William thought. My Uncle Angus, you have paved Magda's path with great difficulties—may both of us help her find a lasting happiness.

Every day Magda expected the bomb to drop, but each day passed without incident. Her brokers, Beatty, Smith and Paige, called to discuss her investments: in the few months since her arrival she had already made a profit and earned Mr. Beatty's respect. But, in spite of her gains, Magda realized that she was no longer interested in what had previously been the most stimulating part of her life.

She and Archie spent most of their evenings in her apartment. There was so much to talk about, so much to plan. There were hopes to share and things to learn about each other. But best of all, they were together—and very much in love. Magda's fear of losing Archie was no longer a constant presence, as weeks had passed since her lunch with Sir Alfred. Archie grew more and more impatient about setting a date for their marriage.

"Why are we waiting?" he demanded one evening. "I don't want to go back to my rooms in the evening. I never want to say goodnight to you again, except in my arms."

"Nor I you," whispered Magda.

"All right, then. Testing time is over. I was positive that you were going to marry me from the first day I saw you, and I still am. Have you any doubts left?"

"I never had any," she replied simply. "I just wanted you to be sure. You knew so little about me when we met, and I was afraid that it might be an infatuation."

"And you do love me?"

"When my heart beats more rapidly, when my knees feel weak, when I spend all my waking hours thinking about you, and when you kiss me and my body goes limp with desire, I know that it's love. I've never been so certain of anything in my whole life." Magda's eyes welled with tears of gladness, and Archie pulled her into his arms. They embraced long and hungrily, filled with their passion for each other.

"What a waste of time," Archie groaned as he let her go. "Here I was, patient and brave while you considered whether this was deeper than infatuation. Shall I quote Elizabeth Browning and tell you in how many ways I love you?" His hands slipped caressingly over the contours of her body and she moved closer to him as she thrilled to his touch.

"I want to undress you. I want our bodies to lie together—God, how I want you—but even more, I want our love to be blessed by the Church and by law. I want everything to start out right for us."

He shook her gently. "Now listen, woman, I will no longer permit you to name the date. I shall see to the certificate and make arrangements with the minister for a simple, private wedding as soon as it can be done. By the way, I never asked you to which Church you belonged?"

"I never told you because I belong to none. I almost became a Roman Catholic when I was in the convent, but I never did."

"It doesn't matter. If you prefer a civil ceremony, we'll have that instead. However, if you truly have no preference, I know Mother will be pleased no end for us to be married in church. So will I, for that matter. Now, I'll listen to no more argument."

"Very well, my lord and liege," she cooed.

"Now that's the way I like my women to answer." In his exuberance he lifted her high in the air. "You seem so tall—I can never get over how light you are. Darling, have I told you that I worship you?"

"You have," she answered, her eyes alight with mirth.

"Good! I thought I'd forgotten," he replied seriously, and they laughed. Everything these days was cause for mirth, every word a treasure. Nothing in the world could ever compare with the wonder of their mutual ardor.

Suddenly, overwhelmed by an emotion stronger than herself, Magda clutched his hand. "Archie! Promise me that you'll never, ever, blame—hold anything against me —that you'll never let me go."

"Silly girl, you talk of the impossible."

"I used to think that something was wrong with me. There was a reason for it and I begged to tell you but you wouldn't let me. It frightens me, sometimes, Archie—I have to tell you."

"You want to tell me something which upsets you, and you want my reassurances that it doesn't matter. Will that satisfy you? You have my assurance that nothing can matter. Magda, dear heart! I've made you cry. I take this oath by my heart and my soul—that I truly believe we have been blessed to find each other, and if ever a marriage were conceived in Heaven, it will be ours. My dearest, is that enough for you?"

"Yes! Oh, yes! Forever and ever, it is enough. I only brought it up because I felt I was being unfair to you."

"Hush! No more. The subject is closed," and he sealed his promise with an impassioned kiss.

Archie dashed up the stairs of the Royal Arms, too agitated to wait for the snail-paced elevator. When Magda opened the door with her usual joyous welcome, he grabbed her hard, almost sobbing with rage.

"I won't let them do this to us. Goddamn it, Magda. He's done it again. He's been good to me, I know—but he thinks he can act like my father, and he *isn't* my father. No father could be so unyielding. He's wanted to marry my mother ever since my father died, and sometimes he really thinks he's in command."

Magda poured out a glass of sherry and endeavored to still her shaking hand. Help me, Papa! she cried silently. I did exactly what you told me—now help me, tell me what to do. Papa! But there was no answer. She drew a deep breath and held it for a few seconds. Trying to remain calm, she took Archie's arm, and led him to the sofa.

"Sit down, Archie, and drink this. Now, tell me what, and how, and who."

"*Who* is my blessed godfather, Sir Bloody Alfred Wilkie-Hume. *What*—is that according to my contract with the bank, I must be ready to travel to various branches to learn the ins and outs of banking wherever they may want to send me. And *how*—is that I must go alone. The bank, says my revered godfather, frowns on marriage for trainees. If I go against their express wishes, it would demonstrate a 'lack of interest' in my career and halt any advancements I may otherwise make. I told him what he could do with the bank and their advancements —I contracted to *work* for them, nothing more and that my private life was my own."

"What did he say?"

"He told me in so many words to stop being a blithering jackass before I wreck my career before it begins— that, if I left them like this, any company would think twice before employing a man who behaved irresponsibly in his previous position. Told me to quiet down and examine it for a few days. Even had the nerve to suggest that I discuss it with you—said a woman was usually more practical."

Magda started to giggle incongruously and a little hysterically.

"Don't darling, don't. Magda, dearest, don't. Take it easy, we'll work it out. Here, drink some water." Archie handed her a glass, patting her back. But she laughed shrilly, and then she cried—her eyes glazing over and words pouring out as though she couldn't stop them.

"We had too much—and no one is allowed more than a little taste of happiness once in a while to give them false hope—to make them greedy for more. And then it's taken away from them. We had too much, Archie. Two whole months of unalloyed joy and wonderment. The gods were jealous—we didn't suffer enough for it and that's not right. Oh, Archie! It came so easily, so naturally, so perfectly—so they're taking it away from us."

"Hush, dear heart! Sh-sh. I shouldn't have burst it on you like that. Hush, my darling. Here, take a sip of this brandy. It'll do you good." He rocked her in his arms. "I swear I won't leave you."

"But, of course, you must." Her eyes opened wide, two oval pools glistening in her pale face. "Don't you see? The gods demand it. We must pay the price—nothing is free. You see, don't you? If we don't we must pay later and it will be even worse—it will ruin the last measure of our love."

She heard, as though from a great distance, Archie's voice soothing her as one would a child. With a shudder, she shook herself free from the horrors which gripped her and downed the brandy Archie held in front of her, shivering as she swallowed the fiery drink.

"Poor Archie. I'm sorry—I didn't think I was hysterically inclined."

"If that is what it was, I hope you never go through it again. You seemed to be in the grip of a nightmare. My dearest girl, there is no need for this agony. I've already decided to opt out of the contract. We'll get married precisely as we planned. I have a private income and a fit farm in England. It's not a half-bad life we'll be going back to—we'll get by all right. You'll love my mum and she'll love you. I'm sorry to let the old man down. He thinks he has to be harsher with me than with anyone else because he's my godfather and can't play favorites."

"But you'll always regret that you didn't do what was expected of you. You'll wonder if your friends will think you expected special privileges. Eventually, in spite of yourself, you'll blame me. No. Wait—" as Archie tried to interrupt her. "You'll never blame me consciously. I know that all our days, all our nights, we'll love each other—but it will be *tainted*." Unconsciously, she used Sir Alfred's word and knew it to be true—not that she was tainted but that her union with Archie would be marred from the beginning. To Magda it seemed like an article of faith: that they had to prove their love by patience if their lives together were to be based on a secure foundation. Then, and only then, whatever Sir Alfred had deviously maneuvered would not matter.

Her flickering thoughts were flashes of truths and half-truths but she faced Archie and explained to him that not accepting the transfer would erode his self-respect.

"I don't understand you, Maggie," Archie said plaintively. "You're urging me to a course of action neither of us really wants. Why, you appear to be agreeing with my godfather. Oh, I could find it in me to hate that man. I'm sure he needn't have been so adamant. But he's always been such a stickler—believes in going beyond the letter of the law, playing the game even if it's damned awful."

"And he's probably also in favor of shackles and pillories," Magda added bitterly. "And of your taking your licks, and the higher you are in life, the more nobly you have to act as an example for the lesser people."

"You must have been eavesdropping."

They fell into an unhappy silence.

"Did you ask him how long you would be gone, and where?"

"Well, first of all, I'm to be sent to some hole in India. From then on, I'm at the disposal of the bank, to be sent to wherever I can learn the different phases of banking in Asia, perhaps even Africa."

"Did he say how long?"

"At least one year, could be two. He said we were young and that a soldier has to put in years more. Then he said being alone would not only place me at the company's disposal, but that young married couples, especially with babies, find it rough going. It was a matter, he said, of not making a bad beginning, perhaps wrecking a marriage. That's why the bank takes a firm position."

"How very altruistic of the bank. What did you say to that?"

"I told him it was stuff and nonsense. That you could take it as well as I could."

Magda couldn't say a word. She just smiled weakly and nodded.

Archie went on. "Then he said that it wasn't his fancy to argue with me—they were company rules and he would be sadly disappointed in me if I failed the first test of reliability. He knows how to rub it in, all right, but I told him what he could do with the bloody job."

"Archie?"

"Yes, my love?"

"Archie, I could wait for you for ten years if I have to."

"What on earth is happening to us! I was determined to throw their bloody job in their faces, and suddenly, here we are planning for my farewell. Why, Magda?"

"I'm not deciding it, darling Archie, only yielding to what is. I know that nothing really can separate us. And I know how your mind works. I'm afraid that the day would come when you would feel you had failed an important test of your integrity. I won't have you plagued with such doubts, or be their cause."

Archie groaned as he gathered her in his arms.

"I don't know. I just don't know. I can't bear the thought of leaving you."

"I wish we hadn't decided to wait for marriage," she murmured, clinging to him. "It's like spurning the gifts of the gods."

"My dearest—my dearest—" he whispered, as they embraced. He refused to release her a moment sooner than a harsh world had decreed.

>>>>>>>>>>>>>>>>>>>>>>>>>>>>>>>>>>>>>>>

PART THREE

Max

1937

>>>>>>>>>>>>>>>>>>>>>>>>>>>>>>>>>>>

CHAPTER EIGHT

<<<<<<<<<<<<<<<<<<<

THE MARKET REPORTS from London, New York, and Paris were not good. The news from Berlin was optimistic, but the political climate of Germany was discouraging. On the whole, Magda concluded, she had gauged the market incisively; though she was a far cry from reaching her million-dollar goal, she had done well enough for Mr. Beatty to ask her laughingly if she'd like a job with them. She might surprise him one day and take him up on it—the days dragged heavily on her hands.

Magda left the offices of her brokers, Beatty, Smith and Paige, deciding to leave her car parked and walk to meet Tasha on Nanking Road. She deliberately chose the Kiangsi Road entrance—it sickened her to see those tens of thousands of refugees from Chapei huddled up on the bund as far as the eye could see, waiting patiently, tirelessly, for assistance. Those damned Japanese!

The sound of distant shooting was now part of the sound of the city; and there were always Japanese warships in the harbor. Japanese troops had surrounded all of the outlying Chinese territories, forcing the inhabitants to flee to the only safe place—the foreign settlements of Shanghai.

It was almost enough to make her take William's proposition seriously. She had always known that he was secretly involved in China's political affairs, but his suggestion had startled her. William had implied that she could double, even triple, her money if she invested in China by providing the funds to smuggle guns into the interior, guns that would be used to fight against the invading Japanese. It would be, he promised, a completely secret transaction, and she would not become personally involved.

"Foreigners are getting wealthy at our expense—why

shouldn't you?" he demanded of her. "Traitors are selling us out to the Japanese. We must fight them, or China will be lost."

Magda had to admit she was tempted. She'd inherited a fierce hatred and distrust of the Japanese. They had already taken Peking and Tientsin. Even Great Britain was being threatened by the Japanese thrust toward Singapore and the Malay States. Was it possible that they could be stopped? The Japanese Navy had grown dangerously powerful, making Japan a world force to be reckoned with. And Japan wanted China—vast, rich China, so vulnerable, with its constant internal warfare.

Magda knew how William felt about all foreigners—he wanted China for the Chinese—but he particularly despised their deadliest enemy, Japan. Magda was in a quandary; she wanted to help him, but financially, the risk was great. Was she prepared to gamble that much?

Magda's thoughts of politics were interrupted by a painful longing. Months of loneliness had made her bitter about her dual heritage. "Why should I have to justify my origins to anyone?" she stormed inwardly. "It was nobody's business but mine and Archie's."

Archie! Her heart leapt whenever she so much as imagined his name. Would these endless days of waiting never come to an end? Almost a year, without his letters to sustain her—

"Oh, Archie!" Magda whispered aloud. Suddenly, she felt such an indescribable aching for him. Her eyes stung with tears of helplessness as she stared blindly into the shop windows on Nanking Road. "Will I ever see you again?"

Maximilian von Zoller, of Sneider and Wolfgang, Inc., Berlin, peered out the window of his office in the Cotton Exchange Building and watched the red-headed woman get out of her car and enter the building across the street. He knew where she was headed—he had seen her often, but never succeeded in his efforts to strike up an acquaintance with her.

With luck, he would catch up with her before she entered the offices of Beatty, Smith and Paige. He straightened his tie, set his hat at exactly the right angle, and raced down the stairs. Too late—she was already inside. Max decided to wait for her at the entrance, introduce himself as she was leaving, and explain that he had tried to find a mutual friend to do the honors.

He rehearsed his lines while he waited patiently for her appearance; then he lifted his hat with a flourish and produced his card. But Magda strolled right by him as though he didn't exist.

Max had to smile at his failure to conquer her reserve. Oh, well, he consoled himself, perhaps I'll get another chance. He decided to walk in the same direction, glancing surreptitiously at himself in the shop windows as he followed Magda. Max was pleased with what he saw there—a tall, well-built, young man, with a clear complexion, a neat moustache, and curly blond hair. He had made a good life for himself in Shanghai, and it showed.

Max let his imagination soar. Each time he saw her his feeling for her grew wildly—so striking, so distant in manner, but so desirable! Max was thirty-two, and it was time, he felt, to get married and settle down. He had come a long way to Shanghai and had devoted all his energies to his work. Now he wanted someone to share his life— and all other women paled before this goddess, this redhaired beauty, so unapproachable, so independent. His blood tingled at the thought of her, as he walked on and turned into Nanking Road.

Tasha looked out of her office window at the hordes of refugees, and knew there was no way she could eat her lunch on the bund, as she usually did on fine days. Even though it was Saturday, she had brought her lunch with her—if she didn't have an excuse, Magda would insist on inviting her to lunch, and it was so awkward to be continually refusing her invitations.

When Magda invited her to share her apartment after Archie left, Tasha refused. "I can't afford it," she said firmly, "And I just swore that I'd never again be obligated to anyone."

"Don't be an idiot, Tash—I'm the one who'll benefit," Magda replied. And Tasha knew she meant it. "It's going to be a long and lonely year before I see Archie again. Don't be so obstinate. I'll tell you what, if it will make you feel better, I'll take a two-bedroom apartment, and you can pay the difference in the rent. You'll be doing me a big favor," Magda argued.

Tasha grinned.

"Some favor, forcing myself to live in a decent apartment instead of the awful place I'm living in now." Tasha was deeply relieved to leave her old rooms in a cheap boarding-house. The food there was greasy and starchy, and it cost Tasha fifty dollars a month out of her small salary as a beginner stenographer. She had often done without lunch and taken the tram to work, hoarding the few clothes she had and cutting off all her former friends —not wanting them to see her poverty.

Every once in a while, the memory of the day her family left flashed through Tasha's mind like a bad dream: the ship slowly leaving its moorings at the Yangtseppo Wharf, the colorful streamers floating in the water, the ship's band playing "Aloha." Aunt Olga had wiped her eyes while the children waved frantically, their faces glowing with the excitement of going to the United States. She was no longer a Wilkinson, but Natasha Guria, Russian orphan, and more alone that she had ever felt in her life.

Tasha shook her head angrily at herself. She had to put it all behind her. Everything was changed now. Besides, what she had gone through seemed like nothing, compared to Magda's losing Archie. Poor Magda! Tasha had seen her—formerly glowing and happy—turn into the old Magda, brooding, drawn into herself. It just wasn't fair.

Tasha tried to leave the building but the whole street was blocked by the Chapei refugees. From one end of the bund, clear to where the old walled city was located, people sat patiently huddled together in one long drab blanket of blues and greys and blacks—a solid mass of refugees surrounded by their meager belongings: whatever clothing they had managed to carry with them, and a few odds and ends of food. In the summer heat, the stench of stale sweat combined with the sick smells of terror and hunger was a palpable thing—so was the hum of thousands of people talking, children crying and beggars whining. All had come to the International Settlement of Shanghai when there was no where else to go. Here they would be safe, even though the gunfire continued without interruption.

And still they came, endless streams of them: the blind led by little boys, the crippled and paralyzed carried on the backs of their sons, or heaped on top of sticks of furniture in rickshaws and wheelbarrows. Babies were strapped on the backs of their mothers or of children hardly larger than the babies they carried. Everyone carried something—bundles, a few scrawny chickens, rolls of straw matting—the pathetic possessions of the poor.

Quick tears of sympathy filled Tasha's eyes. How could she even think of her own misfortune in the face of the sheer misery and hopelessness all around her? The sidewalks, even on the business side of the bund, were packed. Streets were jammed with rickshaws and hand-pulled carts of every variety. Trams, overflowing with refugees, crawled in the traffic snarl from which there seemed to be no escape.

There seemed no possibility of leaving the office. Tasha asked the other employees how they planned to get home but most of them were still looking out of the windows, watching, with horrified eyes, the war taking place in front of them. It was a typically hot and humid August day, and the smell of burning cordite hung heavy in air already thick with smoke and dust.

A dozen Japanese cruisers looked like toy boats in the distance, but the red and blue spurts of fire from the cannons were frighteningly real, as they shelled Chinese positions on shore. To Tasha, staring out the window, it all seemed completely *un*real. This couldn't be happening in front of her eyes!

Every window in the tall office buildings along the bund was filled with spectators. Others ran to the roofs for a better view of the fighting.

Then, a new sound penetrated the existing roar. All eyes looked to the sky as three Japanese fighter planes flew low over the city, and dropped the first bomb on the corner of the bund and Nanking Road—which at that moment was crowded with Saturday shoppers.

There was a terrible explosion, then clouds of dust and the din of falling bricks and concrete. A short silence followed; then two more bombs fell in swift order on downtown Shanghai.

The blasts were followed by the unearthly screaming of the dying and wounded. The pavement beneath Magda's feet shook as if there were an earthquake. But before she had time to understand what was happening, a strong arm seized hers and rushed her into a nearby department store, pushing aside everyone in their way. The man led them through a melee of people, some of whom were trying to run outside and others who were running into the store. Merchandise clattered all around them, and dazed people wandered everywhere. Panic was setting in. But there was no panic evident in the man who had Magda in tow. With his arms clasped firmly around her waist, he used himself as a battering ram, propelling them both through the crowds until they reached the basement. After one quick look around, he pushed Magda and himself under a heavy counter which was attached to the floor.

Booms of thunder shook the building. Each time, a strange and eerie silence followed, broken only by screams of horror and agony. The floors shook, and the walls trembled. Breaking glass crashed above them, and merchandise racks and boxes fell. Someone nearby was crying hysterically; but, other than that, it seemed that everyone was holding his breath and waiting for the holocaust to end.

Finally, when they were certain the bombing had stopped, the man crawled out and helped Magda to her feet. Only then did she recognize him as the man who had tried to approach her that morning at her brokers' office.

"You knew exactly what to do," she gasped, staring at him in some awe. "You didn't waver a minute."

"It was like the recurrence of a nightmare from which I will never fully recover. I have heard all those sounds many, many times. I was thirteen at the end of the war, almost twenty years ago. One may survive, but one never forgets the stark dread." His English was impeccable, if a bit stilted. It had only the faintest hint of a German accent. He handed Magda his card with a flourish and a low bow.

"I am indebted to you, Mr. von Zoller," Magda said, reading the card. "My name is MacDougall, Magda MacDougall."

"I have hoped to meet you, Miss MacDougall, but never imagined it would be under such circumstances." At that, Max lifted his hat, still miraculously on his head, clicked his heels, and kissed her hand lightly—but with aplomb.

Magda controlled an impulse to laugh as she appraised him. It seemed ludicrous for him to conduct himself as if they were being introduced, formally, in a ballroom. But all thoughts of laughter vanished when they turned cautiously onto Nanking Road. The bodies of the dead and mutilated littered the street—they were piled on one another like heaps of old rags. An occasional arm or leg moved spasmodically, then fell back. A stream of blood flooded the street. Magda felt it soak through her shoes. She slipped and grabbed hold of Max's arm to steady herself. Then she gasped and turned pale, as she saw that she had stepped on an arm still holding an old kettle. Gruesome pieces of flesh were strewn along the fronts of buildings. Parked cars were in flames, and streetcars and power lines were tangled together. A sickening stench of burning flesh permeated the air. The corner of the Cathay Hotel had been blown up, and a bomb had thundered through the roof of the Palace Hotel opposite. Shattered glass, red-stained, dotted the streets. A few people staggered numbly by, like zombies.

"But where are the ambulances and police cars?" Max asked, puzzled. Then he noticed the tangled electric wires and gasped. *"Mein Gott!* The telephone wires are severed. Is it possible that the authorities do not know what has happened?"

Max realized that Magda was becoming ill despite a desperate attempt to pull herself together. "Come," he said, taking her firmly by the arm. "Lean against me. Let us hurry. We are going to have to go on. Just don't look."

They ran several blocks to escape the sound and sight and smell of the holocaust, until they reached crowds of people talking excitedly to each other.

"What are they saying? Do you understand Chinese?"

"They are saying that the Japanese have bombed downtown and killed thousands of people. They are guessing. They know nothing."

Fortunately, they were able to ride the rest of the way on rickshaws. There were still no sounds of ambulances or police sirens—communication lines had broken down completely, and for several hours, the rest of Shanghai had gone about business as usual, ignorant that a mortal blow had been struck.

Tasha was home when they arrived. Crying and almost incoherent, she hugged Magda. "I was crazy with worry about you. I knew you were on Nanking Road—several of the men at the office had cars parked nearby and took us all home in relays—none of the back streets were damaged—"

The girls clung to each other for a few moments. Then they separated, a bit awkwardly. Neither of them was given to public displays of affection. Tasha gaped blankly at the strange man who had accompanied Magda home. Magda quickly introduced them, then she excused herself to shower and change.

Max looked around approvingly at the beautifully furnished apartment. It went well with the image he had formed of Magda.

What a self-satisfied prig he seems, Tasha thought, taking an immediate dislike to the man, even after Magda explained that he had probably saved her life.

"Mr. von Zoller, what would you like to drink? I'm ordering tea for us, but perhaps you'd like something stronger. Magda looks exhausted—she really should rest."

"I prefer to wait. I'll have some tea with her when she finishes dressing." Max had no intention of leaving until he had made some headway with the woman he so admired. He ignored Tasha's obvious irritation.

The houseboy, dressed in an immaculate blue serving-gown, brought in a silver tea service and a tray of sandwiches and hot scones. Once again, Max nodded approvingly to himself. She knows how to do things well—she'll be a fine hostess, he grinned.

Before, he had merely been intrigued. Now, he was determined. Max saw that she wore a ring on her engagement finger. But evidently her fiance was not in Shanghai, or she would have telephoned him immediately. Besides that, she had been alone every time he saw her. Surely, there was hope for him!

At that moment Magda came in, freshly bathed and wearing a simple white-linen dress. She was still unnaturally pale but composed.

"Well, I feel a bit more human now," she said shuddering again at the horrors she had seen. "I don't know if you follow politics, Mr. von Zoller, but it's difficult for me to believe that the Japanese would act so imprudently. I'd think they would prefer that Shanghai remain a thriving business community—"

"It felt like the end of the world," Tasha broke in. "All I could do when I came home was run in and out of the building looking for you. Then I worried I'd miss a call."

"Did you have a bad time getting home?"

"More in my imagination than in fact. I thought the whole city had been demolished—I saw the bombs falling —it was all absolutely beyond description." Tasha lit a cigarette nervously and continued, "I was looking out the window when I saw the first bomb drop, right in the middle of all those poor people—it was so horrible, so terribly horrible—some of them had been sitting there so patiently for days—" Tasha ran out of the room, shuddering and sobbing. Magda rose and started after her, but Max put a restraining hand on her arm.

"Forgive me, but it is better, I think, if she cries it all out alone."

Magda was touched by his understanding and concern.

The next day, Max launched his campaign to win Magda. He sent her a basket of flowers with a note: "I trust you are recovered from your harrowing experiences yesterday, and that you will permit me the honor of calling on you this afternoon to pay my respects. Maximilian von Zoller."

Unfortunately for Max, Magda was not home to receive either the flowers or him.

Still shaken by the incredible happenings of August 14th—"Bloody Saturday" as it would soon be known—

Magda resolved her own course of action. She tried to call William and discovered that all the telephone lines were down. Her car had probably been destroyed, and, in any case, was beyond her reach. It was a long ride, but she took a rickshaw to William's house. There she was met enthusiastically by his children and his pretty, shy wife, Lotus, who felt an awed respect for her strange-looking relative. As soon as the amenities had been observed and tea served, William took her to his little office and scrutinized her.

"I'd like to know more about the gun deal, William."

He nodded as though he knew her mission, and explained that, for the most part, the gun smuggling was big business, conducted by influential operators. There were, however, a few minor entrepreneurs who were ready to take big risks in exchange for big profits. William happened to know of a comparatively small shipment where the suppliers had lost heart and were ready to sell their merchandise for a nominal sum and get out of the country.

"How much money are we talking about, and what are the risks?"

"In danger for you, none. In money, it's all or nothing. If the guns are stolen en route, or confiscated by government men, the investor loses everything. If the guns go through, though, the investment is at least doubled, or possibly better. In this case we're talking about an investment of a hundred thousand dollars."

"How can the investor know the money is there on arrival?"

William paused thoughtfully. "There is a cadre of dedicated and patriotic men I know of, who are prepared to risk their lives and their fortunes for the freedom of China. I give you my word that the money is there. Beyond that, I can guarantee nothing; but I *will* say that those entrusted to deliver the guns to the designated point are experienced men of proven honesty. But, Magda, when we spoke the other day, you were not interested. What has changed for you? I am curious."

"My father always taught me that the handling of money should be completely divested of any sentiment or emotionalism. However, I will admit to you, William, that yesterday's attack makes me want to retaliate. If these

107

guns will help drive the Japanese away from China, there is added incentive."

"I am pleased that you are not solely interested in quick profit."

"All well and good, but that is not to say I am *un*interested," Magda replied drily. "I don't have the amount you mentioned on hand, so I will have to get a loan. If the guns do not reach the buyers, I shall be practically stripped of my present holdings. The market has been slow, and I haven't been able to build much. Now—it seems to me that if the suppliers were eager to sell a few days ago, they should be even more eager to sell today. Perhaps the purchase price will be considerably less—"

"I can see that you will not be moved entirely by sentiment," William smiled. "You are serious."

Magda nodded, and added, "And with the present risks involved, what is the best price for delivery? All patriotism aside."

"With the phone out, I cannot get direct replies today. But I'll get the answer for you first thing in the morning."

Magda nodded again. The business meeting was over. She spent the rest of the day with her cousins, enjoying the chatter and affection in the house. William was a kind father and a considerate husband but there was no doubt in her mind that his wife catered to her husband in every way. Magda caught William studying her during the day as though he could read her mind.

"No, Magda. I don't think you could ever be a typical Chinese wife." His eyes twinkled. "It's too late for you to learn obedience."

She chuckled and rose to leave. On her way home, she made another decision: to accept a job with her brokers if they still wanted her. She had to find a way to occupy her time.

An annoyed Tasha met Magda in the tiny hallway of the apartment as soon as she heard the key in the lock.

"That von Zoller!" she whispered. "He's been here since four o'clock and won't budge. He's thick-skinned and arrogant like every German I ever met. I wish you'd send him packing. I suggested a dozen times that you might be late, but he just sits there and grins. Short of throwing him out, I've been stuck with him."

"I'm sorry, Tash. Why is he here?"

"Why do you think? He sent you some flowers saying he was calling to pay his respects—he sounds like a bad novel."

When Magda entered, Max stood up stiffly, bowed low, and kissed her hand.

"Miss Guria tells me you've been waiting for some time. It's too bad I didn't receive your message early enough to tell you that I would be gone for the day," Magda said as she read the card. "Thank you for the flowers—they're very lovely."

"I'm sorry, too. You must have left very early. Your companion tells me she did not know your plans," he said, unconvinced.

"That is correct, Mr. von Zoller."

"I thought that, perhaps, two people who share an apartment would confide in each other."

"You are mistaken," Magda replied with undisguised pique.

"I will know better next time, and give you more warning. Will you do me the honor of dining with me tonight?"

"I'm sorry—I am much too tired to go anywhere."

"Tomorrow then?"

"No, thank you."

"I hope you don't find me presumptuous, but I have wanted to meet you for a long time. Will you please allow me to become better acquainted?"

"Mr. von Zoller, I owe you a great debt for pulling me to safety yesterday, but I must tell you that I do not 'go out,' as you might call it."

"You say that you owe me—I say it was my privilege to have assisted you. But if you claim you owe me anything, may I ask you for at least one date with you? Please?" He smiled appealingly at her.

"If you put it that way, how can I refuse? But I have a better idea. Come to dinner with us some night next week. I have your address—I'll send you a note."

It was not all that Max had hoped, but it was a step in the right direction.

CHAPTER NINE

‹‹‹‹‹‹‹‹‹‹‹‹‹‹‹‹‹

THE WIRE SERVICES rapidly spread the news of "Bloody Saturday" and the Japanese attack on Shanghai. By Monday the unthinkable was bruited around: that the Chinese themselves were responsible for the bombing. It was incredible. But the rumor was substantiated a few days later when Mme. Chiang Kai-shek, in the name of the Chinese pilots implicated, issued a statement explaining that the bomb racks had been damaged by anti-aircraft fires and that the bombs had been dropped by accident. The same thing seemed to have happened in another part of the city, where several bombs had exploded in an amusement park, killing thousands. Then a new rumor began to circulate: that the Chinese had deliberately dropped the bombs to discredit Japan with the major foreign powers and provoke them into taking punitive action.

Chiang Kai-shek offered a strong defense against the invaders, but the Japanese were too strong and too well-organized. Some of the Chinese generals who hated Chiang conspired with the Japanese against him, so that, after two months, Chiang withdrew his troops and left Japan in possession of all Greater Shanghai.

The "new" post office had been built about ten years earlier and had been touted as a symbol of Shanghai's progress. Built on the corner of North Szechuen Road near the Szechuen Bridge, its high mast had flown the flag of various nations. Now it flew the flag of the rising sun. As a direct consequence of the Japanese take over, mail delivery had slowed down almost to a halt.

Magda felt a physical deprivation from not receiving her regular letters from Archie. They had been her sustenance during a long, weary year of waiting. When the mail finally was delivered, she received the immeasurable riches of several letters at one time. Taking them to her room, she locked the door and looked greedily at the bundle. First, she put them in order according to dates, preparing to enjoy a feast; but before reading the new letters, she opened her safe and took out a few of the more recent ones, to mull over them again, to lose herself in reveries of Archie.

In his earlier letters, Archie had sworn that he would remain "enslaved" to the bank only until December—and then, if the situation had not changed, he would feel conscience-free to leave their employ—to return to Shanghai and marry her, and then to England, as they ought to have done in the first place.

Several of these letters mentioned his last transfer, to a small station in India, and his home with one of the bank's officers, and his daughter: "Jennifier is a lonely child who follows me around like a little puppy. She's a sweet child, serious for her age, very lonely in this community where there are few British companions of her years . . ."

In a later letter he had written:

I tell Jennie tales of you and how lovely you are. She cannot get enough of it but must hear every detail, everything we have done together. Tears gather in her eyes when I tell her of my loneliness. She is very sympathetic and it does my heart good and lessens my loneliness to talk about you. She probably thinks she is sharing in one of Elinor Glyn's novels of high romance.

Reading his letters again, Magda suffered a little pang of jealousy—that this child should have Archie's company when she was deprived; but she was glad that Archie had found ears to confide in, as she had with Tasha. Magda had even shared parts of his letters with her and was wryly amused by Tasha's heated anger at Sir Alfred's manipulation. Tasha was so vehemently opposed that Magda found herself defending him, for she could understand his actions, as she could not understand her own intolerant father in similar circumstances.

She did not know whether her father had been wise in the way he directed her life but she knew that he had been motivated by his love for her. She sighed deeply and opened the first of the new letters.

The days grow longer . . . December seems as far away as ever. How did I permit myself to get into this ridiculous position? I must have been mad. The bank doesn't own me. Had I never met you, I might have felt some interest for the places to which I have been transferred; but, on the whole, it is a dull and monotonous life. It's subtropical where I am now, but with nothing of the lush beauty to be found in some tropical countries. The waters breed mosquitos, and malaria is prevalent. There is a club for the British but it is not much to speak of. Were it not for Jenny's sympathetic company, I believe I should go mad for wanting you. Your letters are the source of my courage and my life.

Forever yours, Archie

She had written once offering to join him, in spite of everything. He wrote back:

I will not permit one shred of scandal to touch you. The infinite joy in seeing you again would not be worth having your reputation sullied—the gossips would drag your name in the mud. I want to face the world with you as my beloved wife. I am proud and humble that you love me so much . . . we have waited this long . . .

And so the letters went. Jennie was mentioned once again:

Mr. Denison, Jennifer's father, wants to give her a party on her eighteenth birthday but she doesn't want one. Poor child! There is no one to ask but a few of the local girls of mixed parentage—and her father frowns on her becoming too intimate with them.

Eighteen—hardly a child! The elusive thought slipped away as she opened the last letter. Her eyes were dewy with love. It was August—then September, October, November and, finally, December. Five more months—how many weeks, days, minutes, seconds until they were reunited?

Dearest Magda: I feel it is too much to ask you to keep on with this unsatisfactory arrangement. I hold you in too much esteem to have you tie yourself down when the end is not in sight. I want you to consider yourself free until we should meet again. With my undying devotion, as always, Archie.

The words blurred in front of her eyes. She read the letter again and again, unable to absorb what she read. The thought finally hammered itself in her mind—he couldn't wait out the term, couldn't take it any more. Jennie! The name shouted at her—Jennie was not a child, not at seventeen and eighteen. She was a woman. Had Archie deliberately deceived her about a "child"? Oh, what did it matter, what did anything matter now?

Magda stared dry-eyed at the letters, then she arranged them all neatly in order of date, tied them together, and put them in their box. She put the box in the wall-safe and locked it. She sat upright in her chair with her hands clasped in front of her, trying to erase any thoughts from her mind.

In the days that followed, she was quiet and self-controlled. She ate her meals, she attempted to sleep, and she went about business as though going through the motions of living took all her concentration. She breathed, but she felt dead—Archie had breathed life into her, and, without him, there was no life.

Magda tried to fill her days. A Jesuit priest managed to persuade the Japanese chief-of-staff to let him use a deserted section of Nantau as a hospital and refuge for homeless children. A few houses were cleaned out for the children, and others opened for the sick and dying. Medicines, money, and assistance were desperately needed— and came generously from all quarters. Magda joined those who worked at the shelters, spending long hours using her energies to good purpose. Her knowledge of languages made communication possible among the Chinese people, the French priest, and his English-speaking assistants. She even acted as interpreter for the Japanese general, who spoke execrable German but insisted on using it.

Through it all, though, a sickness hung over her like a pall, every waking hour and deep into the night. Deliberately, she worked until she was physically exhausted—so that sheer tiredness would bring sleep, uneasy sleep, from which she would awaken with a terrible sense of loss. In this half-awakened state of utter despair she faced the cause of her desolation. She lay in bed straining to hypnotize herself into a coma. One day, she prayed, she would open her eyes, and it would all be over. Until then, she did not even want to think of an existence without Archie.

Magda had answered Archie promptly, releasing him and returning his ring. One night, as she sat staring over the racecourse, the full realization of her loss came to her. She knew then that she had always anticipated it. But even that realization made no difference.

Archie returned the ring to her with a message:

"If you ever loved me, worthless as I am, please keep this ring, which was given to you from the fullness of my love. It will never be worn by anyone else. Devotedly yours, Archie."

A month later came the announcement of his marriage to Jennifer Denison. When word came, Magda told Tasha about it simply, and then said, "If you don't mind, we will not discuss it."

The box in which Magda had placed all of Archie's letters had a complicated and secret way of opening. It had always amused her to have a box that no one else could ever open—it seemed to seal in privacy the richness of their love from the outside world. Now she put the marriage notice and the ring inside the box and put the box away in the farthest recesses of the safe, in darkness and oblivion, not to be seen or considered again.

Word came from William that the shipment of guns had gone through successfully, and that Magda had multiplied her investment. Magda went to his house to pick up the money and found it in sackfuls of varied currency issued by the different Chinese banks: the neat small bills from the Bank of Commerce, large bills from the Hong Kong and Shanghai Bank, others from the Charter Bank, the Bank of Cho-sen and the National Bank of China.

"What shall I do with all of this?" Magda cried in dismay. "Can you imagine me bringing this in to deposit? They'll think I've robbed a bank myself, I'm sure."

William gave one of his rare laughs.

"Do you want me to handle this for you? I'll get it changed in an exchange shop."

"Thank you, William. If you'll do me another favor— have a hundred thousand of it changed into American money in a cashier's check? I'll send it to my account in the States—the rest of it into a cashier's check to be deposited here. I don't want to be handling a lot of currency: it looks suspicious when I'm supposed to be investing in stocks."

Magda paused for a moment, then said, "William, I'm ready to continue with the guns as the occasion arises. I never thought I'd be a gun smuggler, but if the guns will aid the Chinese against the Japanese, I'll have done something to help. If the next deal goes through, I'll keep letting the initial investment ride. Oh, one more thing—I think you should receive a percentage of the profits."

William's face was impenetrable as he replied, "My cousin, I know you believe as you have been taught, that all workers should be paid, but I must refuse categorically. I find the idea repugnant, that I should be paid while my brothers are giving their lives for their country. Don't be hurt by my words. It is different with you, Magda—you are just now starting to feel a little for China. I would not want to be in your position when a real decision must be made. However, the rest of your proposition is estimable. I will get in touch with you when and if the occasion arises."

Magda was positive that William was deeply embroiled in China's politics. Exactly how, she did not know, or care to know. From his earliest days, William had been an ardent patriot, and though his attention was now directed against the Japanese, Magda knew that he would never be satisfied until he saw the last foreigner leave his country. She was beginning to fathom the extent of his indignation.

Max von Zoller courted Magda indefatigably. When he first came for dinner at the apartment, she was courteous and distant, offering him no encouragement. But Max felt more sure than ever that he could never be happy without

115

her. He would have to proceed cautiously, though, to gain her confidence. And, far from being discouraged by her remoteness, Max was stimulated.

She refused his entreaties that she have dinner with him, without elaborate excuses or explanations. On the rare occasions when he was able to persuade her to accept, she insisted that Tasha accompany them. Max wanted desperately to be alone with Magda and bristled at Tasha's presence. She made him uncomfortable, as though she were always secretly amused by him. He disguised his dismay as well as he could though—his hold on Magda was too fragile to take such a risk. The more she refused him, the more he was determined to win her with his love.

His persistence finally won out, and he became a regular guest at the apartment. Both Max and Tasha were happy with the arrangement—she could retire to her room and read, and Max, finally, had Magda all to himself.

As the months passed, Magda became accustomed to Max's presence. If Max was relieved when he no longer saw Archie's ring on her finger, he was wise enough to say nothing. When he wasn't visiting, he called on the phone. Sometimes he would send her a small bouquet of flowers he had carefully chosen: perhaps a fresh bunch of violets or a single perfect rose. Sometimes there would be a small gift of little value, but which showed his thoughtfulness: perhaps a Chinese toy on a string or a puzzle to distract her for an hour. Max did not completely recognize his own motives or see that his primary interest in her had changed from desire to overwhelming tenderness. It was the strongest emotion he had ever felt in his life; he was suffused with a longing to help her, to take care of her, and to remove the hurts he saw in her eyes.

Very slowly, Magda came to depend on his presence, to feel a kind of sudden pleasure when they were together. His constant attention had penetrated her defenses: from a great distance, she was drawn back into the world by his affection. Max did all he could to make her happy, and Magda was touched by his concern—by his consideration of her every mood, her every wish.

One day in late December, she announced to Tasha that she had decided to accept Max's proposal of marriage.

"But you can't, Magda, you simply can't. You're just marrying him on the rebound. How can you forget what you had with Archie?"

"Tash—I'm very fond of you and I respect your opinions," Magda began. "But when one chapter of a book is ended, another starts. Unless the book is destroyed," she added pensively. "And I'm not prepared to destroy the book of my life, or leave the rest of the pages completely blank. My whole life extends before me and I want to fill it with the companionship of someone I care for."

"But you haven't given yourself any time. Why Max, of all people? He's shallow, and full of self-importance—"

"He has been very kind and considerate to me. He's much more sensitive than you know, and he understands and respects me. We have quite a lot in common, really. Besides, he knows that all I can ever give him is a deep affection, and that I want him only for companionship. He's ready to accept that as a basis for our marriage. I care for him, Tasha. I'll try to make him happy."

"My God! What an awful prospect! I don't suppose you're blind to the fact that he also likes it that you have money," Tasha said with some bitterness.

Magda was amused. "Of course I'm not blind to it— but neither am I shocked or surprised. I expect it. In Europe a man expects his future wife to provide a dowry —the larger, the more welcome. There is no secret or shame about it. We haven't discussed money matters, but I fully expect to pay part of our expenses. Max doesn't make much money yet, but he will."

"You must be made of ice," Tasha said as she paced the room furiously. "I just don't understand you. I'd fight to the last drop if it were me—I wouldn't give in and accept what's happened."

"What would you suggest, Tasha? That I hide behind a tree and shoot Archie dead? Or would you prefer that I kill Jennie and kidnap her husband?" Saying the word husband was the hardest thing Magda had done but she had to face it. "It's just as foolish to keep fighting when the battle is lost."

"What do you do then, send congratulations to the victor?"

"You try to find some peace and a measure of contentment."

"Well, I wouldn't settle for second best."

"I hope you never have to. And now, I think we'd better leave the subject alone."

"I suppose so," Tasha said dismally. Then, impulsively, she ran over to Magda and hugged her. "I truly hope you'll be happy, Magda—I hope everything works out," she said, and then she ran out of the room, muttering, "But I'll never understand what you see in him."

Tasha was confused and upset. To her consternation, a trace of suspicion hung tenaciously in her mind, despite her efforts to dismiss it. Was Magda marrying Max, even as a second choice, because it was the ambition of every Eurasian to marry a European? How else could she explain Magda's willingness to put Archie out of her mind so quickly? Was it possible to put away the past completely? Such a recent past—just a few months. Could time really heal so rapidly? Why was it, then, that after almost four years *she* still occasionally felt the flood of desolation—the same shocked betrayal she had felt when the only family she had ever known departed and left her behind, as though she were a casual thing to be discarded?

She had to admit that those times were becoming very rare. Of course, she had made a determined effort to forget the past. She supposed that was what Magda meant, and she saw how much harder it must have been for her. Tasha felt ashamed for her doubts. She should be trying to make it easier for Magda, instead of reminding her about Max's shortcomings. But how could she marry him? Tasha sighed heavily. If she had ever seen anyone in love, it had been Magda in those euphoric weeks before Archie left for India.

CHAPTER TEN

TASHA STOOD IN the middle of her bedroom, separating her belongings into three piles: clothes she would take with her, doubtful items, and discards. She still resisted throwing anything away—the habits of economy had been too well instilled in her.

She hummed tonelessly in accompaniment to the trills and arpeggios which came clearly from the next room where Magda was whistling a plaintive tune while doing her own packing. Whistling was one of Magda's minor accomplishments. She had perfect pitch and a clear, full tone, besides the ability to remember every song she ever heard. The only dubious thing about her whistling was how she had become so adept at such an uncouth thing —Magda, the perfectly disciplined product of a finishing school!

In the middle of her ramblings, Tasha realized that the whistling had stopped—had, in fact, been over for some time. She was unaccountably disturbed.

She just doesn't feel like it any more, she thought, and she shrugged away her disquiet. She continued her sorting, but the rhythm of the afternoon had been interrupted. "Silly!" she said aloud to herself. "Mind your own business."

Finally, though, the silence became oppressive.

"Magda! Magda!" Tasha called out. "Come here and look—I've found that locket from my parents that I told you about."

There was no answer. This was most unusual, for Magda was usually polite to a fault. The connecting door between their rooms was shut. Tasha hesitated to disturb Magda, for they both valued their privacy; but nevertheless, she was propelled to the door by her growing anxiety. She knocked. There was no answer. She opened the door a little and looked inside.

119

Magda was on her knees clutching some letters. Others had fallen on the floor, and the safe door was open.

"Magda—Magda," Tasha whispered, but there was no answer or movement. Magda appeared to have gone into a catatonic trance, as though the full and final realization of her loss was more than she could endure.

Tasha ran over to her and shook her, at first gently, then with increasing roughness as fear overcame her.

"Magda! Magda!" she called desperately, "Oh, Magda, dear, don't let it hurt you so!"

Magda's eyes slowly, unwillingly, focused on her. Her mouth opened but only a hoarse croaking emerged—as if she were having difficulty finding her voice. She drew in a few deep, painful breaths and finally some words came, disjointed, gasping, almost incomprehensible at first.

"It's all over—all over. Why did you wake me? I had willed myself to die. The gods were jealous. It was too perfect—How could he do this to me? He loved me! Why? Why? Why?"

The last "why" ended in a long gasping sob, and then the tears came, a convulsion of tears which tore her apart —heartbreaking and retching sobs. Her body shook as Tasha held her in her arms, weeping with her and for her. She knew that Magda at last had to face the terrible fact—that it was really over, that Archie was gone forever.

Then, just as suddenly, the tragic scene was all over. Once again, she became the old, controlled Magda. The emotional typhoon had spent itself, leaving almost no sign that it had occurred. Magda removed herself from Tasha's embrace.

"Sister George would say I was not behaving like a *jeune fille bien élevée*."

"A fig for your Sister George. Aren't well-bred young ladies supposed to have any hearts?"

"Young ladies must learn to control them."

"Bosh! Why don't you burn those letters, Magda? They'll always remind you of the heartache he caused you. Destroy them."

"What rot you talk, Tasha. They are only pieces of paper." Magda gathered up all the letters, tied them neatly together and placed them in her trick box. Then, some of the stiffness left her face and her voice became tender as she whispered: "Destroying them would not change the way I feel. They are all that is left of the love we had, and I will treasure them the rest of my life. They will remind me that once I knew what it meant to be fully alive. Do you know what that means? We touched and a fire swept through us. We looked and could read each other's minds. If one of us laughed, the other did too. Archie can never love anyone like that again. It is a once-in-a-lifetime thing. If I never had anything else, I will have had that. Not everyone is so lucky. I shall love him all my life, and he will never be quite free of me. This I know, and that is the way it must be." She spoke as quietly as usual, but there was an undertone of passion in her voice.

"I could kill that old Sir Alfred Wilkie-Hume," Tasha said hotly.

"He only did what he believed was right."

"For Heaven's sake, are you going for sainthood? He was supposed to be your friend."

"Not really—he was just my financial adviser. How could you expect a well-bred Englishman to tolerate another Englishman—especially his godson—marrying a Eurasian? What could a single ruined life mean in comparison?"

Magda stood up, still a little shaky, and walked nervously around the room, picking up objects and laying them down.

"Come on, Tasha, let's not be maudlin about it. If the truth were told, you might admit that deep down inside you feel the same superiority toward me. Honestly now, you know I'm right."

"No! You're not right, and you bloody well know it. I'm no bloody-minded Englishman who thinks he's above everyone else. You're—"

"Now, now! If you must swear, you should at least try to vary the words a bit." Magda touched Tasha's cheek gently, in an uncommon display of affection, and Tasha looked back at her with tears in her eyes.

"It's just not right, Magda. You're young and beautiful —why can't you wait until you meet someone you could fall in love with?"

"No! Dear God, never again!" A long hard shudder

went through her. "I would kill myself first. There's only so much love in me, and it all went to Archie. The very thought of experiencing that again: the exhilaration, the ecstasy, and the terrible hurt if it doesn't work out—never. Max is fine. I *am* fond of him. He knows the situation, and he accepts it. Besides, we're both neat to a fault."

She laughed at that and, reluctantly, Tasha joined in.

"I suppose that's a slur against me. I'm not untidy—but I don't make a fetish of it like you do."

"Poor Tasha! Don't mind me, I'm unpredictable today, even to myself. I had managed to put everything out of my mind—then, seeing those letters again. If someone dies, it's easier to face than if someone is forever out of reach."

Tasha had never seen Magda so jumpy. She moved from one piece of furniture to another, straightening a picture, rearranging the top of her bureau.

"Let's stop these girlish confidences before I become as sentimental as you. Oh, please, Tasha, don't be hurt by that. Give me just this one day not to be responsible for everything I say and do. By the way, if you're interested, Archie has been transferred to the bank's main office in Hong Kong. He's living in Victoria, with his pure English wife and his pure-white little daughter.

"Oh, yes," she answered the question in Tasha's eyes. "I've kept track of him. I know exactly when his daughter was born—seven and a half months after he wrote the letter giving me my freedom. I think what I find hardest to forgive is that he could not control himself—why didn't he just go to a bordello? Why pick on a foolish girl? Or, as I suspect, the girl was not so foolish and picked him."

Tasha looked at her despairingly. She did not know what to say.

"Are you surprised that I know about him?" Magda laughed bitterly. "It's one of the good things about money —you can always pay for information. Oh, you're shocked. Poor Tasha—do I disillusion you? Don't worry. I'll make a good wife for Max. I'm fond of him, and I can help him with his work. Well, come on, you'd better get your packing finished. The boy will be here in the morning to pick up your things. I'd just as soon keep the apartment, but Max can be so stubborn. I don't know why you won't stay, though. I have to pay the two months until the lease is up, anyway. Think of all the money you'd save."

Tasha felt the blood rush to her cheeks.

"You're always making little jabs to me about money, Magda. Do you want to hurt my pride? I wish I hadn't listened to you and never come to live with you!"

Magda put her arms around Tasha, who was close to sobbing.

"Tasha, my dear, I'm sorry. I don't know what I'm saying. It's a feeble excuse, I know, for hurting my dearest friend. Perhaps I need to lash out at someone, and you're here. It doesn't mean anything—you're the only person in the world I can be myself with, and I'm taking advantage of it. Forgive me, please."

Magda sank into a chair and Tasha's anger quickly left her. In all the years she had known Magda, she had never seen her give way like this before. It is almost as though she had never known her. She was exposing too much of herself—more than Tasha wanted to see.

"As you said, I'd better get on with my packing." She started to leave the room, and Magda stopped her, pulling from her closet a small wardrobe trunk and matching leather suitcase.

"Voilà! For a new start in life, new luggage to get there."

Tasha's eyes sparkled with delight. She was on the verge of refusing them as she did all gifts, when Magda broke in, full of irritation.

"I recognize that resistance in your eyes, Tasha. Don't you dare take away my pleasure! You can be the most aggravating person—can't you accept a gift gracefully? You're always afraid someone will step on your infernal independence. There's a limit, you know. Besides your old trunk needs to be retired."

"Well, don't be so cross about it," Tasha said, relenting. "That old trunk of mine, I would have you know, constitutes my entire inheritance, and it contains priceless rags."

They both laughed, relieved the awkward moment had passed.

"Tell me about the locket. Is there really one or were you just trying to get my attention?"

"I didn't think you heard me. There's a locket, all

123

right. I found it years ago in this trunk, with a packet of letters and documents in Russian, and a gold medal on a chain."

Tasha went to the bureau where she had placed a box covered with worn and faded needlepoint. From it, she drew out a flat case containing a necklace. Dirty red, blue, and crystal beads were strung together with tarnished metal. Loops attached the beaded chain to a large, elaborately decorated locket that was black with age and neglect.

"There they are, my esteemed mother and father. If I didn't have this I wouldn't know I'd had parents."

Magda looked at the pictures thoughtfully. "Your mother was really pretty, and your father—I can see why Max calls you a gypsy—your father sparkles with the magnetic fire of a gypsy king."

"Well, he wasn't. Aunt Olga told me he came from a very old Georgian family, kings at one time. But, as the country kept changing, the family lost a great deal of its power and so my father was more like a minor prince."

"Oh, no, Tasha! Not another Russian prince! I swear all Russia must have been royalty! Every Russian refugee in Shanghai claims to be of royal blood."

"Poor things. It's sad to have to exist on past glories."

"Your father looks dangerous. There is a wild animal in him, like a tiger, ready to jump if you cross him. You have that about you too."

"Thanks a lot."

"No, really. You have the same face with those long, narrow eyes. But he looks like a dangerous wildcat, and you're a soft kitten. Though I can well imagine you with your claws unsheathed. Say, I'm famished. Let's have tea here—I ordered a special one for today. I thought I'd never be able to eat again. You know, Tasha, letting your hair down does wonders for the soul, and for the appetite." Then she added abruptly, "I want to ask a favor of you."

"Anything, Magda."

"Don't be so quick to promise. You haven't a clue what I'm going to ask."

"All right. What, then?" Tasha answered, wondering

if she could eat another slice of the chestnut-cream cake.

"I'm going to visit my family tomorrow. Will you come with me?"

Tasha stopped cutting the cake and stared at Magda with surprise. It was the only time since Magda's return that she had ever mentioned her family.

"If you don't want to go, it's all right, I understand," Magda said, as Tasha swallowed uneasily.

"Of course. I want to go. I just wondered why you wanted me to. I'm honored."

"Yes, indeed. You'll have the privilege of meeting all of my Chinese aunts and uncles and cousins," Magda said wryly.

Tasha had not seen Magda's mother since their school days, and she wondered if the situation between mother and daughter had changed. As she remembered it, they never behaved as mother and daughter but rather as two women jealous of the other's influence on Captain Mac-Dougall. Tasha wondered if, perhaps, the passing of so many years had ended their rivalry and hatred for each other.

Magda wore her lavender-hued going-away outfit for her visit to her family. Tasha wore the soft green dress Magda had insisted on giving her to wear as maid-of-honor for the wedding. She told Tasha that she was tired of seeing her in the black and white which constituted Tasha's entire wardrobe. Tasha admired herself in the mirror—she had forgotten what color could do for her. The green of the dress brought out the flickering emerald lights in her eyes and made her dark hair look like a black-satin turban wound around her head.

"I think we used all of the colors in the paint box," Magda said, joining her in front of the mirror. "I'm all purple and red and you're green and black. I suppose you know you look striking."

"I know," Tasha agreed, both laughing at her apparent conceit. "I'd forgotten how good it is to wear colors. I feel rather splendid!"

"Well, as long as you feel that way about it, here's a little gift from Max and myself for our maid-of-honor."

Magda took a little package from her handbag.

"Please don't make a fuss, Tasha, I do so want you to enjoy them," she pleaded.

"Oh, Magda! How lovely. I'll have to have my ears pierced now. How can I thank you?" Tasha placed the dangling jade earrings against her ears.

"By wearing them in happiness." They smiled at each other and then embraced warmly. It was not necessary to say any more they both knew an old association was ending, new ones beginning.

Magda parked her new lime Citroen on a street outside the Chinese quarter.

"I'm not sure I can drive on any further," she explained to Tasha. They took rickshaws through narrow streets and turned into a cobblestoned alley, where each block of houses consisted of identical two-story brick structures. All that separated one house from another were the drain-pipes which marked off the buildings at regular distances from rooftop to the ground. A high wall, with shards of broken glass sunk into the cemented top, separated the houses from the alley, and at regular intervals stout wooden doors appeared in the walls.

At Magda's command, the coolies pulled up at a door festooned with red-satin streamers inscribed with gold characters. She paid the men and rang the bell that was suspended over the door. No one would have known how tense she felt inside, preparing to face a difficult ordeal.

Shouts and laughter were heard as the inner door was opened and a group of gaily-clad children rushed to the entrance, only to stop shyly when they saw the two foreigners.

Tasha was intrigued as she crossed the tiny courtyard to enter the house. Though she had lived in Shanghai all her life, it was the first time she had ever been in a Chinese home. A Chinese gentleman, dressed in a grey satin brocaded gown, came to the door and smiled when he saw Magda. In the formal Chinese style, they did not embrace. But their faces were full of deep affection.

"Tasha, I want you to meet my cousin, William Chen. William, this is my best friend, Miss Natasha Guria. It is time you met each other."

William put his hand out and shook hers cordially.

"I am so pleased you could come, Miss Guria, I've

heard a great deal about you—all good," he said in excellent English.

They were led into a small living room filled with laughing people, all talking to one another, and Tasha felt a little awkward. Like so many foreigners raised in Shanghai, she spoke no Chinese, except for a few words to the servants. But the bows and handshakes and smiles made her welcome.

Madga ran across the room and knelt before a tiny woman, dwarfed by a heavily carved black teakwood chair. Her face looked like a brown apple, and tears crept down its contours, through a map of wrinkles. The old woman made little crooning sounds of joy as Magda gently wiped away the wet beads with her fingers and with an expression of sweetness and tenderness on her lips. She sat down on a footstool beside her grandmother, stroking her hands while they spoke softly together. The people in the room clapped their hands with pleasure at the happy reunion, but the two were too preoccupied to notice.

The idyllic scene was interrupted as William entered, guiding a reluctant Mei-ling into the room. She was still an attractive woman, but at that moment, her face was tightly set and her eyes hard. Magda rose, her features devoid of expression, as they bowed formally and properly to each other and exchanged the usual courtesies. To Tasha, they were two serpents, rearing up, their tongues darting swiftly, threateningly, at each other. Tasha controlled a shiver—for at that moment, they looked remarkably alike.

The group was silent for a moment, watching the confrontation of mother and daughter, but quickly resumed their conversations. William introduced Tasha to his pregnant wife, Lotus, who giggled and blushed, offering her hand to Tasha, foreign style.

"So happy to meet you," she said carefully, to the applause of Magda and William. But Tasha, embarrassed, did not even know the equivalent in Chinese.

As though a signal had sounded, everyone moved into the back courtyard, which was decorated with red rosettes and pennants with gold characters of congratulations for the wedding. Chinese lanterns were strung between the glass-spiked walls which separated the houses, red candles were lit in profusion, and joss sticks smouldered in front of a statue of Buddha.

Tasha felt strange, seeing Magda in this milieu. It did not seem possible that this chic, poised European woman, who walked and talked so naturally among these Chinese people, was actually one of them. Yet they were all at ease with each other. But she was surprised when Magda went through the ceremony of lighting a few joss sticks, bowing in front of the Buddha, and adding her joss sticks to those already burning in the big brass bowl in front of it. In just a few minutes, the Magda she knew had disappeared into another culture. The old grandmother clapped her hands softly, her face wreathed in a smile as Magda came to her and knelt in honor at her feet. Tasha's misgivings fell away and tears misted her eyes when she saw the devotion and tenderness between the two, as the old lady placed her hands on the bright young head. Perhaps this was the reason Magda had returned to her family, to repay her grandmother in some way for the love and protection this frail old lady had given her when she had needed it most.

The smell of food and drink added to the heavy fragrance of incense in the air. Samshu was served in little china cups and endless rounds of toasts were drunk. At last the many-course meal ended, as wedding cakes filled with poppy seeds, and bowls of oranges, and pomegranates were placed on the red-satin cloth.

All the guests had drunk and eaten well and were full of good wishes as they made their departures, leaving money gifts in red envelopes with their congratulations. Magda stood at the door, graciously accepting the gifts and bowing and smiling as each guest left the house. Finally no one remained except for William and a middle-aged man to whom Tasha had taken an unreasonable dislike.

He was a heavy-set man, elegantly garbed in blue-satin brocade with pearl-mounted jade studs. Magda had made a point of avoiding him, even though he had bowed and smiled obsequiously throughout the afternoon. He came toward her as the door closed on the last guest and began a formal speech. Magda replied curtly to him in

Chinese, drew Tasha into the dining room, and shut the door behind her.

William Chen was seated at the dining-room table, with several papers in Chinese spread out in front of him.

"Let's be careful—Mei-ling's man is sure to eavesdrop. Tasha, will you do me a favor and sign these documents as a witness?"

"Gladly, but a Russian witness carries no weight in Shanghai, as you well know."

"In this case it would not matter very much, but in any case, you're a Chinese citizen," William assured her.

"What rot!"

"Really, Tasha," Magda interjected. "You were born in Shanghai, and the White Russian papers you have are worthless. Don't you remember—you were issued a Chinese passport last year when you went on your vacation?"

"But that doesn't make me Chinese."

"For all legal intents and purposes it does. I want to be certain that these documents meet all legal requirements, though I most earnestly hope that I will never have occasion to use them. For this reason, no one must know about them. You are the only person I trust, besides William, of course. Will you?"

"Of course," Tasha replied slowly, still stunned by the knowledge that she was a Chinese citizen.

"Don't say yes so readily—you're too impulsive!" Magda scolded. "You should never sign anything without knowing the contents."

"If I can't trust you, who can I trust?"

"No one. Don't trust anyone completely, and your friends least of all." Then she smiled mischievously, "Except me—and even then, be cautious. I want you to know the contents."

"Magda," Tasha interrupted. "I'd prefer not to know. You said that no one must know what they contain—I don't want the responsibility of possibly letting something slip without realizing it. Let me just sign it and leave."

"Tasha, it is important to both William and me that you should know the contents, if it should ever come to court. Don't worry about it—I doubt the occasion will ever arise. Now, I am turning over to William the sum of twenty thousand taels. He will offer this to Max as a business proposition, offer to be Max's comprador—you know, the Chinese money-man behind most of the foreign businesses. I know Max has wanted his own business for a long time and has been looking for a comprador. It's a sort of wedding gift from me, but I don't want him to know that I put up the money. The less he knows about my affairs, the better it is for both of us."

"Is this what you mean by not trusting anyone?"

Magda laughed. "You're learning fast. I would be satisfied to shake William's hand on the arrangement, but he insists on these documents to protect me, in case anything happens to him. These papers make it clear that the initial money is mine, that the business is mine to the extent of my investment, and that William is acting as my proxy in all matters. Should anything happen to me, the money will revert to Chen Wen-chu, otherwise known as William Chen, to do with as he pleases. I trust his judgment."

"It's not my business, I know, but wouldn't that put Max in a difficult position?"

"He will be left no better or worse off than if William really were the money-man. Don't worry about Max, Tasha. Now, will you sign?"

"And is Max going to dole out housekeeping money to you from the profits?"

Even William laughed as he handed her the pen and Tasha carefully signed her full name, Natasha Igorovna Guria.

"Well, cousin Magda, this will probably be the last time you sign yourself Magda MacDougall. In two days time you will be Magda von Zoller, German citizen."

Magda turned back abruptly.

"German citizen! Oh, no! I don't like that at all. I may have gone and done the most foolish thing—I never gave it a thought. German citizen!"

"Don't tell me my canny Scotswoman has neglected to have a marriage contract drawn up. My cousin, I'm surprised at you."

"I am shocked at myself, William. What is the German law, do you suppose, on a woman's right to her money after marriage?"

"I'm not certain—but I can find out. Under English law, though, a husband has no claim to any of his wife's property. I believe that, in France, a marriage contract is drawn up showing whether the property of the two parties is considered joint or separate—perhaps it is the same in Germany. In China, of course, the husband has absolute rights."

"I'm not as worried about my rights as I am about the present German government—they change the laws to suit themselves. William, I'm really worried."

"Do you think Max is marrying you for your money?" Tasha asked.

"No, it's not that. It's not even because of the money; it's for Papa. Don't you understand? He killed himself so that the money he left would be safe for me. I would never forgive myself if his sacrifice was for nought. I cannot take the chance that this money go to anyone else but me. Papa left it to me—it's a—sacred trust. I will not permit it to fall into other hands—especially German hands."

Magda's eyes met William's, and a message passed between them. Magda's momentary weakness faded.

"Definitely," she said. "I cannot have anyone checking into my funds."

There was a swift exchange of Chinese spoken very softly, as Magda and William conferred for a few moments.

Then Magda replied, in English, "Don't worry, William. I promise I'll look after it first thing in the morning."

Tasha felt uncomfortable. There seemed to be plots within plots in Magda's life. The atmosphere in the house had become oppressive and she was relieved when they went to make their farewells.

Mei-ling and the gaudily dressed Chinaman were waiting for them. Magda moved past them to embrace her grandmother. At that moment, the man stepped forward, made a deep formal bow, and with an elaborate speech, presented her with a red envelope containing wedding money.

Magda stared at him in disbelief, and Mei-ling broke the silence by chuckling. For a second, it was like a scene from a movie: Mei-ling's face animated and softened by laughter, Magda wearing an amazed expression, and the man with his hand outstretched, holding the envelope.

The man said a few sharp words to Mei-ling, who obediently attempted to smother her derision. A reluctant smile appeared on Magda's face, then was quickly erased, though her eyes still twinkled. Tasha had no idea what it was all about. She saw nothing funny, except in the oddness of this mother and daughter actually sharing the same joke. The man still had a tight smile on his face—his expression sent chills up Tasha's spine. She couldn't wait to leave the house. There were just too many things going on she didn't understand.

When they were safely outside, Magda started to laugh uncontrollably.

"I'm glad you're having such a good time. Perhaps you'll let me in on the joke," Tasha said caustically.

"I'm sorry, Tasha. It's not really all that funny—I guess I'm overreacting. This has been an unbelievable day. It's just that he's such a fool. What a stupid way to try to make an impression on me! *Surely* he must know that the money he was so pompously giving to me was money *I* gave in the first place!"

"Why should he try to make an impression on you? Is that why your mother laughed? I've never seen her smile before—she looks quite lovely when she does."

"Oh, yes, indeed. She can be anything she chooses to be, and she has all the ingredients: beauty, charm, a certain intelligence, and a malicious sense of humor. I'll bet it was her idea in the first place. She was probably getting back at her husband for something he did by making him appear a fool. That's the way her mind works. Somehow, I don't think he's going to take it well."

"Her husband?"

"Didn't I make a proper introduction? He's my latest stepfather, Lee Wing On. He's a horror—gambler, leech, a real scoundrel. He's always pushing Mei-ling to get more money from me. Strangely enough, my sources tell me she's really in love with him, though she hates the very idea of taking my money. She'd rather throw it back in my face. Well, that's the way it is."

At that, Magda firmly closed her mind to the emotions which the day had aroused, and turned her thoughts to overcoming the consequences of becoming a German.

As soon as they returned to the apartment, Magda closeted herself in her room and went over her records. She concentrated on her problem to the exclusion of all else. Finally, she made her decision—but before acting on it, she studied it from all angles, made out a time-table, and was satisfied it could be done.

"I'm sorry, Max," she murmured to herself, "but I must do it. I promise I'll make it up to you."

She made her first phone call to Sir Alfred Wilkie-Hume. He was quite annoyed at being called at his home on business—his houseboy had not gotten her name right, but, after hearing that she was on the phone, he was curious enough to listen.

"Sir Alfred, I regret disturbing you on a Sunday, but it is quite urgent. I need expert advice and immediate action on a situation which has come up. Could you help me by expediting the matter first thing Monday morning?" She explained briefly what she needed to have done. "Mr. Lovejoy would be fine; he is familiar with my account. Yes, it must be completed tomorrow— later would be worthless. Thank you for being so gracious, I'll be there promptly at ten. Good afternoon."

She hung up the phone and said to herself, "I suppose he thinks that evens the score!"

Magda made several other phone calls, checking each one off. The last thing on her agenda was Tasha, who agreed to remain in the apartment the next morning until Magda called her from the bank and asked her to meet her there.

"What's all the mystery about?" Tasha inquired.

"Tasha, dear, it's a long, involved story, and I just don't have time to explain it. I've got so much work to do tonight and I'm exhausted with all the planning. I'll tell you later, all right?"

"Sure, just as long as I'm finished in time to move my things to the Bickerton and get settled. The coolie is coming sometime in the morning to pick up my trunks."

"I'll tell the amah to see that it's delivered in case

you're not here. In fact, I'll tell her to go with the bags and unpack."

"Jolly good, O efficient and great executive!"

When Tasha met her at the bank entrance, Magda's face was aglow, as it often had been when she was engaged to Archie—or, sometimes, when she pulled off a brilliant financial coup.

Mr. Lovejoy was waiting for them in his office. After Magda made the introductions, he said stiffly, "I assume she knows what all this is about?"

"I'll explain it to her later. I assure you, it will be all right."

He scowled at her reprovingly; evidently, he preferred not to rush anyone into signing documents without explanation.

"Very well. I shall proceed with Sir Alfred's instructions to offer you my assistance and to expedite matters."

"You understand that this is highly confidential."

"My dear Miss MacDougall, all bank matters are confidential," he rebuked her, his lips pursed together.

"I'm sorry, Mr. Lovejoy. I meant no offense," Magda said, gazing at him with a helpless expression. Tasha was amazed. Magda, who hated dissimulation, had suddenly become a demure little girl asking for assistance. Her success was instantaneous. Tasha stifled a giggle as Mr. Lovejoy softened to the point of patting Magda's hand stiffly.

"Quite all right, my dear young lady. I shall see that everything is properly executed. I realize that this must be a very emotional time for you. A bank does its best, but it cannot really replace a father or a brother, who should be handling these details for you. Now, Miss Guria, if you would sign here, and here, and here, in duplicate, and here—"

As he passed document after document to Tasha, a fleeting thought passed through her mind—Magda was having her do exactly what she had urged and warned her never to do: sign a paper without first learning its contents.

"Tasha, let's take these papers to the apartment first.

I'll lock them up in my safe—then we'll have to rush to the Bickerton and get you packed for Hong Kong. There's so much to do in such a short time, and I still have more errands to finish!"

"Magda!" Tasha shouted. "Slow down, will you? What's all this nonsense about Hong Kong?"

"Oh—I thought I'd explained. Look, let me run to the apartment and lock these up. I'll tell you on the way." She left Tasha fuming in front of the bank. In a short while they were in her car, driving back to the apartment. "All you have to do is deliver the papers you signed to the Hong Kong and Shanghai Bank in Hong Kong, to a Mr. Southey. He'll know all about it. I thought it would make a nice little jaunt for you, and you'd be doing something very important for me."

"You're being very high-handed about this, Magda, and I don't like it. I have no intention of going to Hong Kong! First you tell me not to sign anything without reading it thoroughly, then you have me signing a lot of papers and won't tell me what they are all about. What is going on?"

"All right. I hope you take this in the right way. You know all those papers you signed?"

"Well?"

"They transferred approximately a hundred thousand dollars to your account in Hong Kong. Just a minute now—don't get all excited. I've protected you from all responsibility, and that took quite some doing. It's now in what they call a revokable trust—though the money is in your account. I still retain full authority over it. And because it's in your account, no one can take it from me. I know how you hate to touch anyone's money. It seemed like the perfect arrangement."

Magda looked over at Tasha and was taken aback to see her sitting very stiffly in her seat, looking hurt and affronted.

"I knew you could be devious, but I never thought you'd take advantage of our friendship," Tasha said with strain in her voice. "I don't think I like you very much at this moment, Magda MacDougall, and I'm not going through with it. If you have so little trust in the man you intend to marry, it's your problem. But I refuse to be used in this manner." Tasha's voice started to quiver, and, for a moment, she could not continue. Then she turned to Magda, trying to control the tears which threatened to overcome her. "But, Magda why? I'm so disappointed in you I can't stand it. I'll never, ever, be able to forgive you for abusing my trust!" The tears fell and she brushed them away angrily. "Why did you do it this way? It would have been so easy to ask me first—you know in the long run I'd have done what you wanted, even if you had to twist my arm a bit. But money is more important to you than anything else in your life—you don't care what you do to protect it. You make me out to be a puppet you can manipulate —all because you don't trust Max."

"Tasha, Max has nothing to do with this. The problem is far more complex. It's my becoming a German citizen. I can't believe that I forgot. The very idea of being a citizen of that country, subject to the whims of that madman Hitler, revolts me."

"Have you been in the Hongkew district lately?" She asked in an abrupt change of subject. "Have you noticed the thousands of refugees crammed up there. They're mostly Jews from Eastern Europe—who escaped with little more than their lives. I've heard they number at least ten thousand, and more are coming in every day. They're telling some stories which horrify me—it's inconceivable that in this day and age—" Magda turned away for a moment, then continued. "I was still in Switzerland when I first heard about the atrocities occurring in small towns in Southern Germany. There were riots and killings and beatings—supposedly instigated by irate citizens, rising in righteous indignation against the evils of the Jews. But in truth, they were orchestrated by Hitler's people, to arouse hatred and animosity. That was only the beginning—it's getting worse. It's the Jews today, tomorrow it could be some other minority. When I see people humiliated and ill-treated because of race—well, you can imagine how deeply it affects me. Hitler could confiscate my money at any moment —Maybe I'm crazy on the subject, Tasha, but I'd sooner throw that money into the Whangpoo than take the chance of one penny going to that gang of thugs!"

Tasha was shaken by Magda's vehemence.

"I could have understood—why didn't you explain?"

"I don't know, Tasha." Magda looked at her helplessly. "I really don't know. I think I've become so accustomed to secrecy that it's difficult to break the habit. Will you help me, Tasha?"

There was no answer. Magda parked the car in front of the Bickerton Hotel. They got out and walked slowly to the entrance, as Magda continued: "If you do decide to go to Hong Kong, it'll take almost the whole week of your vacation. I know that you intended to use it for settling down—it's only fair that I pay you to make the trip. It would certainly make me feel better."

Tasha grew so indignant at the thought of being paid that, before she realized it, the argument centered not on her trip to Hong Kong, but rather that the subject of payment never be mentioned again.

"I suppose you think you've been awfully smart, but don't think you're getting away with something," Tasha warned her.

"No, dear Tasha, I don't think I've been the least bit smart. I should have taken you into my confidence at the beginning, rather than risk your friendship."

That evening, Magda gave a small pre-wedding dinner at the apartment. The only other person present, besides Max, Tasha, and herself, was Dr. Rhinegold, the German consul and Max's friend, who would officiate at the marriage ceremony.

Magda had spent a great deal of time making sure everything was perfect. The table glittered with silver, crystal, long white tapers in silver holders and lilies-of-the-valley in a silver bowl, all set out on a fine white-damask cloth.

Magda had never looked more beautiful. She wore the diamond pendant her father had given her and the matching earrings, and a low-cut ecru lace gown, which made her skin look like faintly flushed alabaster. Her eyes glowed more brightly than her jewels with excitement and a kind of happiness.

Tall and slim, with her hair a flame to flaunt her beauty, Magda greeted her guests warmly. As he entered the room, Max went to her, his arms outstretched, and kissed her proudly and possessively—for once, forgetting his sense of dignity.

The houseboy served an impeccably prepared dinner with all the appropriate wines, and Magda a superb hostess, sparkled throughout the meal.

Max gazed at his fiancée, disbelieving his good fortune. He was usually very articulate, but tonight he talked most incoherently, his eyes fixed adoringly on his bride-to-be. Tasha, observing him, erased all her suspicions that he was marrying Magda for her money; instead, she felt a moment of sympathy for him. She knew Magda very well and feared that she had some hidden motive behind this performance. It was unlike Magda to look so animated—only Archie had performed that miracle—and Tasha found it difficult to accept her friend's change of heart.

Dinner was over at nine, and, as the boy cleared away the last dishes, the doorbell rang as though prearranged.

Max looked at Magda questioningly, as she quickly explained: "That must be Mr. Crichton. He was my father's lawyer and now he looks after my affairs. I hope you don't mind—I know it's late, Max, but I have some unfinished business that involves you. I thought you wouldn't mind if he came here tonight to settle it."

The lawyer entered the room, accompanied by his clerk. Introductions were made, and Mr. Crichton came directly to the point of his visit.

"The late Captain MacDougall's instructions to his daughter were quite explicit, Mr. von Zoller. He instructed her to have a pre-marital contract drawn up in order to keep her assets independent of her husband's. He also advised her to suggest to him that he do the same—that way the question of money may not rise to divide the couple, as so frequently happens. That, sir, is up to you," he said to Max. "I have prepared this agreement, renouncing on the part of Maximilian von Zoller any claims to Miss MacDougall's assets and possessions, except as she may wish to make over to you by testamentary will."

Max's face paled with shock, then colored with torrid humiliation. He turned to Magda and said icily, "Did you think that perhaps I was interested in this mysterious wealth of yours, of which I know nothing?"

"I assure you, Mr. von Zoller," the lawyer broke in

quickly, "that there is no intent to suggest such a thing. Pre-marital agreements are quite common. It is a protection for both the husband and the wife."

Max paid him no heed. His gaze, full of hurt and bewilderment, was on Magda. She went to him and took his hand.

"Max, my dear," she whispered. "Don't brood like that. I can't bear to see you so distressed. Please try to understand—it was my father's wish. He was devoted to me and my interests, and did everything he could to protect me. You must try to see that."

"But why now? At this late date? On our wedding eve?"

"To be quite truthful," Magda said, with a bashful smile, "I had forgotten all about it, even forgotten to notify Mr. Crichton about our coming marriage. When I came across my father's last letter—Oh, Max, dear, please, don't ask me to ignore his final wishes."

They looked steadily into each other's eyes, Max wanting desperately to believe her. Tasha watched them, discreetly, worried and upset, wondering what Magda would do if Max refused. She knew Magda could be inflexible; but she also knew how generous and warm she could be. Max balked for a moment, more for being forced to make a decision than anything else.

"You can be a forgetful little girl, can you not," he smiled, a bit weakly, at Magda. "Perhaps you do need someone to look after you—I will always be there to do so." He kissed her hand and moved to the table where the legal document was spread out. He read it slowly and then signed the paper, relinquishing all rights to Magda's estate.

Dr. Rhinegold and the clerk were the witnesses—Tasha was glad she was not asked to be one. She understood Magda's motives but nevertheless found herself disturbed by the scene.

There is little good which can be said of Shanghai weather. The winters are miserably cold and grey. Once in a great many years, there will be a light snowfall—but it rarely lasts long enough to cover the city in magical white. Instead, it turns immediately into dirty slush.

Then come the rains, dreary rains which intensify the cold with a perpetual dampness that reaches into the marrow of the bones. Finally, out of April, May is born—a month of jubilation. The plane trees which line the streets become, overnight, full of tender green leaves; the sun is warm, but there is enough crispness left in the air to make a person buoyant and alive and full of good spirit. It is a miracle month. Soon, the late-spring typhoons come and the Yangtse Kiang floods the countryside, leaving famine and death in its wake. But all that is forgotten when the month of May unveils its beauty.

So it was, in May, on a perfectly splendid day, that Max and Magda were married, and Magda MacDougall became Magda von Zoller, German citizen and wife.

CHAPTER ELEVEN

WHEN MAGDA ACCEPTED the part-time job offered by her brokers, it was a way for her to occupy herself through a period of utter desolation. However, the position rapidly absorbed her interest and developed into full-time employment. She was part secretary, part financial analyst, part stockbroker. And it was in the last area that she began to achieve a reputation, becoming an authority on the potentials and dangers of transactions in world currencies. Her work was not only fulfilling in itself, but in the last few months it had been her one refuge from tensions brought about by the prolonged visit of Max's cousin, the Baron Waldemar von Zoller.

Max had been both nervous and excited when he first received word that Waldemar was coming to Shanghai.

"He is an extraordinary man, Magda—his family are true Prussians from both sides. He is a millionaire and famous throughout racing circles for his knowledge of thoroughbreds. I believe he has even entertained kings and queens and heads-of-state at his home!"

Max could barely contain his delight at his cousin's arrival—at last he would be able to show Waldemar the fine life he had made for himself in China.

When Magda finally met Waldemar, she found it difficult to believe that the same genes were present in both men. Max was tall, slim and blond, with a certain patrician gentility. Waldemar was powerfully built, shorter, and stocky. His complexion was on the swarthy side; his hair was dark and wiry and cropped very close. His features were heavy: dark, thickly lidded eyes and a clipped moustache, not unlike Hitler's. Though Waldemar was not a physically prepossessing man, Magda, who was particularly sensitive in her perceptions of people, felt the danger of unleashed savagery behind his face—an impression given more credence by his increasingly boorish behavior in the eight months since he had moved in with them.

Magda felt it had long since reached the point that some action had to be taken—one or the other of them had to leave. She and Max had only been married three months when Waldemar first arrived, and Magda looked back with nostalgia on their first months together and their growing affection for one another.

Under Max's guise of fierce pride and self-assurance, Magda had divined a man sensitive to her need for patience and tenderness. He had proved this on their wedding night, when, lying in bed, she had waited passively for the undesirable prospect of being deflowered by a man she only married to blunt her loneliness. When at last he entered her bed, she was unable to control an involuntary shudder.

"Don't be frightened, *Liebchen*," he whispered. "It shall only be if you desire it." Gently, he gathered her slight body in his arms, stroking her as he would a child, until he felt her relax. Lying quietly beside her, he kissed the palms of her hands, her wrists, her arms— stroking, always stroking, pacifying her, gentling her, soft hands barely touching her. Moving up and down over her body, his hands explored the curve of her waist, the fullness of her hips, the sweep of her thighs, the exquisite softness of her stomach; his lips softly nuzzled her neck, then her ears, and kissed her flaming hair. His head went lower, his tongue tasting her shoulders and back. Her body responded to his embraces. Her skin tingled under the ceaseless caressing. Almost without realizing, she took his hands, now so much a part of her, and placed them on her breasts, as her nipples throbbed and hardened. "*Ach,* Magda, *meine Liebling,*" she gasped as he cupped them, his fingers moulding them, massaging them. He put his lips to them hungrily and a sweet pain spread throughout her body. There was no more thought, only feeling. His kisses became hard and urgent and her lips answered his demands. His hands were everywhere, searching, caressing, probing—her body was ablaze, responding to him, aching for him and ready for him. Even the first shock of pain was a sensual fulfillment. And what followed was gloriously satisfying for them both.

Magda went to sleep that night cradled in Max's arms. She was happy to have been awakened as a woman, even if it was not in the throes of her first passionate love. She felt joyously satiated by her accomplished lover, her husband.

In those first months of getting to know each other, they found an unexpected bonus in discussing their work in the evenings: Magda loved to talk about the ups and downs of the stock market to Max, who listened with keen interest; and Max found that his adored wife was as interested in every aspect of his business as he was. Shortly after their wedding, he had met a certain William Chen, who was prepared to finance a company that Max wished to establish. Max had quickly signed a contract with him and became completely immersed in developing his new business, a long-sought and finally realized dream. As both Magda and Max found an enduring satisfaction in their work and a growing happiness with each other, they forged the bonds of friendship and companionship into a strong and rewarding marriage.

Max's initial reluctance to move into Magda's apartment had been based on pride, but, once he had established himself in his own business, he readily complied with Magda's wish to keep her place. Eagerly, he began to rearrange the furniture Magda had purchased, discarding some and adding various Chinese pieces he had accumulated for his own apartment. He hung a piece of Chinese embroidery, fragile with age, delicately faded and muted in color, on one wall, a Chinese landscape scroll on another. Max had long had his eye on a round Chinese screen inlaid with mother-of-pearl, ivory and semi-precious stones, and Magda gave it to him as a belated wedding gift. He was overjoyed and did not permit anyone to clean it but himself. The screen was placed in one corner, arms out around a low chest, on which he placed a tall, narrow Chinese carving and a vase with a single spray of flowers. With imagination and taste, he changed the impersonal apartment into a charming and individual home.

Magda transferred her wall-safe into Tasha's vacated bedroom and made it into a den for herself, where she could work on her private business and read late at night when she wished to without disturbing Max; and he, always sensitive to her needs, understood that she had to have her moments of privacy.

The announcement of Waldemar's arrival caused the first slight rift between them, when Max insisted that Waldemar be given the master bedroom.

"I can't give him the small room, Magda, it would be an insult."

"But it's too small for our big bed—we'll have to squeeze in a cot. It's going to be a tight fit."

"*Meine Liebchen*, it will be for only a few days. He's far too important to stay with us for long."

At that remark Magda eyed him quizzically, but she said no more. She understood the quality of hospitality which gave its best to the guest, but she was determined not to have a permanent visitor in their home. Waldemar knew nothing of her feelings and cared less. He had decided to remain with them permanently, as though it were his right.

From the day he arrived, he changed their lives to suit himself, taking over as if by divine decree. Even the servants obeyed him as though he were the new master. There was an element of ruthlessness about Waldemar which aroused fear and produced compliance.

Magda could understand Max's desire to play the indulgent and gracious host, but it aggravated her beyond measure to see Max's open-handed eagerness to please now twisted into subservience. She had heard enough about his past to know that Max had been, in his early years, the poor relative dominated by his cousin. Max's father had always held Waldemar up as an example, and encouraged Max to emulate his wealthy and powerful relative. Max's eyes were still blinded by his adulation for the man. But, Magda thought impatiently, he was no longer a child, to feel such awe.

During Waldemar's first month with them, the conversation at the dinner table had been in English, but, as the weeks dragged on into months, Waldemar began making comments to Max in German. No longer were his barbs merely condescending. They had become ugly references to Max's background, his ancestry—full of innuendos and underlying threats, sarcastic shafts intended to belittle. For Magda's benefit, Max, ever courteous, would translate false translations, as Waldemar's eyes gleamed with deviltry.

Max never knew that Magda spoke German fluently. In the beginning of their courtship she had not been interested enough to contribute much to the conversation; later, it had become natural for them to speak in English. With the arrival of Waldemar in their home, Magda found it convenient to keep her knowledge of German concealed from both, especially when Waldemar tired of taunting Max and sought greater amusement by discussing Magda. He enjoyed his own outrageous comments, and he looked at her with great innocence while he openly questioned her proficiency in bed.

It was all Magda could do to refrain from walking out of the room. But even in her outrage, she knew she couldn't do that—it would have been an admission that she had understood all the time. Still, it was devastating to watch Max squirm and even more so to observe his cowardice where Waldemar was concerned. In spite of her sincere efforts to make every allowance for Max, Magda felt her growing affection for her husband was colored by pity and some contempt for his refusal to answer Waldemar's taunts.

Waldemar's lascivious remarks continued—there was

little about her he didn't notice. In English, he started to pay her heavy-handed compliments, punctuated by knowing winks, while in German, he relished baiting Max by discussing her as though she were not Max's wife. Max seemed literally to have shrivelled, and he did not even attempt further translations.

One evening when Max was working late, Waldemar was waiting for Magda when she returned from her office. With absolute confidence, he grabbed her by the shoulders and attempted to kiss her. He was honestly surprised when she tried to struggle away.

"Don't play coy with me," he said huskily, still holding her tightly. "You know a real man when you see one, not like that milksop you married." He cupped one breast with a sweaty hand and thrust his thick wet lips on hers, trying to force her clenched lips apart.

"What the hell is the matter with you?" he demanded, so confident had he been on her eager response.

"Do you think you have the *droit du seigneur* in this house?" Magda hissed at him, wiping her lips viciously as she pushed past him.

His first look of astonishment was quickly replaced by a menacing smile as he replied with a sneer, "Perhaps more than you think. I can make you very sorry."

"I doubt it," Magda retorted, striding away to her room and locking the door behind her.

Magda did not mention the episode to Max. Let him continue to believe in the great Waldemar, she raged inwardly. Deep inside she harbored a more awful doubt: if Waldemar went so far as to demand her favors from Max, would Max go so far as to ask her to comply? It wasn't only that her opinion of him had fallen desperately low—but that Magda began to think that Waldemar held some terrible power over Max. It seemed the only possible explanation for her husband's attitude.

She had tried to prevent any deep emotional involvement in her life beyond her work and her affection for Max, but there was one emotion she could not control— a deepening hatred for Waldemar. She hated him for what he was doing to Max and for what he was doing to their lives; but even more than that, she loathed the man himself as much as she loathed and feared the country he came from—and all that she suspected he was capable of *un*doing.

As a true Prussian, Waldemar's greatest interest in life was horses, particularly the breeding of racehorses. His first activity after arriving in Shanghai was to find out who owned the outstanding stables, visit them, and ingratiate himself with the owners. He had built an imposing reputation as a horse-breeder in Germany. Thus, Baron von Zoller was cordially welcomed and immediately accepted by the British community in the city.

Waldemar lived in his riding habit and high boots; his one concession to good grooming was his insistence that his riding boots be rubbed daily with saddle soap and polished to a high gloss. He carried his riding crop wherever he went, as though it was attached to his hand. He thought nothing of coming to dinner, reeking of the stable.

Magda kept hoping that Max, so fastidious about his own person, would find this behavior offensive enough to say something about it to his cousin. But nothing was said. One day when Waldemar walked in with the soles of his boots heavy with horse dung, she could endure it no longer.

"Really, Waldemar," she said sharply. "I appreciate your love of horses, but is it necessary to bring them to the table with you? I find it very distasteful."

Waldemar glared at her insolently and then turned his look toward Max, his eyebrows raised questioningly.

As if cued, Max's face flushed, and his voice choked. He responded to her remark. "Magda, I cannot permit you to talk to my cousin in this manner. Kindly keep your comments to yourself."

Magda stared at him. She had thought him helpless against Waldemar, but never would she have believed that Max would actually rebuke her openly in defense of his cousin. She was about to answer him in kind, when her eye caught Waldemar's mocking smile.

"Max, I need five hundred dollars tomorrow. Bring it to me by ten in the morning," he ordered, still looking at Magda. For the first time, he was openly displaying his power in front of her, gloating over her, challenging her.

At that, Max stood up, holding on to the back of his chair for support. "Herr Schuman in Berlin will be pleased to know I have seen you," he added very softly, in German. Max looked at them both and fell back into his chair.

"This is really too much," Magda said angrily.

"No. It's not too much," Max said, deliberately misunderstanding her words. "I'll bring it to you in the morning. As a matter of fact, I have to meet some people nearby. It will be quite convenient."

"The smell in here is intolerable. I shall have the boy bring a tray to my room." Magda rang the table bell and stood up, her cheeks burning, her eyes glowing dangerously.

"I find it most discourteous for my hostess to leave the table before the meal is served."

Magda looked at him steadily, meeting the challenge.

"When the guest learns not to behave like an ignorant stableboy, his hostess may be prepared to return some courtesy. I find your attitude and your lack of manners deplorable, and your presence in my home intolerable. I trust I need say nothing more. If you want me to speak more plainly, however, I shall be happy to oblige."

The houseboy entered. He had heard the raised voices and trembled with misgivings. Magda gave him instructions, but he looked to Waldemar, as though for permission. Unfortunately for him, Magda caught the look and spoke to him sharply in Chinese. The servant bowed and left the room hurriedly.

It was late when Max entered their bedroom, hoping to find Magda asleep. He was disappointed. She was sitting up in her dressing-gown and reading. He emerged from the bathroom after a lengthy shower—and she was still up, waiting for him. This time she marked her page, put her book down, and watched him expectantly. He still said nothing as he got into his bed.

"Max. We have to talk. You cannot continue to pretend that nothing is the matter."

"Magda, listen to me, please. Waldemar is a horse-breeder. He is used to the company of crude men who speak freely. He is accustomed to rough manners. I often think he loves horses more than people."

"That's not really saying much, is it? Tell me what's wrong, Max. Since Waldemar arrived you have been behaving very strangely, not at all like the man I married."

"You're making too much of it. There is nothing wrong."

"His demands for money?"

"He is my cousin. He was kind to me when I was a lad. Now I can repay him."

"He probably bullied you to death, and you thanked him." She was unable to keep the sarcasm out of her voice. Then she continued, more kindly. "My dear, it does not take a genius to know that he has some hold on you. Tell me about it, Max, please. Whatever it is, I promise not to be shocked. I want to help you. I know many people in Shanghai, and I have some resources."

"Thank you, Magda. Your concern touches me deeply." His words were stiff but there was a voice calling for help inside him, which he denied. "I assure you that it is only your imagination. Waldemar and I are devoted to each other." He coughed, but to Magda it echoed ominously, like a groan.

"Who is Mr. Schuman?"

"He is a mutual acquaintance of ours in Berlin. Magda, please—I implore you, be tolerant of Waldemar. If you have any regard for me, please—I ask you—" he begged, looking at her with bruised eyes. He sighed heavily. "If you don't mind, I wish to sleep," he said as he turned off the light over his bed.

The euphoria Max first felt in hosting his cousin changed rapidly. The smiles, the attention, the willingness to oblige were still there—but now they were defense mechanisms to hide the truth from Magda. The most bitter grief of all was in standing idly by and seeing her love for him change slowly into dismay, disappointment, and finally contempt. Her every change of expression, her voice, told him the story of the disintegration of their marriage.

Max began to develop nervous little habits: a jaw muscle twitched spasmodically; he tapped his knee restlessly with his fingers; he rubbed his hands together when he was addressed.

How long, he wondered, could he keep pretending? How long could he keep the truth—that he was a Jew, despised by the Germans, and a coward without the stomach to fight back—from Magda? How could he tell her that Waldemar threatened to disgrace him, have him dragged into court for using a falsified passport? Falsified because nowhere on it did it say "Jew." He knew that his business contracts could be annulled for the same reason. The business he had founded was already showing a profit and signs of growing lustily. But the worst threat of all was being shipped back to Germany to suffer the fate of all Jews there. And Max never doubted that Waldemar was capable of carrying out his threats.

For his silence, Waldemar had demanded complete obedience in all matters. In return, he had promised Max that, once his own plans were in operation he would leave them, never revealing that Max's mother had been a Jewess. If not—there was little left to the imagination.

Seven months earlier, Max still had some courage. Waldemar, he insisted, had no authority over him. Even if he could get his passport rescinded, even if he could destroy his business, he could not have him sent back to Germany. This was the International Settlement of Shanghai—and Germany had no power over him. There were some twenty-thousand Jewish refugees in Shanghai and Waldemar could not touch one of them.

Max remembered Waldemar's humorless smile—even now, it sent cold chills of fear down his spine.

"You think not, Max? You really think not?" At that moment Max lost his bravado. He knew that Waldemar could do anything he said, any time he wanted.

Max stood to lose everything that mattered—most of all, his beloved Magda, whose desire for him, won with such difficulty, was ebbing, dying. Now, the way she averted his glances, he had probably lost her already.

Why now? Why now, when for the first time in my life some dreams are coming true? Max was filled with anger, helplessness, and a terrible feeling of loss.

The sun filtered through the clouds of the April day, but Max was untouched by it as he left the office. He instructed his chauffeur to take him to an address on North Szechuen Road where he had an appointment. He saw Waldemar sauntering down the street, and he was seized by a sudden impulse to follow him. He cautioned the chauffeur to go as slowly as possible. Fortunately, Shanghai traffic was crowded on all streets, particularly in that section where there was a double electric-tram system and cars crept along at a snail's pace.

Max saw Waldemar stop by a row of buildings which housed several hundred Jewish refugees. There were thousands of refugees scattered all over Shanghai, but most of them were concentrated in this area. He saw Waldemar clap a man on the shoulder, saw the man's face light up, and saw them shake hands as several other men gathered around. Waldemar talked with them for a few minutes, looking expansive and benevolent. The men were obviously pleased by what he said, and they nodded gratefully. Waldemar, waving a cordial hand to them, then entered the building.

Max couldn't repress a shudder as he slumped in the shadow of the back seat of the car. He returned to the office, but his mind was completely focused on Waldemar. How could he prevent Waldemar from going through with whatever nefarious schemes he had in mind? That Waldemar held all the cards he admitted, but despair was no solution. Above all else, he was determined to find a way to spare Magda the shame of being dragged down with him. He had seen his cousin leer at her, and he felt weak with worry. Magda must be made aware of her danger—being a German citizen married to a Jew was, in itself, a punishable offense.

He decided that the best thing he could do was to persuade her to leave him before Waldemar involved her as well. She would have to flee while her passport was still unquestioned. She had money—there shouldn't be any problems for her. Max smiled sadly to himself; the way she now felt toward him, it shouldn't take too much persuasion.

His head throbbed with the echoing of the same questions. Why did Waldemar need him, particularly? Why did Waldemar insist on remaining in their apartment when he could easily afford to pay for his own place? What role had Waldemar prepared for him? Would he have the strength to refuse? Would he even have a choice? Magda! God, how he loved her—all he had ever wanted to do was to make her happy, and now instead. . . this!

150

He rose abruptly and paced the room trying to stem the creeping paralysis he felt whenever he thought of pitting himself against Waldemar. He admonished himself to think positively, to plan some opposition, to save himself, to save Magda.

To his peers, Baron Waldemar Erich von Zoller was a man's man, brusque and earthy. Many were put off by an undisguised hint of brutality in him—others were drawn like magnets by that very trait. Such was his personality that it appeared virile, or so he could make it seem. He was a consummate actor when it served his purpose.

The sporting circles of Shanghai, especially the horsey set, soon knew he was a good man with horses. He had an uncanny way with thoroughbreds, better than any vet, and he was always ready to oblige a friend. He soon became a familiar figure at the Shanghai Race Club and at the last meet had been a guest in the British ambassador's box.

Waldemar was particularly pleased by this accomplishment. It put him on a firm footing with the British community he carefully courted. Who could doubt the credentials of a friend of the British ambassador? He recalled Sir Nigel's delight that his protégé, Waldo, was accepted so well.

The idea of Nigel made him smile sardonically— now there was a man made to his order. He was so generous that he practically asked to be hoodwinked. Waldemar did not remember himself as ever being so ingenuous, so gullible, so suggestible—not even when he had been a child. Only by the greatest exertion of his will power had Waldemar resisted the open invitation. But Sir Nigel had something far more important to offer—influential friends.

All things considered, Waldemar was pleased—he had already accomplished more than had been required of him. When at last he revealed his master plan, his current superiors would no longer be superior to him. Best of all, Max was set up to take the blame.

Waldemar had a late breakfast, perfectly cooked and served. He would brook no less. As he ate, he read the leading papers from Germany, England, and France. The papers were delivered to him daily, as were clippings from other countries, and telegrams in code. He kept the telegrams for last. His mail load was heavy, and he carefully destroyed all letters and messages of consequence after reading them.

He wrote some notes in code in a little notebook and then made his daily pilgrimage to his cousin's bedroom. First, he searched through Max's bureau—not that he expected to find any information, but he had once found a substantial cache of money and pocketed it, knowing there would be no repercussions. It amused him to put Max on guard.

Next he looked through Magda's chest of drawers, again not expecting to find anything, but for the satisfaction of sensing full control over her.

He had long since opened Magda's little safe and checked out the ledgers, dismissing the idea that they were investments. He knew enough about stocks and bonds to know that none of these initials or signs pertained to them. But he had copied the pages carefully and sent the copies off to Berlin, anyway.

Once again, he pored over the ledgers—there were some new entries. If indeed they were investments, then she appeared to have a great deal of money. She was the smart one. He could use her to good advantage: she wouldn't simply give up, like Max. Waldemar smiled. He would let her flounder a little and then would draw her in with a jerk she would understand. That would teach her to defy him. His mouth became dry at the prospect. He spent many enjoyable hours picturing how he would use her in every degrading way. Each fancy ended the same way, with her pleading for him not to discard her. Depending on the mood of the moment, he was occasionally indulgent with her—if she squirmed properly.

Tasha hummed merrily as she packed. She noticed the time—she'd better hurry or she'd be late for her luncheon date with Magda. She stopped for a moment and peeked out of the window to take a few deep breaths of the fresh spring air. The whole world was coming alive all at once on this glorious day in this most glorious of all worlds. She stretched out her arms as though to embrace everyone in it and resumed her packing. It was going to be a rich and colorful wardrobe this time —something for which she had to thank Magda, who had influenced her away from her eternal black and white. She owed Magda so much, but, most of all, for Barry—if she hadn't gone to Hong Kong she'd never have met him!

Barry! Barry! she sang. That was a name to conjure with, a name with a lilt to it. Barry Winters—beautiful, blond, bashful, Barry. She giggled. Well, hardly bashful. Thoroughly, irrepressibly, magnificently American Barry—casually attractive, strong and tall like a Hollywood movie star. Well, maybe not quite. But to Tasha, he was Clark Gable and Dick Powell and Robert Taylor rolled into one. She stood up and stretched again from her tiptoes to the tips of her fingers, a wonderful stretch like a cat. Tasha, Natasha, the pussy cat, that's what Barry called her. For pure joy, she laughed aloud.

It was time to meet Magda and tell her the good news. She'd be so pleased. She'd been trying to persuade Tasha to move from Shanghai to Hong Kong for a long time. But it was Barry who had really been responsible.

Sweetest, most wonderful, darling Barry, I wish you were here right now. She hugged herself, tingling just thinking of him. If it has to end, she promised herself, I'll never regret it, not for a single day.

She studied her face in the mirror. "I wonder if it shows. I wonder if Magda guesses. I'll bet she wishes she and Archie had gone ahead instead of waiting and wasting all that wonderful awakening—keeping it all for a man she didn't even love. Poor Magda!"

By mutual agreement, Tasha only saw Magda when they met for lunch, even though the von Zollers lived very close to the Bickerton Hotel. The hotel was a glorified boarding-house, one of the oldest and most reputable in Shanghai. It had originally been one house in a terrace and had been run by two English sisters. They were strict about whom they accepted as boarders and firmly enforced a Victorian code of behavior. The hotel prospered and gradually, one by one, absorbed all the houses in the terrace. The two sisters had long since sold out to a Chinese cartel, but with a proviso written into the sales contract that the same code of behavior be strictly observed. Barry approved of her living there.

At first, it had been a plus to live so close to Magda, but not any more. Tasha still disliked Max. She thought he was a phony—to use Barry's word—bluffing to hide a weak, pretentious man. But he was a prince compared to his horror of a cousin.

Waldemar! Even the name sounded like a curse. He was so sure of his superiority and behaved with complete indifference to hurting anyone. She'd met him only a couple of times but, to her, he was evil incarnate. "Get out, Magda," she thought aloud. "That man is dangerous!" Magda had changed since his arrival. She was even more withdrawn than she'd been after Archie left. She would have to get Magda to visit her once she was settled in Hong Kong—anything to get her away from those two monsters.

Tasha jumped into a rickshaw and rode to Marcel's Cafe on Nanking Road. Today she would insist it was her treat—she really had something to celebrate.

Magda was waiting for her at the entrance, and Tasha squeezed her arm in anticipation as they were led to a table.

"Hello, Tasha. You look as though you were ready to fly!"

"You're a mind-reader. I'm really going to take wing. My sweet boss arranged a transfer for me to Hong Kong. He's being transferred there himself as top man, and I, Natasha Guria, am now his private secretary with a big boost in pay. Isn't that scrumptious?"

"Congratulations! That's wonderful. It's a perfect opportunity for you to emigrate. Once you get there you've got to make some effort to get a visa—for the States, preferably. I've told you that since your Aunt Olga became an American citizen she could help you enormously by sending you a notarized affidavit of support, I think it's called, so you'll be allowed to enter the country. Tensions are building up all over the world—something terrible is going to happen, and soon. When and where I don't know—but it's in the air, and you've got to be ready to leave China on a moment's notice."

"Please, Magda, please not today. I just want to think of the wonderful things that are going to happen."

"Not by any chance because Barry is stationed in Hong Kong?" Magda smiled affectionately at Tasha. "He made all the airlines rich, he's crossed over to Shanghai so often. Not to mention that you switched your summer vacation to go to Hong Kong at Christmas."

"Oh, Magda! That was wonderful! Barry took me to the Christmas party at the American Consulate. I told you all about it, didn't I?"

"If you have, I've forgotten," Magda said kindly.

"Well, I had this deep-garnet dress made especially to match that necklace—you know, the one from my parents. I thought that at least it was an antique and different from anything I'd ever seen. I scrubbed it with ammonia and it came out all gleaming—it was hard to believe they were the same old dirty beads. Everyone admired it and someone told me that they thought the stones were real."

"Why don't you have the necklace appraised?" Magda suggested for at least the third time.

"I guess I should—but I hate to be disappointed. Barry said I looked like a princess. Of course he was joking but—" Tasha broke off when she saw the suppressed mirth in Magda's eyes. "You shouldn't have let me go on. I must have told you the story a dozen times."

"You enjoy telling it so much I would not deprive you for the world. Now let's get back to important things. Has your aunt ever replied to you?"

"Well, I wrote to her, but the letters were returned 'address unknown.' There's nothing else I can do."

"You must find some other way. Have you told Barry? Maybe he could tell you the best way to go about getting an immigrant visa?"

"No, I haven't told Barry. I don't want to. He might think I was expecting something from him and was twisting his arm." She blushed. "Magda, darling, let's not talk about it any more. I just want to be happy today."

"Poor Tasha, how I do overwhelm you with my unsolicited advice! You know, my dear, I chide you about being impulsive—but I envy you. I wish I could be as carefree as you are, really."

"You'll come and visit me in Hong Kong? Promise me."

"I'll take it under advisement," Magda smiled. "Of course, I will." They stood up to leave and Magda leaned over and kissed Tasha on the cheek.

"Be happy, dearest Tasha. Enjoy your love," she whispered, and walked away rapidly, her eyes moist.

Magda came right home after her lunch with Tasha. Except for the servants, the place was empty. She went to her room, undressed, and took a leisurely bath. She brushed her hair until it shone.

She dressed in a comfortable kimono and then took the precaution of checking to see that no one had entered the flat since she arrived. She locked her door and put a chair under the knob for further protection against interruptions.

Then, very carefully, so as not to disturb anything, she opened the top drawer of her bureau. It appeared to be all right. Then the next. She smiled grimly. He was getting careless. Too sure of himself. She wondered what he expected to find there; perhaps he was some kind of a pervert, the kind who enjoyed handling women's underthings. She'd heard of people like that. The thought of his filthy hands touching her intimate apparel made her stomach churn—it was almost as if those thick, clammy fingers were touching her body.

If only she knew what he was after. Or was he just looking for anything which could incriminate her in some way? There was no doubt that he was blackmailing Max, but why? Max didn't have enough money to tempt anyone, certainly not someone like Waldemar. She suspected he would take any graft which came his way, if only for the sheer enjoyment of making someone squirm, but he wouldn't be laying such complicated plans for small gains. She would have to stop letting her repugnance get the better of her mind.

She had to start analyzing the facts she had on hand, add them to her suspicions and come up with an answer. It didn't matter if the answer were, in itself, a question —if it were the *right* question.

Magda opened the safe and again, very carefully, removed the top ledger and opened it. Well, the plots in the

156

mystery books really worked— the strand of hair she had placed in the book was gone! With a smile that would have reminded Tasha of Mei-ling, Magda added a few haphazard figures, turned back a few pages, underlined a few numbers, crossed out others, and wrote in a few meaningless words.

Don't overdo it, Madame Spy, she cautioned herself. She closed the book and returned it to its exact place in the safe, first placing one hair in the last entry and one under the safe door before closing it.

A bad situation existed—and something was causing it. Therefore, someone would have to act to prevent disaster, and Magda knew it had to be her. First she had to discover what hold Waldemar had over Max, and then, she had to find out just what he was planning.

CHAPTER TWELVE

≪≪≪≪≪≪≪≪≪≪≪≪≪≪≪≪≪

WHATEVER THE SITUATION in Shanghai had been prior to the Japanese invasion of 1937, by 1939 it had deteriorated into a maelstrom of political unrest. Communist organizations flourished and had a stranglehold on labor. Atrocities and force were the order of the day. The Chinese municipalities under the military rule of Japan were subjected to strict regulations and were pressured by Communist threats.

The Japanese made no secret of their ambitions: They wanted to be the ruling power in the Far East, and were making physical inroads into China. In the previous year, they had taken Peking, then Canton, moving closer to Hong Kong, through what had once been considered British territory. They had seized the nine most important ports and cities in China, but the British were not prepared to go to war. They had a longtime friendship pact with Japan and closed their eyes rather than upset the diplomatic relations which existed between the two countries.

Shanghai had become more isolated than ever and retreated behind the shaky wall of treaties. "Bloody Saturday" had been a ruinous blow to China's growing prosperity and hit Shanghai hardest of all. Foreign commitments and investments had taken a tremendous loss —but much more was involved.

In this climate, secret societies proliferated to a point of anarchy. They were all-powerful in the Chinese areas and their influence was potent. Magda knew a little of the two main underground societies in Shanghai, the Blue and the Red. The Blues, also known as Dragon Seed, had at its head a Mr. Dzu Bing Lok. He was probably the single most important man in all of Greater Shanghai. Magda knew of his reputation for good and evil—the stories she heard were contradictory, but they were enough to upset her and to terrify her about her participation in gun-running.

He and his aides most certainly knew of the entrepreneurs who, frightened of reprisals and risks, sold out to comparatively small speculators such as Magda. But, as long as the arms deals remained small and infrequent, he ordered hands off. There was no time, however, that he couldn't have had the trading stopped and awful punishment meted out to those who disobeyed.

Magda's investments in arms were paying off handsomely. She bought in increasing amounts as the occasion arose. She had been fortunate that, in such a risky business, only two of the shipments had failed to arrive at their destinations. But these losses were more than compensated for by the amounts she received.

She had the bulk of her growing wealth deposited in various banks in Switzerland and England, but mostly in the United States. She intended to have substantial accounts outside the country to draw from if she decided to leave China.

Magda knew her marriage could not last long. Living with a man for whom she felt affection and respect was one thing, but living with a man who had become weak and corrupted by fear, even if she pitied him, was impossible. The marriage was held together only by the residue of loyalty and the shreds of their affection. Magda was determined to remain with Max until she could find some way to help him out of his situation. How, she did not know—but she would find a way. Only with Max's freedom would she ever feel free herself. She had to save him to save herself from self-condemnation. Max had given her so much of himself, and she had given him so little. If she could help Max it would, in a way, balance the books.

At least I have money, she thought; it might not buy happiness, but it can buy safety to some extent. However much it took, whether for bribes, or to buy a passport, whatever was required, she would provide. If only she knew the cause—it was difficult enough without having to work in the dark. And it had to be soon. Max was so sunk in despondency that he had lost all sense of self-preservation. It was as though mind and will had left him. He had abandoned hope. Even his refusal to confide in her was a surrender to what he had accepted as inevitable.

Magda knew she needed help and advice, and, as usual, turned to William Chen.

A few months earlier, Magda's beloved grandmother had died as gently as she had lived, in her sleep. Magda paid for a lavish funeral to do her honor and attended the procession in a closed and curtained limousine, weeping her tears alone for the one Chinese person she had loved unreservedly as a child and who had so loved her in return.

There was no need ever again to go to the little house where her mother, Mei-ling, lived with her present husband, Lee Wing On. But there were certain things about Mei-ling's income which had to be straightened out, and Magda used this as an excuse to meet with William.

Because of the arms operations, they had to take precautions never to be associated in any way, in order to fully protect Magda from any consequences. This William had insisted on. He had gradually divested himself of the actual duties of comprador to Max's business and had put a relative in his place. He still acted as legal advisor, and he put in an appearance in Max's office on set days, just in case. Should Magda need to reach him, she would call the office on those days. If Max or the typist answered the phone, she spoke in Chinese. If the phone were answered by the Chinese clerk, she would hang up. But when she called at the times specified, William answered. Their code was simple, as was their conversation. In it, he would insert a street and a time. She then drove to the specified place, parked her car, and entered a waiting limousine. At times, it would take her some place to meet him; at other times, William would be in the car. She left all the details to him, trusting his discretion completely. For her, only money was at stake—but he was risking his own life as well as the lives of many others.

Magda was certain that William was perilously involved in Chinese political affairs, but she knew better than to ask questions. To all appearances, William was a member of the upper class, highly regarded in his profession. Though not wealthy, he was respected as a member of a well-known Mandarin family, highly esteemed in the Republic. He was also known as a lawyer, specializing in Chinese law in regard to the treaties, and, to some extent, international law. He appeared to be a man whose main interest was to rise in his profession. His most obvious eccentricity lay in wearing his Chinese gown in a westernized Shanghai. Magda claimed he did so to show his intolerance for the Europeans. But, with a twinkle in his eyes, he insisted that he preferred the gown because of its superiority of design, comfort, efficiency, and beauty.

He was also a member of a patriotic society dedicated to undermining Japan's power in China by any means it could. Its main function was gathering information, and, to this purpose, William was studying Japanese when Magda arrived.

"I wish I had your gift for languages. I find it difficult to make Japanese sounds. They are like the Japanese, hard and cold, with a staccato beat like the rat-a-tat-tat of a machine gun—and like the people themselves."

"Japanese? Somehow, I never thought of learning it. I think I will study it, too."

"Don't you ever stop studying? What is your latest?"

"Well, there are so many Russians here, I thought it might be interesting to learn a whole different alphabet. But why are you bothering with Japanese if you find it so jarring?"

"Max is doing so much business with them that I

160

thought it would be useful. Also for my law practice; there's a good deal of litigation with Japanese companies."

His face was always inscrutable, but even his voice was without inflection as he gave his reasons. His secret society, known as The Vengeful Dragon was a cell connected to the labyrinthine Dragon Seed, or Blue Society. Disclosure of any information to anyone, regardless of family ties, was tantamount to a death sentence—and for William death meant less than dishonor. His word was more binding than a legal contract to another man. As austere in appearance as he was in character, his face was the color of old parchment. He had an aquiline nose—surprising to those who thought that all Chinese had short flattened noses—and a mouth which seemed carved into his face. Magda thought he was the finest man she had ever known. Though she had loved others more, only to William did she give her complete trust.

She looked at him now with deep affection.

"I'm very proud to be related to you, William," she said impulsively.

"Well, little cousin, what exactly brought that forth I don't know, but it gives me great pleasure to hear." A warm smile lit his face. "That leads us directly to another relative. We must discuss your mother's finances. Do you intend to continue giving her the extra money you allowed for your grandmother?"

Mei-ling had had an income of a hundred dollars a month left in trust for her by Angus MacDougall. Magda had bought the little house for her grandmother's security and had added another fifty taels a month for the old lady's extra comforts. When she died, the house had been left to Mei-ling. Magda had expected that. She agreed immediately that the extra money could continue to be paid, but not through a trust.

"I want the capital to be placed in your name and the interest of fifty taels a month paid to Mei-ling. I don't want her to be able to touch the capital—mainly for her own protection. And, William, when Mei-ling dies, the initial sum is to go to your eldest son for his education."

"So you will find some way to pay me," William said, displeased. "How can I turn down a gift for my son? Now —you must know that the main problem is with her hus-

161

band. It is a great loss of face for Wing On that he does not handle his wife's affairs; she suffers from it because he claims that she does not put enough pressure on you, her daughter, who should be obedient to her mother and stepfather. He is a foolish man in many ways, but he is also shrewd and very greedy. It is good that no one but I know much about you and your affairs—I don't believe you even told your mother your married name or where you now live."

"My mother and I have spoken little, except for meager words of greeting, and even that little has stopped since Meh-meh's death. Neither of us has any interest in the other, and that is the way I prefer. As for Wing On, if you think it is necessary to stroke his ego, tell him that by Chinese tradition, my duty lies with my husband and not my mother, and that therefore I cannot do more."

"If he were more reliable, I would suggest that he be made your mother's administrator—but seeing the way he went through the five thousand dollars I was honor-bound to turn over to him after their marriage has made that impossible. Would you be prepared to give him a small amount every month, to allay his loss of face? If you agree, I shall do it in such a way that he can preserve his pride. Otherwise, the gift may do more harm than good."

"Whatever you think is proper, William. I leave it up to you. Perhaps I take advantage and leave too much up to you, William—but let it be made clear to them that I will not listen to continuing demands from either of them. And I want no contact with him."

"Magda, I think also that it would be a good idea for you to see Mei-ling and talk to her. Wing On's animosity toward you is due to hearing false stories about your wealth, and Mei-ling's anger toward you makes it worse. It is sad to see such bitterness between you two—shall I arrange something?"

"It goes against my better jugment, but if you think I must—but away from Wing On."

"You leave the burden of advice on me."

"But naturally. What else are cousins good for?"

They both laughed and William said seriously, "All right, Magda! Now tell me what your problem is. I know you have one which disturbs you deeply—you have given only half your attention to the matter we discussed."

Magda told her cousin about the problems in her home.

"If it were only a domestic problem I would try to live with it. To paraphrase a saying, 'What I reap, thus have I sown.' But in all seriousness, I do not believe that Waldemar is simply an ex-millionaire living off his cousin's generosity, with a little blackmail thrown in. I am certain he poses some deep threat to Max, and beyond that I am very suspicious of his motives and the fact that he is in Shanghai at the same time that thousands of Jews have come here for refuge.

"It is too much of a coincidence. I believe that Waldemar is attached to the German SS and is here officially. He could be here just to cement ties and trade with Japan, though that doesn't sound like his kind of operation. More likely, he's arranging something with them—we know that there are German experts training the military in Japan—"

"Max has been receiving guidelines from the German trade commissioner to push Japanese sales," William added thoughtfully.

"Anyway, it's still only supposition on my part. But I cannot believe that his only goal is squeezing a few dollars from Max. He is the type of man who enjoys using his power over people, and Max is too beaten to fight back. Waldemar would like to see me in the same position, I know."

She told William about discovering Waldemar's visits to her room.

"I trust that—"

"Don't even say it, William. You may rest assured that there is no mention of our private deals in writing anywhere. I decided that long before I first discovered he was inspecting the contents of my safe. It is in our heads alone."

"How did you come to suspect him in the first place?"

"Very simply. My maid told me under oath that he came regularly to our bedroom. She and her husband are deathly afraid of Waldemar—he carries the aura of a predatory animal—enough to make anyone coil from him."

"Do you?"

"Indeed I do. With loathing. It would be foolish not to, but he will never know it. He is a vindictive and conscienceless man, vicious by nature and made more so by training—a perfect member of the Third Reich. All I need do is watch how he plays with my poor Max."

"What did you do about the ledgers?"

With some pride, she told him how she doctored the books.

"I have seen him peering at me with great concentration at times, as though he could read my mind. It is the only vaguely comical thing in my life at present."

"Magda, this is no joke. I am most concerned by what you tell me. It is very disturbing for me as well as you. I need to do a great deal of thinking. Let me out here. I'll get in touch with you in the usual way as soon as I find out more about Waldemar von Zoller. Until then, we had better not see each other, unless something important arises."

When Magda arrived home that evening she heard her husband's voice raised almost hysterically. She was a little amazed to find he had the nerve to talk back to his nemesis.

As she opened the door, Max immediately stopped what he was saying and leapt to his feet. Courtesy was as inviolable to him as boorishness was to Waldemar, who sat with his booted legs spread out insolently.

Magda greeted the men and slipped into her room, leaving the door slightly ajar. They were, naturally, talking in German, as Max continued speaking:

"You are draining me. It has to stop. If I keep taking money from my business, my comprador will become suspicious. There is no logical reason for me to be withdrawing money. I have a big deal coming up with some Japanese, but I cannot make the sale when you are constantly demanding money. My dealers are already refusing to grant me more credit because you take all my money and I cannot settle with them."

"You were always a whiner. This stupid business of yours. Idiot! I should have known you couldn't succeed in anything. Why, I made more money in a week than you make in a year, and you would have me ask you for pennies. Your business is not my concern. I need money, and you have no alternative but to get it for me, have you, dear boy?"

"Do what you will. Nothing can be worse than the hell you are putting me through!"

"Oh ho, what a big brave man is this talking! That would be the way to lose the business altogether, would it not? And also be shown up for a traitor, and a thief, and a few other things—like Mr. Schuman?"

"That was you! You!" Max shrieked. "God in Heaven —to think I worshiped you as my savior, my friend. Perhaps if it all came out I could prove—"

"Think twice before you speak. Your word against mine and my proof? *Your* word, Max? How much weight would that carry? You are a weakling. Are your few dollars worth your life? I don't know how much longer I can hide the facts—and if you make scenes like this, it will hurry the day. What about your beloved wife? *She* earns good money. Didn't you write me that she had money of her own? A good *hausfrau* should be willing to help her husband. Get the money from her. I will not live like a beggar—I want that money and I don't intend to keep asking for it. You understand?"

"I will never ask Magda for money. She has put up with enough from you."

"I think it's time I withdrew my kindness and taught you a lesson."

Magda heard the threat in Waldemar's voice and came into the room. Max was flushed and sweating, and when she entered he sank limply into a chair.

Max barely touched his food at dinner, and Magda only made a pretense of eating hers. Waldemar ate heartily and, without any further conversation, went to his room. Soon they heard him playing his flute. It never ceased to amaze Magda that a man such as he, brutal and aggressive, should play a musical instrument with such sensitivity, choosing the most sentimental of German songs.

Max sat at the table glumly, utter hopelessness engulfing him. "I should like to wrap that goddamned flute around his neck," he muttered, and almost broke down when he saw the compassion on her face. "Magda, I must tell you . . ." his voice faded away as he looked at her despairingly. Max stood up, straightened his shoulders, and walked away without another word.

I have to get out of here, Magda thought. I absolutely must get away for a while.

Torn with pity for one and revulsion for the other, she found her own will crumbling. All she could think of at the moment was escape.

PART FOUR

Hong Kong

1939

CHAPTER THIRTEEN

<<<<<<<<<<<<<<<<<<<<<<<<<<

23 Haiphong Rd. Flat D
Kowloon

IT'S REALLY GREAT here. Do you know Hong Kong well?
Of course I saw it on my last vacation but it's different
when you live here, especially after living in Shanghai. I can't get over how beautiful it is and how peaceful.

This is just a note to let you know I arrived safely and
am settled in a fantastic little apartment Barry found for
me. It was a real find and I can meet the rent comfortably—actually things are a bit cheaper here. Anyway,
Barry rented the place in my name before I arrived. He
told me I wasn't to feel at all pinned down about it, as it
could be rented any time, but that he was afraid to let it
go. How thoughtful he is, and, of course, I love it. It's in
Kowloon, just a short rickshaw drive to the Star Ferry. In
a way it reminds me of the Bickerton, one of a long
row of tall houses, but it's terribly narrow; each floor is
only the width of a room plus a narrow hallway and stairs.
The last owner converted it into individual flats, one to a
floor. The front room faces the Haiphong Park and has a
small terrace outside the windows which can't, by any
stretch of the imagination, be called a verandah. But it's
kind of fun to open the window and water my plants—
my own little garden. Between the front room and the
bedroom, there is a large closet, or a small bathroom and
kitchen combined. At least it has a cupboard and a hot
plate and some utensils and dishes. Maybe I'll learn to
fry an egg. I can hardly wait to have you visit me.

Tasha

Shanghai, April 9, '39

How delighted you sound about everything! I'm so
happy for you. I've been thinking very seriously about

taking a short vacation so don't be too surprised if you see me soon, but you mustn't put yourself out. By the way, in the future, please write to me c/o Beatty, Smith, Paige, Suite 386, Cotton Exchange Bldg. Shanghai. Mark it personal. Thanks.

Magda

Kowloon, April 12th

I'm loving Hong Kong, by which I mean all two hundred odd islands and the peninsula, more every day. People don't seem to be as restless and full of tensions here. It's mostly house parties rather than night clubs. I've met more friendly people here in a few weeks than in Shanghai all my life. Of course, that's all due to Barry. He is welcome everywhere and that makes all the difference, I suppose. I've even been invited to a few English homes, can you imagine? (That would put Gladys Coswel's nose out of joint!) Anyhow, when the British accept you, they're just as easy and pleasant as can be, though a few still choke on my name. (Russians are *persona non grata* here.) I get a little rebuff now and again and give it right back. The other day at a party, a girl said, making sure she was overheard, "I'm sure you must be a Russian princess, at least, like all the other refugees in Shanghai." And I said, "My father would not like to be called a Russian prince. As a Guria from Georgia, he felt the Russian tsars were upstarts," and left her with her mouth open!

I've got to thank you for insisting I have my father's papers translated. It does make a difference to know you come from a family who helped make history, at least in his part of the world. I went to the library to do some research on Georgia. It had every variety of ruler and invader, including the Ottoman Empire and Byzantium. As far as I can make out, I'm likely a mixture of Armenian, Persian, Turk, with a little Mongol thrown in, and Russian. Of course my mother was a full Russian, but I'm beginning to doubt if anyone is a full anything, so much for pure bloodlines the Germans are talking about. You know, I urged myself to hold my head high and be proud of what I was. I never quite succeeded—but since I've been reading about the Georgians I'm really smug about my ancestry. No wonder I've that barbaric air about me.

169

I treasure my necklace now and wish I hadn't given away the gold medallion. It was an emblem of my father's status and it would be a nice thing for my children to have. You see, I've become as much a snob as anyone. I almost wish I hadn't inherited my mother's fair skin and was born all tawny like my forbears. How's that—forbears, no less! I can understand now why your father was so proud of being a MacDougall and William, a Chen. I suppose we must all find a way of being proud of ourselves or we're nothing.

Oh, Magda, my dear! I'm so happy I wish I could share it with you. Barry has been a perfect angel. He bought a small car and takes me everywhere. A friend of his has a motor boat and we take wonderful little picnic trips to the islands dotted all over the place. He told me that only a few of them were inhabited—something to do with lack of water—can you imagine being surrounded with water and having none to drink! Remember "The Ancient Mariner"? "Water, Water, everywhere, nor any drop to drink." I'm becoming such an authority on Hong Kong.

Well, enough of that. I've been scribbling away on this and that because I couldn't make up my mind whether or not to tell you that I saw Archie and his wife the other day on the street. I was with Barry and we stopped and introduced each other. Barry liked him and suggested we stop and have tea at the Peninsular. It was sort of funny. You know, the dining room has an imaginary dividing line, like the equator, between the British side and where we others sit. Well, I sort of pushed Barry into our side, and Jennie looked very uncomfortable, as though we were breaching some sort of protocol. Of course *I* loved it. Jennie is a frail-looking girl, and very young. She's pregnant again. I suppose you could call her pretty—she's got that transparent kind of fair skin, with blue eyes and pale lashes and eyebrows, and that sort of ashen frizzy blonde hair. At first she seems to have a shy manner—timid and helpless—but she isn't. She giggles a lot and talks in a sort of high-pitched whisper as though every word were a special secret she was sharing. It's· "my husband" this, and "my husband" that. I could choke her!

I thought you might like to know. Archie is kind and thoughtful to her, though I think he was getting a little irritated by her constant reference to "my husband." I can't imagine his ever being in love with her. He is very thin. He's aged a lot and is ever so solemn and quiet. He's got a lot of grey scattered in his hair. I wonder what caused it—maybe a bad conscience.

After we left, Barry said. "She's going to drive that man crazy if she doesn't quit chattering constantly in that squeaky voice of hers. He's a more patient man than I'd ever be. Better never let me hear you babbling away like that or I'll gag you." Do you think that's a proposal?

Tasha

Shanghai, April 15, 1939

No, I don't think that was a proposal, but it's certainly leaning that way. I was interested in hearing about Archie. I hope he and his wife are happy. The way they're going at it, they're going to have a very large family.

I'm planning on visiting Hong Kong shortly to settle some business and also take a little vacation. I need a change.

Magda

Kowloon, April 18th

That will be simply scrumptious. I do want you and Barry to get to know each other better—you're the two people I love most of all in this world. I must have done something right in my life to be so happy. The American girls here are green with envy at my snaring (not really, at least not yet) such a prize from under their very noses. (All adorably turned up—they must have a special brand of noses in the States!)

The other afternoon when I left the office, Archie was waiting for me. He pretended he was just passing by, but I saw him standing there, and then he walked up and stopped. You know, I really used to hate him for what he did to you, but now I just feel sorry for him. He looked so sad, not on the surface but deep inside. I remember when you both used to look at each other and laugh at nothing and you—well, I'd better not get into that. It's such rotten luck. Anyway, he hemmed and hawed but I wouldn't open the subject for him. I knew he wanted to talk about you. Finally he broke down and asked how you were, and I simply raved about how well you're doing; I even raved about Max (shame on me!). I wanted to make him feel really bad, but instead his face cleared and I heard him murmur, "Thank God, thank God." I wanted to make him feel worse, not better. I'm such a fool sometimes.

I'm told the weather will be wet and muggy in May, and impossibly hot as summer approaches. Then, it's typhoon time, and even worse than Shanghai. Anyway, whenever you come it'll be perfect for me, and I'll take a couple of days off from work.

Don't you even dare talk about staying in a hotel!

Tasha

Shanghai, April 24th

. . . Tasha, my dear, you *are* a romantic. It's been almost three years since Archie and I have seen each other. Certainly he is interested in me as I am in him, but don't exaggerate a natural interest into a broken heart. We are both married and the whole episode is behind us.

I have decided to take advantage of your invitation and spend a few days with you, if you are absolutely positive it will not put you out. It will be such a relief to get away from this depressing atmosphere. I'll be flying over and will cable you as soon as my passage is confirmed. Don't worry if you're at work—I can find my way to your place, just leave word with the manager to let me in.

Magda

An exuberant Tasha was at the Kai Tai Airport to meet Magda when she arrived in Hong Kong.

"I've got the afternoon off—my boss is an old dear! Barry will be over this evening and we're going to a dinner-dance. I hope you brought something really gorgeous to wear—I want you to knock everyone's eyes out. Oh, Magda, it's so good to see you!"

The visit was a complete success. If Barry was put out by his exile from the apartment he gave no sign of it. He came over every evening and endeared himself to Magda by his unconcealed delight in Tasha, who had bloomed into her own type of wild beauty. If eyes could blaze with pure elation, hers did. If anything, it made Magda a little fearful for Tasha—it resembled so closely her own episode with Archie. She desperately hoped that Tasha would not get hurt. But at least, she sighed a little enviously, Tasha had not waited for marriage. She left the thought unfinished—it was useless to look back and regret.

Magda almost wished she had the right to ask Barry his intentions toward Tasha, but she knew she could not. She did try to bring up the important question of Tasha's obtaining a visa to some other country in case of war, but, as usual, Tasha brushed it aside, saying:

"Oh, Magda, there's time enough to worry about that."

For her own part, Magda kept postponing her visit to the bank, trying not to think about meeting Archie there, though her heart beat more rapidly in anticipation of such a meeting. At last, she could put it off no longer. She was due to leave in a couple of days, and there were important matters to straighten out concerning her deposits in Tasha's name.

Magda took extra pains with her appearance that day, and in spite of her self-discipline, she was visibly nervous when she entered the bank. Her business was soon finished, and she left with some relief, but more let down than anything else. Scolding herself for being a sentimental fool, she slowly descended the wide marble steps. There, at the bottom, she saw Archie waiting for her.

She stood very still, feeling a weakness in her knees as he loomed in front of her. He advanced slowly, his right hand reaching out in unconscious entreaty. Suddenly, she lost her footing and stumbled down the last stair, and he ran to hold her steady.

The old electricity was still there. Their fingers touched. And a shock sparked from their fingertips and lit their bodies. As through a mist she saw his face flush and little beads of perspiration gather on this cold day in May.

"I just heard that you were here. I—I couldn't stand not seeing you at least once more. There is so much—can we—?" He looked at her helplessly, still holding her hand as though he could not let it go.

Magda took a deep breath, trying to control herself, but her mind was empty of everything but Archie's presence.

He looked at her questioningly, unable to speak. She nodded.

"I'd hoped so. I have a cab waiting around the corner—just in case—"

They walked like zombies down De Vores Street, turned at Ice House Road and entered the waiting cab. Archie gave the driver an address.

They sat in the car, silently, each in a corner. Magda never could remember how they reached the restaurant. The taxi came to a halt, and Archie jumped out. He paid the driver and held his hand out to assist Magda. A simple gesture of courtesy, except that as she stepped out of the car, his arms reached out, as though with a mind of their own, and wrapped themselves around her. And she came swiftly into them, as though propelled by a force other than her own.

For a long time they lingered there, paralyzed by the spell of being together. The driver left. The street may or may not have been deserted, but for those few moments Magda and Archie were alone in the world—their own private world. Magda raised her head to look at him and their eyes met with the knowledge they had always had of each other. Their lips met and clung as though ordained from the beginning of time.

Somehow, they walked into the restaurant and were shown to a private room Archie had reserved—a strange dining room, had either of them been in a mood to notice. There was, indeed, a table set for a meal, and chairs. But the most important feature in the room was a very wide divan, with a high, caned back and sides. A thin pad covered the caned seat and there were drapes in front, to be drawn if needed. Magda and Archie stood in the middle of the room, oblivious to everything around them, staring at each other in a state between disbelief and wonder.

The waiter stood by impassively.

"You want to order?"

"Later," Archie said absently.

"Maybe drink now?"

"Later."

A knowing smile crossed the waiter's face as he paid more attention to them; then he went to the windows and let down the bamboo blinds, leaving the room in semi-darkness, before shutting the door quietly behind him.

When they were, at last, alone, Archie drew her to him and they stood close, embracing, her head on his shoulder—as they had stood so many times looking out on her apartment verandah. But now a new element was added: she had been lost in a dark world of hopelessness and she was found again. Magda felt weak with exaltation.

For a time, they simply stood together, silent and still, their heartbeats coming together. Somehow, sometime, they got undressed. Their mouths pressed together in a timeless kiss, their hands explored each other as if they were children finding unbelievable treasure, their bodies pressed hard against each other. They moved like sleepwalkers to the divan, completely aroused by primordial instincts and hungers. Every touch, every movement brought them quickly to the height of passion, to that exquisite peak which is a kind of madness, and then to the throbbing wonder of complete fulfillment.

Their passion spent, Magda and Archie lay quietly together, her head resting comfortably on his chest, an arm flung around him, her fingers gently molding his flesh, his hand lazily tracing the contour of her hip. Suddenly she started to laugh.

"Did you know we were lying on an opium couch? Perhaps we should order a couple of pipes."

Very carefully, he moved her arm and raised himself up; scanning the room, he grinned, then leaned on one elbow, his free hand again stroking her, caressing her face, her neck, her shoulders, as though his fingers were trying to memorize every inch of her, with his eyes following suit.

"I am already hallucinating. You can not be real. You are a dryad, a vision—so impossibly slender and yet so fully rounded. You must be a creature of my dreams and fantasies. I don't believe you have any bones."

"That, my love, is my heritage from my Chinese mother. She's very slightly built, with fine bones."

"Chinese mother? You must be joking." He examined her so-familiar face critically, tracing every feature.

"Does it matter to you?" she asked in a still, emotionless voice, pulling herself away.

He drew her close to him and kissed her very tenderly.

"Oh, my dearest Maggie. Is this what you tried to tell me all those sad years ago? You've been hurt! My dear, it's only in these outskirts of the world where such prejudices exist."

"Not according to Sir Alfred. He told me it would ruin you to be connected with me in any way."

"He's a hidebound old snob and has no right to speak for anyone but himself. A girl I know, Ann Heathcott, who's a sister of a friend of mine who, by the way, has a far longer pedigree than old Humey—well, she married an Indian rajah, black as shoe polish, and they were not only accepted, but celebrated."

"An Indian rajah is a far cry from me."

"Nonsense. My godfather is no spokesman for England. But certainly you couldn't have thought it would matter to me. You knew how I loved you, Magda MacDougall. Why did you persuade me to leave?"

"He threatened to ruin us both. I didn't accept that, but I did think, that, perhaps, if you completed your contract—"

"May God forgive him. I never shall. How dared he take that right? He's messed up my life for the last time and I'll damned well tell him so. My God! Magda! To think—"

"I tried to tell you—twice—"

"And I was too much of an opinionated prig."

"He would have destroyed your career if you hadn't—"

"The hell with my career. Dearest heart, what have we done to each other? Oh, Magda, what are we going to do?"

In answer, she took his hand and placed it on her breast. The response was immediate as he brought her roughly to him. His passion was almost brutal, and she responded to it ardently, almost crazed as their feelings were heightened by the desperation they shared. Finally, he rose from the divan, and she smiled at him with such sweetness, such tenderness that he knelt down again by her side and gathered her in his arms.

"You are more perfect than I ever dreamed you," he murmured between kisses. "Your body glows from a light within you." Magda soothed the lines between his brows. He had changed so much since they first met—

he was now fully a man. "What an utter fool I was—when a gift like you fell into my arms—to let anyone—even you—pull us apart," he whispered between kissing her fingertips.

"I think it is time I pulled us apart for a while," Magda said and with a polite "excuse me," she picked up her clothes and went into a small, curtained-off washroom.

She emerged a short time later, dressed and jubilant.

"I must say the accoutrements are quite complete here. Would you care to use the facilities, sir?" She waved him courteously to the curtains, her face flushed and lovely, her eyes twinkling.

"You little devil," he said, grabbing for her.

"Oh, no," she moved deftly out of his reach. "I'm ravenous and you must get back to work."

"I'm bloody well not going back to work this afternoon. No way. I'll phone in sick."

"After you were well this morning? It wouldn't go down too well, I should think, Archie. How lovely the name sounds. Archie," she repeated happily. "Do you know—I refused to even think the name—it was too unbearable. I tried to erase the sound of it from my mind or I'd have gone mad. Go along, you big bully, and get dressed. We have about half an hour. Let's have a quick lunch and then you can rush back. Someone might have seen you leave with me."

"Are you still being logical and making decisions for both of us?" he called out from behind the curtain. "Quite frankly, right now I wouldn't mind if the whole thing burst wide open in my face—except, of course—" He walked out of the bathroom, running his fingers through his freshly combed hair. "Magda! What are we going to do? I refuse to part with you. We've wasted too much time without each other—there is so much to talk about. But Magda—you know I can't leave her. I can't let poor little Jennie bear the brunt of my errors."

"It's very simple, Archie. Just tell me that you don't love me and I'll never see you again."

"You're cruel to taunt me. You know you are my one and only love and always have been. This last hour and a half means more to me than anything that can ever happen to me again in my life. We belong together. I recognized that from the moment I first saw you. You know that you will forever be my obsession, my dream come true."

He knelt and buried his face in her lap. She stroked his hair and caressed his cheek. There was pure joy just in touching him.

"We've both been cheated," she mused, after a long pause. "I want my portion of happiness, Archie. This you cannot deny me."

"Or myself. But I can't leave Jennie. You must know that. She mustn't suffer for my sake."

Magda looked at him in stupefaction—was it conceivable that Archie, who presumed to love her, was not aware of what he had done to her?

"It's all right to hurt me to save her? Is it always going to be Jennie and never me that you consider first?" Magda demanded passionately, her eyes blazing with the bitterness she had stifled for so long.

"Dear God! What have I done to you!"

She looked at him, her eyes veiled.

"What did she do to you, is more the question. Take off her clothes? The better to seduce you?"

"Magda! You mustn't think or say such things. It was all my fault. I was older and more experienced, I should have—"

"What? Beaten her off? Don't be so naive. She wanted you and she fought for you as I didn't, and she won the battle. Then, of course, she conveniently became pregnant. What could an honorable English gentleman do but to break one commitment to fulfill another!"

"Don't, Maggie. Don't say such ugly things. You're destroying yourself."

"No! I am not! And I am not the sweet and gentle heroine of some Victorian novel, who waits patiently on the sideline and accepts the blows unkind fate bestows on her. I feel bitter and ugly. I have to let the poison out or I'll choke on it. She's the thief, not I. She knew what she was doing. She played her games and won you, while I waited for my knight to return. Well, not any more. Now you know what I'm really like. Your respected godfather would say I am running true to form—a bad and vindictive loser." She turned away, then wheeled around, her words slicing his heart and hers. "Oh, Archie! My dearest Archie! We've both been so foolish—You'd better go—"

"Go? God, Magda, I can't leave you like this. I don't want to leave you ever again. I swear to you, Maggie, I never intended this to happen. I've been so hungry for you all these years, I lost my head. Can you forgive me for taking advantage of our meeting?"

"Are you sorry?"

"Sorry? Me? How can I be, knowing for certain that you love me as I love you. But what can we do? We're both married."

"Marriages have been known to be broken."

"You know I can't leave Jennie. She's pregnant again. She's little more than a child herself and quite dependent on me."

"She must have known I was going to reappear, and gave herself a head start."

Archie smiled wanly, but a smile nonetheless. "You know you can't hurt me, no matter what you say. Come here."

They stood there, embracing each other, close, as though their nearness could ease their desolation. Then they sat once again on the opium divan and made plans—tentative ones at first—to communicate privately and to rearrange their lives as best they could.

Archie called his office, with no further arguments from Magda, and explained to his immediate superior that he had gotten lost in the twining streets and alleys of the New Settlement.

It was too late, he said, to attempt to return before the bank closed for the day, as it would take at least an hour to get back. Even if Archie had known that word of his lapse would reach the ears of Sir Alfred—now the director of the Hong Kong and Shanghai Bank at its head office in Hong Kong—in his present mood, he would not have cared.

The days of intrigue began, as Magda's mind spun intricate webs of deceit. She refused to be cheated of whatever hours of happiness she could have. If it meant a secret arrangement for the rest of her life, so be it. For Max, she had hardly a fleeting thought. Archie came first, would always come first. If there *were* an interloper, it was Max. If she could have left him at that moment, she

179

would willingly have done so, but first she had to try to get him out of the mess he was in.

Archie would have to manage somehow. She was certain that, given his code of honor and time to consider, the afternoon would never have ended the way it did. That his honor was slightly tarnished, she excused on the grounds that he had been "done to," rather than doing. Their lives had been ruined by following convention. Therefore, a fig for convention from now on. Magda smiled to herself a little grimly. Tasha had said she would fight tooth-and-nail for her love. You were right, Tasha, she silently addressed her friend. "I've been well taught. What's good enough for English Jennie should certainly be good enough for Eurasian Magda. It's my turn now."

Archie's position with the bank required that, from time to time, he visit the many branches of the Hong Kong and Shanghai Bank, including those located in dozens of small towns along the coast. When he found that the one located in the Portuguese settlement of Macau had not been visited for some time, he arranged to go there for a complete examination, which would take several days. When he told Jennie about the trip, she wanted to accompany him, but Archie, a little sick at heart for the deception, persuaded her that it would be bad for the expected baby.

Magda told her friends she would be flying back to Shanghai on an early morning flight and absolutely refused to permit Tasha to hang around the airport waiting for the plane to take off.

"It's been wonderful, Tasha. I've really enjoyed myself," she told her and meant it. "I'll be back as soon as I can arrange it."

And so, Magda and Archie planned to spend three days and nights together in a little villa in a sparsely settled area in the hills of Macau. They had an unspoken pact that neither of them would mention their personal entanglements for the duration. This they kept.

In anticipation of any problems, Archie registered at the Royal Macau Hotel and put in enough appearances there to make his stay plausible. Macau was filled to capacity with weekend gamblers and it was all too likely that he might meet some acquaintance from the British colony.

On the first evening in the villa, Magda experienced unexpected shyness when she greeted Archie at the entrance. The dream had become reality, even if only for a few days. She was welcoming her husband home after a day's work. But her self-consciousness was of short duration. When Archie saw her in the door that evening, he smiled joyously and ran the last few steps to swing her up in his arms.

It rained steadily for the entire three days, but had there been a typhoon, it would not have mattered to them. Early each morning they went for a walk, huddled in sweaters and raincoats. The only sound they heard was mongrels barking. Archie carried a sturdy stick to ward off stray dogs, who barked from a distance but ran away at a shout or the wave of a stick, only to approach again, each time a little closer—teeth showing in ugly snarls, hackles bristling in starved bodies. But nothing was ugly or fearful or dangerous to the lovers, armored as they were in their bright happiness. The world belonged to them. They ran hand in hand, climbing through the weeds and watched the sun rising through the morning fog. In the distance, they could see the shadowy hills of Mainland China. Once, they stood on a steep hill and looked down on the harbor below, marveling at a solitary junk disappearing into the mist, leaving only a wake of silvery waves.

Every evening, when Magda saw Archie open the gate, she felt grateful that another day had been granted them. The next hours belonged to them, when the mere presence of each other was enough to fill them with enchantment. A simple touch was electrifying, and in the quiet of the deep night they embraced with a rapture that left them lying together in complete harmony and fulfillment, exhausted.

But each morning, a feeling of uncertainty hung over their goodbye as Archie left for the bank. Would he ever return, or would he be stopped by some chance incident? Their paradise was a fragile one.

Their years of loneliness were forgotten. The drained

look vanished from Archie's face and once again he was as she had first known him: part light-hearted, beguiling "Bunny," part serious, poetic, sensitive man, and always her ardent swain.

Magda put away the feelings of bitter disappointment which had gnawed at her, and she gave her love unrestrained, without fear or doubt about the consequences. She was tender, passionate, and happily uninhibited, spending hours while Archie was at work, decorating the little rented villa or going out to the fields and picking wildflowers and arranging them into bouquets. She had dismissed the part-time servants in order to ensure complete privacy. It gave her pleasure to cook for Archie, preparing unusual and delicious meals. He noticed everything and appreciated the tokens of her love. For this magical interlude, she became the wife she had hoped to be, and Archie became her beloved husband.

For three days, time stood still for them. On the evening of the third day, Magda knelt next to Archie and said to him, "Will you hear my confession?"

"Never again will I stop you from telling me whatever is on your mind," he replied gravely.

"My life began upon the day you took me to that house of assignation which pretended to be a restaurant. But to me, no spot on earth was ever more beautiful. When we left, I intended to use every means in my power to hold on to you, to get back all the years which were stolen from me. I saw Jennie as a conscienceless opportunist, a Jezebel, a thief. I felt no consideration for her—I decided to out-Jezebel her, and nothing could stop me.

"I want to tell you this because I have lived a lifetime in these three days. We may or may not meet again. But if and when we do, it will be like this, without recrimination and without regret." Then she added provocatively, "And I would do it all over again and more!"

For this Archie had no answer but to draw her into his arms. Outside, nightfall came early and the rain droned steadily. Inside, Magda and Archie huddled closely together in front of the fireplace where the embers hissed and crackled. Red flames spiraled upward and cast a glow over the two faces, revealing that they had united in body and spirit in a love which, they were confident, would endure forever.

The next morning Archie left as though it were just another day, without saying goodbye, as they had agreed. Magda planned to take a later launch, going first to Hong Kong, then to the airport, and on to Shanghai. She took one last look around the house before she left, and she saw the note Archie had propped up on the mantelpiece.

"What can I say to you that you don't already know?" he wrote. "I'll let Shelley speak for me once again:

> 'All love is sweet,
> Given or returned. Common as light is love
> And its familiar voice wearies not ever.
> They who inspire it most are fortunate,
> As I am now; but those who feel it most
> Are happier still.'

"As I am now. Yours forever, Archie."

CHAPTER FOURTEEN

MAGDA OFFERED NO explanation for her prolonged stay in Hong Kong. But Max, with his acute awareness of every facet of Magda's personality, noticed a subtle difference. There was a softness, a gentleness, a glow which had not been there before. She did not even answer Waldemar's remarks with her usual harshness. She smiled at him absently.

To Waldemar, the lessening of her antagonism meant she was becoming more submissive to his bullying. Max, far more perceptive, knew that something important had happened. As a man deprived of his wife's affection, his mind jumped to the conclusion that Magda had once again met her first love—that Tasha, in Hong Kong, must have arranged a meeting and the old love affair been rekindled.

Max was convinced that the intangible difference in his wife was that now she was a woman fulfilled in love—something she had never felt with him. For him she had only pity, a terrible thing for a man to swallow. With his last ounce of pride, he determined to end all physical contact with his wife, though night after night he lay in bed wracked with desire for his precious Magda, so close and available.

It was a bitter form of self-flagellation, but in a strange way it made him stronger, as if, being less of a man in one way, he became more of one in the rest of his life. Out of his desperation grew a determination, which started with Waldemar. Waldemar—not a man but a plague which made rank everything it touched. And a plague had to be exterminated at its source. Waldemar, himself the man who had the power to destroy him and everyone close to him, including all of those wretched refugees, was that source. Max became certain that Waldemar intended to harm them by some trickery. So he, Max, would be their ally, would justify his existence by being Waldemar's exterminator. For the first time in months, Max felt at peace with himself. With calm resolution, he gave himself a purpose in life—the purpose of death. With it, as an added dividend, came insulation from fear. Magda would be freed; and his fellow Jews, for now he was aligned with them, must learn of Waldemar's real intent and then be warned of others like him who might follow.

A few days after Magda returned, there was a phone call. Waldemar answered it since most of the calls were for him.

"Wrong number," he said disgustedly and slammed down the receiver.

"Oh? Who did the caller ask for?" Magda inquired.

"Some damn Chink, asking for Jig Wong or some such name. Who can make out their names. They all sound alike." He left the room, and soon the sounds of a flute being played filled the apartment.

"It's incomprehensible," Magda declared.

"You mean his music? Even a devil can have some redeeming quality," Max said bitterly. Magda looked at him soberly. He had aged twenty years in the last few months.

"Max," she said impulsively. "I hate to see you so upset. I'm sure I can help—if only I knew what troubles you. If it's money—"

"No one can help me, Magda. I'm just sorry for involving you in my problems—" Max made one of his formal half-bows to her. "I know how upsetting the invasion of my cousin has been for you."

"Max, why don't you leave? Forget about the business. Go to the States, or South America—whichever would be easier to arrange. I know that for some reason you are afraid of Waldemar, of something to do with Germany. Then leave! It can be done. Take a new identity—I have contacts who could help you and enough money for you to start over again."

"You are very kind, Magda. Very thoughtful . . ." For an instant there was a gleam of hope in his eyes, but it soon faded. "I'm afraid it is too late for me."

Magda felt her old irritation. Was Max just a weak and helpless man—a man without inner courage, without the will to fight?

"Nothing is too late until you decide it is," she said a bit harshly. "Well, I think I will go to the office. I left much unfinished business and stayed away longer than I expected."

"It is very late now. Would you like me to come with you?"

"No, don't bother. I'll call up the night watchman and see if the building is still open. I've got the keys to the offices, but not to the building."

She dialed a number and spoke rapidly in Chinese.

"It's all right," she said cheerfully. "There are others working late. I don't know how late I'll be, so don't wait up."

Magda picked up her purse and a light coat and left. From the moment she heard about the wrong number she had been impatient to leave. It was a signal from William.

This time William was waiting for her in the car.
"What is it?" she asked.
"Wait."

185

They were let off a few minutes later, walked quickly around the block, entering an empty shop for which William had a key. He carried a small suitcase with him, and when they entered, he opened it and took out a black wig.

"Here, put this on. Your hair is too memorable."

"We're really getting into a cloak-and-dagger act," Magda responded: "Is all this necessary?"

"Have I ever asked you to do the unnecessary? Yes! That wig really makes a difference. Now, change your coat for this one—it has a Chinese cut. That's fine. Ordinary-looking and hard to remember."

"I thought your driver was completely trustworthy."

"He is loyal to the cause, but this is personal and I prefer to take added precautions. We will leave the shop by the back entrance; I have a cab waiting for us."

"My word! You certainly came prepared. Or is this merely a bad movie?"

"Little cousin, you take this too lightly. We have a great deal to discuss and we must do so where we'll be inconspicuous."

At that, Magda's nerves started to tingle. For the first time she realized that she could be in real danger.

The driver let them off at a Chinese amusement park, where they pushed their way through hordes of pedestrians, peddlers hawking their wares, and a large group of maimed and mutilated beggars with their eternal whining of "nya-nya ta-ta," hands outstretched, tugging and pulling. Finally Magda and William reached the entrance which was surrounded by foodsellers with portable stoves, cooking spicy foods which emitted penetrating odors.

William bought two cones of sunflower seeds and presented one to Magda, smiling as she expertly spit the seeds between her teeth, letting a spray of shells float down.

The park teemed with people sitting on benches, at small tables, or visiting the sideshows. A merry-go-round with dragons and other mythical animals was jammed with customers whose loud talking and laughing and shouting almost drowned out the blare of music. Gymnasts were performing remarkable feats and children juggled

186

with knives for pennies. From one gaudily-decorated tent could be heard the falsetto singing of a Chinese opera.

"This is the first time I've ever been to an amusement park," Magda chuckled. "I could really learn to enjoy this."

"You look very lovely when you laugh," William said, smiling at her. "You too seldom do."

"This is the first time you've ever paid me a compliment."

"That is true." William paused thoughtfully. "Perhaps this is the first time I have really looked at you carefully. Remember—I have known you since you were born."

"I think you simply don't like anything about foreigners, and now I don't look foreign. Admit it, William."

William laughed. "Let me just say I prefer Chinese."

They walked on until they found a bench occupied only by a blind musician who strummed his two-string instrument and sang in a high, reedy voice. William gave him a coin to move on, and, with a wide, toothless smile, the musician disappeared from their sight.

"Magda, I have important news for you. As you guessed, Waldemar von Zoller is working for German Intelligence. His authority supersedes the German consuls in both Shanghai and Hong Kong. As far as we've been able to ascertain, he has *carte blanche* in everything but money—there is great power, but little pay. We find that his millions were a myth. His family was wealthy and influential before the war, but most of his estates were mortgaged to the hilt. He joined the Nazi Party as an informer and saboteur when Hitler was rising to power, and he used his position to avoid paying his debts. Few people have the courage to oppose the bullying tactics of the ruffians who became powerful along with Hitler."

"But what can his purpose be here? It puzzles me. Surely China is outside the German sphere of interest."

"True, but not Japan. The two countries are closely knit, and that is what concerns us. You know the expression that one hand washes the other? Well, German experts are in Japan training the military. Germany and Japan have signed a friendshp pact; Germany and Italy have formed a union and recently Japan joined them.

"You may know that Max recently received instructions from Germany to concentrate on Japanese accounts.

I assume all German companies here have received the same instructions."

"But what has all this to do with my poor Max? We can assume that Waldemar has some sort of hold over Max, but, surely, squeezing him of every penny and making him jump on command can only be Waldermar's private little game. Why does he bother with it? What good can Max possibly be to him?"

"My guess is that Waldemar seeks to infiltrate business, and get on good terms with important Chinese businessmen. For this, he needs a respectable front, and a cover. Max provided that. In checking on von Zoller we have found some unexpected bonuses. But that is not for you."

William's investigation had found that Waldemar was not in China in the usual occupations of troublemaker, saboteur, and spy, but was there to provide the Japanese military authorities in China with information which would further harass the British and weaken their overseas operation. This would serve two purposes for Germany—it would cement their friendship with Japan and serve their long-range plans. In William's mind there was little doubt that Britain and Germany would soon be at war.

"Yes, yes, I know that nobody wants another war, except for those two insane countries. Europe is still recovering from the last one."

He offered Magda a cigarette and lit one for himself, the light of the match momentarily revealing a face burning with fanatical patriotism.

"We Chinese are willing to fight to the death. We love neither England nor Germany, but in my mind England is the lesser of the two evils."

"But, William, how does this affect Max? I'm in great sympathy with your cause, but helping Max is my primary aim. From what I have gathered, he is terrified of being sent back to Germany, so whatever happened, whatever put him so disastrously in Waldemar's hands, must have happened there. I've tried to explain to him that, whatever he did, he can't be sent back to Germany, since Germany forfeited her rights of extradition at the end of the war. Instead of being tried by German courts for something he may have done, he would be tried by a Chinese court and that is nothing to be afraid of."

"He has every reason to be afraid. The Chinese municipal governments are under Japanese authority, administered by puppet Chinese mayors. Japanese pressure could easily force Chinese magistrates to extradite a recalcitrant German citizen."

"I still fail to understand why Waldemar would jeopardize his mission for the comparatively small sums he extorts from Max."

"Don't ask me what inspires people to act as they do. It could be some perverted thrill he gets by forcing people to do his bidding, or just plain greed. Waldemar's job is to produce information to aid Hitler. The means and manner of obtaining money is left up to him. If he wishes to rise in the hierarchy of the Third Reich, anything and everything is justified."

Magda was shocked to hear from William of the inroads Waldemar had made in the British Embassy, and of his invitations to parties on British warships, not to mention contacts he already had made among Chinese businessmen and politicians.

"I am myself to blame for some of these introductions, through my desire to assist Max in his business," William stated. "We know that Waldemar has already elicited important information about secret British naval missions, which was relayed not only to Germany but also to Japan, especially those regarding movements in Asiatic waters. He is an octopus with his tentacles reaching out in all directions, grasping at everything, big or small. Our contacts in Berlin inform us that Hitler is very impressed with him."

"We must do something, William. Help me to get Max out of this!"

"It pleases me that you are so devoted a wife," William said drily, and Magda flushed. Though in a way she was living a lie, she disliked dissembling in any way to William. She started to explain, but, before she could say a word, he held up his hand.

"No, Magda. It is not necessary for me to know. As long as I can, I shall help you in every way in my power. I've given your situation a great deal of reflection. You must remember that you are a German citizen, my dear Magda. We do know that he has attempted to obtain information about you and that you are under his authority. He can make it very unpleasant for you. He knows you have some money but no idea how much. This is very important to him. You must be extremely careful."

"What can I do?"

William's advice was simple: to avoid discussions with either Max or Waldemar; to watch everything that took place in the apartment; and take note of all phone conversations, from whom, to whom—and the nature of each. In other words, to be alert at all times.

"Do you know anyone in Hong Kong who might have access to the head of British Intelligence? Not necessarily a friend? If we can prove what are now only suspicions, we will have to contact someone in authority."

"I can only think of Sir Alfred Wilkie-Hume. He's the director of the Hong Kong and Shanghai Bank, in Hong Kong. But he's hardly a person I could approach."

"That is not the question. We must be able to reach those in real power, and I don't mean the governor. He is a political appointee and I distrust them all."

"I will think about it. I'm ready to do whatever you wish."

"It might be dangerous." He studied his young cousin intently.

"It would be more dangerous to do nothing."

"Very well. Don't be surprised if you get new servants."

"I shall check with you on everything."

"Now to touch on some private matters. Wing On has been making ugly noises again."

William continued, telling her that Magda's stepfather claimed that Mei-ling had been cheated of her rights and was stirring up all the trouble he could. Wing On refused to accept a pittance, when he felt that by right Mei-ling should have had at least half of MacDougall's assets. In any case, he had no intention of being told how to behave by a half-caste girl who belonged neither to the white nor the yellow.

"He talks with a big mouth and nothing but air comes out," Magda said wearily.

"True enough, but the air fouls the atmosphere which we all must breathe."

"I refuse to meet with him, William, but I will talk to my mother if it can be arranged privately in your house. If he is there, I will not come. It's time for us to settle this,

190

once and for all. Perhaps now we can speak as one woman to another."

"I am happy to hear you say that. It will be arranged. Just say nothing you will regret."

"William?"

"Yes, Magda?"

"Thank you for being such a good friend to me."

"Little cousin, I'm very fond of you." A smile crossed his face briefly. "Come, it is time for my Chinese lady friend to return to her western ways."

Magda went to the arranged meeting with misgivings. She felt unexpectedly nervous. But then a whisper of hope appeared deep inside her. Was there any chance of being friends with her mother at this late date?

Mei-ling had not been told of Magda's visit. When she saw her in the bedroom, she was furious at the deception.

"What are you doing here?" she demanded, spitting out the words. "What evil do you bring me now?"

Nothing has changed, Magda thought dismally. She started to explain what she had in mind, but Mei-ling was in no mood to talk. The very sight of Magda brought out the worst in her. Though Magda was now a head taller than her mother, she felt herself shrinking back into a terrified little girl. Almost fifteen years had passed, but Mei-ling's attack was no less virulent, as she glared at Magda. "You are not my daughter! Your red hair is like the fire of disaster. You accosted my second husband and tempted him with your youth, just as you stole the love of my first husband and took his money for yourself. Your viper's fangs are forever in my flesh!"

The years had made Mei-ling more vengeful than ever, and Magda felt sick as her mother praised Wing On.

"Now I have a true husband, a husband who will be with me in my old age, not one who leaves me at will, a Chinese husband who listens to no foolishness from his women. You spurned his attempts at friendship and he shows his anger to me. You taunt him with your money, which should be mine, and throw him a bone as if he were a dog. He is no beggar. He wants his rightful place and his rightful share of my money, which you stole from me. This he has explained to me."

Mei-ling continued, her wrath unabated.

"Your cousin, William, told me that it was your generosity which gave us a decent living, but now my husband has explained it properly. He says that William panders to your wishes because he hopes to gain more money from you, and that you have already given him much. My husband does not lie. When he says he will do such a thing, this he will do. So do not ask me to tell him that you agree to increase my income. I shall delight to see you groveling at my feet, begging for my mercy. That is where a daughter belongs, not telling her mother what to do—this is not the way of the Chinese. You are nothing. My husband will see that we get our rights. He knows how to do this—he is a man of great brilliance. Soon, he says, Japan will rule China, and he has made many friends with them—"

It could have been the expression on Magda's face which made Mei-ling realize she had said too much. She put her hand over her mouth and quickly tried to rephrase her words.

"He hates the Japanese, as do we all, but he is clever, more clever than you who thought to steal from me—" On and on went the tirade.

Magda knew that her overtures of friendship, and her effort to give her mother a generous financial solution without getting Wing On in control, were useless. All the meeting accomplished was to bring to the surface all of her mother's bitterness. It was no use. Her mother truly believed all the things she said. Spurred by Wing On's constant arguments, her hatred for her daughter had become even more pronounced.

There was no need to say more. Mei-ling returned to her mah-jongg game, and Magda returned to her office, where she reported the conversation to William by phone and told him that no further offers should be made to Wing On.

Lee Wing On, with the special intuition of the shrewd, the greedy, and the suspicious, had a feeling about the invitation to his wife from Lotus. His wife and William's were not on especially intimate terms, and he wondered at the reason for the invitation.

Having nothing better to do, he decided to watch the house and see what happened. With the patience of a successful opportunist, he watched the Chen house from a corner tobacco shop. His hunch paid off when he saw his stepdaughter's car drive down the street and park at the corner of the block. He saw her get out and walk briskly up to the door and enter.

Wing On knew very little about this peculiar woman, his wife's daughter, with the outlandish name of Magda. His wife constantly complained about her and the shameful way she had behaved. He had done his best to keep the sparks stirred, since his mischief frequently brought some money into the house. The only time he had seen her was at the wedding dinner his mother-in-law had insisted on having. He still felt resentful about her treatment of his cordial congratulations at the party. His self-esteem had been punctured, and he had lost face when his wife's income had not been turned over to him to handle. Surely he was master of his house. William had recently tried to persuade him to accept a small income—and that was when he concluded he had something to bargain with. Just what, he didn't know, but he was determined to find out. Naturally, he had refused the offer—nothing less than a thousand taels would do—maybe even five thousand. Better not be too greedy, he thought—if there was more to be gotten, there would always be another time.

Mei-ling had no idea how much money Magda actually had, but he planned to find out and get a share. Was he not the husband of her mother! There must have been some trickery when the English court awarded the money to the daughter. Wing On knew he had no chance of collecting anything in the courts. He had a great deal of respect for William's ability as a lawyer, but he'd frighten them into thinking he'd sue—they would not like a scandal.

Wing On saw Magda leave the house. He did his best to keep her in sight, and jumped on a streetcar at the corner where she had driven. The traffic was stalled as usual, and he managed to get a cab. Ordering the driver to follow her car, he watched while she parked in front of an office building. She entered the building and disappeared into an elevator. Carefully, he watched it stop on the third floor.

Wing On took the elevator to the same floor and studied all of the office doors. He had learned enough English to speak it, but he could not read it. He told the elevator operator that he had an urgent message for the red-haired lady but he did not know how to read the English on the doors. Obligingly, the elevator man told him which office it was, and Wing On laboriously copied down the English letters and returned to the street.

He was pleased with the first step he had taken. Now, how could he follow her home? It was too expensive to keep a taxi waiting until she came out—it could be hours. He looked around. There were several cars parked nearby, with chauffeurs waiting for their wealthy masters. He started a conversation with the one who looked the most likely to take a small bribe, confided in him that he was working for a lawyer and was watching a woman who was suspected of cheating on her husband. He and the chauffeur had a long talk about the ways of white women— no Chinaman would permit such behavior from his wife. A good beating was what most of them deserved.

Wing On told the man that he had no idea what time his quarry would leave her office. He had worked hard to trace her so far, but he had no car and he needed to follow her to see where she went, probably to the arms of her lover.

They had another good talk, and Wing On offered him a cigarette. By this time he was sitting in the car with the chauffeur. The question of money came up after some time, and a sum of money was agreed on. His master, the chauffeur said, usually worked until six o'clock, sometimes later, but he had to be there waiting. Wing On could stay in the car unless the master came out early; then he would have to leave immediately. He agreed that if the lady came out any time before five, he would follow her with Wing On. But no later. They bargained some more, and he agreed to wait until five-thirty. But the chauffeur insisted on a dollar as good will. Reluctantly, Wing On parted with a dollar, offering two or more if he followed her.

Magda emerged from the building at four-thirty, and Wing On watched her get into her car and drive away.

He followed in the big limousine. If all went well, there would be nothing to stop him from having such a car. He, too, would have a chauffeur dressed in uniform, he thought, as he settled back in his seat.

CHAPTER FIFTEEN
◄◄◄◄◄◄◄◄◄◄◄◄◄◄◄◄◄◄◄◄

THAT MORNING, WALDEMAR had slept late as usual and he enjoyed a leisurely breakfast. He made a few phone calls, read his newspapers, and waited for his mail—the important event of the day. When it arrived, he received his latest instructions from Germany. After studying them, he went through the familiar routine, tearing some pages into shreds, burning others. All the while, he was making notes in his own private code. He had two notebooks—one kept in his pocket at all times, the other locked and hidden in his room. He was sure that no one in the household would dare to rummage there. He had them all, including the servants, under his thumb. Even Magda was sagging under the strain. It was a pleasure to wear down her resistance to his authority.

How was he to get a substantial sum of money from her? If there was anything about her to be discovered, he had not yet found it. Recently, he had managed to open the box in her safe, but there were only sentimental love-letters in it, not even worth reading, and an old-fashioned ring. He put them back and closed the box with its intricate trick opening.

The doorbell rang, and the servant told him that there was a Chinaman outside who wished to see the master.

"Show him in," Waldemar ordered.

The houseboy ushered in a Chinaman dressed in rich brocade. He was plump, his face was rosy with good living and was wreathed in a wide smile. Waldemar inspected him carefully. This could be an important businessman, perhaps looking for some business from Max.

Waldemar greeted him cordially and waved him to a seat.

"Something to drink?"

"Very kind. Please, some tea." The man gave an even broader smile and bowed. This was the way to be treated—gentleman to gentleman. The houseboy served the tea and left hurriedly at a nod from Waldemar.

"Please, you are Mister von Zoller?"

"Yes. What can I do for you?" Here comes the offer of a bribe, Waldemar thought with relish.

The Chinaman stood up and bowed.

"Please to meet me. I Mr. Lee Wing On. I stepfather to your wife, Magda. Man to man, I want talk about Magda's money. It is for men of house to talk business, not for lady of house."

Waldemar's eyes opened for a moment in stunned surprise but he quickly recovered his nonchalance, while gloating inside. Magda a half-caste! Well, well, he would never have believed it. So that was her secret. He would take an oath that Max did not know. That fool! How proudly he had presented his wife and boasted about her breeding. It was difficult for Waldemar to hide his exultation. The whole picture was clear now. He had heard how those who passed as white protected themselves, and he knew of their pride in being accepted by white society. That weakling, Max, had been properly duped—not that he was any bargain himself.

"What can I do for Magda's father?" Waldemar asked courteously.

"Stepfather, please. Never would a true daughter of me act in this manner. She would have been well beaten. Magda's father leave much money. Because she look English, she gets all the money. She give my wife small money every month. My wife, she fool, she take money. I not fool. I tell her, I make plenty trouble. If Magda no give money my wife, maybe even I go court. In China, Chinese law must be. Money of number one husband must belong wife, not daughter."

Feeling he had made a splendid case for himself, Wing On settled back comfortably in his chair, and he lit a cigarette. This husband of Magda's was a fine man. It was right to deal with another man. Women were fools. His wife was a fool, accepting that pittance all these

196

years. He would show the whole Chen clan who was the smart one.

"Tell me, Mr. Lee, what kind of money are you talking about?"

"You pay me five thousand taels, I am satisfy. No ask more even if Magda have plenty."

"We must be fair about this, Mr. Lee. I don't want to see you cheated. How much money do you think Magda has?"

"You her husband. You know."

"Maybe if she cheated her mother, she has cheated me."

"I think maybe twenty thousand, twenty-five thousand. She works, she make much money also."

"Mr. Lee, you were quite right to come to me. We men must look after our rights. I shall see that you get your money."

"You give me some money now for goodwill."

"I'm sorry, I don't keep money in the house. Besides, I must discuss this with Magda."

"I want money quick, no wait long time. Must wait, I make much trouble."

"How much money do you think I carry on me? I only keep enough on hand to meet the day's expenses."

"You give me five hundred taels goodwill money. Ten percent. You no give, I wait for Magda. Must have money, no nonsense."

"I will give you nothing until I discuss this with Magda. How do I know you are telling me the truth? How do I know you are Magda's stepfather? Maybe you are trying to steal from me."

"I show you Magda is my wife's daughter. I have picture."

Wing On took out his billfold, very nearly empty, as Waldemar's sharp eyes noted. He took out a picture of a little girl, dressed in a starched, very frilly dress. She wore a big bow in her hair, and her hand rested on a carved, marble-topped teak table. A pretty Chinese woman was standing next to her, dressed in a beautiful cheongsam. Both child and woman looked, without expression, at the camera.

Waldemar studied it. There was no doubt it was Magda, looking rather sulky; in fact, Waldemar thought, very much as she appeared most of the time. He decided there was more he could get out of this fat man. He took out his billfold.

"This is all the money I have with me. One hundred and twenty dollars. I'll keep twenty and I'll keep the picture. That's it. You come and see me again next week and bring me everything you can find out about Magda's money. I'll have some definite arrangement made by then. I'll tell you this much—if your story is true, I promise that you'll get all the money you asked for."

"Next week too long time. Must get this week, Friday."

"Very well. Friday then," Waldemar said agreeably and showed Wing On to the door.

The servants heard a sound in the house they had not heard before. Nervously, they peeked in the living room —the bad master was laughing. They didn't like the sound of his raucous roars and hurriedly shut the door.

Magda and Max returned to the apartment that evening and Waldemar greeted them jovially. He offered them drinks and seemed in extraordinarily good spirits, which immediately put them on guard. He chatted idly for a few minutes. But their instincts made them wary. Waldemar inwardly whetted his appetite for the kill. Magda was reminded of nothing so much as a bird of prey waiting to pounce. Finally, she excused herself to freshen up for dinner.

"What's the hurry?" Waldemar asked, lazily. "I want to tell you of a most interesting visitor I had this afternoon."

They looked at him attentively.

"Magda's stepfather visited me." He pronounced the words triumphantly. But if he expected any reaction, he was disappointed.

"I hope you had an enjoyable afternoon. I myself do not much care for his company," Magda said coolly.

Max looked stunned.

"Didn't you know that Magda had a stepfather, Max?"

"I have never inquired about Magda's relatives," Max replied stiffly.

"And I'll be bound she never volunteered any information. That was naughty of you, Magda. Even Max might have shied away from marrying a half-caste."

"What are you talking about?" Max demanded.

"I am talking about Magda's Chinese stepfather, Wing Wing something—some ridiculous name."

"Lee Wing On is his name," Magda informed him quietly. "My mother's name is Lee Mei-ling."

"You—you're half Chinese?" Max stuttered, his mouth half open in utter surprise. "But that's impossible."

Waldemar burst out into vulgar guffaws.

"You two are really a pair. Magda, meet your Jew husband; Max, meet your Chinese wife." His eyes studied first one, then the other, enjoying the results of his outburst. "What a pair you are! You deserve each other. Each lying to the other, each hiding your shame. Max, a Jew, hiding his disgrace, pretending to be a full-blooded German—an Aryan, no less! Magda, you with your arrogant airs, trying to pass for white, nothing but a half-breed whore—"

Max came out of shock long enough to say with some of his old spirit, "I cannot permit you to talk this way about my wife. I care nothing about this 'so-called' discovery."

"Naturally, anything is good enough for a Jew dog," Waldemar spat back.

Max went over to Magda with dignity, relieved that he was no longer living a lie.

"Magda, believe me, there was never any attempt to deceive you or anyone else. I have always considered myself a true German, loyal and patriotic to my country. I fought once for Germany and would again if called. It's people like Waldemar who have made the word *Jew* sound like something obscene."

"How dare you talk of me as though I weren't here!" Waldemar shouted, his face suffused with rage. "All I have to do is to expose you for the dirty Jew you are and you know what will happen to you. Be very careful what you say and how you say it—I am not a tolerant man. Remember, I am your only safety."

"Now that you have burst your bombshell, Waldemar, such as it is, I'm sure you'll excuse me. I need to wash some filth off me." Magda stood up calmly. "For your information, I am neither ashamed nor in hiding. And after meeting a full-blooded European like you, I have become more proud of my Chinese heritage."

"Don't you dare talk to me so insolently, you bastard of a lusting man and a Chinese whore! I'll show you what you're good for—to give satisfaction to a man's needs—I'll show you how a real man treats a woman like you!"

"Stop talking to my wife like that," Max cried out, rushing at Waldemar, who brushed him aside and sent him crashing into the furniture. Waldemar took a step forward and gave Magda a resounding slap across the face. "That's the way to treat garbage like you."

Magda fell back a couple of steps with the force of the blow and stumbled against one of the dining-room chairs. When she got to her feet, she clutched a steak-knife in her hand. Her face was dead white except for the livid mark on her cheek.

"Waldemar!" Her voice shook with the passion of her fury. Then, more softly, but no less deadly, she said, "If you place a hand on me ever again, you will die a death inflicted by my people, who know even better than you villains how to cause a death of infinite variety. If you take one step toward me now, you may well kill me but first I shall gouge out your eyes with this knife. I'll rip your face apart and take pleasure in doing so. Don't think I can't manage that, if I die doing it!"

Max still half-stunned on the floor, made a desperate effort to reach Waldemar, trying to pull him down, but Waldemar kicked him brutally in the groin and gauged his chance of taking the knife away from Magda. Seeing the chill resolution in her eyes, he laughed at her contemptuously.

"You don't think I'd ever touch your filth-contaminated body?" he mocked. "That was to teach you a lesson you'll not forget easily. Now listen to me, you two mongrels, I want no more nonsense from either of you. Don't think that because this is Shanghai that you're safe, either of you. I know all about this treaty business and it means nothing. There's always force. Smuggled out on a German freighter, how would it be for you?"

Magda looked Waldemar straight in the eye and said, "We could report your threats of blackmail and kidnapping. How would that sit with your new friends, Waldemar?"

"How much sympathy would you receive, and who

would believe you? One of you a Jew and too cowardly to admit it, the other pretending to be white, ashamed of her Chinese blood. That won't go well on either side, am I right, Magda? From what your stepfather said, I don't think your mother would make a good character witness for you."

Waldemar stated his terms: all of Magda's money, and complete compliance with his orders. He spoke again of his mysterious business and how he needed a staff of people whom he could expect to carry out his orders without question.

"I have already a good-sized staff, but I can use you as well, Magda. You meet many people at your office. Your stepfather told me you were very wealthy, and he also hinted about your Chinese investments. I can find out a great deal more from him about you. He wanted five thousand taels for himself, which I generously told him I'd pay. The fool."

"Why should Wing On ask you for money?" Magda asked, genuinely curious.

"I let him understand I was your husband."

"Congratulations. You two have a great deal in common—blackmailing, for one."

"Don't go too far. I told you I'm not a tolerant man."

"Oh, my God! Magda! What have I let you in for?" Max moaned helplessly, still twisted up in agony.

The telephone rang and Waldemar answered it. His face showed concern.

"You should have called me immediately," he growled. "Is the vet there? I'll kill him if he hurts Concert Lady. I'll be right over. The damned butcher," he muttered, slamming down the phone. "Doesn't know how to treat a frisky horse! Fool!"

He turned to his victims. "I'll give you a few hours to decide. You know the consequences." He picked up his coat and left the apartment.

"If that man were one-tenth as concerned with people as he is with horses, the world would be a better place," Max said bitterly. Painfully, he rose to his feet, still bent double. There was a deep gash on his forehead where he had hit his head. Slowly, he straightened up and faced Magda. "I have no words to tell you how much I regret this—this terrible—this insult and brutality to you. I used to think I was a man of pride and self-respect. He has stripped me of everything, even the ability to protect my wife."

"It's all right, Max. He's a powerfully-built man. You had no chance." She sank into a chair. Her fury was spent, leaving her physically exhausted. But the experience had sown seeds of hatred in her as well as a healthy fear. Not only she, but also William, could be endangered if Waldemar's prying opened up their secret arms deal. Magda was deep in her own thoughts when she realized that Max was talking in a sort of monotone, as much to himself as to her.

"I, Max von Zoller, no longer exist . . . some other man has taken his place . . . perhaps he, too, never existed, except as an imitation of Waldemar. I never consciously pretended not to be a Jew. I thought of myself as German and was proud."

"Don't torture yourself, Max. If you're trying to explain to me, what on earth made you think I'd care? Nobody except that travesty of a government in Berlin cares about it."

"That's not true. Even before Hitler, though many Jews in Germany were wealthy and had prestige, they were always a breed apart. After my mother's death, I deliberately cut her side of the family out of my life. We never mixed much with them after her marriage to my father, anyway. She'd go on a little visit, but my father never permitted me to go. I don't remember knowing any of them. She was a beautiful woman, and my father was a tyrant with dreams of becoming rich and famous. He squandered away all of her money. On the von Zoller side of the family, there was little respect for my father, and none at all for her. She was like a shadow in the house and, I say now with shame, maybe I was a little glad when the source of my difference from the other von Zollers passed away."

"Stop it, Max. I won't listen to your wallowing in self-recrimination. We must plan our next move; let's not waste time regretting our pasts."

"I grieved for the woman with the soft voice," Max continued, not even hearing her. "She was afraid to mother me too much because my father would disapprove. She used to come to my room secretly when she thought I was aseleep and kiss me gently and hum sad little songs, and then she'd leave. Sometimes when she left I would cry unaccountably. I felt torn. I wanted to hug her and be hugged back, but I knew it was unmanly."

Magda looked at Max with sympathy and some irritation. Melancholy over what was past, regret over that which was irreparable, was an exercise in futility, but Max seemed to need it. She couldn't understand his not wanting to retaliate, and his complete submission to Waldemar. It was not a common trait with the Jews she had known. There had to be something more. Or was she losing her perspective in trying to understand him? Was he simply a weak man with no backbone?

Max went on. "I used to be a willing slave to Waldemar and proud that he even suffered me around. But I've been through hell since he arrived here—I still haven't recovered from the shock of finding out what he's really like. Can you understand that I had no resistance to his will? There's so much he has against me. He's been hoarding and twisting things, trying to make me guilty of his acts. Tonight I would have killed him if I could have. I ask you to forgive me—I never had my intention of lying to you about my race."

"But I did the same to you, Max, and yet you showed only surprise, not revulsion. Doesn't it matter to you?" she asked.

"Perhaps if I am truthful, it may have in the beginning. But now, all I know is that I love you as I never thought possible, and I am filled with disgrace that I did not defend you better. Leave me, Magda. Leave this house. Waldemar can only bring you misery and humiliation."

"You forget that I too am a German citizen now. It might not be easy to leave here without a passport, if the consul nullifies mine. What do you know of Waldemar's official position?"

"As far as I know he has little money and no official position. But he has powerful friends in Germany."

Magda tried to probe further into Max's reasons for fearing what Waldemar could do, but Max spoke only of his shame, of losing the business he had worked so hard to build, of the disgust with which his fellow Jews would regard him, as a traitor of the most despicable kind. "But my only deceit was in the way I looked—I am so blond, so German in appearance, it was so easy—"

To his surprise, Magda burst into laughter, a little wildly as though she could not stop.

"We're really two of a kind, Max. How ridiculous —both pushed into pretense because of our appearances. Laugh, Max, it really is funny. Both of us so justified." Her speech was interrupted by her uncontrollable mirth and, as suddenly, she stopped. "Well, are we going to be destroyed because of a couple of blackmailers? We'll call them on it, Max. We'll even wear little labels so that no one is under any misconception. Maybe we'll even set a new style, every one in the world wearing little labels admitting their secret shames. Then, having no secrets, there will be no shame. Everything in the open—the world one vast confessional. All right, Max. Enough of the nonsense. Forget about the business. You're good at your work; you can start again. We don't need passports; we can buy them, and go to another country where Waldemar can't reach you. But we'll go honestly, as what we are."

"Did you say 'we'? Do you mean that you will go with me?"

Magda drew a deep breath. Was she really ready to go with him? She hadn't meant to say it but her subconscious had said it for her. She looked at her husband: at the once fine rosy complexion full of good health and self-esteem, now grey and lined; at the hopelessness in his eyes; and she knew he could never make it without her.

"Yes. I meant it, Max. I'm ready to start over again. Perhaps we can make it. We can try."

"You would come with me?" He repeated the words in a sort of wonder. Then, his eyes brightened, and he stood up straight.

"You make me very proud. I cannot tell you what it means to me. Now I have the strength to say that I will not accept your sacrifice. I treasure your saying it, but I will not ruin your life. It's just not possible. But, there is something which is very important to me—suddenly more than my life—and I must face it alone. I will not drag you down with me. More than anything else in the world,

I want you to find happiness. Tell me just one thing—that you do not despise me."

"You belittle yourself." In spite of herself, some exasperation crept into Magda's voice. "It would help if you showed some fight, as you did tonight."

Max smiled tiredly. "He has all the ammunition, more than you know. It's useless to talk about it. But I have a plan I hope to carry out when the right time comes, if only I have the courage."

"You will, Max, you will," she said encouragingly, going over to kiss him lightly on the cheek. He seized her hand and held on to it desperately; then, with a deep sobbing groan, he relinquished it and went to his room.

Magda shook her head in sorrow and compassion—there was no way to help him. She forced herself to put it all behind her, and made an urgent call to William. He had to be told of Wing On's actions without delay.

The following morning, Magda stayed home from work. She was sitting in the living room when Waldemar sauntered in for breakfast. He gave her an annoyed look.

"Why aren't you at work?"

"I didn't sleep much last night. I don't feel well."

"So, the lady is not made of stone. I almost admired you yesterday—that is, if I could admire such as you."

"We all have our limits," Magda replied meekly, as she managed to stifle a sharp retort. William's advice to go along with Waldemar's wishes was going to be increasingly difficult, especially if she was to appear compliant.

"Let's talk about money and influence. Turn over your money to me immediately. With my influence, I can save you and Max a lot of trouble. If you obey me completely, and do what I tell you to do, when the time comes, I shall see that you and Max get your passports stamped for whatever countries you want and will help you get your visas. I suggest the United States—they are a decadent mixed breed of people themselves and you will feel comfortable there. But, remember, no more insolence, and only if you obey without question."

"What would you expect me to do?"

"Nothing beyond your powers. For now, to listen to

gossip, and tell me everything. Do you have entrée into Chinese society?"

"No."

"Can you get in?"

"I have no contacts."

He looked at her thoughtfully.

"Don't lie to me. I don't believe you. Whom do you know of importance?"

"You have lived with us for nine months, very long months. You know our lives. You know we are not socially inclined."

Waldemar looked at her with narrowing slits of eyes and said harshly, "You are not cooperating. I'll give you another chance. When Max was boasting about his well-bred wife, he told me you spoke French fluently. That is good—I may soon have a great deal of contact with them." He smiled secretively. "Chinese, of course, you know. That is also good. You can be very useful to me. Cooperate fully with me and you'll make the kind of money that would put your few thousands in the shade. For my business I will need information about people so that I can be prepared for any eventuality. Do you understand?"

"Is it necessary that I understand?"

Waldemar laughed good-naturedly. "You are a smart woman. You accept the situation as a reality. If you would give in a little more, we could get along famously."

He walked over to her and she drew back rigidly. His smile disappeared immediately and he snarled, "You should be flattered that I, Baron von Zoller, even look at you. When I am through with you, you will be happy to be in a brothel, where you belong." His anger made the scar on his face stand out as he looked at her threateningly, his fists clenched.

The servants chose this moment to enter the room. They were dressed in outdoor clothes and came in bowing, first to one, then to the other, both talking quickly and interrupting each other with explanations. Magda listened patiently as they told her that the man's father had died, and he should inherit the farm as the eldest son, but that, unless he went to claim it immediately, his brothers might seize it. During the lengthy and involved explanation, the maid went back into the kitchen. She returned,

206

ushering in two Chinese men. Once more, a long conversation ensued.

"What the hell goes on? Where's my breakfast?" Waldemar roared.

"It seems we have new servants," Magda replied evenly.

"Do you mean to allow them to leave without giving notice?"

"How could I stop them? Besides, according to their customs, they have acted honorably by training these men in the likes and dislikes of this household, particularly yours," Magda added drily.

The new servants bowed low to Waldemar and the would-be houseboy said, "Oh, yes, master. Me velly fine houseboy. I bling young fella, make him coolie, teach him how shine you boots. I be number one houseboy. Velly fine."

The other one, bowing low and smiling obsequiously, said, "I cook more betta, he," pointing to the cook whom Magda had employed for years. "He tell me how you like."

They rushed out, and almost immediately, returned. The houseboy was now attired in an immaculate blue serving-gown and was carrying a heavy tray which he set down and from which he served, while the cook observed —his face full of anxiety.

The new houseboy pulled out a chair for Waldemar, who said over his shoulder to Magda, "They already know who the *real* master is here."

With the air of a gourmet, he tasted the dish of scrambled eggs, kidneys on toast, and crisp bacon. He nodded approvingly and the servants left the room, smiling and bowing to them both.

"Does the *real* master then approve the hiring of the new servants?" Magda asked with mock humility.

Waldemar laughed. "I like your spirit. It will be a pleasure to break it. This cook has done the kidneys to a turn. I like them a little bloody."

"You would," Magda uttered under her breath, but he heard her and grinned amiably as she went to the kitchen to pay the old servants and instruct the new ones.

Unless otherwise arranged, Magda and William now

met once a week at the Chinese amusement park to exchange information. It was a simple solution, without the former complications. First, she went to any hotel where the lobby had a great deal of activity. A short while later a Chinese woman, beautifully outfitted in a cheongsam, left the ladies' lounge and deposited a small suitcase at the desk. With her flawless pale complexion, her large brilliant almond eyes deftly outlined to increase the slant, shining black hair smoothly and severely drawn back to form a figure-eight, Magda's lissome figure moved with a natural grace through the lobby, drawing all eyes. Such, though, was her dignity and poise that no man thought to accost her, not a Chinese lady of substance as she so obviously was.

The doorman was gallant and ordered her taxi before those of others waiting. This was a true Chinese lady of the old school, not like some of these modern Chinese girls who tried to ape the Europeans with heavy makeup, hair frizzed ridiculously, and cheongsams slit to their hips.

On this June day, the weather was fresh and the air fragrant. Lotus flowers bloomed along the green pads which floated on the still pond. Heavy clusters of purple and white wisteria added their heavy perfume to that of the gentle violets which formed patterns along the paths. Plane trees, in full leaf, rose high around the park and gave shade from the sun. Doll-like children, dressed in brilliantly flowered pants and tops, and others dressed in the Western way, played games, giving forth shrill shouts of glee as their mothers watched them affectionately.

Magda was lost in thought as she walked slowly through the park toward the usual meeting place.

She was torn between her desires and a growing sense of duty compounded with compassion. It was not like her to have spoken so impulsively as she had when she offered to go away with Max—she wanted desperately to separate herself from him. She ached whenever she remembered Archie which, these days, was almost constantly. That was where she belonged; it was about time she thought of herself. She had been cheated enough; she owed Max nothing. As she argued with herself, she knew it was useless. Somewhere along the line, a feeling of pity and responsibility had developed toward him, and she knew she could not leave him to face his future alone. Their childhoods had a strange similarity. But where her mother's cruelty had made her hard and self-sufficient, Max's father's despotic ways had made him weak, malleable.

Ahead of her was the pagoda-shaped summerhouse where they met. It housed a rock waterfall, where, balanced on the topmost rock, perched a stone toad. Sun-dappled and serene, it crouched, imperviously spewing a trickle of water. In such a scene of peace, it was unfit to discuss a man's depravity, nor to consider anything but the beauty of nature. She sighed as she entered the little building.

William was waiting for her.

"You seem pensive, my cousin," he greeted her. "But, nevertheless, you are a living illustration of Chinese beauty."

"Don't forget the Scottish blood that got thrown in."

"How your life would be changed had you not had the MacDougall hair! It is a shame."

"I don't know whether that was a compliment or not, but I'll admit that I enjoy this masquerade. There's a kind of exhilaration in living in someone else's body. But it does seem that we take exaggerated precautions not to be seen together."

"There's a saying, 'An ounce of prevention is worth a pound of cure.' Do you not think Max would put two and two together if he knew that his comprador and his wife were old and good friends?"

"Yes. Of course, you are right, as always. Well, I have some new information for you."

Magda told him of the incoming calls Waldemar received and of the arrival of the new servants, at which William nodded his head approvingly. She told him that a Sir Nigel Lewisholm appeared to be Waldemar's closest associate; that Sir Nigel was on the board of directors of Matheson's, one of the most respected and powerful companies in China; and also that he was the owner of a breeding stable and a director of the Shanghai Race Club.

"I believe he is heavily involved in raising funds and

helping administer the Jewish Refugee Welfare League in Shanghai."

"I am starting to get a clear picture of what is taking place. It is so base, it does not bear thinking about."

"Tell me, please."

"Not yet. You have done well, Magda. We must not rush things, nor do anything which may arouse any suspicion on Waldemar's part. Tell me, what does he want from you besides your money?"

"Only that I introduce him to important Chinese businessmen, such as I meet in the office. He wants to hear any bits of gossip about people. He even offered me a bribe, told me that I could make a great deal of money which would put my few thousands to shame. I wonder if he supposes he has me completely under his thumb."

"He considers everyone as corruptible as himself. It is important, if unpleasant, to let him for now. To that end I can obtain an invitation for you to attend the ball Mr. Dzu Bing will be giving shortly."

"No! Not him."

"What have you heard of Dzu that you say 'no' so rapidly?" William's voice was full of exasperation. "You must not be so ready to judge what you don't know. He is two men in one: a notorious bandit on the one hand and a philanthropist and patriot on the other. Besides which, he is the most powerful man in Shanghai—probably in all of China."

"I think I'm afraid of him. I've heard that he is the head of the Blue Society, that he knows everything and has the best intelligence bureau in the world."

"Probably true."

"Does he know of my involvement in the gun purchases?"

"I cannot say yes or no."

"He knows about the guns, though?"

"If he doesn't I'd be most surprised. But he also knows that the men we supply are patriots who would willingly give up their lives for the cause, as would I."

She hesitated to ask the question in the back of her mind—not fully prepared for the answer—but she forced herself to ask about Wing On, and what had happened to him. It was most unlike him not to have shown up for his meeting with Waldemar where, presumably, money was waiting for him.

"He was set upon by rogues who stole his money and his clothes and left him badly beaten. His tongue was torn out and placed in a bowl beside him. He almost bled to death."

The answer was cold and impersonal, and Magda shuddered.

"Cousin William, was it your doing?"

"No, cousin. Rest easy on that. With the hint you gave us we found that he was selling such meager information as he had to the Japanese. He was followed. Blackmailing you is of little concern to our people, but the consequent probing by Waldemar could have led to me and, through me, to the others. It was too big a problem for me to answer alone. I had to tell my compatriots. Perhaps wrongly, I pleaded for his life because of Mei-ling. He was a traitor, and he deserved to die. A wounded cur is a dangerous animal. He was warned that his eyes would go next if by one single action or gesture, he attempts contact with anyone. Mei-ling believes, as he pretends to, that it was a matter of street bandits."

"Does Mr. Dzu know of this?" Her voice shook in revulsion.

"I truly doubt that Mr. Dzu would be interested in such minor matters. Magda, we can't afford the luxury of remorse or guilt. There is work to be done, if we are to get proof of Waldemar's treachery."

Thus, they joined forces for a common cause—she to help Max, he to aid China. Magda was sympathetic with William's goals but ridding Max of his cousin's tyranny had become a passionate crusade with her. Somehow, too, the situation in Europe seemed more real than the situation in China, and she said as much to William.

"You talk of Europe and I talk of China," he responded. "Right now Japan is deliberately pouring opium into the areas it rules in order to weaken the inhabitants and keep them from rebelling. But we, unlike your Europeans, will fight to the death. We will not capitulate. Even a coolie knows that the person who pays what is demanded is an easy mark—it encourages him to ask for more and more. If he gets it, the pattern is set—and the coolie will continue to scream for more. On the other hand, he will run away from those who refuse his demands and will bow to those who show a fist or threaten to kick, just like those countries who quail before Hitler."

"I agree with you that war is inevitable in Europe. But in none of the newspapers I read is there any mention of collusion between Japan and Germany," Magda responded.

"It is an unavoidable force of nature. Take two aggressive countries, both war-indoctrinated, industrialized, arrogant, militaristic, both brought to a frenzy of patriotism, conscienceless where their causes are concerned, of different cultures—one Oriental, one Occidental—but alike in their ultimate goals. It is almost like two opponents playing a mighty game of chess.

"In this version, each king must first subdue his own side of the board with the aid of the other. When each king is supreme, the two antagonists will face each other for complete domination of the board."

"What a terrible idea," Magda said, shuddering. "World domination."

"Indeed," said William. "But we are seeing the early signs take form. Tell me, Magda, is *your* war against these great powers, or is it against one man?"

"Something of both, I suppose. If it weren't for Max, I doubt that my efforts would be so intense. I am not neutral; I would applaud any success you have over the Japanese. I would also be very pleased, if, in helping Max, I could aid Great Britain. For you it is much simpler. I envy you your singleness of purpose—all who are enemies of China are your enemies, too."

"You read me well, cousin. I abominate all people who use my country as a marketplace, use our wealth as a source of their power. It is intolerable. However, at this time in history we need British help against the Japanese. If, as we have reason to believe, Germany sides with Japan, then you and I will have a common enemy.

"Now that I have spoken at such unnecessary lengths, tell me, Magda, besides being a part of the effort to save Max, what makes you want to help the British when they have treated you so badly?"

She shrugged. "I don't know many English. But my

father and Sir Alfred are of the same breed. Whether their intolerance is general I don't know. Yet, I can wipe away neither my education nor my loyalty to my father's people. He himself hated the English at times, but he served the whole country. He would curse me from his grave if he knew I had a way to help them against their worst enemies and did not. Besides, there is another factor. Even more than I despise Waldemar, I despise what Germany is doing."

"Well, England is our only source of help for Max. If we can succeed in getting documented proof of Waldemar's actions, and thereby expose him, Waldemar will be shown to his government as incompetent and he will be recalled. Then he will not be a threat to Max or to you."

"Poor William, I think I am more trouble to you than all the Chens put together."

"You mean as Elder Brother? Believe me, this is a far cry from such duties." He looked at her fondly as he stood up and gave her his hand.

"Come. Let us go. The time has come to act. You told me that the only person you know of real importance in Hong Kong is Sir Alfred. Are you prepared to see him?"

"If I must. Do you have enough ammunition for me? Enough to make a point?"

"Yes. They will be shocked, I think. Now remember, Wilkie-Hume is only the path to the real person. Do not talk to the governor. He is a jovial, well-respected man, but he's a stubborn fool. It's one of his assistants you must contrive to reach. We know this much—that he is unassuming in appearance and holds a moderate position on the governor's staff. In actuality, he has more genuine influence than the governor. I will give you no hints, for we are not sure of his identity. This you must find out for yourself. You must not speak openly to anyone but him."

"How, William? I do not know how to go about it," Magda replied.

"I have no doubt that you will find a way. Max will be your inspiration. You must persuade Sir Alfred that your errand is of sufficient importance that he should help you make these connections without being given any actual facts. The sooner you leave, the better. I shall have such documentary proof as we have obtained delivered to you before your flight. It is time to act."

CHAPTER SIXTEEN

◄◄◄◄◄◄◄◄◄◄◄◄◄◄◄◄◄◄◄◄◄

MAGDA HAD INFORMED Archie of her arrival by means of their private post-office box, and they planned to meet on her first evening in Hong Kong. She was torn between joy at seeing him again, even though it might well be the last time, and apprehension at the prospect of making an appointment with Sir Alfred. It was not an interview to which she was looking forward.

It was a humid, sultry day when Magda arrived at the Kai Tak Airport in Kowloon. Her eyes lit up when she saw Tasha waiting for her.

"You must have an extraordinarily generous boss to let you off to meet planes."

"Oh, I'm pretty good at my job," said Tasha with no false modesty. "Besides, it's so hot that no one is particularly eager to work."

In spite of the debilitating heat which made everyone's clothes stick to their bodies, Tasha looked fresh and alert, her eyes dancing, with a quick smile for her friend.

Tasha rattled on all the way to the apartment, looking at Magda surreptitiously all the while. Barry had suggested that there was something up between Archie and Magda, but she had scoffed at him. They were both too straight-laced, she'd said. But now she wasn't so sure. There was an anticipatory gleam in Magda's expression, something reminiscent of other days. Oh, well, it wasn't her business and if Magda was playing a double game, good for her. She deserved more happiness, even if it was temporary. That gutless Max and that brute, Waldemar—a Nazi if there ever was one—they were really giving Magda a bad time. Barry had told her some stories about the Nazis—Oh, Barry! Why haven't you asked me to marry you? I know you love me; you show it in a hundred ways. What's stopping you?

"I know it's not because I gave in to him," Tasha murmured to herself.

"What did you say?" Magda asked, shaken out of her own daydreams.

"I didn't realize I was talking out loud." Tasha flushed.

"Do you want to talk about it? Or shall I forget you said anything unintentionally?"

"I guess there's nothing much to tell you. I'm sure you've guessed that I'm living with Barry. Of course, not openly."

"Oh, my dear Tasha, what a goose I am. I wasn't thinking very clearly. I should have reserved a room at a hotel. I'll do it right away. I'm sure the Peninsular will have one."

"Don't you dare. We'd be really hurt if you did that. Besides it won't hurt him to have house privileges taken away for a few days," she laughed.

"Why do I get the feeling that, in spite of your obvious happiness, there's something wrong?"

"Well, I can't help wondering why he never talks about marriage. I suppose he just doesn't care enough and that makes me a little sad—because I'm so crazy about him."

"No, it can't be that. I've seen the way he looks at you."

"Then why? Can you tell me why? I keep telling myself I don't mind, but I do. Very much. I wonder if my being Russian and maybe hurting his career—"

"It sounds all too familiar," Magda said evenly.

"Magda! I'm sorry! I didn't mean—"

"My dear, it's ancient history."

Magda took several deep breaths before she entered the bank to keep her appointment with Sir Alfred. She had been passed from one secretary to another, after insisting on the interview. Finally a time slot was found, but she was told the meeting would have to be very brief.

So much depended on this meeting—her future and safety included. But no one seeing Magda would have guessed she was nervous. On this blisteringly hot day at the beginning of August, with the humidity higher than the temperature, and the threat of a typhoon heavy in the air, Magda looked remarkably cool and comfortable in her sleeveless lime-green dress and white accessories. It was too hot to wear a hat, and she carried, instead, a parasol to shade her from the sun's rays.

A clerk ushered her into Sir Alfred's richly-furnished office. He stood, tall and forbidding, behind a handsome Queen Anne desk, as though to protect himself from having to shake hands.

"Magda." He nodded in greeting and waved her to a seat as he sat down stiffly.

"Sir Alfred." The amenities, such as they were, over, Magda came directly to the point. "I have some important information about a German spy in Shanghai, and I need to get in touch with whoever is in charge of British Intelligence."

"This is not my province. I'm in banking, not in government service."

"I understand that your time is very limited, Sir Alfred. Please don't waste it parrying words with me. I am no more at ease in this situation than you are. But this has to be done. In your position, you probably know more of what goes on than the governor himself."

"Even if your assumption is correct, which I don't admit, this mysterious agent you mention is evidently not known officially. Otherwise, you would not need to inquire. How would I know that you are not seeking information instead of giving it, or, furthermore, forcing him to reveal his 'cover,' I believe it is called. There is another fact—that Germany and Great Britain are at present in what I hope will be a lasting peace pact. Chamberlain has done a great service to ensure peace with honor, and I have no desire to muddy any waters. You've come to the wrong person." He stood up in dismissal.

"I see I was as mistaken about your patriotism as I was about your one-sided sense of honor. I brought this confidential information at great risk to myself. I have no reason to like you, but I had thought that where your country was concerned, you would put aside your personal dislike and disapproval of me. I can't let this matter drop, and I will have to seek some other source. I only regret that in so doing I may unintentionally raise the very suspicions I hoped to avoid."

Magda rose to leave. For once her face revealed her emotions—her scorn was paramount.

"What reason do I have to trust you?" he responded vehemently. "You are married to a German!"

He saw her stunned stare, and for a fraction of a moment he had the grace to look away. But almost immediately he took up the offense again. "You are even prepared to cheat and spy on your husband, regardless of your motives in marrying him. Nothing matters to you but your own selfish gains. You are all alike—treacherous and devious. At the *first* opportunity you are ready to sell out your husband, as I presume this spy is, and to try to insinuate yourself back into Archie's life. Poor little Jennifer. She had tears in her eyes." He closed his mouth sharply, suddenly aware of what he was saying.

"Dear Sir Alfred. It is good to see you are as unprejudiced and objective as ever, and to know that you're more involved in the domestic problems of your employees than you are with the good of your country. For your information, far from the spy being my husband, I'm here for the express purpose of saving him. Goodday, sir."

His mouth dropped. "Stop. I'll listen to you, though I make no promises. What information do you have?"

"As you said, this is not your province," Magda retorted. "What I have is not for you; not for anyone in fact, but the top man in British Intelligence. It will be better for him to judge the relative importance. All I ask is that you bring us together."

"I am sure you realize that you are most insulting," he said coldly.

"That is my pleasure."

"I shall get in touch with you."

"May I suggest that you dispense with the services of your secretary in this matter? The fewer people involved, the better. I am staying, at present, with Miss Natasha Guria—here is her address and my phone number."

"Ah, yes, your Russian friend," he accentuated the "Russian." "I trust she hasn't the same idea of marrying above her station in life. A word to the wise for her—Americans object as much to Russians as we do to half-castes. I doubt if there is any future for her with the young American from the consulate."

Magda laughed in honest amusement.

"I'm disappointed in you. Where is the sharp wit? The twist of the stiletto? Tut-tut, Sir Alfred, you use too heavy a bludgeon. I'm disillusioned. Goodday, sir."

"Your opinion disturbs me not at all, Mrs. von Zoller," he said to her departing figure. He paced the floor a few times after she left, his back as straight as though a rod had replaced his spine. He pressed his temples with his fists and rubbed them slowly. "What devil gets into me when I'm with that bitch? I sounded like a petulant schoolboy." He muttered to himself. "Where is my self-control? I'm even talking aloud to myself. That woman plays havoc with me."

He fixed himself a drink from his private stock and dabbed his forehead with his handkerchief. He sat quietly until he felt his vexation with both Magda and himself simmer down before making a phone call directly to the party in question.

"What is that name again?" asked the voice at the other end of the phone when identification had been confirmed.

"Magda von Zoller."

"Von Zoller. That's very interesting. Do you know anything about her and why she came to you?"

Sir Alfred relayed the information requested.

"How is it you know so much about her?"

"I have known the young woman most of her life," he said and explained the circumstances briefly.

"I'll set up a meeting and get in touch with you. Will you be available this evening?"

"Why do you need my presence? I prefer to stay out of any further dealings with this person."

"Sorry, old chap, but it's necessary. I need you to identify her before making myself known. All right?"

"Very well. I'll await your call."

Magda stepped off the ferry at eight p.m. and took a

218

taxi to the address she had been given. It was a fairly long drive and she tried to figure out where she was heading. But her knowledge of the city was limited. She gave up the effort and concentrated on marshaling all her facts and preparing herself to present them in the best way. When she and William had reviewed them, they sounded foolproof, but now she could see the gaps, the lack of actual evidence. A great deal of her conjecture was based on little documentary proof. Magda began to feel a lack of confidence in the eventual success of her mission, but she shook herself out of it. Her nature refused to admit failure without trial. Even courts, she told herself encouragingly, often accepted circumstantial evidence.

The taxi proceeded from the commercial center of the island into the residential area. She caught the name on a sign—Queen's Road, East. They were in the suburbs now. Soon the car turned left into one of the side streets and stopped in front of a house which seemed identical to the other residences on the street.

Magda dismissed the taxi and rang the bell. A houseboy ushered her in and courteously led her to the living room. It was filled with modern Chinese furniture, ornately carved, but cushioned and comfortable. There were a number of fine Chinese scrolls on the walls and a particularly beautiful inlaid screen in one corner. Vases and carvings were placed on the mantelpiece and on side tables while a sculpted Tientsin carpet in rich deep-blue with a dragon motif covered the floor. Someone had gone to a great deal of trouble to furnish the room lavishly, but it still had an impersonal emptiness to it.

The servant followed her in and apologized that the other guests had not yet arrived. Since it was early, would she care for something to drink?

She shook her head and sat in one of the comfortable chairs, willing her body to relax. She must stop thinking negatively, she instructed herself; in fact, she must stop thinking about the meeting altogether or she could never hope to convince that all-important man from British Intelligence of the facts she so earnestly believed.

Think of something else, she commanded herself. It

was not difficult. The thought of Archie was ever present in her mind—to be conjured up effortlessly.

Her mind drifted back to that afternoon. Every detail, every word, was singularly clear, as though she were indeed reliving the events. She had gone to their rendezvous with the knowledge that it could well be their last time together. Perhaps she would say nothing of that possibility; why ruin this last tender meeting—if that was to be their fate? There was still a chance that Max could be saved in spite of himself, with the help of the Hong Kong authorities; if not—she groaned with the ache that twisted her insides. She had no sense of disloyalty to Max; he was her duty, but Archie was her life.

She and Archie had agreed to meet in the same little restaurant which had been the scene of their first reunion, and which had become for them their own special place. As always, they were drawn together by a kind of electricity that swept them into each other's arms. For a few precious moments, they just stood there, clasped together. This embrace was all that was necessary—their minds blank of everything but the presence of each other. He covered her face and neck with kisses tender and sweet. Finally, their mouths met and clung. The tip of his tongue searched for and found hers; his hands sought her breasts and the shock of passion thrilled through her body. Her nipples hardened, demanding his caress; she felt the pressure of his body swelling against hers. Their bodies clamored savagely for satisfaction of mutual ecstasy. Suddenly, Archie pushed her into a chair and dropped into another, several feet away.

Magda looked at him wonderingly, as his eyes devoured her from a distance.

"I can't trust myself to speak sanely when I am near you because I want you more than life itself." His mouth was dry, and he swallowed hard several times before he could continue, his voice sounding dull and tired. "When you're away from me, I feel more alone than I ever dreamed possible. But, my dearest Maggie, I also feel I've become unworthy of your love. I promised to love and care for my wife. Poor Jennie—she finally had the baby, and neither of them is doing well. The baby has colic, and Jennie is ever nervous and upset. The doctor gives her pills to calm her nerves and different formulas for the baby, and neither of them works. Oh, Maggie, we—we—must not see each other again." He turned his eyes to the wall.

Feeling the shock of Archie's words, Magda's heart plummeted to the ground. She felt hollow, as though all her vital organs had collapsed. She felt a piercing pain stab her, and she wanted to double over in agony. Instead, she lit a cigarette and tried to appear calm. The bitterness she always felt because Archie gave Jennie prior claim to his loyalty flared up once again, and it could not be denied.

Perhaps hardest of all was losing a moment she had been prepared to remember—a last time of lingering tenderness and love.

Archie was still talking, still facing the wall. "I dread this more than I can say, but I know we must not meet anymore. We should never have met here, of all places —it is too fraught with memories." He brought his eyes to face hers.

"You are tired of lying, of sneaking around." Magda's voice was steady, but she stubbed out her cigarette so that he would not see her hands shaking as her anger grew. "It's not worth it all to see me. Is that what you're trying to tell me? That I'm not worth it?"

Archie came toward her, his palms out, entreating her to understand. But she pushed him away. Magda focused on him, unflinching, while inside her, she felt her whole world coming apart.

"Maggie, dearest. You are worth everything. Oh, Maggie. Please don't diminish what we have. If there was anything in the world I could do without hurting her, I'd do it."

"*Someone* is going to be hurt, Archie. You have to decide whether it'll be Jennie or me. Twice in my life I've fallen in love. After the first time, I swore that never, never again would I allow myself such devastating feelings. There's a terrible irony in falling in love with the same man twice. It's really a joke, isn't it? Isn't it, Archie? Isn't it funny that the same man should twice tell me to get out of his life? Why don't you laugh, Archie? It's really very funny. Go ahead, laugh."

"Don't do this to us, Magda! Please? What can I do?"

"You must do what you will. When you married Jennie, I died inside. I never came fully alive again until I saw you—almost three years later, and it was as if not a minute had passed. There is a bond between us which must have been welded by the gods, for nothing could destroy it."

"Magda—please—"

"If you hold your honor so high, and your vows so sacred, why didn't you hold to the one you made to me? Why, Archie? I have to know. Is your sense of honor as twisted as your godfather's? Is the vow you take before a minister sacrosanct, but the vow you gave to *me* worthless because it wasn't witnessed?" She felt a sour satisfaction in her words, knowing the hurt she was inflicting, though with each word she felt something precious slipping away.

"Did your Alfred Wilkie-Hume give you his permission for that marriage? Did he say to you: this one you may not have, but for this one you have my permission and the bank's? And did you obey?"

Archie put his hand over her mouth. "Hush! You mustn't say things you know to be untrue. My God, Magda, what have I done to you? I thought only of my own sacrifice, I didn't think of your hurt."

"You never have."

"Hush! Don't ever say that. I'll never leave you— never let you go. Never."

Unable to restrain himself a moment longer, he seized her and smothered her with kisses, paying no heed to her struggles. Soon her furor turned into ardent uncontrollable passion, and her sense of betrayal faded away. They reached out for each other in desperate longing; hungrily and greedily they satiated themselves in each other's arms. But nothing had changed between them. Magda still felt betrayed—now more than before —having lost a memory she had hoped to recapture for all time: the ecstatic, trusting surrender she had known in the fresh wonder of love.

So lost was she in the vivid recall of that afternoon, Magda did not hear Sir Alfred enter the room. And she was startled when she heard him apologize for being tardy.

He was his old self again, the person she had known as a child—dignified, controlled, with stately courtesy.

"I apologize for this afternoon. I must have felt unwell from the excessive heat to have spoken as I did."

"I too, apologize. I don't often lose control of my tongue. Will the gentleman I asked to see be here?"

"Apologies are again in order, this time for taking rather dramatic steps. The person to whom you refer is behind that screen." For the first time, Magda noticed that the screen partially hid another entrance into the room. "I would not consent to the arrangement unless you were told and agreed to it. I shall leave now so that you two can confer."

"In that case, I shall also leave. This is a very one-sided arrangement."

"Be reasonable, young woman. I admit that it's rather more dramatic than is to my liking, but he explained to me that his effectiveness depends on his anonymity."

"Has it occurred to either of you that my cover is also imperiled? Unless *you* identify him, an imposter might be behind that screen. And I would be in danger?"

"Come, come, m'dear."

Magda smiled at the expression, and Sir Alfred, noting it, found his lips twitching upward, if a bit reluctantly.

"Aren't you exaggerating your difficulties in making a simple trip to Hong Kong?"

"Let me elaborate, Sir Alfred. When I went to the German Consulate to have my passport stamped, the official took it, checked it, and left the office. When he returned, he told me that there was some problem which would have to be cleared up and that it would take several days. It was not difficult for me to discern Waldemar's hand in this. As soon as I agreed to Waldemar's demands for money, the passport was released. But I was warned that if I made any attempt to leave China, it would be irrevocably canceled."

"I shall come out," said a quiet voice from behind the screen. There was the scraping sound of someone pushing back a chair.

"Before you do, it is only fair to tell you that, in exchange for the information I have, I want safe conduct for my husband and myself to enter and remain in Hong Kong."

"I knew it was too much to expect you to do anything for the sake of your country. You're running true to form," Sir Alfred interjected acidly.

"If it were still my country legally, I would not be in this position."

"You've lost your wits. What you want is not to be had for the mere asking, and you know it."

"All I'm asking is to be able to enter and remain here in case of war. I wish I could simply remain, but the German consul has jurisdiction over me, even here."

"Not in Hong Kong," said the clear voice of the hidden man. "We are under British law here and intend to keep it that way. Now, do you have any documentary proof of what you are about to tell me?"

"I prefer to say no more. You are only a voice to both of us, and voices are easy to impersonate."

At that moment, a man stepped out from behind the screen. He was thin and wiry, with short brown hair, and horn-rimmed glasses—altogether a most forgettable-looking person. But behind the glasses, unnecessary ones, his eyes were twinkling with amusement.

"I think you deserve a high mark for caution, Mrs. von Zoller. Perhaps you will introduce us, Sir Alfred, and allay Mrs. von Zoller's doubts."

"Mrs. Magda von Zoller . . . Mr. Chapin Desmond, Third Secretary in the service of the Government of the British Crown Colony of Hong Kong. Now if you'll excuse me."

Sir Alfred took his leave abruptly, leaving Magda and Mr. Desmond to inspect each other.

"Perhaps I could persuade you to join our service. I think you would do admirably," he said, half seriously. "You are, of course, talking about Baron Waldemar Erich von Zoller."

"Perhaps you already know all about him." Magda tried not to show her disappointment. "My information is useless."

"Not at all. In our slow, plodding way we do try to keep up with anyone who is invited so rapidly into inner British circles as von Zoller has been."

For the next hour, Magda talked and answered questions. She showed Desmond copies of Waldemar's little notebooks which the new servants had photographed for her. She also showed him proof that Waldemar was connected to the German S.S.: scraps of mail he had torn up, some half-burned letters describing secret arms deals Germany had made with Japan, which William's men had discovered.

As she talked and showed her bits of proof, Magda became more confident. Mr. Desmond's intense interest and occasional probing questions spurred her on. She told him about the Captain of the British Navy cruising on the Whangpoo, of his parties on board to which Waldemar was a frequent guest. Some of the information was based on hearsay, but even this helped provide a clearer picture of Waldemar's activities.

The words poured out. Magda had never talked so freely of her doubts and despair to anyone other than William. She thought she was speaking only of Waldemar and Max and of the political situation in Asia and Europe, but in so doing, she was exposing much of herself to the man across from her. She sensed he was a man of deep convictions: a silent man who spoke only when necessary and a strong man who made no promises he could not keep. He was not a man to vacillate, to change his mind continually. Unbidden, the thought of Archie flashed into her consciousness.

Magda immediately dismissed the comparison before it had time to take root in her mind.

She explained to Desmond that her husband was a Jew who had not registered as one, and she described Waldemar's threats to both of them. She told him of her hopes that the disclosures of Waldemar's activities would destroy his effectiveness and that he would be recalled to Germany—thus freeing her husband from his threats, which she had no doubt Waldemar would carry out, even if he had to use force.

Desmond looked at Magda and shook his head.

"It's not a very sound plan, you know."

"Neither William or—I don't care for it too much myself, but whether it helps Max or not, Waldemar must be exposed for what he is, as a warning to those who give their trust too easily."

Magda admitted that her husband had not confided fully in her, and that there might be more to his story than just being a Jew—but, if that were so, it was even more essential that he receive British protection. At least in Hong Kong he would be guaranteed a fair trial for whatever crime it was that Waldemar held over his head. Once again, Magda reflected how radically Max had changed since his cousin had arrived.

"He is so terribly—" she hesitated, trying to find a tactful word.

"Afraid? There is nothing shameful about fear. It is probably the most honest emotion, and we all experience it at some time."

Encouraged, she told him of Waldemar's efforts to subjugate her as he had her husband: his demands that she arrange for him to meet influential Chinese, and her pretense of giving in to him, even as far as providing him with money, in order to gain time.

"I would say you've been very busy. But why are you so certain there will be war between Germany and Britain? Do you have evidence why the peace treaty Chamberlain signed with Hitler is not valid?"

"Only my assumptions. But they are based on hard facts. You may consider my suspicions a bit far-fetched, but I am convinced that Hitler has decided to take Europe and plans to concede Asia to Japan. The British seem to be blind, deaf, and dumb in the face of his madness. Forgive me my bluntness. Germany!" Magda shuddered. "I've lived in the same house as that Nazi for almost a year. He doesn't know that I speak German and that I understand everything he says. He is so full of disdain for Max that he speaks without caution. To hear his arrogance, and his supreme confidence—I know that there is a basis for my suspicions. You should hear Waldemar sneer at the Munich Pact, and at the agreement not to invade Poland—then you wouldn't have much faith in Chamberlain's 'peace with honor.' "

"There is no doubt that you are thoroughly convinced, Mrs. von Zoller," Mr. Desmond said resolutely, leafing through the papers she had turned over to him. "Tell me, in this list of names, is there any one Waldemar visited more frequently than the others?"

Magda didn't answer immediately, and Desmond eyed her questioningly.

"By all accounts this man is extremely well known and

226

is a philanthropist. I dislike embroiling him more than is necessary."

"My dear Magda," he said, using her first name without realizing it. "You have done an excellent job of spying. I use that word deliberately, since this is no game for the squeamish—not if you want to win."

Magda gave a little shrug. "You're right, of course. I hesitated not only out of squeamishness," she caught his eye and smiled a little sheepishly, "but because I'll be making serious accusations and all I have to go on is hearsay."

She took some papers from her handbag. "These reports are from servants who were carefully placed in the homes which Waldemar visits most frequently. First, let me describe the situation. Usually he is the picture of good humor at the homes he visits. Lately, though, in direct contrast to his moods at home, his behavior with his friends is depressed, brooding, very subdued. Every time Hitler succeeds in another brilliant coup, Waldemar finds a reason to visit his English friends. The people we have placed in these homes quote him as loading his conversations with such remarks as: 'Christ! I'd give anything not to have to return to Germany—this man Hitler is the devil incarnate, the bloody things he's doing. Of course, Hitler is not a true German, he's Austrian. How pleased I'd be if only I could go to England—I'd work at any kind of a job, be a stableboy if necessary.'

"But this one is the most serious. It was taken down by a stableboy immediately after the conversation took place in Sir Nigel Lewisholm's stable. Our reports on Sir Nigel show that he is very active in the Jewish Refugee League in Shanghai; on the board of directors of many charitable institutions; and an officer of the Shanghai Race Club. He's a genuinely decent man from all accounts. You know him?" she asked when she saw Desmond raise his eyebrows at the mention of Lewisholm's name.

"I know of him."

"Then you probably know why I—I don't like to bandy names about unnecessarily. But we think this is an important lead into Waldemar's plans. First, you must know that Waldemar's only love is for horses, and he is known for his uncanny relationship with them. He had made good use of this talent to reach out to horse-owners —Lewisholm being one. Sir Nigel called him when one of his best horses was ill, and Waldemar stayed up all night with it. This is a verbatim report of the conversation they had on the following morning—at least of the part pertinent to our investigation."

Desmond took the sheets of paper from Magda and read:

Nigel Lewisholm: By Jove, Waldo, you can't possibly return to Germany. A man like you does not belong there.

Waldemar v. Zoller: The worst thing is that I may be forced to go to war against my good English friends. There are times I feel closer to you than to my own people. Forgive me for being sentimental, Nigel. It's a German characteristic. At least it used to be.

Nigel L: Look here, old man, if there's anything I can do, you let me know. I have good friends in high places.

Waldemar v. Z.: I'm afraid war is inevitable, and in that case, I'd be interned as an enemy alien.

Nigel L.: Not so, old boy. Not so. Not if someone with my credentials guarantees your good faith—and you can rely on me.

Desmond scanned the rest of the sheets, saying, "I'll go over these more carefully later. Yes, I can see many possibilities in this, but as you said, it's hearsay. It gives us a few leads but we need *real* proof to be able to pursue it. Do you have anything else?"

"That's all." It was difficult to disguise her disappointment.

"Magda—excuse me, Mrs. von Zoller—"

"I prefer Magda, if you please. The name von Zoller has a sound of unmentionable filth to me these days."

"Magda suits you better. Sharp, alert, crystal-clear —Are you prepared to continue the investigation?"

"I fully expect to, especially if I can rely on your help."

"All the help I can give you. What do you plan to do next?"

"Bring him the money I promised. It should keep him

228

satisfied for a while. He thinks I'm an easy mark, as my American friends would say. But it will give me time to obtain more substantial proof. In the meantime, I hope that Max—well, he feels so—"

"Magda, we both know how important this is. But I must tell you that I can't promise to expose Waldemar—it may not be to our best interests. However, I do promise you that we will work something out for your safety, so don't worry about it. And definite proof that he is corrupting our people will seal his fate. Now, how do I get in touch with you?"

"I have a private mailbox in the building where I work."

"What about a simple code for greater safety? Do you think you could manage to remember one?"

For the first time that evening she laughed. "Do you know any of Shakespeare's plays?"

"I'm familiar with several." He looked at her quizzically. "Ah, I think I see. Start with *Julius Caesar.*"

Magda began to recite from Scene One, word for word, including stage directions.

Desmond chuckled. "That's quite a gift."

"Just a sharp memory. That's why I find languages so simple to learn."

"Which languages?"

"Chinese, for one. I assume you know I'm half-Chinese?" He nodded. "Several Chinese dialects. English, French, German, some Italian. I've been studying Russian lately; the Slav languages are quite a challenge —knowing Latin and Greek is no help. I'm studying Japanese now. My cousin was studying it and having difficulty, so I started to work with him and, in doing so, I've learned it fairly well. He is very annoyed with me."

They both laughed. "So would I be. It's getting very late. I wish I could escort you home but I shouldn't be seen with you, in case you're being watched. I'll send you home with my driver."

"I'm living in Kowloon."

"He's gone on longer trips for me. Take care of yourself. Waldemar sounds like a pretty nasty customer. Whatever you do, be very, very careful. We need this proof— but not at the expense of your life."

"You risk yours."

"It's my job. It'll be safest for you, Magda, to continue to act as though you were cowed. And keep in touch with me. If you're ever in danger, call this number and someone will know how to reach me."

They stood up. He was barely as tall as she. They shook hands cordially, and Magda wondered if she would recognize him if she saw him in the street. His appearance was so ordinary, he might disappear in a crowd. Looking at him, it was difficult for her to believe he had any importance or influence, and yet she was oddly comforted and encouraged by his interest.

Waldemar was playing his flute when Magda returned to the apartment. At least he wasn't playing his usual sickeningly sweet love-songs which, coming from him, seemed almost obscene; but no more did she like the jubilant martial music of Wagner, which seemed to auger badly for the times.

The houseboy came in to pick up her luggage as Waldemar entered the living room.

"Well, did you bring the money?" he greeted her.

"How much time am I buying for Max with this?"

"It all depends how much *this* is," he countered playfully.

"Will you leave him alone and in peace?"

"You are in no position to bargain with me."

"You're foolish to drive him so hard. He could make good money from the business and you would profit more."

"If I remained long enough to profit—but I believe in taking what I want *when* I want it." He laughed at the contempt in her face, which she could not completely disguise. "Do I shock you? Poor little one! Well, don't waste my time." His eyes shone when she shoved the packages of bills at him. "So, you had it, after all. Your stepfather did me a favor. I wonder why he never showed up again. Who knows what other information I could get from him? You think he didn't believe me?"

"You probably scared him off. He was always a very timid man," she replied with a touch of irony.

"Do I look like someone to be frightened of, *Liebchen?*"

Magda did not know which side of Waldemar she

230

hated most—his brutality, or his twisted sense of humor.

"I've kept my side of the bargain, now you keep yours. Leave Max alone."

"Only as long as it suits me. Now, see how quick you can be about arranging those contacts I need—I can't believe that you have no connections. You'd better make it soon. I have ways . . ." he threatened.

"What if I can't?"

"You will be very sorry. And don't try anything. No, Magda, in your place I wouldn't try anything clever. Just because I joke a little with you, don't think I wouldn't have you both shipped off to Germany. I'm not a man to play games with. I'm warning you for the last time. Maybe I should give you some proof."

"I'm going to my room."

"Did you see this Archie of yours in Hong Kong?" he taunted.

Magda froze. Had she been followed?

Waldemar's bellowing guffaws followed her as she tried to walk without faltering to her room. She closed the door behind her and leaned weakly against it, fighting back a terrible sickness deep inside her.

CHAPTER SEVENTEEN

MR. DZU BING LOK was a man of overwhelming curiosity, a trait which led him to Magda. He owed a great deal of his success to his curiosity about people, their idiosyncrasies, and their actions. He had learned to trust implicitly his interest in certain people, and, due to this extraordinary curiosity, he had the most thorough intelligence service in Shanghai—perhaps in all of China and the Far East.

All of his information-gathering activities were directed to a single cause—himself—and used to increase his wealth, his influence, and his almost complete power in Shanghai. Even the Japanese who controlled the Chinese cities making up Greater Shanghai were second in power to Dzu Bing Lok; they accepted his apparent friendship and repaid it handsomely by leaving his affairs alone. Mr. Dzu was capable of causing so many problems that even the men behind the puppet governments preferred to keep his good will. Strikes, rioting, anarchy—all were within his power.

It was a time of political chaos in Shanghai. There were diverse parties within parties and secret societies within secret societies, all of which made deep inroads into the country. Communists were the power behind labor and used their power in raids, piracies, kidnappings, public executions, and acts of terrorism. A mere suspicion of disloyalty was followed by assassination. It was not unknown for a suspected traitor of any organization to have his eyes and tongue torn out and placed in a rice bowl as a warning. Atrocities became a daily occurrence as the fighting elsewhere in China was duplicated in Shanghai.

The residents of the foreign settlements in the city continued to act as if all were normal, even though they saw men killed on Nanking Road, the main street of the downtown business district. They, too, were content to leave Dzu Bing Lok alone. Strange and terrible things happened to people who interfered with his affairs. His notoriety penetrated throughout Greater Shanghai, further inland, and even to Hong Kong. His name was enough to create panic, and most were eager for his approval. He could make a man wealthy within twenty-four hours—or dead, if he chose.

Two societies in particular, the Red and the Blue, ruled in Shanghai, and the man at the head of the Blue Society was Mr. Dzu. It was purposely not the best-kept secret in Shanghai, and the fear and respect the fact inspired kept Mr. Dzu above the chaos. He was like a giant octopus whose tentacles stretched into all of the underground activities: gambling, prostitution, extortion, and infiltration of the powerful labor guilds. Above all else, he was the absolute king of the opium trade.

His was the brain which manipulated the affairs of the foreign community, the top businesses, local politics, and all other matters of importance. He was a director of several foreign banks and of the cotton mills and a member of the Chinese Chamber of Commerce. He also owned a controlling interest in the leading American newspaper in Shanghai.

Dzu Bing Lok was also a humanitarian. His educational and philanthropic interests were as extensive, in their way, as were his activities in the underworld. He supported free schools and hospitals for the poor, and provided free burials to beggars.

Most assuredly, his was a dual personality. Only in China could such a man be accepted as a dedicated patriot and leader of his people. He spent millions of dollars buying airplanes for the Chinese Nationalists and was an intimate friend of their leaders.

One evening, while going over the business of the day, Mr. Dzu saw a notation about the man, Lee Wing On, who had had his tongue pulled out by its roots.

"Our work?" he asked his lieutenant, pointing his finger at the item.

"Not on our orders, or a more thorough job would have been done. It is the work of patriots, members of a political group within the Blue Society."

"Tell me more," said Dzu Bing, casually, his interest stirred.

His chief aide related the incident as well as he could. A thorough investigation had not been made of such a small event, and the aide was annoyed at his lieutenant's failure to find out more. He was being made to look inefficient in front of Mr. Dzu, and that was a serious matter.

"The man you describe—Chen Wen-chu—which family Chen is it?"

"He is descended from Chen Ping Lui, a Mandarin from Shangsi Province; his grandfather was Chen Hsui Chu, a magistrate in Shanghai, whose eldest son, Wen-chu's father, died serving General Ho. Chen Wen-chu, called William in the English fashion, is now Elder Brother of the family and a lawyer of good repute. He is permitted by the Society to buy and send limited arms to a growing number of patriots camped near Hangchow."

233

"Hm-m. If I remember correctly, he is a worthy man."

"Your memory is without compare."

"I want complete information. Complete. And soon."

Mr. Dzu entered the brokerage firm of Beatty, Smith and Paige. Two bodyguards, who accompanied him everywhere, checked the room, giving it a quick and efficient search which the staff accepted as a matter of course as soon as they heard the name Dzu Bing Lok. The news of his appearance spread rapidly. Mr. Beatty came out from his office, his hand outstretched, a welcoming smile on his face.

"Goodday, Mr. Dzu, it's good to see you again." Though Mr. Dzu smiled back cordially, Beatty knew he had not been recognized. "I'm sure you don't remember me; we met for a very short time at the races at last year's Champion Sweepstakes."

"Yes! Yes, of course. I believe you held the number of one of the horses who placed in the sweepstakes."

"By George, what a memory! I wish I had it."

Dzu smiled. His memory was one of the traits of which he was most particularly proud. He should have remembered this man, but he was so typical of his people—medium blond, medium height, medium everything —how was one to distinguish among them?

"I hope I may have the pleasure of doing something for you," Mr. Beatty said warmly, thinking what a coup it would be if this man of tremendous wealth became a client.

"Yes, Mr. Beatty, if you would be so kind. You have a woman working here whose name I don't recall, but it is said that she has hair like the blazing sun."

"You must mean our Mrs. von Zoller."

"That, I believe, is the name. Your names are very difficult for my people to remember, I have heard from friends that she's very well informed about foreign currencies. Is this true?"

"Indeed. She is very shrewd about the market in general, but world currency is her specialty. I'll have her sent for. If you care to follow the clerk to a private office, you can discuss your interests without interruption."

When Magda heard that Mr. Dzu was waiting for her, she felt unnerved. What did Mr. Dzu want with her?

It was ludicrous to think he had come for professional advice—he had an empire! William had mentioned something about an invitation, but most certainly Dzu did not go about checking out guests for himself.

The guns! It must be the guns!

She felt a chill of apprehension but entered the room coolly. She gave him a formal bow to which he responded, studying her with frank appraisal. He saw a woman of restrained elegance who looked taller than she was because of her extreme slenderness. A strong man could snap her in two. She was as willowy as a bamboo tree and as graceful as the goddess of love. Her eyes were like two dark pools of mystery in a moonlit face. Her hair was the deep, rich red of the setting sun. Truly, she would please any man.

Mr. Dzu's eyes approved of what he saw, and he did not fail to consider the possibilities. He had reached such a pinnacle of wealth and power that he considered no woman beyond his reach.

His eyes were alert with sharp intelligence; his complexion dark and pock-marked, his nose flat, his lips thick and sensuous. Short and squat, he was a man of compelling ugliness, which, somehow, became part of his aura of monumental power, blending with his earthy sexuality, which attracted as much as it repelled. His lusty appetites had brought many women—European as well as Oriental—to his bed, and none of them had been forced.

Magda, having been forewarned about him, felt a strange mixture of revulsion and attraction. Mr. Dzu exuded power of such magnitude that it did not have to be emphasized or proved in any way. It was itself a magnet which drew powerfully and Magda felt its pull. He sat there with calm assurance as he studied the exquisite young woman.

"I hope I can be of some service to you, Mr. Dzu," Magda said in impeccable Chinese. Dzu was pleased. She did not conceal her lineage. But he carried on the myth.

"You speak excellent Chinese for a foreigner."

"But I am sure you know that I am half Chinese," Magda smiled and her face lit up with perception.

235

Mr. Dzu enjoyed the turnabout. Again, he approved of this woman who was neither afraid of him nor unconvincingly coy. Without any explanation, he proceeded to ask her about herself, her way of life, her preferences. And, equally without hesitation, she answered his questions with candor and, unexpectedly, a marked relief in throwing off all disguise and pretense. It occurred to her that she had talked more about herself in the last few weeks than in her entire life. She must curb it. But, in spite of her usual reserve, she was flattered by Mr. Dzu's interest and probing questioning. He went on:

"I have met many Eurasians, as they are pleased to call themselves. They come in several categories: those who pass for white; those who accept their lives straddling a fence, as it were; and those who accept the Chinese way of life. How do you stand? Are you Chinese or are you British, within yourself?"

Magda considered the question thoughtfully.

"Had you asked this of me a few years ago, the answer would have been immediate—British. That is how I looked, how I was educated, but most of all, it was my father's dearest wish. I idolized him and obeyed him in all matters."

"What about your mother?"

"We are as strangers to each other."

"Surely you owe her a daughter's respect."

"I owed my father more. He ruled my life, and my decisions are still based on his advice."

"And now? How do you feel now? Where do your loyalties lie?"

His voice was very soft but Magda knew the importance of her answer—it could be dangerous or advantageous to her. This, she thought, was the reason for the interview, though she could not guess at his purpose. She looked at him steadfastly.

"Mr. Dzu, you are the most important person in Shanghai, and I am less than a dot on the surface. Why, sir, do you ask me these questions?"

He smiled, delighted at her boldness.

"May I not be permitted to pursue my sheer curiosity about a fascinating woman? I see before me a woman who would grace any man's home, one who could live in

236

a palace, if she so desired," he bowed low as though inviting her to share his. "One who could have her every wish granted—but instead, I find her working in an office like any underpaid menial."

Magda shook her head in denial, her eyes twinkling.

"Very well, if you say so," he continued, "like a well-paid secretary. So I wonder about this woman. What kind of life does she lead? How does she think? How does she feel? Also, I ask myself, how can I use her in ways other than the obvious, though, I assure you, the obvious would be very much to my liking. I also ask myself: underneath the pale skin and red hair, is she Chinese or Western?"

"Mr. Dzu, you do me honor with your interest. I thought I had answered the question, if only to say I don't really know."

"But I must press you for your answer. I am intrigued."

"In that case—I find a great deal about China to admire, and also to dislike, but this, I'm sorry to say is true about all countries. I find myself more European than Chinese, which is, in many ways, a burden. And it is only recently that I have realized I am also Chinese."

"You are very honest with me. I like that. I must confess that I myself prefer being devious."

They both smiled, enjoying each other's remarks. Magda felt a strange sense of ease in talking to him. She had to remind herself that he was a dangerous as well as a powerful man, who could, on a whim, have her killed. That he had little respect for life other than his own was a well-known part of the legend about him, but she felt no fear.

"Now, Mrs. von Zoller, tell me. Which currency in the world do you suggest for a quick-profit investment?"

Magda named three, and added her choice for the most immediately rewarding one, giving him facts, background, and figures.

"I am impressed with your competence and thoroughness. You deserve your reputation. Well, I shall think about it."

They did not shake hands in the foreign manner but bowed to each other. Once again, he admired the grace and poise of her movements, and the slender small-boned body, which, he decided, was more Chinese than Western. He visualized her in a close-fitting cheongsam, and he found the image enchanting.

In the other office, he made a point of telling Mr. Beatty how pleased he was with the service provided, and that his secretary would be in touch.

Two days later, Magda received an invitation with gold letters embossed on red paper. The envelope was addressed to her apartment, in beautiful flowing Chinese script.

"Who on earth can this be from?" she asked innocently.

"It must be one of those comprador banquets," Max said tiredly. He had changed even more in the last two months; he rarely spoke and remained apart from any discussion, his face stamped with blank resignation rather than despair.

Waldemar took the invitation from her, and a gleam of triumph glowed in Magda's eyes, which she quickly lowered.

Waldemar read it aloud. "Dzu Bing Lok?—Club Paris—reserved entirely for his friends—Dzu Bing— where have I heard that name? I know! He's the top man around here. I've heard that he rules the city. This is a real stroke of luck. You've deceived me again, Magda," he said, giving her a dangerously threatening grimace. "I told you not to play games with me. Why didn't you tell me you knew this man?"

In spite of herself, Magda shuddered. No, he was not a man to play games with. As he loomed in front of her, he became a nightmare creature, and for a second, she saw before her a slithering, fanged brute with red eyes and clawlike hands, approaching her. She managed to laugh at the image, if a little shakily. She must not let him get to her.

"Oh, do sit down, Waldemar. You look ridiculous, and you don't frighten me by your theatrics. Mr. Dzu came to the office a few days ago to inquire about investments. That's the depth of my 'knowing' him. But I remembered how sweet and kind you always are, so I tried to make a good impression on him. *Voilà!* The invitation."

"You see how successful you can be when you make an effort? No doubt he recognized your Chinese blood."

"Probably."

"To show how much I appreciate your efforts I want you to get a very special new gown for the occasion. Spend as much as you like. I will pay for it."

"Save your money. I have no intention of going."

"You will be sorry if you don't obey me. All three of us will go. The Chinese are hospitable, and you can say your husband's relative is visiting you. I want you to look magnificent. Aren't you pleased that I want to show off your beauty?"

"How nice of you. I'll be delighted to get this beautiful gown and accept your generosity in paying for it, considering you have all of my money."

"No! Magda! No! Oh, Magda, you didn't. What have I forced upon you?" Max looked at her, devastated. He had not known about the money. All the hard-won serenity drained from his face. He gulped painfully and left the room, his shoulders hunched like an old man's.

Magda ran after him into the bedroom, more sorry for him than she had ever been. She was furious with herself that her sarcastic remark had inadvertently revealed to him what she had done. She put a hand on his arm, trying to ease his distress.

"It doesn't matter, Max. Don't let it worry you. It's only money." She wished she could tell him that it had all been a delaying tactic, but the knowledge that his wife was fighting his battles was just one more searing humiliation for him.

Magda took unusual pains with her toilette on the evening of the ball. A mischievous demon inside made her resolve that for this one night, she would play down her European appearance and enhance the Chinese. Maybe it would prove something to her.

Her eyes had a distinctly Oriental cast, something she had previously disliked. They were almond-shaped, almost lidless when open, revealing two dark pools. Tonight she carefully elongated them with an eyebrow pencil, emphasizing the upward tilt, then, in the Chinese fashion, she brushed some rouge lightly on her upper eyelids, starting from the center and gradually widening the area upward, then down the side of her cheekbones, letting it fade away into the contrasting pallor of her face. Then the final touch, a dot of lipstick at the inner corners, and Magda was startled at the change the makeup had elicited. Her eyes shone back at her like enormous, multifaceted black diamonds, reflecting light. She dusted her face lightly with powder, brushed her eyebrows, and chose a pale-rose lipstick. Her hair had been dressed for the occasion, and it swirled smoothly around her head—a brilliant, burnished-copper helmet.

She studied herself carefully, a little stunned by the effect of the makeup, so rarely did she bother to use any. Tonight was different, though—tonight she would look Chinese in her gown of dull bronze silk, shot through with green lights. It was a Westernized version of a cheongsam, with a stiff, high collar, but cut away at the neckline to disclose her alabaster shoulders and arms. The effect was dazzling.

The silk clung to her, showing every gentle curve of her body, exaggerating the slenderness of her waist and the fullness of her hips, tapering smoothly down. The gown was slit on one side only to just above her knee, exposing one shapely leg, and reached to the tips of her high-heeled shoes. And as the gown molded itself to her body, so did the dragon which was embroidered on it in bronze and gold beads and sequins. Its tail flicked at the slit in her gown as though it had emerged from there and attached itself to her. Its body encircled hers, the dragon's head coming to rest below her breast and its red tongue forked up, darting fire. Hesitantly, afraid to overdo the effect, Magda tried on a pair of long dangling jade earrings intricately mounted on gold—they were an heirloom gift from her grandmother.

Magda surveyed the entire effect in the long mirror and discovered that she was ravishing. She looked at herself rather shyly, not fully believing her own image. She had always considered herself reasonably attractive. But tonight, as though seeing herself for the first time, she was both disconcerted and entranced with her reflection.

She picked up her wrap and her beaded evening-bag, opened the door to the living room, and stood there, rather bashfully, in front of the two men.

"Beautiful! Dazzling!" ejaculated Waldemar, his eyes shining. "What you would do to the fellows in Berlin!"

Magda ignored him, and her eyes went to Max, seeking —what? Approval? She didn't know. After his initial gasp of admiration, Max instinctively sensed her vulnerability. He went to her, took her hands, and kissed them. Her hand crept into his, and a smile of indescribable sweetness trembled on her lips as she gazed at him. Love and pride surged within him and, taking her firmly by the arm, he brushed by Waldemar without a glance and led her outside to the waiting limousine, feeling himself her protector. For some wonderful and unknown reason, his strong-willed Magda, so firm and secure, needed him.

Waldemar followed them out to the car, a little bewildered that Max had taken the lead. Both men looked distinguished in their formal black-and-white: Waldemar, powerfully built, swarthy of complexion, autocratic; and Max, tall, erect, and extremely blond, by all appearances the true Aryan. Bloodlines, Magda thought, surveying both of them, do not always behave as prescribed—as she had good reason to know.

Once there had been a huge estate owned by a British gentleman on Bubbling Well Road, which at that time was far from the hub of the city. He was thought to have some Indian blood but he was so fabulously wealthy that the blood taint did not touch him, for where wealth is great there is no taint. Everyone, even those in the highest social and diplomatic circles, was flattered to be invited to his palace, for it was that in all respects. The gardens were magnificent and he had a staff of gardeners to see that the rolling lawns were always well groomed and trimmed—to the last blade of green grass. The garden was designed so that there would always be some trees, bushes, and plants in bloom at any season. A large, arched, glass conservatory housed rare and exotic plants.

The large manor was designed after Blenheim House in England, and the grounds also held several small houses and cottages for guests, each with its own garden and surrounded by trees. The entire estate was protected by an elaborate wrought-iron fence, with the owner's coat of arms worked in at regular intervals.

Then one day, the owner disappeared, and the estate

was put up for sale. A cartel of investors bought it and turned it into the Majestic Hotel, the most expensive and exclusive hotel in the Far East. But, after the 1937 invasion of Shanghai, the flow of wealthy visitors slowed down to a trickle. The hotel could not afford to remain open and the estate was divided into smaller parcels, becoming the center of Shanghai night life for both the Chinese and the international cafe society.

Amusement parks, cabarets, and nightclubs all vied with each other in glitter and noise. One of the largest and most spectacular was the Parisian Club, where Dzu Bing Lok held his annual ball.

The ball, its decor, its guest list, and everything about it, was a matter of public interest as soon as the date was set. Big-name bands were flown in for the occasion, and top-flight entertainers from different countries were hired. Caterers prepared the finest food: specialties from around the world, food and drinks from every nation. As soon as one year's ball ended, planning and preparations for the next one commenced.

The Parisian Ballroom could hold several hundred couples. The guest-list included Mr. Dzu's friends, his acquaintances, and his enemies. Generals and admirals came in full-dress uniform, replete with medals and ribbons; so came ambassadors and their ladies. Princes of industry and commerce mingled with extortionists; society ladies were indistinguishable from high-class call girls. It was truly democratic. There were those who were invited for expediency and others who were invited because Mr. Dzu had taken a liking to them. Some were friends of friends, invited as a special favor. There were others who couldn't afford the right clothes, so mysterious and anonymous checks would arrive in order that they would not lose face.

There were two explicit rules for this ball. Rule number one was that no business was to be discussed with Mr. Dzu. Those found engaged in business discussion or meeting others for that purpose were never invited again. Mr. Dzu's guards, waiters, and aides always had their ears and eyes open for any kind of misconduct and for other useful information.

Rule number two was that no guest should seek out Mr. Dzu or approach him unless specifically invited to do so.

Sometimes he attended the ball only long enough to give a welcoming speech; at other times he remained at his table and nodded to a few intimate friends. Occasionally he left his table and spoke to one or two individuals. At such times, even the most highly placed among them felt pleased to be singled out by this one-time orphan and beggarboy, who, at five, was already streetwise, and who earned his first pennies taking drunken sailors to meet his "sisters."

When Magda entered with her two escorts, the large ballroom was already filling up as were the side rooms, bars, and lounges. They were stopped in the foyer, where each invitation was checked by a Chinaman dressed in formal European attire. He wrote down each guest's name, then he passed the invitation to another, who checked it against his list. Waldemar was courteously welcomed, and his name was carefully entered in the list. After this formality, they were greeted by a receiving line of hosts and hostesses and shown to their tables or, if they wished, left to mingle with the other guests. Only a few were directed to Mr. Dzu's table, at his request.

Even in a crowd of beautifully garbed and glamorous women, Magda caused a stir of interest when she entered the main ballroom flanked by Max and Waldemar, both standing a little prouder for the effect she made, and for the heads turned toward her.

She posed there a moment, transported by the elaborate fantasy in front of her, lips slightly open in delight at the fairy-tale surroundings. A thousand light bulbs shone down, making pinpoints of dancing red and gold and bronze flame on her hair and gown, until she seemed to be a living part of the illumination.

The decor this year was in the Versailles tradition. The hall was divided into geometric shapes banked by flowering plants. In the center of each section, a fountain shot up a thin stream of wine which tumbled down into a marble basin elaborately decorated with maidens being chased by Pan. Each fountain spouted a different wine: in one, a deep burgundy splashed ruby droplets, as did a pale rosé; in others, purplish claret, pale golden sauterne, and the deep amber of chablis flowed; while in the enormous central one, a clear, bubbling champagne sparkled.

Only by the greatest exertion of will power could Magda restrain her impulse to clap her hands at the extravagance of color and lights and perfumes. She felt as if she were a child being shown magical wonders. The orchestra was playing haunting little French tunes in keeping with the decor. Magda knew them well, and the words and music bubbled up inside her. She laughed aloud at the thought of herself suddenly whistling along with the orchestra, as she was tempted to do.

She glided around the ballroom, her eyes glowing with delight, the dragon on her gown undulating with every movement of her body—like a live companion dancing with her—and her hair glowing like the tongue of fire breathed up by the dragon. Many eyes followed her and wondered who she was. Here was a new face in their midst—she must be someone special, to have the features and the figure to wear such a gown. In it she was provocative, alluring, and just a little dangerous.

Her two escorts trailed her closely: Max in proud acceptance of his wife's beauty; Waldemar, triumphant in his entrée to the inner sanctum of the powerful.

The flutter caused by her arrival stirred Magda with elation.

Even the look of admiration from Waldemar pleased her ego. For the first time, she accepted his compliments as genuine tribute. It still amazed her that she, whom she had always considered rather dull and provincial, would be looked upon as glamorous. She was inclined to laugh at herself for being so easily flattered. But nonetheless she enjoyed it, especially the gleam she saw in Mr. Dzu's eyes as she drew near the balcony. If his reputation were true, he was a connoisseur of beautiful women.

From his very private and well-protected balcony, Mr. Dzu saw Magda and her party enter. His eyes devoured her movements around the ballroom, vicariously enjoying her open delight. He must remember to congratulate the designer; he had outdone himself this year. He was flattered by her decision to wear a Chinese-style gown, certain it had been chosen with him in mind. He wondered if the dragon was meant to be himself consuming her. That was a tantalizing notion, but, at the same time, he had long since learned that those who tried to please him usually had ulterior motives. Dzu shrugged his shoulders. He had her dossier, knew all about her that was to be known. The outcome would depend on her.

He said a few words to his chief aide. Soon Magda and her party were being escorted up to Mr. Dzu's table. She caught his eye from below and smiled at him with unrestrained pleasure as he bowed his head in greeting. She knew it was no light thing to be summoned to Mr. Dzu's table.

Heads turned and watched her progress to the balcony. There was a rustle of interest and gossip as to whether she was Mr. Dzu's new favorite.

"She is married to the tall blond one," someone said.

"What difference does that make?" said another. "He could not be the first man to close his eyes when a fortune is to be made," he added enviously.

Every conceivable precaution had been taken to guard Mr. Dzu's person. A balcony was built on the narrow side of the hall, at the corner of which Mr. Dzu's table was set up. Thus, he was protected by two walls. No one could sneak up behind him or on one side of him. His complete privacy was assured since no other tables were placed on the open side of the balcony. A hand-picked phalanx of armed men stood on guard at each possible point of entry, protecting Dzu, and in addition, guards were stationed for the safety of the powerful Chinese who occupied the rest of the balcony. They were invited each year for the occasion: ex-Mandarins who had managed to escape the revolutionary upheavals inland and found refuge in fortified homes in Shanghai. Rarely did they emerge from their retreats or condescend to mix with the white community. On special occasions like this, they sat apart, and watched, with wry disdain, the ill-smelling barbarians they despised, the men and women who exploited their country. Every one of the Chinese belonged to some secret society and nursed long, involved plans for exterminating the hated foreigners.

The entire row of tables directly under the balcony was occupied by other guards dressed as guests. But there all similarity ended. Their bodies were tensed to spring up on a moment's notice. They held guns hidden below the tables, with hammers cocked, as well as knives ready for throwing. Similar men were placed elsewhere in the room at strategic points, alert for any attack.

Dzu Bing Lok's security was so tight, and his person so guarded, it would have been a foolhardy assassin who tried to break through. Dzu's men were known to shoot first on the slightest provocation. They were carefully selected from his private army of some fifty thousand soldiers, reputed to be the best trained and armed brigands in China.

The von Zollers passed through the cordon of guards who scrutinized them carefully as they climbed the few stairs to the balcony. They were greeted by Dzu's chief aide and led to Mr. Dzu's table, where several other guards stood at attention, hands on their guns.

One of Dzu's idiosyncrasies was that he never wore European clothes. For this occasion, he had dressed in a black-silk gown, with a brocaded vest fastened in front with black pearl studs. He was quite oblivious to the armed men all around him as he greeted Magda and her party with a warm and courteous welcome. Immediately chairs were provided by his aides, and an array of food and drink was presented.

Magda was not unaware of the singular honor done her, nor was she immune to the implicit flattery behind it.

"You bring radiance to my table, O Princess," Dzu said in Chinese.

"You do too much honor to my humble self."

"Humility is a pearl of virtue, but I think that pearls are not your jewels," he responded. "No, I would like to deck you in jewels of splendor: the emerald, the ruby, the sapphire, the black opal with green-and-red fire, and jade of true color. Diamonds, of course, hard, indestructible and brilliant, to take second place to your own brilliance. Would you like this?"

"What woman would not and still be a woman? But this one must remain a jewel of less value in another setting."

"Do you then hold your marriage vows sacred? I

have heard otherwise. I have heard of one who did give you a sapphire of little value."

"You know much of my unimportant self. I am at a disadvantage." Magda felt the blood flow to her face, but to take offense against a man who evidently had had her thoroughly investigated would be useless, she knew.

"I take great interest in you. I understand you have made several trips to Hong Kong recently."

Does he know about my meeting Archie? Magda wondered, feeling ashamed and embarrassed at having her privacy invaded. She hoped that none of her discomfort was visible to the discerning eyes across from her. To show any weakness before him was defeat.

At that moment, Mr. Dzu noticed that Max and Waldemar were sitting awkwardly, ignorant of what was being said, pretending interest in the scene below.

"I must beg your pardon, gentlemen. I have been so carried away by the exquisiteness of Frau von Zoller, which can only be accomplished when East and West meet in perfection. If I may, I shall keep her here with me, but, in the meantime, permit me to provide some entertainment for you."

At his signal, Dzu's secretary brought two lovely Chinese ladies to the table and invited the men to dance.

"Are you upset by my plain speaking, Goddess of Grace?" Mr. Dzu resumed the conversation where it had been interrupted.

"Your words of poetry and praise overwhelm me into speechlessness. I would be pleased if you would call this insignificant one by her given name—Magda."

"Magda!" he repeated after her, feeling the sound of it. "It is a strange name, hard on the tongue, without description or flavor. Should we get better acquainted, I shall find a more fitting name for you."

"I fear it is unlikely that our paths will cross again, for truly I must admit to you—who have already shown me much honor—that my one desire at this time is to leave China. Do I offend you by my straight talk?"

"It seems we both indulge in it. No, I find it refreshing. Is it with this man who awaits you in Hong Kong that you wish to leave this country?"

"It is to escape the threats of one who would hurt me

247

and my husband. My life has little significance, but what there is, I would keep intact."

"If you wish to tell me more, I will listen."

"I have heard it said that one must not speak of business, or such matters, at your ball."

"I make the rules, and I can break them."

"My affairs are of too little importance to wear down the ears of such an important man as yourself. I spoke only to tell you why my efforts are directed toward leaving China."

"Do you not feel Chinese, then? I regret that."

"As I told you on another occasion, I was raised otherwise. In the last two years only have I felt a unity with my mother's people. Lately, the cause of China has touched me deeply."

"If China and Britain were to come to war, to which side would you give allegiance? I am most interested. I have never thought there was a choice; for me, there is but one."

"Mr. Dzu, if only you knew how much I have at times craved the simplicity of one direction," Magda said with unexpected passion. "How simple life would be to know there was but one path—and to follow it."

"I have been told that you have hidden in shame all signs of your Chinese heritage, and that you pass as white."

"That you have heard of me at all surprises me. I am not one who moves much in either society. I wonder at your interest."

"Do you not look in a mirror and see why a man's eyes follow you? Surely you must be the most modest of all women."

"I have offended you. This I did not wish to do. I will be bold and say to you that I have come to a kinship with you and would prefer that you thought kindly of me. Or do I doubly offend you by being overbold?"

"You speak not as a modest Chinese lady, but more as I do. I prefer candid words to subterfuge—though I rarely get them, especially from a woman. Usually, I desire a woman, rather than delight in her companionship. With you it is both." He smiled at her knowingly, then continued. "Now, how may I take away your fears? If you wish to remain in Shanghai, I offer you my protection. You would find it adequate, even against this man, your husband's cousin, who attempts to use you both for his own gain."

He smiled at her astonishment. "I know much, and will know much more."

"Mr. Dzu, I came here only at your invitation. Never did I think to presume to burden you with my misfortunes. Do you believe this?"

He nodded. "Else I would not listen. I am weary of those who come to me only for favors."

"Then let me return to our earlier conversation about loyalties for a moment. Certain knowledge has come to me, and I would like to use it for the sake of Great Britain. It would, at the same time, ensure the safety of my husband and myself."

"You have great love, then, for this country of your father's?"

"Not love. I was raised by my father to consider myself completely of his country. My father loved me greatly, even to the point of sacrificing his life so that I might be financially secure. I owe this to his memory."

"I admire your respect for him. And China? Did your Western education teach you to consider it inferior?"

"You ask me questions I find difficult to answer, because I have never fully thought them out for myself. But with you, I must be honest. Never have I said to myself that I am half one thing and half the other and must choose to love and respect only one. But, my father taught me to make a choice and stick with it—or be lost in a hole from which neither side would reach out to save me. He told me I was in a precarious position in the world, and he said, 'White is better.' So I believed him and continued to believe that my father's people were all brave, all righteous, all just." She paused, lost in deep thought.

"You think that China is corrupt and intolerant?"

Magda smiled a little sadly. "I have found the qualities you mention as much a weakness of the country of my choice. It seems that all nations suffer from these frailties as well as stupidity."

"And will you continue to be all Western and no part Chinese?"

"What can I be? My appearance has made the decision. I am weary of having to make a choice."

"Wherein lies your trouble, and how do you require my assistance, were I to offer it?" Dzu asked, abruptly coming to the point.

"You have great resources for information gathering," Magda answered bluntly. "I need to have indisputable proof that the man of whom we speak is Chief of German Intelligence in Shanghai; that he is sowing whatever discord he can to make the British situation more difficult; and that he is infiltrating the British hierarchy in Shanghai with harmful intentions. Above all, I need to prove that he is receiving information from them and is using them without their knowledge."

"Tell me, Magda, why should I help you with this? Germany is no enemy of ours and I do not dearly love this England who has in the past defiled us and used our country for its own gain."

"Because, Mr. Dzu, in weakening England, you aid Japan. That is the monster who intends to devour us. What China must begin to do is to treat every suspected ally of Japan as a deadly enemy of China and make their enemies our friends," she replied vehemently, noting a gleam in Dzu's eye. "I think you're testing me," she continued, reproaching him. "I need not tell you things of which you are far more cognizant than I." He smiled and did not answer.

"Above all else, I *hate* Germany," she finished explosively, her face blazing with passion. "Whether my mission assisted me or not, I would do everything in my power to help destroy her."

Mr. Dzu looked at her approvingly. She was stimulating company. He could tell that she was attracted to him, as he was to her. It was too bad that she was otherwise involved. He struggled, and then made a firm decision.

"Have you had assistance up to now?" he asked her.

"What I had must come to an end."

"Will you tell me who aided you?"

Magda shook her head. "My husband and I are in great danger. I wish not to mention any names."

Dzu Bing Lok produced a card, wrote something on it, and handed it to her.

"You read Chinese?"

250

She nodded.

"Should you find yourself in any kind of trouble, or even the hint of it, call this number—it is good even in Hong Kong—and say these words. Assistance will be forthcoming immediately. This is my gift to you. Don't use it rashly, but only when you sense the need."

"It gives me great relief to have your protection."

"I would have that protection go deeper and further, but, in the meantime, guard this well and see that it does not fall into hands other than your own. Best destroy it and memorize the words and number. This man, your husband's cousin, sounds as though he has qualities I could use in some of my business transactions."

"That is very likely," Magda said calmly. Evidently Mr. Dzu was not finished testing her. "But I believe you would be hard put to place a price on his loyalty, or, for that matter, his presumption that he could replace you. He is not a fool and, yet, he is a great fool."

"Should I then shiver with fear?" They both laughed at his remark. "I fear I have kept you from the party too long. I see there are many looking this way, waiting for me to release you to their attention. Please permit my secretary to introduce you and your party to some of your compatriots. About the other, you will hear from me."

They stood and bowed to each other as friends. Her eyes showed him her deep thanks for which there were no words.

She took his promise as a vow of assistance. Mr. Dzu did not make such offers lightly, and Magda was content.

CHAPTER EIGHTEEN

◄◄◄◄◄◄◄◄◄◄◄◄◄◄◄◄◄◄◄◄◄

On August 24th, the world was shocked to read in the newspaper that Germany, arch enemy and blatant critic of Communism, had signed a nonaggression pact with Russia. Slowly and inexorably, Germany's vast plan of conquest was unfolding. This latest move meant grave trouble for those European countries not already dominated by Germany and Russia, two giants who seemed determined to divide the continent between them.

Waldemar walked around with ill-concealed elation. He was, in fact, so confident of his power over Max and Magda that he made no attempt to disguise his contempt for the Allies and sneered openly at the Munich Pact. He was in high spirits these days.

Magda had an uneasy feeling that Waldemar had changed courses and that she and Max were now of little consequence to him. But, rather than easing the tension within her, this indifference to them increased her suspicions of imminent danger.

Max also had changed. He had turned a deaf ear to Waldemar's insults some time ago and had more color in his face lately, as though he were slowly recovering from an illness. Magda noticed the difference in him and wondered at its source.

Except for occasional taunts from Waldemar, the cousins rarely spoke; then, only when Waldemar wanted something. The most recent occasion was when he demanded that Max set up a banquet for several people he had met at Mr. Dzu's ball. That also worried Magda. Waldemar brought up Mr. Dzu's name too frequently to please her.

Perhaps Mr. Dzu had already changed his mind, had decided that, of the two, Waldemar could be of more use to him. He was not accustomed to being rebuffed and she had let him know that she was not interested in his thinly-disguised invitation. Her doubts gnawed at her, but in spite of Dzu's prolonged silence, she forced herself to believe he would keep his promise.

Max was the real problem on her mind. He was adamant about not leaving. Magda was certain that she would have no difficulty getting away—but there was no escape for her unless Max was first freed from Waldemar's domination.

Shanghai itself was a city gone mad. The powerful radicals who ruled the local Communist Party had recently instituted a ruthless special department which enforced discipline and carried out the terrorist policies of the High Command.

Chiang Kai-shek moved his capital to Chungking after he failed to defend Shanghai. To Magda, reading the Chinese newspapers, it appeared that every section of China was at war—as much with internal disorder as rebellion against the invading Japanese.

Every day that passed brought Magda closer to the conclusion that she could not wait much longer before taking action. Fortunately, money was no problem. Thanks to the gun-smuggling operation, she was a wealthy woman, and she had invested her money wisely and successfully in the United States. She also had several large accounts in London banks and a secret numbered account in Switzerland.

Magda thought wryly that if her personal life had been chaotic, at least her business acumen was sound—she had correctly gauged the financial situation. For the last two years, business in Shanghai had been slipping badly: most of the cotton factories had been destroyed in the Japanese invasion and, of the four hundred or more silk and weaving factories, at least three hundred had been burned. There was terrible unemployment, and thousands of persons fled inland, returning to small family farms.

Foreigners had been leaving Shanghai at a steady pace, too, though it was doubtful whether they'd be any better off at home with a world-wide depression facing them. Political unrest was at a peak, but in Shanghai and Hong Kong night life was wilder than ever, as the people threw themselves desperately into fleeting escape in a world which threatened to explode at any moment.

Daily, Magda waited for word from Mr. Dzu. None came. She stayed home frequently these days, hoping she would discover something crucial to lift her failing spirits, but all she heard were the same discussions Waldemar had with his subordinates and with Nigel Lewisholm. He came to the apartment one day, a big red-faced man with blunt good humor. He shook hands with her, commiserating as though they shared a secret.

"Damned fine fellow, your cousin. Damned fine man. Wish there were more like him. You tell your husband not to worry. I'm pulling some strings for all of you."

Waldemar led him away before he said any more. That

was the closest Magda ever came to a picture of Waldemar's activities, and it only left her puzzled.

She considered other solutions, but it all came back to Mr. Dzu. He was her sole possible source of aid. She had always known that William eventually would have to withdraw his help. He had to account to his society, and they were primarily interested in Japan. For the first time in her life, William was reluctant to talk to her. She felt his attitudes were altered, and not in her favor. One day, he admitted to her that, though he abhorred the Communists' actions, they were at least fighting the Japanese more successfully than the Nationalists under Chiang. He hated their reliance on Russia, but Chiang also received aid from Russia. William owed allegiance to neither party but to the expulsion of Japan from China's borders. Having said this much, he closed his mouth, as though he had overstepped due caution.

All that remained were the two servants in Magda's home; and they were there more for her protection than for actual domestic service.

As August drew to a close, Waldemar grew tense, but his eyes were bright with expectation. He even stopped taunting Max. But Max did not react to the change in his cousin. He remained completely aloof from Waldemar and remote from Magda, except for an occasional word to her in the privacy of their bedroom. She could find no conceivable reason for this and wondered if he were losing his mind.

Magda sat one evening, utterly dejected, feeling completely alone in the world. All that she and Max shared was the space enclosed by the four walls. She picked up a book but did not open it, as thoughts ran, unbidden, through her mind.

Dzu had no intention of doing anything; he had simply toyed with her. What on earth had made her take a few words, lightly said, so seriously. And Chapin Desmond must have lost interest, or perhaps he could do nothing—what was one spy, more or less, to them? Even if proof were found, what made her think that Waldemar would be recalled? What on earth had persuaded her to believe in their help? Magda tried to dismiss Max's problems from her mind, but then the memory of Archie only stung her more deeply. He had shown so clearly that he put his marriage ahead of their love— Oh, what was happening to her? Was she sacrificing her pride and dignity in a vain cause? She had to put both of them completely out of her mind.

She was so lost in her dejection that Max called her name three times before she heard him.

He spoke very softly again. "Magda!"

"Yes, Max. What is it?"

He put his finger to his lips.

"Softly," he whispered. "He hears everything."

At that moment, the telephone rang and they heard Waldemar answer it. His cocky voice came through to them crisply, harshly.

"I'll be right over, old boy. You have so many accidents with your animals, you should have a resident vet. Just joking, old man. You know I'd never let a horse suffer unnecessarily. Send a car over right away."

A few minutes later, they heard the door slam and both of them drew relaxed breaths.

"Now tell me, what is all the secrecy about?"

Max's eyes had an almost feverish brightness to them as he answered. "I am going to ask you to leave Shanghai, to find a way to leave so that Waldemar does not try to stop you. It is difficult for me to make any request of you—I have caused you so much grief through my foolishness."

"Oh, Max. Don't go on so," Magda said, trying to keep the irritation out of her voice. "The only thing you're guilty of is being a German."

"You mean a German Jew."

"You're no more responsible for that than I am for being a Eurasian. Well. I finally said that horrible word. Didn't hurt a bit."

"Magda, I want to talk about something else, something besides self-pity."

"Max, my dear. I didn't mean it that way. I wish I could help, but you keep turning down all my suggestions. I can't understand it. Is it your pride that won't let you take aid or money from me? Money can buy almost everything, including false passports."

"No, Magda. You can do much for me, but not that way. It's too late for me, but not for you. Go to Hong

Kong and don't come back. On no account return. Don't let any thought of me jeopardize your safety. Don't underestimate Waldemar. He is with the Gestapo—a Nazi not only because he desires personal gain and future power, but because he likes terrorizing the enemies of the Third Reich. He enjoys the blood of others." Max came over and put his hands on her shoulders. "Believe me, Magda, don't take him lightly."

"You don't have to explain Waldemar to me, Max. Don't forget, he's been here almost a year."

"Listen to me, Magda. He has some plan for which he intends to use me. I suspect what it is. But until I know for sure, I cannot act. Whatever it is he plans, I shall bear the brunt of it, and if you're still here, you will be forced to share it. It will not be the first time I have been his scapegoat, all neatly tethered for the kill—a real kill, like the time he murdered a man who sought repayment from him on a large loan."

"So that is what you've never told me."

"I couldn't stand to show myself to you as such a fool," he said simply. "But somehow it doesn't seem so important any more. I shall tell you the whole story. Waldemar asked me to help him cover up the crime, but he told me a different story—that he was helping a wife to escape from her brutal husband, that this man discovered them and threatened them with a gun and, in the fight that followed, the man was killed. Oh, yes! Certainly, I helped him. I was the perfect patsy. You must remember that I was raised to see him as the epitome of German courage and manhood. I idolized him in a way I find difficult to believe now."

"Is this the Mr. Schuman he frequently refers to?"

Max nodded. "It amuses him that I should be accused of his crime. Somehow, he managed to frame me for the murder. When it finally occurred to me that I, who was innocent of everything but helping him, was being implicated, he apologized and said that the least he could do was help me out. But what he did was to collect all the evidence of my involvement in covering up the crime —evidence which he now holds over me."

"It sounds incredible that he could have known then that it would ever be of any use to him."

"Waldemar always prepares to use people. I look back

256

now and realize—I'm not the only one. He has a genius for manipulating men, women, even children. He has files on everyone. Sometimes he doesn't use the information for years. But when he does, his victims are as helpless as I am. He has collected all kinds of proof, and, even if it were only his word against mine, whose word would be taken? When he persuaded me to leave Germany without first registering as a Jew, he made it seem as though I were running away from guilt. He said he was covering up my Jewish blood—my God, I thought he was so noble—even his making me take money from the business—If Mr. Chen wanted to, he could have me arrested for embezzlement. He must know how much I have been taking—God, how I hate misusing his trust. There isn't anything Waldemar overlooks as evidence against me."

"All these years you never realized what he was doing? But you're not a fool, Max. How could you permit yourself to be deceived like this? I can't understand such—such—"

"Didn't you make excuses for your father?" Max said sharply and then, seeing Magda wince, he apologized. "I'm sorry. I had no right. It is just that when you love someone, you find reasons to trust them. Waldemar was the hero of my dreams—it is hard to believe that now. But, Magda, this time I believe I know what he is planning, and I will defeat him." His voice rose, his face was flushed, and his eyes had a fanatical gleam.

"Under all the layers of the person I thought I was, I have found that a true man exists—one I can respect. It has taken a long time. At last I am a man ready to act, but first you must go, so that the way is clear. Don't believe that Waldemar is all bluff; it's only partly true. For underneath that, he will do all he threatens. He'll do to you what he's done to me. Don't think there is anything in your life he cannot uncover and rearrange to make it sound despicable. I know you are brave and clever and proud but in this you can't stand in his way."

He paused to draw a deep breath and then continued quietly, "I repeat—I can only act if you leave Shanghai. Your presence here hinders me. Please—go away and never come back, hide from him."

"Come with me, Max. We'll escape him together."

257

He ignored her words as if she had not spoken. "Ask for British aid; they may help you. Renounce your German citizenship. Denounce me. Say that you married me under false representation. It doesn't matter to me. The only thing I care about is your safety. Make any excuse you can and leave without his suspecting you will not return. This is absolutely essential. Whatever you hear, don't come back. Don't wait for me. Go immediately. I know that war will come soon. I'll stake my life on it. By then, it will be too late for you—you'll already be an enemy alien to Britain." Max spoke passionately, with an intensity and spirit he had been without for so long. Suddenly, he stopped pacing up and down the room and he knelt by her chair, taking her hand in his.

"Remember only one thing about me—that I've always loved you, always wanted you to be happy. I love you this moment more than I can say. I never knew I could love so dearly that another's life would mean so much more to me than my own."

"Oh, Max! My dear Max—" was all she could sigh as she looked at him with sympathy and understanding—more than she'd ever felt for him.

"Find happiness for yourself. It's the only thing I want. Even if Archie had returned, I would have said to him: take her, she was always yours."

Magda stiffened and removed her hand from his. "How did you know about Archie? I never mentioned his name, and I'm sure Tasha never did."

"Waldemar told me," Max said simply, rising to his feet. He walked away softly. "He has read everything in your box with the trick opening. He told me he found the letters quite ludicrous."

A deep indignation erupted within Magda—to such a devastating degree that she felt weak. For the first time she understood the compulsion to kill someone and knew herself capable of doing so, cold-bloodedly and with premeditation.

"I'm sorry I told you," Max said, seeing the expression on her face. "He told me only to make me jealous, to make me hate you; but instead, it pleased me to know that once you had been so happy. I only wished that it could have been with me. I felt jealousy only because he gave you what I never could."

The passion had left his face. Now he spoke quietly and deliberately. "Go and forget this sad, bitter year. Find a new country. Please go and never return—and make it soon, for the time is growing short. Promise me this, Magda, if you ever felt any love for me. I have a job to do, and I can only do it when I know you will be safe from the consequences of my actions. Trust me, my dearest."

Magda's attitude toward Waldemar became more aggressive. She answered him sullenly and defiantly, and one evening she culminated her campaign at the dinner table by brazenly taunting him for being a gullible oaf.

"You think you know so much about me and my assets," she scoffed and then stopped dead, as though she had said too much.

"So! You think you fooled me. That is not easily done, believe me. I know you have considerable money in Hong Kong, but you will transfer that to me if you care for your own safety and your husband's. I shall arrange to send someone with you to Hong Kong to prevent your double-crossing me. Believe Max when he says I can and will do what I say."

Magda was overjoyed—her plan was working. "You don't frighten me, you're like the air in a balloon!"

Waldemar leaned back in his chair and studied her. "There are times I am inclined to obey my instincts and pack you off to Germany. Do not test my patience too far. You will bring me every dollar you have, and this time I'll have your accounts thoroughly checked. You can take my word that I am capable of doing just that."

"I don't care what you do," Magda flared. "I won't go if you send someone with me!"

"Idiot! Don't you understand what I can do to you?"

"And what exactly is that? Push me too far and I'll ask for Chinese citizenship. I was born here and I have friends."

"Max really picked a prize when he married you. All right, on this item I will agree. No one will follow you. Today is the twenty-ninth. You will take the plane tomorrow. I will be generous and give you the full day to settle your affairs. The reservations for your return will be for the following day. If, for any reason, you are not on that flight, I shall have you arrested by the German authorities for grand theft and have you sent here for trial. There will be no difficulty about the verdict. Don't think you can out-fox me with all that nonsense about international law. There was never a law made which could not be circumvented, if one has friends in the right places. I'm an expert in these matters." He laughed humorlessly at her consternation. "I've had this planned for a long time!"

As usual, Waldemar had ignored Max as if he were not even there. When the meal was over, Max went to his room, and Magda followed him soon after.

"You were magnificent!" he whispered. "You've done exactly the right thing." He paused. "But you must not believe anything he says. Until you leave, he will watch you like a hawk. We can do nothing from here. But from my office I shall make other reservations for you in Hong Kong. If you have the faintest suspicion of any danger whatever, go into hiding in the other hotel. I do not know Hong Kong, but I will ask Mr. Chen, my compradore, about it—he is very trustworthy." He looked at Magda anxiously. "You don't think this is unwise?"

She shook her head, feeling sorry that she had kept so many secrets from him. She looked over at him, seeing the childlike glee in his face because he was putting something over on Waldemar, rejoicing to be a man again, for Magda.

Impulsively, she threw her arms around him and kissed him unrestrainedly.

"*Ach! Mein Magda! Mein Herz, mein lieb Herz. Mein Liebchen.*" He lapsed unconsciously into German as he murmured the words of love he had held back for so long. His eyes were awash with unashamed tears as he embraced her tenderly.

CHAPTER NINETEEN

MAX SAID GOODBYE to Magda at the apartment, knowing it was for the last time. His arms tightened around her, and he kissed her passionately, as if to make up for all the lost months in this one moment. She responded to the heat of his emotion and then, for a few minutes, they simply clung together, trying to say with their eyes what was in their hearts.

Waldemar witnessed the warm embrace and was satisfied at least on one point: Magda would not permit anything drastic to happen to Max if she could prevent it. Nevertheless, it was just as well he had taken the precautions he had to ensure her return.

He had always doubted his control over this strong-willed woman—at times she appeared compliant; at others she damned him with those strange eyes which stared right through him and made him wonder what she was thinking. She was truly an enigma. Her Chinese heritage gave her an air of mystery that even Waldemar could not penetrate.

As he riveted his gaze on the scene in front of him, his lips tightened. He felt a gnawing uneasiness in his stomach, which he refused to admit was jealousy. Ridiculous! He had no need to envy anyone.

Magda insisted on going to the airport alone. She took a cursory look at the other passengers. Most of them were Chinese. A couple of elderly priests sat patiently reading the Bible next to a Portuguese couple and a heavy-set man with cropped, pale hair who was completely immersed in some technical magazines.

They all found their seats. Fortunately, the plane was not crowded and Magda managed to sit by herself. She noticed that the blond man had taken a seat on the opposite side, a couple of rows behind. She felt relieved—at least she would not have to worry about being pestered with conversation.

The take-off was smooth. She unfastened her seat-belt and relaxed. Her mind went back to Max as she had seen him last, his eyes glowing with sacrificial fervor as he kissed her one more time. Magda had no alternative but to go.

"Poor Max! I wish I had given him more of myself," she thought with remorse. Deep inside she wept for their lost life together. It was not the same as regret. She could not regret leaving him. It was more a requiem for someone who was gone from her whole existence.

There was a sudden period of turbulence and the plane lurched and went into a deep dive. She was jolted forward, slipping to the floor before the plane could right itself. Magda picked herself up and began to straighten her twisted dress. In doing so, she caught sight of the man with the cropped hair. He was staring at her intently. She would have thought nothing of it if he hadn't immediately, on catching her eye, buried himself in his magazine. She felt a spark of amusement at catching him in the act—but at that moment she realized who he was—Waldemar's man!

What a fool she'd been not to have noticed sooner. Even Max had warned her to be constantly on her guard.

Magda figured he'd been given careful instructions. First, he'd follow her to the bank to be sure she withdrew the money. Then he'd see that she returned to the hotel Waldemar had chosen and keep guard on her until she left the following morning for Shanghai. She was certain that was what he'd been told, and that any deviation from it would be suspect.

Suddenly a sickening fear overwhelmed her—what if Desmond wasn't able to help her. She'd heard nothing from him. She had no new information to give him, either.

Her mouth went dry and she could not swallow. Magda could not still the dread which swelled and choked her. She felt once more the helpless terror of her childhood. Papa! she'd called then from the very depths of her soul. But there had been no answer then, and there was none now.

She was all alone. No one in Hong Kong even knew

she was coming. Max never expected to hear from her again, and she hadn't been able to contact anyone from the moment Waldemar had arranged her flight.

She tried to calm the unnatural thumping of her heartbeat by taking deep breaths. But she knew she was shaking uncontrollably. She tried to dispel the fear which filled her by using logic—that it was only the paranoia of knowing that she was being followed, that eyes were prying into everything she did. She shuddered. Logic had nothing to do with a rapid pulse and a cold sweat on her forehead—or with a terrifying sense of impending disaster.

Mr. Dzu had said to call when she felt trouble coming. He must have known it would happen. She would call the number he had given her. His people were experts; they would know how to protect her. What if he weren't interested anymore. Angrily, she dismissed the possibility. He had to be. His people would hide her. But first, somehow, she had to see Mr. Desmond. He had to give her the safe-conduct pass. She must persuade him. She couldn't remain in hiding forever.

Slowly, her confidence returned. Fear is defeat, she kept reminding herself, as she floundered between choices. Should she go first to the Grand Hotel where Waldemar had booked her? That way it would seem as though she were following his instructions. But, at the very thought of his spy dogging her, a convulsive shiver brought back her horror. No! She couldn't. She had to elude him right away. Who knew what Waldemar might have arranged for her once he thought the money was safely out of the bank?

First she had to get out of the Kai Tak airport in Kowloon, cross over to Hong Kong by ferry, then go directly to the Repulse Bay Hotel where Max had made reservations for her in case she needed them. It was a highly respected luxury hotel, far from the ferry. Nothing untoward could happen there. First, she'd call the number Mr. Dzu had given her, then she'd get in touch with Desmond—No. Maybe she should go directly to the bank. But she would be followed there. Then what? Everything seemed to depend on Desmond's help—she was counting on it, maybe too much. And what if the card from Dzu was only a macabre joke, he was fond of jokes—

"Stop it, Magda MacDougall. What's got into you? What about using your own wits for a change? It's all right to rely on others but no one can do your thinking for you," she scolded herself. All she really had was herself, and she knew it.

She took out her compact and put on a fresh lipstick. In the mirror, she saw the man watching her, and all her new-found courage fled in the face of those cold blue eyes, the stolid sullen glower, the tight mouth. Obedience to orders was all he knew. Magda felt numbing panic.

She wished she could pray. But to which God? Her mother's fat-bellied Buddha? Her father had no use for his strict Calvinist faith. And she had grown up with nothing. To Sister George's God? If only she could. It was strange to think that, of all the people she knew, outside the convent, Archie was the only one who had any genuine faith, which was probably why he felt so strongly about Jennie—he couldn't lightly break his vows.

"I'd always be second, wouldn't I, Archie?" she whispered aloud. "Some sort of behind-the-scene mistress? And you'd always feel guilty, wouldn't you? It's just not good enough."

For once, the thought of Archie brought no solace, only a greater loneliness than she'd ever felt before.

The plane lurched sharply as it dove down to make a perfect landing at Kai Tak airport.

The passengers hurriedly trooped out and proceeded to the office to get their passports stamped. There was a rush to get out quickly and escape the stifling, stale heat of the terminal building.

Some of the passengers tried to shove ahead of each other in the narrow aisle, while others refused to let them through. It was the usual incoming routine. One little Chinese gentleman managed to squirm through, making little mewing sounds of apology as he slid by; everyone let him pass rather than bother to stop him. As he passed by Magda, he slipped an envelope into her hand, which already held her passport and landing pass. He whispered one sibilant word in Chinese—so softly that she almost imagined she heard it. Then he was through the gate and out of sight. Magda casually opened her handbag as if to make sure she had the right papers, moved some papers around, and slipped the envelope in. She desperately hoped that the man who was watching her had not noticed anything. But the little man had been so quick and skillful that she doubted even the person behind her had glimpsed the transfer. She looked into the mirror again, pretending to smooth her hair, and she noticed that the man, whom she had nicknamed "Hans," was at least ten feet away. He was trying hard to shove ahead, but a stout Chinaman in front of him refused to budge. It seemed to give him a great deal of satisfaction to curse Hans luridly in Chinese, smiling all the while.

It brightened the day a bit for Magda as she hurried out to the street, abandoning her luggage. All she had that was valuable and necessary was in her large handbag. Clothes she could always replace.

She rushed into a waiting taxi and directed it to the Star Ferry depot. At that moment, she realized her error. The man would also be taking the ferry to Hong Kong—that was where she'd have to lose him.

When the boat tied up in Hong Kong, Magda disembarked quickly, noting that the German was not far behind her. She entered a taxi and gave the address of the Grand Hotel, where Waldemar had made her reservation. Once inside the lobby, though, she left by a side exit where a line of cabs was waiting. Hurriedly, she got into one, promising to pay the driver extra if he'd hurry to the Repulse Bay Hotel. For the first time she felt almost relaxed, thinking she had succeeded in evading her pursuer. She kept looking back but could not identify anyone in the cars behind her.

The driver pulled up at the hotel. Magda scrambled out, shoved some money at him, and ran up the wide steps leading into the hotel. Inside, she asked the desk clerk for the key to her room and informed him that her luggage would follow. She hurried into a waiting elevator. Then her heart sank. Through the wide, open entrance, she saw Hans running up the stairs three at a time. In the reflection of the glass door, she saw Hans arguing with the reception clerk.

Magda hurried to her room and locked the door behind her. As an afterthought, she braced a chair against the knob. Without even taking off her hat, she sat down on the bed and brought out the envelope. "You wonderful, unbelievable, dependable Mr. Dzu," she murmured. "You came through."

Somewhere in the distance, the elevator banged open and she heard quick footsteps in the corridor. For the moment, however, she was safe in her room. She rarely drank liquor, but for once she wished she had something to calm her nerves. Her hand shook a little as she broke the seal of the unaddressed envelope and found another envelope inside. It was addressed to the Minister of Home Affairs in London. She opened the envelope carefully and looked for the signature. It was, as she had guessed, from Nigel Lewisholm.

Taking a deep breath to calm herself, she started to read rapidly. The first paragraph of the letter was full of news about friends of friends. Magda wondered where it was going to lead, as her eyes moved impatiently down the page. Then the name Waldemar von Zoller seemed to grow large and fill the sheet. She forced herself to go back and reread it slowly until she found the meaningful paragraph.

. . . You remember some time ago I mentioned a good friend of mine by the name of Baron Waldemar Erich von Zoller. He's a German, but one of the old-timers, you know, the decent kind, not like the bunch they have today. You may have heard of him, he used to own and breed that magnificent line of racehorses, the Zorros. Remember when Zorro Historian won the Derby? Well, Waldo (that's what I call him) built up his stables after the war and overextended himself. Then came the Depression and, on top of it all, Hitler and his not-so-merry men. Well, old Waldo couldn't swallow them, and he left the country. He was forced to give up the estates his family had owned for generations, all on a technicality. Some big-wig in the Third Reich has it now. Waldo is in Shanghai with the last of the fortune he managed to save. He's helping out his cousin, a decent enough chap named Max. Max is half-Jewish and you know how they're being hounded. Waldo is fond of his cousin, though I gather he's a bit of a helpless fellow, no fight in him. Waldo has some sort of consular job and has managed to keep Max's name off the listing of Jews. (They all have to register these days. Poor devils. Thank God, it could never happen in England!)

, Now, this is the reason I'm writing about him, old man. I want your help in getting him into England. At present he is spending his time helping the Jewish refugees in Shanghai. He has contacts all over Europe and is doing a magnificent job. His cousin, Max, is supposed to be helping him with what he's doing. Oh, but that's beside the point. I'm behind him all the way. He can't stand this Nazi bunch and wants to take refuge in England in case of war. Well-educated sort of fellow, speaks English perfectly, lots of class, no nonsense about him. He'd fit in anywhere. He thinks he could be useful to us and knows quite a lot about the German hierarchy.

He is positive that war is inevitable, and, though he admits he does not want to fight his own people, the thought of having to work under Hitler and his regime is abhorrent to him. I promised I'd do what I could. He's an all right chap and I'll back him to the hilt. An absolute master with the horses. You should see them when they're hurt and rearing quite uncontrollably. All he has to do is put his hands on their necks and gentle them a little, and I'll be damned if they don't quiet and let the vet do his job. I'd appreciate your help no end, old chap.

Magda clasped the letter to her breast in elation. Thank you, Mr. Dzu, brilliant Mr. Dzu. You have literally saved my life. This is it. This will do it. She read on:

By the way, do you remember last summer at—

There was a knock on the door. Magda felt as though the bottom of her stomach had dropped out—she was so frightened she could hardly breathe. She was certain it was Hans. It had to be he. She froze for a long moment; it seemed as if hours had passed before she thought lucidly again. The letter, where could she hide it? It was her passport—it would also be her death warrant if Waldemar knew—

There was another knock, even louder. Under the mattress? In the desk?

Once again there was a knock and a voice called out:

"Magda! Are you there? Open the door."

"Archie!" she gulped and ran to remove the chair and unlock the door. The next moment she was in his arms.

Archie looked at the chair turned over on the floor and steadied her as they walked into the room. He held her tightly as she clung to him, trembling.

"Hush, hush! My darling, hush! It's all right. What's going on? You're shaking like a leaf." He kissed her and stroked her head as if she were a child, until she quieted down. "Now what's all this about? I received a phone call from your husband that you might be in danger—"

"Is anything the matter?" asked a voice from the doorway.

They both turned around and Magda felt fear grip her again when she saw the man from the plane, his face set in ill-disguised anger.

"No," Magda said, coolly, in control of herself. "There is nothing the matter. Why should you think there is and what concern is it of yours?"

"I thought I heard a scream and I came to see if I could help."

"Very thoughtful of you, but you see you were in error. Please leave us and shut the door behind you."

"No. Your husband instructed me to watch over you and to see that you were all right."

"There is no need for any help. Everything is fine. Now get on your way," Archie said, taking a step forward.

"Not so fast. Who are you?" The man put his hand in his pocket. "Something's wrong here. No one told me you were being met, or staying at this hotel. My instructions were—"

"To get out," Archie said in a harsh voice.

The man started to ease his hand out of his pocket but Archie leaped forward, flung himself at him with a clenched fist and struck him on the chin with his full weight. It caught the man completely off guard, and he fell back hard, striking his head on the open door. He lay unconscious on the floor, his right hand outstretched and cupping a set of brass knuckles.

Magda shuddered.

"What the bloody hell is happening here? What does this have to do with you?"

"This is the Nazi way, Archie. This is the way of Max's cousin. He's been threatening me, and that's the end result." She pointed to the ugly weapon and sighed shakily.

"Hey, now! You're not going to go hysterical on me, are you?" Archie asked anxiously and took her in his arms to calm her. Her pulse steadied and she drew away, smiling a little tremulously.

"I never knew you could move so fast," she murmured, looking up at him with new respect. "I learn something new about you all the time."

"I've been wanting to hit someone hard for three long years. Mostly myself," Archie answered ruefully, flexing his swelling fist. "Now, what's all this about?"

"How did you know to come here and why was Max calling you?"

"Let's get this brute out of here first." Archie took hold of the prone man's shoulders and Magda grasped his feet.

The corridor was empty as they dragged him to a room with an open door, and left him lying on the floor. Archie removed the brass knuckles, while, to his astonishment, he saw Magda go through the man's pockets and examine the contents. He opened his mouth to say something, but Magda cried out triumphantly, "Just as I thought. Heinrich Bergmann, German Consulate, Shanghai; and here's a note from the German consul here: 'To whom it may concern: We would appreciate any service you can render to the bearer in the performance of his duty, signed, Wilhelm Messinger, Consul General, Hong Kong.' You see, that's how he got into the hotel. I saw him showing the desk clerk a paper. You really came in the nick of time, my darling. But tell me now how you knew to come here."

"All I know is that your husband called me long distance. He sounded frantic, said he'd been trying for hours to get me but the lines between here and Shanghai were jammed. Said he'd found out that you were being followed on the plane, some strange story about a Mr. Chen from his office who'd been called by one of your servants from the airport to say that his mistress was in real danger—that the man following you was known to be brutal. Couldn't really make too much out of it. Your husband was so distraught that it was pretty garbled, but I got the message that the threat to you was real. It all sounded crazy, but when he said, 'Don't let her return here. Keep her there by force, if necessary,' I decided it was no time to hang around for an explanation—so I rushed here. Your turn now. What the devil goes on?"

"It's such a long story and there's no time to explain . . . I must go to the bank immediately and see Sir Alfred."

"Curiouser and curiouser, as Alice would say!" But there was no joking in his voice. "And what may I ask, does my godfather have to do with this? I'd think he'd be the last person in the world you'd ever want to see."

"Archie, my dearest darling. Not now. I'll tell you everything, at least as much as I can, on the way. But we must hurry. Please!"

She pulled him to the door and they were halfway down the corridor when she stopped and looked into her bag.

"Oh, my God! The letter!" She ran back to her room, Archie following. The letter was lying on the floor where she had dropped it.

"This could well be my safe-conduct pass out of the mess I'm in. Hurry, Archie, let's go. I don't dare stay here any longer."

In the taxi, Archie waited silently for Magda to start talking. Finally, she said, "Would you mind waiting until after I'm through with Sir Alfred? I don't know how much I'm free to tell you."

"You owe me no explanations after the way I let you down," he said stiffly. "I can understand your lack of trust in me, but why do you have to deal with that bloody bastard after what he did to us? I find it hard to be *civil* to him."

"You know I'd trust you with my life—I wish you *had* my life, for all time. But this is something that not only involves me—please be patient just a little longer."

"I have no choice, have I? But I'll tell you one thing. I'm going in with you."

"No, Archie. You mustn't. This is not your problem."

"I'm making it mine."

"Don't you understand? Your being there will only make it more difficult."

"Magda, stop telling me what to do and what not to do. I'm involved now, whatever it is. If nothing else, I can see he doesn't bully you. We won't discuss it further."

Magda stole an affectionate look at him. She reached out tentatively for his hand. He returned her glance intently, his face sober. As they looked at each other long and steadily, his eyes seemed to penetrate her thoughts. Finally, he smiled at her with great tenderness and pressed her hand reassuringly. There was no more said between them as they rode to the bank.

Together they went to Sir Alfred's office, knocked, and entered.

He blinked in surprise when he saw them and rose slowly, his face stiff with anger at the intrusion.

"Do you have an appointment, Archie?" he asked, his voice icy.

"No, sir, I haven't. I brought Magda here to see you. I know she is in great physical danger, and I want to be assured that she will be given protection."

"Why should that be my concern?"

"I don't know, and I don't want to. What I do know is that she came to Hong Kong without telling her friends, with the express purpose of seeing you. I should think you'd be the last person she'd want to see, but I assure you most solemnly that, should anything happen to Magda, I shall hold you responsible."

Magda listened with rapt wonder.

"How dare you talk to me like that! Does it occur to you that your concern should be for your wife and children and not this woman who has forced her way into your life again by telling you ridiculous stories?"

"What I do and what I do not do is no concern of yours, Sir Bloody Alfred. You interfered with my life for the last time when you sent me away. It has been hell ever since. So, I have no reason to honor you or answer to you. But if you have used your position and authority to torment her, I will not hesitate to take whatever means necessary to make it public."

Sir Alfred turned to Magda in fury. "Well, Magda, I trust you are satisfied with the trouble you've started. You have successfully managed to separate me from my godson, whom I looked upon as my son."

"If separating me from the only woman I will ever love is a mark of your affection—" Archie began hotly.

"How dare you? How *dare* you have the gall to say this when you have a lovely wife like Jennifer? Are you completely shameless?"

The two men glared at each other. Archie's face was dead white, a vein throbbing in his forehead; Sir Alfred was nearly apoplectic. Magda looked on with mixed emotions, but she was grateful for Archie's open declaration of his love.

"You prove my point, Magda von Zoller," Sir Alfred said bitterly. "All your kind—you cause nothing but misery—as though the worst of both races festers in you. And you are doubly dangerous because you entice men with your appearance. You have made a fool of Archie."

Archie approached him with a clenched fist, trying hard to restrain his fury.

"Gentlemen," Magda said firmly. "While you are both discussing me as though I were not here, valuable time is being lost. I have an extremely important document with me. You, Sir Alfred, are my only link with the person to whom I must deliver it without delay. At our last meeting I was asked not to contact him personally—that's the only reason I am here. It's important for England, and it will be enough to get me the safe-conduct pass I need."

"I will use every bit of influence I possess to keep you from being allowed to remain here," said Sir Alfred. He looked at her grimly, leaving no doubt in Magda's mind that he intended to carry out his threat.

"Archie, dear, will you please leave us alone? And thank you for what you said. I'll never forget it."

He smiled wryly. "Today's my day. I've hit one man and let out all the anger I've felt for years. I'll wait outside."

"Don't you have any consideration for Jennie's feelings, her reputation?" Sir Alfred tried to speak calmly, appealing to Archie one last time.

"Magda's life is worth more to me than a few words of gossip," Archie replied vehemently.

"Poppycock! A lot of fiction to engage your sympathies. This is Hong Kong, not the wilds of Borneo."

"I've just struck a man with this." Archie pulled out his swollen and bruised fist. "And the man I struck was wearing these." And he pulled the brass knuckles out of his pocket. "He was ready to attack, but I beat him to the punch."

"Incredible! It sounds like a bad movie. Still, I suppose I must believe you."

Archie gave a mock bow and left the room, closing the door quietly behind him.

"Why don't you leave the boy alone?" Sir Alfred demanded.

"Why you don't leave us both alone would be more to the point. Who gave you the right to judge, gave you the right to talk to me as you do? I listened to you once, hoping that everything would work out. You think you won that round, but you heard Archie. You did a terrible thing, and Archie and I and your precious Jennie suffer for it. It has brought two unwanted children into the world. Jennie could easily have been someone's beloved wife, instead of a suspicious, unhappy woman. And you are responsible," Magda finished with some bitterness. "You and you alone.

"I have a document to deliver. You are the connection," she said, weariness in her voice. "Please make it. And when I see the gentleman I shall ask him to make other arrangements. I never want to see or talk to you again in my life."

Sir Alfred stood stiff, staring out of his office window. Then he turned around, his mouth pursed tightly, his nostrils flaring and white. Without deigning to face her, he dialed a number, gave the requisite information, wrote the answer, and left the slip of paper on the corner of his desk for her to pick up.

Archie was reluctant to leave her alone, but Magda insisted.

"I'm under orders. I'm not permitted to tell you his name or why he's sending a car for me. Please, darling, go back to work now. I can't tell you what it's meant to have you stand up for me. You were so wonderful in there. I've never known what it feels like to be defended like that. Thank you, my dearest."

She went on. "I think the crisis is over, at least for now.

This man I'm seeing will make certain that I'm protected. I'm sorry to be so mysterious, darling, but, believe me, it's necessary."

"God, Magda! If anything happens to you now that we've—Oh, Magda, I hope it's over soon. I don't like to think of your returning to that hotel," he grumbled. "I'll call there later on. If you're not there, leave me some sort of message."

He waited with her at the bank entrance until a limousine drew up. Magda kissed him lingeringly and then she was gone.

Chapin Desmond was waiting in the house on Queen's Road when Magda arrived. Just seeing him gave her a tremendous sense of security, and his warm greeting and concern reinforced her relief.

After the initial courtesies, she told him every detail of what had occurred, omitting only William's name and Mr. Dzu's.

"In the one case, he is a close friend of mine who has jeopardized his own safety to help me, and, in the other," she smiled a little wryly, "I could be in even more danger than from Waldemar. I would tell you if I could."

"Very well, let that go for the time being. This letter is very useful. It is my experience that the German mind is inclined to tortuous paths, but this Waldemar of yours appears to be even more devious than most to design such a far-fetched scheme of infiltration."

"I don't think Waldemar always acts by prearranged plan. Instead he seizes each opportunity to instigate an operation as it opens up. I think I understand the way his mind works. He appreciated Sir Nigel's naiveté, had inside knowledge that war was coming soon, saw where he could expand his personal power to a more important field than China, and used the circumstances to his advantage. But—" she hesitated.

"Yes, Mrs. von Zoller," he encouraged her.

"He is a true megalomaniac—it gives him extraordinary pleasure to manipulate people and to let them know about it. Max is not important to his plans but I think I am. Oh, certainly there is the money; he likes money but that is the least part of it, I think. He enjoys having supreme power over his victims, as it were. Do I sound dramatic,

Mr. Desmond? There are just no limits to Waldemar's self-confidence, and he acts accordingly."

"I'm very much inclined to agree with you. You are very discerning and analytical. You could be more useful to us than you are, if you wished."

"When this is over, I wish only to be left alone."

"Well. What do we do about you, Magda?"

"Give me what I asked for. A safe-conduct pass so that I can remain here in safety even if war breaks out. My husband insisted that I come alone, saying that I would have a better chance for British protection without him."

"He was right. It's one thing to give a former British citizen temporary refuge and quite another to slap the German Consulate in the face."

"I suppose it's futile to hope that I could ever regain my British citizenship."

"I've already contacted London about your position. The safe-conduct card arrived with my superior's recommendation. That usually would be sufficient, but you have a powerful enemy here."

"Sir Alfred."

"I mention no names but you are not to worry. I will not hesitate to use pressure if necessary, but I'd prefer to get the governor's signature diplomatically. By the way, you know, I'm quite serious about your working for us. We have investigated you quite thoroughly."

"You and everyone else. Perhaps I belong in a museum —or on a laboratory slide!"

"Bitterness does not become you. You are conspicuous and that is the price you pay for being so visible. It would be in the national interest if you'd agree."

"Is that an ultimatum?"

"No, indeed. The paper you ask for is forthcoming in any event. But it would make it simpler."

"How much influence does Sir Alfred Wilkie-Hume wield?"

"Considerable. He is usually a pleasant gentleman with a strong sense of justice. Whatever did you do to him to make him turn against you, if I may ask a personal question?"

"You may ask, and I'll tell you, though I'm surprised you don't already know. You said you'd investigated me. Surely you must know that I was once engaged to be

275

married to Archie Monteith, Sir Alfred's godson. Sir Alfred did not look favorably on the union—he detests Eurasians. Well, he broke it up successfully, and has never forgiven me, even though I was the victim."

"Why, the hard-nosed old bastard! Excuse me, Magda. I had not heard that piece of information. Now the pieces fit."

"I don't think the respected baronet would advertise it."

"Forget about it. I can promise you what you want, just give me a couple of days."

"Mr. Desmond, there is no more time. War is coming much sooner than you expect."

"Of course, you don't know what I expect, do you?" he asked softly. "Be patient for a few days; in the meantime, I shall see that you're fully protected. German consul or no German consul, no one can force you out of here without our say-so. This is Hong Kong. You'll be safe enough."

"Waldemar's reach is very long."

"Don't you worry about anything. You may be assured that everything will be looked after. The man who assaulted you is long gone. I made a phone call shortly after you arrived." He smiled at her reassuringly.

"Mr. Desmond, I trust you absolutely but I won't feel safe until I have that precious permit in my hands."

"It's as good as there. All it needs is the governor's signature, and I'll hurry it up. Think about my offer, please, and let me know. Sleep well tonight; there'll be someone on guard."

"I never thought I'd enjoy hearing that," she said gratefully.

CHAPTER TWENTY

‹‹‹‹‹‹‹‹‹‹‹‹‹‹‹‹‹‹‹‹‹‹‹‹

MAGDA SPENT A restless night and in the morning she lay curled up on a couch. Weary after days of tension, and with the soft radio music lulling her, she fell into a deep slumber.

The radio music was suddenly interrupted. A jumble of sound awakened Magda. "GERMANY INVADES POLAND" blared the voice on the radio. "The Third Reich declares that it can no longer tolerate the mistreatment of the German people, nor the denial of their just rights after they have lived in Poland for generations. To answer their pleas, the armies of the Fatherland have launched a drive to liberate them from their Polish oppressors."

It took a few moments for the full impact of the news to penetrate. Magda jumped to her feet.

"It's happened. It's here. The war has begun!"

The radio announcer quoted reports from countries around the world—the free countries, England, France, Australia, Canada, the United States, Sweden, even the small countries with Germany right on their doorsteps, all denounced Germany's actions.

Magda listened to the words, repeated over and over, then turned the dial to a Chinese broadcast station. They were still far more upset about Russia's turnabout in signing a nonaggression pact with Germany. They feared it would curtail her military aid to China, which they desperately needed in their unending war against Japan. Russia had obligingly supplied both Chiang Kai-shek and Mao Tse-tung with weapons. In recent years, Chiang was said to be moving away from Russian influence, all very diplomatically, as he was now receiving aid from the United States.

In the announcer's appraisal of the world situation, he took some satisfaction that Europe was experiencing what had plagued China for so many years.

Magda bathed and dressed. She was too restless to remain in her suite and decided to go to the lobby to hear how the public was reacting.

A pleasant-faced English policeman was waiting for her by the elevator.

"Good morning, Mrs. von Zoller," he greeted her. "I trust you had a good night's rest. I'm assigned here to see that nothing happens to you."

"Thank you, Officer—?"

"Sergeant Detective Mulhaney, mum."

"I'm extraordinarily relieved to have you here. I

thought I'd go down to the lobby. I suppose that's all right?"

"Oh, yes, mum. We don't expect any trouble. Just a precaution. But don't step out of the hotel unless you inform me. I'll take my position by the registry desk, not to embarrass you. I'll be able to keep my eagle eye on you from there." He smiled jovially and Magda responded in kind.

Magda bought a newspaper but was too keyed-up to sit and read. She strolled over to the large glass entrance and stepped out onto the courtyard, a wide platform which was, in a way, an outdoor extension of the foyer. It stretched out about fifteen feet in front of the steps which led down to the street level. From the open doorway, she saw Mulhaney leaning nonchalantly against the counter, chatting with the desk clerk. From his attitude he certainly didn't think there was any chance of imminent danger; nevertheless, she felt safer just knowing he was nearby.

The area was deserted except for the solitary Sikh doorman who stood at the entrance. Magda greeted him politely and took a few steps forward, to enjoy the slight breeze which blew in from the bay. The intense heat of the Hong Kong summer had subsided a little, and the day seemed clear of rain. It was incredible that the dramatic events of yesterday could have occurred in this tranquil hotel, terraced so snugly on the side of the hill with every suite looking down at the calm waters below.

A number of limousines were parked on one side of the road. Most of them were owned by the hotel residents and had liveried chauffeurs sitting at the wheels awaiting their orders for the day. There were also several rickshaws around, and Magda wondered idly at their presence at this luxury hotel—it hardly seemed a profitable place for their hire.

One of the motorcars which had been sitting in the parking area for some time contained three foreigners besides the Chinese chauffeur. One of the men, stocky, with close-cropped blond hair, constantly watched the hotel entrance through a pair of binoculars. Suddenly, he gave a satisfied grunt and pointed up to the courtyard.

He donned a cap and sunglasses and ordered the chauffeur to draw up to the curb next to the hotel steps.

Several of the coolies who had been standing around simultaneously crossed the street. They huddled nearby the car, watching the three men curiously as they got out. The chauffeur honked his horn angrily at the coolies to drive them away from the car—but that only brought more of them over, each one deliberately drawing his rickshaw in front of the automobile.

From her elevated position in the courtyard, Magda, watching the little scene, suddenly straightened in shock. She recognized, in spite of the long-billed cap and the dark sunglasses, the person of Hans. She turned around and walked swiftly back to the hotel entrance where she was relieved to find Mulhaney watching her.

"I don't feel too well. I think I'll go up to my room and rest." Magda hesitated for a moment, wavering, but, in the end she did not tell the policeman about the three men on the street, whom she knew, without any doubt, were waiting for her.

Mulhaney noted her pallor and accompanied her to her room, somewhat concerned.

"P'raps you should have a bite of lunch. Would you like me to get you something?"

"Don't leave the hallway," she cried out, and then regained her poise. "I'm not in the least hungry. I just need to lie down."

"Don't worry, mum, an army couldn't move me from here. Just call out if you want me."

She shut the door and leaned against it in relief. Police protection was not enough. She knew what she had to do. Without further hesitation, she called the number she had memorized some time ago for such an emergency.

A singsong voice answered, "Lum Fat Restaurant."

Magda said the words Mr. Dzu had given her. There was silence and she repeated them slowly and clearly.

"You have wrong number, lady. For big reservation you call this number."

At the second number she was once again asked to wait, and this time a cultured voice answered in classic Mandarin. She gave her name and was recognized immediately.

"Ah, yes. You are at the Repulse Bay Hotel. You have

been under our surveillance since you arrived in Hong Kong. Is there any problem?"

"There are three men outside whom I wish to evade. Can you arrange a hiding place for me for a few days?" she asked in the same Mandarin he had used.

"That is no problem."

"I have an English policeman protecting me now. He must not know."

"That poses a problem, but a small one. I will call you back in five minutes."

Magda picked up the phone at the first ring.

"All is arranged. In exactly one hour, you will tell your policeman that you are too nervous to remain in your room and would like to take a stroll on the beach. He will naturally accompany you. No matter what happens, go on down the stairs to the road and leave everything to us. In one hour, no sooner. There are things to arrange. And bring a scarf with you."

Mulhaney was pleased to see a little color back in her cheeks and readily agreed that a walk on the beach would do her good. Magda picked up her handbag and a scarf, and left the hotel accompanied by the officer.

When they approached the steps, Mulhaney frowned. "Never saw so many rickshaws gathered in one spot. I wonder what's up?" There were indeed several more than had been there previously, but Magda's attention was riveted on the automobile still parked in front of the hotel. She found herself clutching Mulhaney's arm.

"Nothing to be afraid of, mum, they won't give us any trouble." He patted her hand and smiled at her comfortingly.

When they had descended the last step, an elegantly dressed man climbed out of the car and handed Magda a card.

"Bruno von Scheft of the German Consulate, at your service, Frau von Zoller." He clicked his heels and bowed in a stiff, official manner. She looked at him questioningly, her grip on Mulhaney's arm growing tighter.

"Our consul, Herr Messinger, would like to have a few words with you, and he has sent me to escort you to the consulate."

"I have no wish to see the consul, Herr von Scheft. If you will excuse me," and she started to walk away, but the other two men, one of whom she recognized with an inward shudder, got out of the car and stood in front of her.

"You must remember you are a German citizen, and when the head of our government here requests your presence, he is not to be dismissed like a shopkeeper."

"You will present my courtesies and tell him that I have nothing to say."

"I must insist you come with me. Let us go, we are wasting time."

Mulhaney's face had been growing red with suppressed anger. "May I remind you, gentlemen, that this is the Crown Colony of Great Britain and the only law here is British. If Mrs. von Zoller does not wish to accompany you, she need not."

"My good man," the vice-consul said, speaking as a man accustomed to the use of authority in addressing an underling. "You will do well to hold your tongue. This matter is beyond your scope. I speak as a representative of the sovereign nation of Germany and with the power vested in me."

Hans seized Magda's arm.

"Take your hands off this woman," Mulhaney ordered, and when Hans showed no signs of obeying, he came down heavily on his wrist, almost pulling Magda down with the force of his blow.

While this altercation escalated, the coolies closed in. Then, as if on cue, several things happened at once. The three Germans were attacked, and Magda was separated from Mulhaney, who was pushed violently to one side. A rough hand was clamped over her mouth and she was carried bodily and thrust into the rear seat of a strange limousine, which had, in the meantime, maneuvered its way into the suddenly cleared place in front of the Germans' car.

The coolie who carried Magda remained with her, followed by another man. The last thing she saw as the car sped away was the three Germans lying on the ground, covered by a mass of kicking, yelling Chinese. Of Mulhaney, she saw nothing. But she heard his stentorian voice shouting obscenities from some unseen vantage point.

Once they were inside the car, Magda's scarf was tied, firmly over her mouth and she was forced to lie on the floor. When the auto slowed down after they turned off the hotel road, she pointed to the scarf and gestured that it was hurting her. There was a brief discussion in a dialect she did not understand; then the one who had carried her in made two gestures—one finger on his lips for silence, one drawn menacingly across his throat, his meaning clear. Magda shuddered inwardly. He looked capable of carrying out his threat, but she nodded that she would comply, and the scarf was removed from her face.

After several miles, the limousine stopped, and she was moved to another car with a different group of men. They drove for a long time through a series of narrow, tortuous alleys. Magda knew they were heading for the waterfront long before they reached it, by the pungent smell of salt water and refuse. The car halted once more. One man gave Magda a wide-brimmed straw hat to put on, the kind the native Hakka women wore, with a short veil almost covering her face and hair. Then a large shawl was draped over her shoulders and she was led down a short ramp, and into a sampan. Magda suspected that they were in Aberdeen, one of the vast typhoon shelters which harbored thousands of boats of all sizes and types. She was too busy keeping her balance in the tiny boat to pay much attention to anything else. They were rowed to the outskirts of the harbor and tied alongside the largest, most elaborate junk Magda had ever seen. A short ladder was lowered, willing hands helped her aboard, and she was escorted to a lavishly furnished stateroom. Almost immediately, she heard the throb of an engine as the houseboat moved away from shore.

Magda went over to a curtained window and watched the trail of muddy water the houseboat left in its wake. She felt safe, her tensions gone for the first time in weeks. This was the best idea she'd had in a long time, even though it was a shabby trick to play on Desmond, after all his concern for her. Determinedly, she erased the notion. For the next few days, she vowed to herself, she was not going to think one serious thought. She should rest mentally as well as physically, until at last she was herself again.

Magda examined her surroundings with interest, and was amazed by the quality of the room's elaborate furnishings. The walls were paneled with inlaid tiles of ivory and mother-of-pearl separated by finely carved strips of black teak. The room was both dining room and game room, with assorted marble-topped tables—the one by the window was used for Mah-Jongg. The tile trays were set up and a rosewood box held a handsome jade quartz set. Square windows placed on each of the four walls gave a complete panoramic view, though heavy velvet curtains were drawn at present.

Before Magda had a chance to investigate further, the door opened and a servant woman entered, bowed and beckoned her through a door on one side of the room. Magda spoke to her in Chinese, but the woman looked at her blankly and then said a few words Magda could not understand. Magda tried all the dialects she knew, but the maid showed no comprehension, answering in her own gutteral language.

Sankka, Magda decided, that's what it must be, the language of the river people. She knew that there was a large population of them living in the typhoon shelters around Hong Kong Harbor. She tried to remember what she had heard of them: they lived independently of the shore people; many of them never set foot on land from the day they were born to the day they died—only for that final trip were they buried in sacred soil of China. The Sankkas had known no other way of life for hundreds of years and were supposedly the descendants of the sea pirates who used to roam and plunder the coastal villages.

Perfect keepers for me were I kidnapped instead of rescued, Magda reflected as the woman brought her to a bedroom, equally luxurious but very small and with a tiny bathroom adjoining. The servant pulled back a folding screen and with a broad smile exposed several Chinese gowns on hangers. Then, with a final bow, she made the sign for eating and left Magda to attend to her toilette.

Washed, changed, and fully refreshed, Magda returned to the lounge. The table was set with fine porcelain and ivory chopsticks and a steaming bowl of soup. Its aroma made Magda's mouth water. She hadn't realized how hungry she was, nor could she recall when she had last eaten. One well-cooked dish followed another, served by the same woman who, Magda judged, had been assigned to watch over her.

At though cued by her last sip of tea, a man, exquisitely gowned in the Chinese fashion, entered the room from the deck side. As soon as he spoke, she recognized the voice she had heard on the phone.

They made the usual formal exchange of greetings, and, regarding her curiously, he asked, "Do all Western women have the same adventurous life as you?"

She laughed, completely at ease. "It is not of my making. Adventure and danger seem to seek me out, not the other way around. May I thank you for saving me from it."

He waved his hand gracefully. "It is my business."

"I am sure Mr. Dzu would be more than pleased by your ingenuity."

"I know nothing of names," he replied coldly, "and would not mention any if I knew. You are subcontracted to me, and for this I am well paid. Now, these are my instructions for you. You will keep within the confines of this suite, which I trust is to your liking. During such times as the boat returns to the harbor, you are to make no overt effort to gain anyone's attention. Should we, in the course of the week I have arranged for you to be aboard, be passed or contacted by the Harbor Patrol, you will go to a place reserved for that purpose. You are here by your request, and I am sure you can understand the reasons for these precautions. Have you any questions?"

"It's difficult to be without exercise."

He scowled at her reprovingly. "The women of this country, which I understand is partially yours, have spent most of their lives without any exercise. I do not think that a week will deprive you greatly. Nevertheless, I will make an exception: on dark evenings, you may walk on the deck—with the understanding that you do not attempt to engage in any conversation with members of the crew."

Magda nodded, a little overwhelmed by his businesslike attitude—so in opposition to his speech and dress. "I shall see you in a week." He rose, bowed and left the room as silently as he had entered. She realized for the first time that the junk had stopped moving; then she heard a faint phut-phut like that of a motorboat, and the junk started moving once more.

Magda experienced an eerie, stabbing isolation. She was somewhere in the Hong Kong waters, headed for who knew where—with people whose language she did not understand and with all lines of communication cut off.

For three days, Magda reveled in her tranquility of mind and body in her luxurious prison. Every day she was massaged by her maid and soothed with aromatic oils. The food was both plentiful and delicious. In the evenings she was accompanied for her walk around the deck, not by her maid, but by a surly man who gripped her arm as though—she giggled a little hysterically at the thought—as though she were going to jump overboard.

During the days, she distracted herself by studying the Sankka language and conversing with her maid, who, shy and distant in the beginning, had gradually become quite open. To her satisfaction, she discovered she could learn it easily, and her vocabulary and ability to speak it expanded. Magda enjoyed the peaceful calm—after so many days and nights of fear and anguish.

She particularly liked the evenings, when the setting sun changed the muddy waters into molten gold, and she could sit by an open window and watch the black-shadowed waves chase each other. It had a mesmerizing effect. Magda began to see in the sparkling waters, pictures of herself and Archie when they first met—of the sweetness and innocence of their love.

The beating of the waves echoed against the old song they had cherished. It reflected musically all the depth and passion of their emotions—especially hers when she first realized what being in love could feel like—from that first unexpected kiss—

She smiled in memory of that breathless moment. What had become of that repressed, reserved young woman? But even in that happy memory she asked herself the question which had long been buried in her mind: Had that repressed girl—who once swore never to become involved with anyone—deliberately destroyed her own happiness because she was afraid of being overwhelmed by passion? Afraid of risking involvement? Certainly she had persuaded Archie to leave for India against his wishes. Had she somehow hoped that he would overpower her logical reasons with his love for her, that he would not be convinced?

Magda could not find any answers to these questions which had haunted her for years. Instead she looked regretfully at the darkening sky. The gold had disappeared, leaving only blackness and the pounding of the waves.

"But it's still there, Magda," she told herself. "The gold will be there tomorrow as it was yesterday, and will always be there if you will only seek it."

The junk returned to the harbor after three days at sea, to pick up fresh water and food. It dropped anchor far from shore, and boatloads of necessities were stored below deck. While they were in the harbor, Magda was moved to a tiny crawlspace under the deck. She understood the necessity—it took only one person's prying eyes to wonder what a foreigner was doing on the boat and call the Harbor Patrol to investigate.

She listened to the clanking of chains, the thudding of footsteps, and the sound of many voices shouting and laughing. The crew were enjoying their brief respite from their time at sea, hearing news from their friends and families. The head men from some of the boats came aboard to drink with the boat's captain until their crews had finished unloading.

For Magda, in her cramped quarters, it seemed to take forever before she heard the last boat leave for the dock. When the junk was under way again, she was mercifully released from under the planks, choking and gasping for air. She had never known what it was to suffer from claustrophobia, if that were what she had just experienced. The feeling of being penned up, the knowledge that she was, to all purposes, truly a prisoner, made her tremble. Her earlier sense of isolation became oppressive; even the knowledge that Mr. Dzu was behind her rescue was dimmed in her fears that, if anything happened to her, no one would ever know. She had seen the boats of prostitutes being rowed out to foreign freighters anchored in the bay. It forced her to imagine what her life might have been had her mother sold her. Foolish thinking, she knew, but she remembered the hooded eyes of the man she had talked to. A businessman, he had called himself. She shivered. Magda changed her mind—she had to get off the boat and back to Hong Kong.

She wrote a letter in Mandarin and gave it to her maid. In broken Sankka, she instructed her to see that it was delivered to the head man. The maid's face paled; she shook her head violently and ran out of the room, as though even touching the letter would scar her. Soon the captain of the boat came to see her. He looked at her angrily and asked her a question. But his voice was so harsh and his accent so slurred that she couldn't understand a word he said. Then he shouted something and banged his fist on the table. From the little she could understand, it seemed he thought she was complaining about the way she had been treated. She opened the note and showed him that it was not so, but he brushed it aside. He probably cannot read, Magda surmised. Few of them could. In the end, he took the letter from her, thrust it into his corded belt, and left the room. From that point on, the maid timidly served the meals and rushed out of the room. There was no more conversation, no more friendliness from anyone on board. Magda felt even more alone.

Somehow she lived through the next two days. At last, on her sixth day at sea, she heard the phut-phut of a motorboat approaching the junk. A few minutes later, the nameless man entered her room, holding her letter. His lizardlike eyes looked at her, unblinking.

"You have seen fit to try to break our arrangement," he said harshly. "Even more seriously, you have disobeyed your instructions not to speak to any member of the crew. You have asked your amah the name of this junk, how many men on its crew, even my name and position. You realize that breaking security can have very bad consequences for you."

Magda listened to him with growing concern; his recitation of her "crimes" made her realize how much in danger she was at that moment.

"You must believe that I did not intend to pry. I am interested in languages and speak several Chinese dia-

287

lects, but I had no knowledge of Sankka. I was merely trying to learn the language. By asking simple questions of my maid I hoped to master the vocabulary. Besides, there is no reason why I would want to gather information which would be harmful to you who have come to my aid —for whatever reason."

He looked at her steadily for a few minutes as though trying to read her mind; then he nodded his head and called out for some tea.

"Why do you wish to leave before the week is over? Have things not been to your liking?"

"I have never lived so luxuriously in my life."

"Then why?"

"I started to feel like a prisoner," she answered honestly.

"Have you considered how you will explain your absence to the British authorities who had you under their care?"

She looked at him blankly and shook her head.

"Will you tell them that you did not believe they could protect you adequately, and that you sought more qualified assistance?"

"Oh, no!"

"Then what?"

"I will say that I was kidnapped for my safety and am being released at my own request. Furthermore, I wish to thank my benefactors to the sum of ten thousand Hong Kong dollars."

"You think the authorities will not consider it a kidnapping for ransom, because you word it thus? They are not fools. At least not completely so."

"What, then, do you suggest?"

"If you wish, for the sake of your reputation, to be considered kidnapped, I think you must not be so diplomatic about my feelings. Now, don't you feel that ten thousand dollars is too much?" He looked at her innocently.

"Oh, no. Not at all. Any less would not be taken seriously."

A smile flickered at the corners of his thin mouth. "You show good judgment. Write your letter and I shall take it with me when I leave."

"I would like, if it is possible, to include another note, asking if my position in the community is safe."

"Write it, and I shall see if our security will not be threatened."

Placidly sipping a cup of tea, Magda penned the letters. She chose her words with care and handed the notes to her host, trying to hide her relief from his penetrating eyes, pleased that she had chosen the right answer to his cupidity.

CHAPTER TWENTY-ONE

◄◄◄◄◄◄◄◄◄◄◄◄◄◄◄◄◄◄◄◄◄◄◄◄◄◄◄◄

GERMANY UNLEASHED ITS furies with a blitzkrieg into Poland on September 1. Two days later, Great Britain and France declared that a state of war would ensue if Germany did not immediately withdraw her troops from Poland. They did not. On September 4, World War II commenced. The fact that it had been anticipated did not allay the shock any more than the finality of death removes the grief from a bereaved family.

It was war again. Pacifists wept that the horror of 1914 had come once more, and that the countries of the civilized world had not yet found a way to peace among men. In countries not yet at war, people took sides and neighbors became enemies overnight.

Magda, in her prison retreat, heard nothing of the war, and missed the hollow death knell which jolted the British Empire out of its lethargy at last. In Hong Kong, faces were tense, waiting for orders, and wondering how the war in Europe would forever change their lives.

Chapin Desmond had been sending home classified reports of dangerous activities by the Japanese, but the British Foreign Office still thought it was only necessary to mention British gunboats and the enemy would scuttle away. Desmond wrote to his superiors, enclosing documented proof of massive Japanese military positions nearby. In due time, military experts were sent to examine Hong Kong's defenses. They ordered huge guns placed along the coast and around the island in fortified positions; thus, they declared Hong Kong impregnable. They were positive that if Japan were so foolhardy as to attempt to invade Hong Kong, it would be by sea.

But after war was declared in Europe, Japan became more openly belligerent. Desmond reported that Hong Kong was flooded with Japanese agents, but headquarters responded that he was not to touch them or in any way disrupt relations between Japan and Great Britain, which were, on the surface, still friendly. Though he was one of the top men in British Intelligence, his constant warnings that Japan was a real threat were ignored. He was known to be an alert and thorough investigator, but the War Office had elected to disregard his entreaties; British experts on the Far East said it would be suicidal for Japan to challenge the Western powers and that their fighting capacity was overrated. In their smug superiority, they ignored all information to the contrary and brushed away as insignificant the Japanese victories. Even Winston Churchill was quoted as saying that "nothing could be more foolish from the Japanese viewpoint" when he was informed of the movement of Japan's navy toward Malay and Burma.

The head office of British Far East Intelligence in Singapore was reputedly the most lax, corrupt, and inefficient of all its departments. Desmond, frustrated by the apathy and irritation of the London office, expected daily to be recalled to England. In fact, he almost hoped he would be.

There, he could employ his efforts defending the country itself, and his experience could be used to greater capacity. In the meantime, he gathered his facts doggedly, determined that, when he returned to England, he would be able to present them directly to the right people. He was, in another way, equally frustrated in his efforts to locate Magda von Zoller who, despite his promise of protection in Hong Kong, had disappeared without a trace.

Clear-witted, discerning, at times brilliant, Chapin Desmond was considered by his associates to be dedicated to his work and totally dispassionate. He had trained himself never to become emotionally entangled in any of the investigations handled by his department. And he warned his assistants to beware of the same.

He was surprised and a little amused at himself for

permitting this extraordinary Eurasian woman to make such a crack in his armor. There was something about her —her gallantry in fighting the odds against her, her adamant refusal to yield to pressures that others might find overwhelming—something so controlled and yet so vulnerable about her, that it aroused his sympathies, and something else, he didn't know quite what. He was determined to help her in every way he could. If only he could find her again!

On September 6, Sir Alfred, once more unwillingly involved, entered the house on Queen's Road. There he found Desmond and showed him the ransom note which had been delivered to him at the bank. He informed Desmond that the handwriting had been authenticated, that the money was available. Carefully checking the procedure given by the kidnappers for payment of the money, Desmond arranged for the terms to be strictly met. Magda had enclosed a note meant for his eyes only: "Am I properly protected to come out of hiding?" she asked, and he wrote his answer readily.

Magda was released the following day. With her release she was handed a note from Desmond which said only, "Request granted."

Magda was returned to Kowloon as she had asked, but only after many car changes during a trip that took several hours. Shortly after dark, she was let out of the car several blocks from Tasha's hotel. There had been no way to let Tasha know she was coming, but the manager of the hotel recognized her and let her in, a little taken aback by her disheveled appearance. Miss Guria, he told her stiffly, was away on business, but, he was certain, her dear friend Frau von Zoller would be most welcome to take refuge in her apartment.

The first thing Magda did was check the mail which was usually left on a brass tray near the elevator. There was a bulky letter for her from William. She had hoped there would be some word from him, but before reading the letter, she turned on the radio and heard for the first time that the war had been declared at last. Surely now, she thought, they'll be warned about Japan and take precautions.

When the report of the war news had ended, Magda put the letter to one side to enjoy it more after she soaked luxuriously in a steaming bath. Then she slipped on a comfortable pair of lounging pajamas, borrowed from Tasha's closet, and opened William's letter.

Magda read the letter for the second time and each time she read it, she felt deep regret and more than a little remorse.

Max was dead.

She stared off into space and could not conjure up his face, only the anguish she had caused him which tore her apart. If only—if only, she thought. The world is full of "if onlys." Poor Max, dear Max, you asked for so little and I couldn't even give you that!

The tight knot within her finally loosened, and she was able to weep, as much for his passing as for the hurts he had suffered and for the loneliness of his death. She, who rarely cried, wept for all the lonely ones in the world, and for the man Max could have been. Finally she wept for herself, and for so much she could not understand.

Exhausted, Magda rinsed her face with cold water and brewed some tea. As an afterthought, she poured in a jigger of brandy, shuddering as she drank it. But it warmed the chill in her heart. Then she picked up William's letter and read it again. It was written as usual in Chinese, and dated September 3, 1939. After the usual greetings of good will, she read:

My dear cousin, I very much regret telling you that Max is dead. We received word that you had been kidnapped and that your whereabouts were in doubt. I never saw a man so distraught. Max was half-insane with fear for you and hatred for Waldemar, for he never doubted for a moment but that his cousin was responsible for the act.

The letter went on to describe all the incidents which had led to Max's calling Archie and how he heard of Magda's kidnapping the following day:

Waldemar was himself fuming with rage and in his own way as worried about your disappearance as Max. From his ravings, Max gathered that you had not withdrawn the money from the bank and that, in Waldemar's opinion, you had arranged the kidnapping yourself in order to deceive him. He threatened all manner of dire revenge against you and Max. Seeing his state, Max was convinced that you were not in Waldemar's hands.

He came to the office on the following morning with a calm look on his face, as if he had made a decision. As you have realized by now, Max had confided in me to a certain extent, and I welcomed the friendship between us. I knew that it was in a mood of real happiness that Max wrote a long letter to you and gave it to my keeping. When the ultimatum sent to Germany by Great Britain was announced, it was tantamount to a declaration of war, and Max wanted to be prepared for any eventuality. I knew he had something mysterious planned. When he was finished writing this letter, which took several hours, he left the office, after telling me he had left me some instructions, in case of trouble. I knew I would never see him again—but a man has to do what he must.

On the evening of September 2, the two servants in your household heard a great deal of shouting and scuffling. They opened the door to the living room slightly and saw Max holding a gun on Waldemar. He was talking in German—they do not understand this language—and he was making a long speech. They thought he was very nervous, as his voice seemed hysterical. Waldemar was watching him like an animal poised to spring. They saw Waldemar leap at Max and the two men engaged in a deadly struggle over possession of the gun. Waldemar was the stronger of the two, and obviously more accustomed to fighting. He grabbed the gun from Max's hand and managed to point it away from himself, toward Max. My two men, who are not innocent of bloodshed themselves, remarked with some shock at the savage glee with which Waldemar's pulled the trigger. Max died instantly, shot in the heart. He slumped forward in a heap at Waldemar's feet, his hand, under Waldemar's, still clutching the gun. Some instinct made Waldemar look up at that moment, and he saw the two men staring at him. He pulled the gun from Max's grasp, and took careful aim at them. One of my men is expert with a knife, his aim unfailing, and he was ready. He could have sliced Waldemar's hand cleanly off or pierced his heart while Waldemar was taking aim, but at the split second of decision, he decided that their instructions had not included murder—unless it was to protect you. They hurriedly closed the door, and disappeared from the house and reported back to me.

The story of Max's death was buried in the newspapers, a simple announcement of suicide by a man of unsound mind. I enclose the clipping.

This is purely conjecture on my part, but I believe that Waldemar will persuade the courts that, in your absence, he is the legal heir to Max's interest in the company. Should this happen, as I am certain it will, it would suit my purposes well. If he does come into the business, it will give me a perfect opportunity to keep an eye on him and his contacts, not only with the Japanese but with those of our people who deal with him. Unfortunately, there are Chinese traitors who do not hesitate to work with our enemies for their own gain. Well, they will receive short shrift from us. It would also give me great satisfaction to see Max's killer get his just reward.

Business in Shanghai is in a state of paralysis, but otherwise life goes on as usual. We expect to hear of war any moment now—and have, since Germany's army entered Poland. The nightclubs are full from dusk to dawn, and the atmosphere is one of hysteria. A stream of Germans are pouring out of the French Concession of Shanghai, and moving to the International Settlement. They don't want to be in French hands once war is declared.

A double-strength police force has been ordered for the Hongkew district, where there are so many thousands of Jewish refugees. I think it's a wise precaution. These people have no love for the Germans, and since they had no chance to fight in their own countries, they may well do battle here. The Japanese, who are in power in Shanghai, though not officially in the foreign sections, remain very quiet. For now, no one is anxious to disturb the status quo.

My final piece of news is of a lighter nature. I chanced to be at the same banquet as Mr. Dzu—I know him, but, to the best of my knowledge, he does not know me. However, he sent his aide to invite me to his table, and then asked how my ravishing red-headed cousin was—saying how wise and delightful you were, and that he hoped that, on your return, you and he would become better acquainted.

My dear cousin, it is time that our private business arrangement come to an end. Please write, and tell me how to dispose of your investment. I am sending this and the enclosed letter to Miss Guria's address—I feel it is the safest place, even if she may not yet know you left Shanghai.

The letter ended with news of his family and his sincere expression of grief at Max's death.

Magda carefully folded the news clipping about Max's death and placed it in a secret fold of her wallet. The hatred which flared up at times as though it might consume her was at that moment replaced by an icy resolve: that sometime, somehow, Waldemar would answer to her. The clipping would remain with her as an amulet for revenge, until Waldemar was destroyed. She tensed her features grimly. She had hoped for a purpose in life—was that great purpose to be the pursuit of ugly, lusting vengeance instead of love? She knew one thing: someday she and Waldemar would meet again, and she had to be prepared.

She fingered Max's letter. It took a tremendous force of will to break the seal and open the envelope. It was like reading the letter from her father after he had killed himself. Was it her destiny to have a series of men who loved her destroy themselves in her cause? The thought was a nightmarish one, and she shuddered inwardly.

"My beloved wife," the letter began.

When you read this I shall be dead—at peace for the first time—I was going to write "in my life" but of course I won't be when you read this. So, for my peace in death, do not mourn for me, or be offended by my action. I must do it, and I have delayed this long only to be sure you were safe from any repercussions.

I have dreamed of this moment as others dream of glory; of a time when no one can attack me, or you through me. But more glorious than this last release is the knowledge that, in dying, I shall bring death to the man whom I hate most in all the world—less for what he did to me, than for what he contrived to do to you, my dearest one, my wife.

This is a love-letter I am writing you, one which I could never send in life. Perhaps you will not deny me, in death, the extravagant words of devotion which I have stifled for so long. Knowing that you never completely reciprocated my love is a small price to pay when I consider the joy you brought me for a few precious months—the only real happiness of my life.

I go back to those months greedily and treasure every memory of the time when you started to respond to me with affection, when you really saw me, and looked forward to our life together. These are the memories which gave me the endurance to live this long—long enough to do the thing I must do. In these last months, there has been only one thing on my mind: to destroy Waldemar. There are so many good reasons for his death. I could pick one of a hundred and it would justify my action, but if I speak of a personal one, do not think I am indulging in self-pity or self-condemnation. I want this last day of my life to be positive—not negative. I want to tell you everything that has led up to this moment, for within it is the reason that has kept me alive this long, and why I must accomplish it before Waldemar and I both die. It is something I must explain, so please, open your heart and mind to the cause of my actions.

What happened to the Jews in Germany, I never applied to myself. How easily one can fool oneself! Then Waldemar came into our lives, constantly attacking me, using the word *Jew* as a curse; telling me tales of German Jews who obey the master race in fear. Suffering every kind of humiliation and, still, on their knees, begging for life—a worthless race of whiners, contemptible, a race which the master race was determined to exterminate as they would rats. These are the things he said, and I began to believe them. I am ashamed, but I *believed*. Once a man of pride, suddenly I found myself shriveling in my own esteem. I could not believe what was happening to me. At the word *Jew*, I wanted to hide, to cringe, even to erase my shadow. He tortured me with his loathing for me and my people. What people? My poor mother who died when I was a child?

I had no Jewish traditions to sustain me. An accident

of birth had suddenly become a sin of vital proportions. I had become a pariah in the eyes of those I considered my countrymen. I was heartsick with what I was.

But recently it has changed for me. I have been reading the history of my people, my newly-found people. For the first time, I can look at myself and know who I am. It has taken me a lifetime to find I come from an indomitable and proud people, a people who have been subjected to every form of vilification, and who rise again and again. If I were to live, I would devote myself to work for a movement they call Zionism. I would help found a country for my people, that they may never again have to cringe before man's intolerance.

Forgive me, my dearest Magda, that I am taking so long to finish—it has been a long and difficult process for me. And now I will come to the point of what I want to tell you.

It began the day I discovered that Waldemar had been visiting the Jewish refugees. Knowing him, I was sure that whatever he appeared to be doing, his true purpose was utterly malevolent. I met with them, not mentioning my connection with Waldemar. I simply told them I was a businessman looking for possible employees. There was little language problem, for their common language, Yiddish, is based on German.

I managed to gain their confidence, and I heard Waldemar spoken of in glowing terms. They told me how he was bringing out their relatives who were still in hiding in their home countries. These people had been unable to bring out much money in the flight. What they had went for bribes and extortion. They did, however, bring with them such valuables as they had, jewelry and pieces of art—as much as they could smuggle out. Waldemar refused all payment for his services; but they insisted, in their gratitude, in thrusting upon him these precious things, which he reluctantly accepted.

At first, few trusted him with the hiding places of their loved ones; but he managed to rescue several Jews and brought them safely to Shanghai. Then he became a savior to them: beloved, trusted, almost worshiped. Many, who had previously reserved judgment, came to him with their stories and their last possessions of value, which they offered him to save those they loved.

Ah, Magda! The stories I heard would break the heart of a statue or create in it a heart to grieve for the sufferings mankind wreaks on their own!

It seems that, after the first survivors, very few of the later ones were saved. Always, it seemed, the police got there first, or there was some unforeseen disaster. These, my people, were gracious and generous in their despair. They never blamed Waldemar for the failures. When the disappointments became too frequent and they lost heart, one or two would again manage to escape and be brought to Shanghai, full of harrowing tales of danger and of how the rescuer went to extraordinary lengths to save the refugee's life—even as far as endangering his own. One success made up for fifty failures.

I tried in vain to awaken suspicions of Waldemar's purpose, but nothing would convince them that this wonderful and charitable man was playing any part in their betrayal. They needed, desperately, to believe in hope and human kindness; they were easy prey for human scavengers such as Waldemar. Finally, we come to the basis for Waldemar's satanic plans and to the reason he still needed me. First, though, let me add up his success to this point. His prestige increased every time he gave his authorities the names of those in hiding from the Gestapo, for their capture showed the invincibility of the Germans. His exploits made him many friends in high places, and his dedication to the German cause was unquestionable. He possessed the many articles of value—some of them priceless—which it had delighted him to accept from the very people he deceived. And finally, he had proved to the British through his friend (I believe it is Sir Nigel Lewisholm who anonymously pays for the escape expeditions) that he is a man of great humanity.

But he needed a scapegoat for the inevitable end of this project, and who was more fitting than I? It was conceivable that he might want to play this game again, in which case his reputation had to remain unblemished.

Bit by bit, I heard that "poor Waldemar" was becoming disillusioned about his cousin Max—himself part Jewish, and for that reason to be trusted in this work—who was given the important job of planning the escapes. But, lately, Waldemar would sigh, reluctant to accuse his cousin, hinting his confidence may have been misplaced, that perhaps the reason for so many failures was more than just bad luck. He told those who gathered around him so trustfully that from now on he was feeding his cousin false information. Then he urged all those who still had their relatives in hiding to act quickly, for soon, he said, it would be too late. The Germans were spreading throughout Europe and it would become impossible to carry out any kind of rescue mission.

Magda, I thought I knew the worst Waldemar was capable of. But in my wildest imagination, I didn't even scratch the surface of this monster's mind.

It is less important to me that I shall carry the weight of his guilt than it is to persuade these people of their misplaced trust. Now that I feel instinctively that you are safe, I will delay no longer. I have left a letter with Mr. Chen asking that, on my death and that of Waldemar, a letter disclosing all his horrible plots against them be circulated to these unfortunate people, so that they will not trust those who may come after him. It is too late to save the victims who have already confided in him. They are being hunted down even as I write.

My plans are made. I have a gun and I shall use it triumphantly. All the ghosts of those he betrayed and those still alive whom he has persecuted will be with me to give me strength and courage.

There will be one less fiend to carry out the sadistic cruelties which Hitler's madness has demanded. I cannot pray. I have never learned how. Nor would I know to which god to pray. Certainly not to the god of the Jews, who is neither strong nor loyal to his people. And not to Christ, whose message of love has taught people the greatest intolerance. No, I could not pray to him, however worthy his mission, for in two thousand years it has failed.

But in my heart there is one hope: that one day there will be a country for the Jews in the world, where they can gather together and proclaim to the world, "We are Jews. This is our homeland. We will defend it to the death, but we will take you with us!"

Magda, I have left you my business. It is a good one, and my share should amount to a large sum. You can trust Mr. Chen implicitly. I ask only this of you—if you don't need the money, sell the business, to him preferably.

And it will give me great satisfaction if the proceeds could go to the Zionists.

Dearest and beloved Magda. On this last day of my life, let me conjure you up in my mind again, so that I can keep your beauty and your worth as a comfort to me in the end. I ask your forgiveness for having dragged you into my troubles. You had your own private agony to suffer, though I did not know it until Waldemar spat it out.

Perhaps the day will come when people are accepted for who they are as individuals, and not judged by their blood or their ancestors. My only advice to you is that you hold yourself proudly for what you are, and that you honor yourself. You have great strength and great integrity, and you are not easily persuaded against your will. You have a spirit and a determination which will not be conquered. It is a gift beyond all else I wish had been bestowed on me.

In dying, I will cause one man to die. I hope, in doing so, to save the lives of many.

I love you very much, and I hope that in your life you find the happiness you deserve. I die in peace, and, I hope, for some purpose. Were I a courtier of old I would go into battle carrying your banner and die with your name on my lips.

Max

Magda's emotion was too deep for tears. She felt his pain as though it were her own. He was so near her in spirit that when she finished the letter she spoke to him as though he were with her.

"Dear, sweet Max! I did not ask for your love, which brought you only pain and grief. But Max, my dear Max, I shall always cherish it and wish I had been half worthy of what you gave me. I wish I had loved you more . . . but please believe me, I gave you all I could."

And then, silently, so that he would not hear, she sent a prayer to whatever god might be listening: that Max might go to his eternal peace still exultant in the belief that he had killed Waldemar.

"God, give him this one thing," she prayed.

One of Max's wishes *was* hers to grant. She wrote to William and told him that the money she had invested in the firm was his, but that the money belonging to Max was to be given to the Zionist movement.

I depend completely on your caution and judgment to handle it, she wrote. As far as our private business is concerned, I'd like it all to go to the Chinese refugees. I know, my dear William, that a hundred thousand dollars is not much when it reaches thousands, but let it go to those poor souls who wish to escape from Shanghai. It is not likely that I shall ever return.

William, dear friend and cousin, if you would do one other favor for me: let a rumor be started. Arrange it so that it grows and cannot be traced, and let the rumor be that Waldemar is making a fortune from the objects given to him by the Jewish refugees. There is no way in which the letters Max spoke of can be sent, and this may do as well.

There is nothing like hearing of corruption and embezzlement to disenchant people. Let the rumors be insidious: from servants, business associates, even to the consulates. Let it spread among the Europeans, let it spread like a plague, to dishonor this blood brother of the devil. You know the form the rumors can take. And if they can convey even a little of Max's good intentions and Waldemar's evil ones, then let it be so. If nothing else, it will make these people, who so eagerly trust Waldemar with secrets which mean life or death, think well and hesitate.

You will be pleased to know that I have been informed that I may remain here under British protection.

Should you encounter Mr. Dzu, please tell him that I, too, found the situation humorous and I shall always be indebted to him for his help. If the use of my money brought him a smile, he must know I am happy.

I miss you, dear William. I cannot think what I would do if you were not in my life. I wish you could visit Hong Kong—it would be such a comfort.

CHAPTER TWENTY-TWO

MAGDA'S RELEASE HAD taken place three days after the declaration of war and she was surprised how few people had responded passionately to the situation. Instead of flags waving, instead of long lines of men waiting to enlist, life was going on as usual. The only enlistees were applicants to join the Royal Volunteer Corps, which had been founded as a Crown Colony National Guard unit and which included men of different nationalities prepared to defend Hong Kong.

What happened to the colony's former German residents, Magda did not know. There seemed to have been very minor, half-hearted action. Guards were placed in front of the German Consulate, but, by a strange coincidence, and to the relief of the local British administration, the consul and his close aides were all on holiday in Japan. On later inspection, it was found that the consulate files had been cleverly emptied of all papers and records.

One evening, Magda received a call from Chapin Desmond, asking her to meet him in the house on Queen's Road. This time, happily, there was no need for the intervention of Sir Alfred. Chapin greeted her cordially and congratulated her on her escape. She asked him not to question her about the kidnappers, saying she hoped the incident would be permitted to remain closed.

"You must know that we can't let it drop. However, since you've been safely returned, the investigations will probably be superficial. I shouldn't admit that to you."

"Thank you. By the way, Sergeant Mulhaney was not to blame. He told me not to move out of the hotel without letting him know, and I foolishly disobeyed him."

"That is not the point," Chapin replied, his mouth set sternly. "We can always make excuses. The fact is that he was negligent in his duties."

From the quiet, rather nondescript man she had previously regarded, she saw that there was steel and intensity behind his official facade.

"Enough of that. This is what I called you for." He handed her a stamped, sealed, and signed document which proclaimed her to be under the protection of the Government of the United Kingdom of Great Britain. "But I have even better news for you. There is a good chance of your being reinstated as a British citizen. I've been checking on it for some time and had the legal office in London chase it down. It's something to do with the British Nationality Status of Aliens Act. I quote, 'A British woman who married an Alien and acquired his nationality could, if the husband were an enemy alien (which a German citizen became on September 3, 1939), on her return to the United Kingdom receive her British nationality by naturalization without fulfilling the residence or other requirements.'"

As he read, Magda's eyes widened with incredulity. As the words reflected their joyful meaning, she impulsively came forward and kissed their herald. Then, blushing, she stood back.

"I think I deserved that," he said, to cover her embarrassment. "It's better than you expected, eh!"

"I don't believe it yet. I can't believe that such a wonderful thing could happen to me."

"Believe it," he smiled, all the more appealing because his smiles were so rare.

"How can I thank you for all your kindness?"

"No need for thanks," he replied gruffly. "I'm very pleased for you. However, it would help if you were working in some capacity for the administration in Hong Kong."

Magda recalled his suggestion of several weeks past, no longer minding that it was being made formal.

"I'll see if I can't arrange a spot for you. You'd make an excellent translator. That's is, the position comes under my department, as third secretary. The pay is rotten, as in all government jobs. With that recommendation, how about it?"

"I'd like it very much."

"That is step number one. Step number two is to get you to England. I have something in mind for you in

British Intelligence in London. You'd fit admirably—now, mind you, this is only a suggestion. It would still have to be implemented by the front office in London. But I think I can swing it—I have some influence there. Would you like me to make preliminary inquiries?"

"It would be satisfying to work in some capacity useful to the war effort," Magda answered thoughtfully. "Everyone here seems to take the war so casually. I can't understand it."

"They're experiencing a common disease stimulated by relief that they're not in the war zone."

"But they're crazy," Magda exploded, shaken out of her usual calm. "Don't they know they'll be in the middle of it here? And worse for them because there's no place to go. This is the perfect time for the Japanese to take things in their own hands. You must know that!"

"You forget. I'm in charge of information, not action," Chapin bristled, and she stiffened at his rebuff. "Sorry, Magda. Didn't mean to snap at you—I'm frustrated, too. Now, let's get back to you. I'm expecting to be recalled daily, and if I'm to arrange for you to work for Intelligence in London you'd better let me have your decision soon. Is there some reason that makes you unsure? I was sorry to hear of your husband's death but that does leave you at a loose end. I'd imagine you'd want to do something."

Magda flushed inexplicably. "I really don't know yet. It seems such a final step—to commit myself. It's like recasting myself in a role I'm not ready for. I need some time to think about it. Please don't think I'm ungrateful. I'm just not accustomed to have someone arranging things for me. I do thank you, Chapin."

They shook hands. As was usual for their meetings at the Queen's Road house, he departed first as a precaution. Today, pausing at the door, he said, rather shyly, "By the way, thanks for the 'Chapin.' "

Magda filed her application but had no idea when the option to restore her citizenship would take effect. But, whenever that would be, there was one thing she had to do first, and that was to settle Tasha's affairs. Tasha was so much in love she simply refused to consider the future. She laughed at Magda for her concern and called her an old worrywart. So be it, but the "worrywart" was about to take some positive action.

Magda called Barry and explained that she had something important to discuss regarding Tasha. They arranged to meet at the Happy Dragon Restaurant near the racecourse because "it's too far from town to be frequented during the noon-hour rush," she said.

"Why all the secrecy?"

"I'll tell you at lunch."

They met at the entrance of the restaurant.

"What's up?" he asked.

"Really, Barry, do you think I'd bring you all the way here if I could say what I have to in one sentence? I'm hungry, let's eat first."

She had already ordered the meal. The restaurant specialized in Peking food, and as one delicious dish was followed by another even more delectable and accompanied by rice wine, Barry relaxed.

"Okay, now give."

"I'm very concerned about Tasha's future."

Barry stiffened perceptibly but Magda pretended not to notice.

"For years I've been trying to push her toward getting a visa for the States, but she's made little or no effort in that direction. I don't suppose you have any idea of what it's like to be a White Russian in China. The Soviets are represented, but Tasha isn't listed with them, which means she has only a worthless Chinese passport. For a long time Russian refugees in Shanghai and here were considered the lowest stratum of society, even lower than the Eurasians. Tasha wasn't a refugee, but the stigma still existed . . . How much do you know about Tasha's background?"

"All I need to know. Before you continue, Magda, let me tell you that I don't welcome this conversation, and I'm not sure I want to hear any more. I'm shocked that you, her closest friend, should fill my ears with stories of Tasha's low estate in the world."

"And I'm appalled that you take me for a gossip, you bloody fool!" she answered. "If you think I'm interested in wasting your time with meaningless scandals, you don't deserve to belong to the diplomatic corps. Now, will you listen to me without interrupting? I have to tell you

Tasha's past in order to describe the position she's in, okay?"

Her eyes met his, signaling first her irritation, then her sincere good will. Magda proceeded to tell Barry of the sisters, Olga and Luba Lenova, daughters of a diplomat in the service of the Imperial Russian Embassy; of how one of the girls, Olga, married an American, Edward Wilkinson, a small businessman of no wealth or position. Of the other daughter Luba, Tasha's mother, who married a member of the Russian Embassy—Igor Guria, a prince of a small Georgian country, a dot on the map of Russia. She told him of the death of Tasha's mother and of Igor going off to fight the Bolsheviks, leaving the child with Olga; of Olga's love and care of Natasha who was raised as one of her own, in spite of her own large family.

Barry listened with interest but his face tightened when Magda related the ugly details preceding the Wilkinson's departure for the States.

"I wish you'd get to the point," Barry grumbled, at which point Magda lost her temper.

She shot him a withering glare. "Look, Barry, if you're not interested in helping Tasha, we'll just forget it. If what I have to ask you weren't so important, I'd give up right now and let you go on in happy ignorance of what Tasha's future may be if she doesn't get some help right now. If war should come, and it's bound to—and if foreigners are forced to leave, or the Western powers decide to evacuate, which is a definite possibility—Tasha will be one of the victims. She has no passport or visa to any country. You have been protected all your life, Barry. You have no idea what that means. Please let me tell you what I have in mind."

She gave him all the details of the transfer of her securities from Shanghai and their deposit under Tasha's name in Hong Kong with herself as trustee, and how, without Tasha's knowledge, she'd had the interest on the securities deposited in Tasha's savings account.

"If Tasha knew, she'd probably refuse it. She'll have to know soon and if she doesn't take it, it will rot there. It's her money; she earned it. Right now there's enough to take her to the States and support her for a few months until she finds a job, which with her experience shouldn't be too difficult. Her boss likes her and I wouldn't be at all surprised if he managed to transfer her there. The main thing is to *get* her there. Now, this is my idea. The money in my bank has been in her name for well over a year and should prove to the State Department that she isn't indigent. I can, if necessary, have the money transferred to the States and held in escrow until her citizenship is ratified."

"Your throat must be dry by now." Barry poured out some tea, and Magda drank it thirstily. Barry had stopped pacing up and down the room and was listening intently.

"Barry, I need your help to persuade Tasha to act immediately. She won't listen to me but she'll listen to you. In the States she'll meet people and make friends and have a good time, but most important, she'll have a country and security. She needs to belong somewhere."

There was complete silence when she finished speaking.

"Well? What do you say? Will you use your powers of persuasion? You're very quiet."

"I'm sure," Barry replied rather coldly, "that Tasha should be congratulated to have you for a friend. I'll consider what you've said and act accordingly. When do you leave for England?"

"There's no telling when or if I will, but I want to be prepared. One of the reasons I'm so worried is that Tasha will never ask for help—whatever the circumstances. We can't wait too long. We must get started before I leave if I'm to arrange about money matters. Besides, I want to be sure she asks her employer for a recommendation. It's important. Well?"

Barry stood up, for some reason obviously annoyed. "I have every intention of doing what I think is best for Tasha," he asserted. "Certainly you must know what she means to me. I'll consider what you suggest. Goodbye."

He left abruptly and Magda smiled to herself in satisfaction. The bait was cast—would the fish bite?

Magda's work at Government House kept her busy, but there was a deep void in her life which nothing could fill. Archie had made no effort to contact her. The days crawled by. Magda felt both relief at not hearing from him and yet as if the ground had been slipped from under her feet and she were left suspended in space.

Empty day followed empty day until Magda resolved

to act. Perhaps some good had come from her voluntary imprisonment. She had learned to explore the possibilities, and find her own solutions.

"I'll take your offer to work in London for British Intelligence if you still want me," she told Chapin one afternoon at closing time.

"Good. Of course this is only my idea. You'll still have to be accepted, but I anticipate no problems. Will you be ready to leave as soon as I send for you? I'm expecting my recall at any moment, and I'll get you fixed up as soon as I can."

"Mr. Desmond," Magda said wearily, "I've had all I want of adventure and danger. I want a quiet life where I can work in peace, preferably where there are not too many people. I hope you don't think I'm asking too much?"

"If you don't, who will? Actually, what I have in mind should suit you to a tee if it works out. It will be departmental work and highly confidential—not only the work itself but where you are and what your work is. You'll have to be trained and you'll be completely checked out. That is usual, of course, for any kind of secret service work."

"I understand. If you think me capable, I'm prepared."

"Your capabilities will have to be proven, but I'm confident that I'm not mistaken. I can't say any more right now."

"I'm ready at any time. The sooner the better."

"Good. I'll set the process in motion."

"I hope I'll be in your section."

"We'll have to see." Then Chapin added impulsively, surprising himself, "How about dinner with me tonight to celebrate?"

"What about your cover?" Magda replied.

"My dear, what could be more natural than for me to go out with my beautiful new assistant?"

"In that case, I'd love to. By the way, could I have some address in London, or a private post-office box number to which I can have mail sent?"

"Is it necessary now? The fewer people who know where you're going, the better," Chapin cautioned her.

"I don't want to cut myself off completely. I would

trust my cousin, William, with any secret. I also want to keep in touch with Tasha."

"I suppose I could give you my post-office box number in Chelsea, where you can reach me in case you have any questions. If you wish to use that address, I'll put any mail for you aside. Do you want it now?"

"If you don't mind. I like all loose ends made tidy." She changed the subject. "By the way, there's one thing you never told me. What did you do about Waldemar?"

"He played right into our hands. I recommended that we permit him to come to England. Not too soon, for it would make him suspicious. That's top secret. You see, I've already taken you into my confidence. Now, about tonight, say seven-thirty? And how about the Peninsular Hotel? They have a good band, and dancing is one of my weaknesses. I assume you're still living with Miss Guria?"

"Yes, but I'll be moving in a couple of days to the island. A pleasant, quiet place called the Island Hotel."

"I know it. Good choice. See you later then."

Chapin watched her leave, admiring her smooth, graceful walk. You're breaking every rule in the book, old boy, he cautioned himself, but it didn't change his inclinations. "What an ass he was to let her go . . ." he sighed after she left. "If I had a woman like that, damned if I'd give her up."

When Magda arrived at the apartment, Tasha rushed to meet her and embraced her wildly. Her face was flushed with happiness and exultation, her eyes flashing green fire. Barry was standing in the living room, both sheepish and elated.

"Magda! Oh, darling, dearest Magda. You'll never guess. Barry and I are going to get married." She gazed adoringly at Barry who returned her look with his own soulful glance.

"I've notified the consul and put up the banns," he said calmly, as if talking about the weather. But the big grin which spread across his face belied his voice.

"When Barry decides to do something, it's right now." Tasha praised him proudly. "Oh, Magda, I couldn't be happier. I don't want a big wedding—just you to stand up for me."

"That will depend on when it happens. I might have to leave on a day's notice."

"We'll do it before you leave. Dearest, blessed Barry, say you'll arrange it." She turned to him as though Barry had only to say he would, and it could be done.

"You'd better believe it, even if we have to resort to a Buddhist ceremony."

"Don't say that," Magda hissed sharply.

"Just joking." He was surprised by her vehemence. "I'll get in touch with the consul and he'll rush things. He's met Tasha and knows what a jewel I have. Excuse, me, ladies, I must go. I'll be back soon."

He embraced Tasha as though every minute apart from now on would be an eternity. There was a new possessiveness in him and radiance in Tasha, which spelled a joyous future for them. Magda's eyes misted a little at their happiness.

Tasha collapsed in a bubbling heap when Barry left and shook her head in wonder.

"I couldn't believe it. He called me at work about four this afternoon and told me to get off early, he had to see me. He sounded so cross and I couldn't imagine what had happened. He didn't get down on his knees," she giggled. "I think I'll get him to do that one day. Anyway, he just told me we were going to get married, that there was no time for fuss and he'd already told the consul. Then he kissed me so hard my mouth hurt, and held me so tightly I thought my bones would break."

She sighed rapturously. "I knew he loved me but he never talked marriage, and I wasn't going to bargain for it. I wanted him to be free to decide for himself. I thought the State Department frowned on Russian intermarriages, and that he had to put his career ahead of me. It hurt some, but I decided not to let it affect our lives together. As long as he wanted me, he was the only man I would ever want."

"Did he tell you what finally settled matters for him?"

"He'd been sort of engaged to a girl back home, someone he'd known for years, practically grown up with. His mother is very fond of her and keeps pushing him to send for her. Lately his mother wrote that she was thinking of taking a trip to the Orient and would bring Ellen with her. Barry was really worried. He'd been trying to break it off gently, in fact he kept hoping she would, so she wouldn't get hurt. Isn't he wonderful?"

"Yes, he is. I'm very happy for you, Tasha dear."

"I asked him about the Russian thing. You know it's always been at the back of my mind, that it would wreck his career if he married me. You know what he said?" Tasha sighed blissfully. "He said he could always get another job, but never another me!"

It felt good to bathe and dress up for a date. Magda couldn't remember when she had last gone out for a purely social engagement.

Chapin Desmond was full of surprises. Such a quiet man. But actually he wasn't so quiet—he only gave the studied impression of slipping into the background. Magda had been with him often enough to realize that his mind was very sharp and alert to every nuance, and that he had an acute sensitivity to what should be omitted and what was important.

It would be a relief to be with someone with whom she could be herself and not feel that she was playing a role, as she had been for the past year. There was probably no one besides William who knew as much about her as Chapin did.

For this special evening, Magda selected a flowing white-chiffon gown worn over a pale-green satin under-slip, which gave the faintest shimmer of green highlights through the transparent material. Almost as an after-thought, she decided to wear the diamond earrings and pendant her father had given her, and she brushed her hair until it blazed deep red-and-gold.

The doorbell rang and Magda went to let Chapin in. For a moment he was motionless, transfixed. He had always thought she was striking. But as she stood before him now, she sparkled incandescently as though lit from deep within. She was dazzling. It was more than good looks or her unusual coloring—she had that indefinable something, a distinction in her bearing which put her in a class above mere beauty.

"You look like the sun shimmering on an ice cap," he said admiringly.

"Well, then, perhaps I may be able to cool off this humid evening."

"No, not that. You'll just freshen the air with your loveliness."

"You are very gallant, Chapin." She smiled, a genuine warm smile which made her seem more animated than he had ever seen her before.

"Are you ready?" he asked.

She nodded, picked up a light scarf and her bag, and they went outside to the waiting cab.

He escorted her proudly to the table reserved for them and beckoned to a waiter standing beside a table on which a bottle of champagne, previously ordered, nested in a bucket of ice. The waiter immediately uncorked the bottle and, after Chapin tasted and approved the wine, filled their glasses.

"This is our own private little celebration," Chapin said, raising his glass to her. "To you, Magda, to a good start in a new life, and I must say you've made a smashing beginning."

"Thank you, Chapin. It's wonderful to see this other side of you."

"I'm glad you like it. I hope we'll do this more often in London."

"Will you be leaving soon?"

"I've been recalled, but, remember, the sooner I get there, the sooner I can start pulling the right strings for you. Things are pretty chaotic right now, but I'll get you there if I have to go straight to the king. By the way, how's your Japanese now?"

"A couple of months of conversation with a Japanese for true sound and timbre, and I'll pass."

"You're fortunate to have such a talent for languages."

"Talent's a funny thing, really. You're born with it and can't honestly take any credit for it, except to be modest. I must agree, though, that it's a gift. They come quite easily to me."

"Well, I have a recommendation to make. How about Polish?"

Magda laughed. "You sound as though you were offering me a choice between peanuts or walnuts."

Chapin groaned. "What a fool I am discussing work with a pretty girl on a night when we're celebrating. I should have my head examined. Let's dance, shall we?"

"That was wonderful," he said, leading her back to their table.

"You continue to amaze me, Chapin. You dance like a professional."

"I enjoy it—it's one of my few social graces." His last words came out slowly as he watched the expression on her face change from animated pleasure to a frozen stillness. He turned his head in the direction she was looking and saw the tall figure of Archie Monteith, whose wife was clutching his arm.

He swore under his breath, determined not to allow Magda to be hurt again—it just wasn't fair. Nor was he going to permit the bloody bastard to ruin this evening.

"Speaking of dancing," he began, watching her valiant effort to turn her attention to him, "the Peninsular has an excellent band, but it's not what I feel like tonight. There's a place near here that specializes in South American music, and I won't be content until I show you my tango. Shall we go?"

"Oh, yes, of course. I'd love it," Magda replied with feigned enthusiasm, still shocked not only by seeing Archie so unexpectedly, but also unnerved by her own reaction. When he had not tried to contact her after her release, she struggled to put his ghost away with other tender memories of the past, but she now realized that she could never escape her feelings for him.

There was one more hurdle for her to overcome. Archie was standing near the ballroom entrance, staring at her, mesmerized. They began to move slowly toward the door.

When Chapin and Magda passed, Archie took a step forward, preparing to speak to them. But Chapin firmed his grip on Magda's arm as he felt a tremor go through her. He tossed Archie a nonchalant half-salute as they exited, saying, "Come on, Magda, old girl, there's a tango waiting for us," and he hurried her out.

The last thing Magda saw was Archie's white, drawn face, his body slowly swivelling around, his eyes fixed on her as she glided out on Chapin's arm.

>>>>>>>>>>>>>>>>>>>>>>>>>>>>>>>>>>>

PART FIVE

London

1940–1942

>>>>>>>>>>>>>>>>>>>>>>>>>>>>>>>>>>>

CHAPTER TWENTY-THREE

THE H.M.S. *Queen Victoria* made an uneventful and tiresomely long trip from Hong Kong to tie up at Southampton in February, 1940. The deck was lined with passengers eagerly watching the mooring of the ship and scanning the crowds on the dock, searching hopefully for familiar faces.

Magda stood by the railing, unconcerned, not expecting to be met by anyone. Thus, she was delighted to see Chapin Desmond standing a little apart from those waving handkerchiefs and shouting messages. She waved exuberantly at him—surprised out of her usual composure by her delight that he made the effort to meet her.

He gazed at her approvingly when she stepped down the gangplank. She looked smart and glowing in her sheared beaver coat and Russian-style fur hat.

"Good that you got yourself a warm outfit where you could still have a choice," he said, as they greeted each other French-style, kissing each other on both cheeks. It seemed the natural thing to do.

"I've been in England before, and I can still remember how bitterly cold it gets here. I didn't know whether or not rationing was in effect here—or what I could buy."

"That will depend on the length of the war. People here are optimistic it will be a short one."

"What do you think?"

"Hard to tell," he replied. "I hope so, but only if it comes out the right way."

Magda felt a little shock go through her—that anyone could even consider otherwise. Despite her familiarity with Germany's military power, it seemed impossible to believe for an instant that Great Britain might not emerge victorious.

Chapin got her through Customs in record time, and

soon they were in his little Morris heading for London. The sun was making a valiant effort to pierce through the leaden sky, occasionally gilding a stand of trees, picking out a timbered cottage which rose mysteriously from the mist, or bringing to sudden life a thread of trickling stream. An omen of things to come? Magda wondered.

They drove in companionable silence. Neither felt the need to chatter idly. They were completely at ease with each other, and relaxed.

Magda broke the silence, saying, "I hope you managed to get me a hotel room for a few days. I've been warned that London is booked solid."

"Done better than that," he answered with a broad grin. "I got you an apartment. That is, if you want it. You'll see."

A few hours later they pulled up in front of an old house, with a tiny garden around it. It stood out like something out of a madman's dream—amidst the tight grouping of small shops and dreary flats. An elaborate wrought-iron fence separated it from the street. And there it grew—the maddest of all architectural nightmares, with turrets, fretwork, mullioned windows, and elaborate little verandahs, all strewn around as if by a careless hand. At the very top, it was capped with a round crenelated tower.

"Isn't that something?" he asked admiringly.

"I don't believe it," Magda breathed. "It can't be real. I feel as though I've been drinking absinthe and might be hallucinating."

"You like it?"

She nodded enthusiastically.

"What's it called? It must have a name."

"What else but Hatter's Castle Secundus."

"Of course. How dense of me. Do I get the turret on top?" she asked hopefully.

"M'lady must not be greedy. That is being held by guards night and day in fear of invasion. But you get the next best thing. Do you see that gargoyle peeping out at the left side? The one holding up the balustrade? That's yours."

"Chapin, you're a magician. How on earth did you manage it?"

"Oh, I pulled a few strings," he said complacently. "What are strings for but to pull? Of course, I sold my immortal soul. Come on, I'll take your luggage up. We've four flights to climb."

The surge of patriotism, the intense indignation at Germany's tactics, the excitement of fighting a war against injustice, which had originally stirred the nation, had deteriorated. Newspapers were calling it a "phony war," and both the British and French governments were beginning to hope that it would be a limited war, with most of the action confined to the north and east of Europe.

Magda followed the reports in papers from around the world and shared the shock and feeling of hopelessness endured by small countries who surrendered to the threat of German invasion—frequently without a shot being fired. The atmosphere was tense and uncertain, and she was reminded of the calm preceding a typhoon, when the air was stilled only hours before the rampage and fury of the elements took over.

In this climate of a country at war for its life, Magda proceeded to go through her renaturalization process. The day came when she was finally granted her papers as a British citizen, and only when she held them in her hands did she realize how much being British meant to her. She felt like a whole person again and knew the stirrings of national pride.

The position to which Chapin had considered her eminently suited was that of cryptologist. As he had warned, she had to go through grueling examinations and checks, until she felt that every thought she had ever had was exposed to the examiners at Intelligence before they accepted her. But it was worth it. She was thrilled by the work. It took concentration and an analytical approach, a superb memory and a subtlety of imagination.

Cryptology, she learned, was a science, with rules and mathematical precision. Sophisticated equipment was constantly being adapted to the breaking down of codes. Chapin told her that the examiners who accepted her had been impressed by her grasp of languages in general and, in particular, her almost uncanny perception of inconsistencies or too many consistencies in a code. But Magda herself was fascinated by the whole new world of study which utilized her special talents.

Her life took on a routine and, moreover, a meaning. At last, she knew that she was doing something constructive. In the evenings she volunteered for Red Cross work or studied the history of cryptology. She and Chapin found they had many things in common, and when both had free time, they spent it together.

The hours of her days and evenings were well occupied, and memories of Archie did not stab her as frequently as they once had.

She had agreed to see him once more before she left Hong Kong. He had telephoned and begged her to lunch with him in a small teahouse on the outskirts of Kowloon.

How predictable he had been, embracing her, then launching into his usual promises that they would somehow steal time for each other again. But Magda, tired of his entreaties, stood firm—the time had come to break with the past, and she tried to make Archie understand.

"You said it once, Archie—we're best apart. Anyway, it's too late. I've decided to go to England. My plans are made."

Archie's eyes lit up.

"Magda! That's perfect. I've put in for the RAF, I'll be gone any day. Dear heart, don't close the door on me, let me see you in London."

"I don't think I could. Not any more, please, Archie. It's no good—let it pass," she said and he gave her such a forlorn frown that all the things she felt, all the things she wanted to say, went unspoken. The good common sense had melted away. All that was left was their intense need for each other.

"We'll wait and see," Magda had whispered weakly, close to tears.

Then she said: "Archie, remember this number," and she repeated the post-office box number Chapin had given her. After that, she rose quickly from her chair, and left the restaurant without saying goodbye.

Their arrangements for an evening out had to be on the spur of the moment, for Chapin was frequently called to the office without advance notice. This was one of the lucky nights, though. They were both without commitments. Chapin brought over Magda's mail, for she still

319

used his private post-office box number at Chelsea Station; it was simpler, for the time being, than arranging one for herself. He had three letters for her: one from William, a thick one from Tasha, and a typed envelope with no return address. As she handled it, Magda felt her blood run first hot, then cold. She had a strong premonition of what it contained.

"Don't mind me," said Chapin, glancing over the titles of several books on her desk. "My word, you're really getting into this stuff: *Traité des Chiffres, Kryptographik* by Kluber, and here's one in Italian. Look, go ahead and read your letters. I'll try my hand on the old German—it's been a long time since I tackled it."

"Let's go now, Chapin. I'll read them later."

They went to Enrico's, in Soho, which they both liked, but the evening did not go well. Magda tried to disguise her misgivings and nervousness with feverish gaiety. This was so unlike her that it would have alerted anyone, even someone less perceptive than Chapin.

It's that bloody swine, Monteith, he thought angrily. Why the hell doesn't he leave her alone? He had noticed her sharp inhalation of breath when she saw the anonymous envelope. He looked at her with compassion and the dismal knowledge that he could do nothing to help her. There was only one person who could upset Magda like that. Chapin had a burning desire to give Archie a good hiding. For all his slightness, Chapin could give a good accounting of himself to a man twice his size, but it was rare that he was ever called upon to practice his skills.

"Sorry to cut our evening short, old girl, but I'm going to have to go back. Do you mind if we leave early?" he asked, easing her out of her misery as diplomatically as he could.

"Oh, no!" she said eagerly, then realizing that she sounded too enthusiastic, "In fact, yes—I—I have a bit of a headache."

He left Magda at the entrance of Hatter's Castle. They both understood that he would not be coming up for his usual nightcap. He waited until he heard her footsteps fade away, then went on his way, his mind occupied with Magda and what he felt for her.

In her room, Magda stirred the last embers of fire in the grate and threw on some more coal. She undressed, wrapped herself in a quilted robe, and, sitting as close to the fire as possible, first read the letter from William. Then, she forced herself to wait, next reading Tasha's long, rambling letter full of news from home. With no further excuse, she studied the typed envelope—even before she opened it, she knew it was from Archie.

Don't open the letter, she warned herself. Think, Magda, think.

Think how pleasant, how comfortable and uninvolved is your relationship with Chapin—we're both the same kind, quiet, same sense of fun, same interests, unemotional.

Unemotional? Once long ago, perhaps. What had set her on fire then, made her passionate, demanding, needing Archie? No! She mustn't let it happen again. Destroy the letter, Magda. Nothing was worth jeopardizing her present peace of mind.

Pushing these thoughts from her consciousness, Magda carefully opened the envelope and saw the familiar handwriting. Slowly she read:

My dear Magda: I'll be in London for a day or so. It does seem foolish that two people who have known each other so long and are so genuinely fond of each other should not spend a few hours together. I am sure we can be good friends and act in a mature way. Time in London hangs heavy on my hands and I would like to show you some of my favorite places. Jennie and the children are with my mother at the farm.

Let me know in care of Brown's Hotel. I usually stay there when I'm in London. I'll be there on Saturday and Sunday this weekend, or you could phone and let me know when and where and if.

Please!

Archie

A very cautious and friendly letter; certainly not one to find fault with. Magda was distinctly annoyed. Then she laughed at herself. She had not wanted any further entanglement with Archie and, if this letter were any criterion, neither did he. Was it really possible? Could they

321

just be good friends—joke and talk and go on long walks, have the companionship they had once enjoyed—without the destructive passion which had absorbed them both?

She noticed the date. It had been sent three days ago. Tomorrow was Saturday—there was no time to write. She would have to call and leave a message. She worried about what to do and what to say, but all along she knew she was going to see him—just to see how it could work out, of course. If it didn't, it would be time enough to call a halt. She had learned her lesson.

The fire was cold now. The embers were all that remained. Magda hadn't realized how long she'd been sitting there. She shivered. She had discovered that in London, even colder than the wind, the rain, and frost, were the icy cold sheets which her body could not warm up. This night, with a hot-water bag at her feet, she fell asleep, for the first time in months, with a warm glow of anticipation . . . of a fire that smoldered no matter how she tried to quench it.

They met by the Marble Arch in Hyde Park. It was early May and the sun was gloriously bright. The flowers did not know it was wartime—they only knew it was spring, and they lifted their heads joyously—daffodils and sweet-smelling purple crocuses. The trees bore new green leaves scattered on dark branches like small pieces of jade sparkling in the sunlight.

Archie was waiting near the Arch. As soon as he saw Magda, he rushed toward her. She faltered at the sight of his tall, slim figure, so familiar, and yet so strange in his uniform. Then her steps quickened, and they almost ran into each other's arms. Six months fled. Three years fled. They held hands and walked through the huge park, stopping to throw little pebbles into the lake and watching the swans glide by in proud disdain. They sat on benches like hundreds of other couples who had taken advantage of this day in spring. The couples looked alike: all the men in uniform, and many of the women. Archie and Magda went to a little teashop and feasted on buttered scones and seed cake and drank cups of strong tea. They peered in the windows of all the shops, and they talked, oh, how they talked, trying to make up for all those lost months.

They stopped at a foodshop and bought some cold cuts and a bottle of wine. Seeming to wander aimlessly, they strolled past Threadneedle Street, turned down another street, then turned down a narrow alley and still another. Finally, they stood in front of Magda's place. Archie stared at the curlicued building. Then he confronted her with raised eyebrows. She met his eyes, trying to be serious, and they both burst into laughter.

"It isn't possible. It must have been built by blind hobgoblins! What's it called?"

"Tut-tut, don't know? Why, Hatter's Castle Secundus."

"I think I'll rename it Merlin's Folly—certainly only a warlock could have waved his wand and created this." He stroked her chin and whispered softly, "Perhaps he will wave his wand again and turn it into our castle of dreams."

Carrying their packages, they ascended the four flights of steps up to her rooms.

The next morning, Magda awoke as if in a dream. She smiled as the dream became reality, snuggled back into Archie's arms, and slept sweetly. Loneliness was banished. She woke again to the sound of a crackling fire, of water bubbling on the stove of her miniature kitchen, and to the smell of fresh, hot bread. Most importantly, there was Archie smiling down at her. She raised her arms lazily, and he sat on the edge of the bed and hugged her.

"You are sweet and fresh and tender and I think I shall eat you," he murmured between kisses and nibbles. Once again, desire filled them, and once more their bodies clung together in passionate abandon, illuminated by a brilliant morning sun.

At last they lay still in happy exhaustion.

"You are insatiable," she said with contentment in her voice.

"Greedy," he corrected her, smiling. "Sorry?"

His hands roamed over her body. Her fragile beauty seemed like a miracle, a gift, and he couldn't bear to let her out of his arms. But she pushed herself away from him, laughing, and jumped out of bed.

"It's going to be another lovely day, darling. Let's not waste it!"

323

"You call this wasting the day?" he grumbled, joining her at the window. Magda pointed to the right.

"Can you see that silvery line? That's the Thames way off there. Can you see it?" She laughed. "Of course, Chappie says that if I saw the Thames at all, it would be in the other direction, but I insist it is the Thames. What is in a person's mind is reality to that person," she added imperiously. "Therefore, that is the Thames."

"If you say it's the Thames, then I believe you," Archie assured her. "Well, now that we're up, let's get cracking!"

"Did you have something in mind?" Magda asked.

"Just for the heck of it, I thought we'd pretend to be tourists and take a bus to Shakespeare country. What do you think?"

"It's crazy, but what fun! Are the tours on?"

"Easy enough to find out."

The day was sunny but very cold. They walked briskly; Archie had his coat collar up and his RAF cap pulled down over his eyes.

"What I can see of you looks very debonair, airman," Magda teased, her breath forming steam in the air as she spoke through her scarf.

"The tip of your nose is very lovely, lady of my heart," he responded, taking her arm to help her over a curb. Without his realizing, it remained there possessively.

"Do you know something? I don't feel as though I ate any breakfast. Suddenly, I'm ravenously hungry."

"I was thinking the same thing, but it seemed so silly to say so. There's a little place nearby, I seem to remember, where they serve hot chocolate and a bun. Over there, next to the newspaper shop."

They walked over. The shop was empty except for the two of them. Magda sat down at a spindly little table, while Archie gave the order and went to buy a newspaper.

It was overheated in the small room, and Magda removed her hat and scarf. She looked up and smiled at Archie when he returned to the table. He traced her face with his finger, wonderingly.

"Every time I see you, I am startled again by how beautiful you are. It's always a surprise. I keep thinking —I can't be so lucky, this girl can't be my girl. I feel I should do something extraordinary to deserve your attention—like performing a heroic deed or making you laugh. Should I wiggle my ears and become Bunny again?"

Magda couldn't restrain a giggle. "You are a goose, and I do so love you when you're in this mood. I wish it could always be like this with us, so carefree and happy. Will we ever be able to throw off the unhappy past when we see each other? Do you think we can, Archie?"

"Yes, we will, I promise you that. Believe me, my dearest heart, each minute we have together will be preciously guarded. Our time together will be secret and private, and nothing will intrude into our rare, enchanted world."

"Is that a solemn promise?" Magda asked, her voice a whisper.

"I cross my heart and hope to die. I love you so much my heart overfloweth." He tried to say it lightly, but there was a seriousness in his eyes and his voice. They looked at each other as though, indeed, a special grace had been given them, a world of their own within the larger one.

The day beckoned to them, and Magda and Archie were determined to enjoy it.

"Let's see if there's any mention of tours today," Archie said as he opened up the folded newspaper to the front page. The ultra-conservative *London Times,* which did not believe in big headlines, had one blazoned under its banner, two inches wide. GERMANY STARTS INVASION OF LOWLANDS. Sunday, May 10, 1940. Then came the three-column story, reporting that the largest German force yet mustered for a single maneuver was already overrunning the borders of Holland; Denmark was under attack; and another group was deployed toward Belgium.

This was the closest the war had come to Great Britain. The "phony war" was over; the brief, inconsequential skirmishes were things of the past.

"I must make a telephone call immediately."

Archie left the table and returned in a few minutes. "This is it, my sweet."

He asked the young girl who was minding the store to call them a cab. Silently, Magda put on her hat and

325

scarf, and they went outside to await its arrival. In these last minutes, Magda watched another man emerge in Archie, strong, courageous, and more precious than ever.

They faced each other. He took her hand and kissed her ring finger.

"I wish this had my ring on it," he said solemnly with no effort to lighten the words. "If we never see each other again, my sweet, don't regret our love, for that will never die. So many things have happened, and so many things have gone wrong for us, but the one right thing was that we met and that we fell in love. For me that is the only thing in my life that has meaning. I wish you bore my name, so that I could leave you something of me. But you must know that yours is engraved on my heart for all eternity."

Tenderly, he brushed away the tears in her eyes. They held each other close for that one moment which time always stopped for them.

"May I come to see you when I return?" he asked.

She nodded—she could say nothing.

The driver honked his horn. Archie touched his cap to her and entered the cab. He looked straight ahead as the cab rolled away, but Magda watched the road for a long time after the car had disappeared into the distance.

A vow was forming in her heart—henceforth, she would be generous and undemanding in her love. If her road led to Archie, she would never again question his devotion nor ask him for more than he was free to give. Perhaps they would never have the trappings of a traditional love—a family, a home together—but they had each other's love, and that would be enough for a lifetime.

CHAPTER TWENTY-FOUR

‹‹‹‹‹‹‹‹‹‹‹‹‹‹‹‹‹‹‹‹‹‹‹‹‹‹‹‹‹‹‹

ON SUNDAY, MAY 10, while London was enjoying the arrival of spring, the curtain rose on the great European tragedy. Poland, Norway, and Denmark were mere dress rehearsals for the devastation which followed.

Magda, along with the rest of the country, read the news reports in a state of shock, as one disaster followed another and the lists of British casualties grew. The famed Maginot Line, on which the French had placed their faith, was overwhelmed and the fall of France began. The British Expeditionary Forces, three hundred and fifty thousand strong, were hemmed in on all sides, leaving only one way out, through the open port of Dunkirk.

Magda had a large map of Europe pinned on her wall and followed every movement of the war. Newspapers from all over the world were delivered to her desk; it was part of her job to scan foreign papers for items of interest to British Intelligence.

Chapin had been gone for a week on some secret mission, and she missed his constant presence. She had never fully appreciated how much she depended on his company, his dry wit and his comforting, realistic sanity. He finally returned during the desperate defense of the Netherlands, and she burst out with her bottled-up feelings. She condemned the Allied Command for not taking more bold and decisive actions. They were fighting a defensive war, and the Germans out-maneuvered them every time. Why was it, Magda demanded that the Allies were always too late with too little?

"They're doing the same thing as in Hong Kong. There, they're deliberately blinding themselves to the Japanese threat, as though hoping that if they close their eyes it will all go away."

"It's too bad you're not doing the Allied planning," he said sardonically.

"I know I'm being insufferable, but it's sickening. I eat and live with it and can't sleep at night."

"Have you heard from Archie?"

"No. I doubt if the RAF are allowed to write at this time. Even the postmarks could give them away," she answered, shaking her head at him as she realized what she had admitted. "You know me too well, Chappie. Sometimes I'm almost afraid of you. Do you have a little antenna hidden in your head? I don't suppose I really mind your knowing—you know everything about me there is to know, anyhow."

He shrugged. "I just thought you might want an ear or a shoulder."

She took his hand and pressed it to her cheek.

"I'm not too accustomed to shoulders, but I'll keep it in mind. An ear is something else. Sometimes I think I'll go mad if I can't tell my worries to someone. That's one of the disadvantages of not being a wife." She smiled a bit shamefacedly. "You are so good to me, Chappie. I just can't thank you enough."

"Then don't."

Chapin called Magda two days before the full disaster struck the Lowlands. It was May 26. Bad news was pouring in from all fronts, and the BEF was surrounded at Dunkirk. Magda received a sudden phone call from Chapin.

"Your office has consented to release you to my division for the present. I'll pick you up in half an hour. Bring along warm sturdy clothes. We may have to rough it. Be sure you have heavy gloves and woolen stockings. I can't tell you anything more now."

"What's happening?" she asked him when they were on the road.

"We're preparing to evacuate the BEF from Europe. There will be French and Dutch and Belgians among our own. I've been put in charge of Intelligence, and I'm going to depend on your sharp ear for speech discrepancies. We'll be taking all possible precautions after they land. It's a perfect opportunity for illegal entry."

On June 4, the last boats arrived back in England.

The statistics which Chapin later showed Magda indicated: "People saved: 338,226, among them 26,000 Frenchmen, some Dutch and Belgians. Over four thousand craft used."

It had truly been a miracle. The whole of England had acted as one unit, with valor, strength of purpose, and complete dedication.

Clothes, blankets, food, and money came from every part of the British Isles. Those who had been lethargic in their previous support were spurred to new heights. England was united in a manner which only great tragedy or fear can produce.

The one thing that Hitler and his Third Reich had not counted on was that, instead of accepting defeat, the British were now dogged in their determination to fight to the last man, even if they had to fight with bare hands—which at present was about all they had. Their navy was tattered. All too few planes had survived the holocaust; tanks, mobile equipment, guns, all were abandoned in Europe. But the men were back home and that was what mattered.

Dunkirk became a rallying cry. It lit a torch which warmed the hearts of all Britishers, filling their eyes with zeal. A signal defeat became a moment of glory, an almost holy experience. It showed the capacity of man to triumph over terrible odds. For Magda, it kindled a new loyalty, and her heart filled with love for her country.

Driving back to London with Chapin, Magda was tired, but it was an exhaustion filled with satisfaction at their accomplishment.

"I'll never forget it, Chappie, if I live to be a hundred. Those small fishing boats manned by children and old women, their hands wrapped in scarves. People making trip after trip under gunfire and everyone absolutely confident they would carry it off. I never saw so many different kinds of boats in my life: tugs, trawlers, private yachts, ferry boats and fishing boats. There they were, all getting out into that grey sea with breakers large enough to capsize them. My dear, I was so proud of being British, even only half-British."

"Does that still bother you?"

"Not really. I feel as though I'm really a part of everything that's happening. Even though it's so sad, there's still a resurgence of spirit and faith which penetrates everyone and everything. We are all together in this, and it makes no difference who or what you are. I feel a little like Columbus, as though I could kneel and kiss the ground of England. For the first time, I know what it's like to be devoted to a country and ready to die for it—like William feels about China. Oh, how I do babble!"

In drowsy silence they drove on, Magda tucked under a plaid blanket, still seeing the sea of tents which had lined the beaches along the coast, and the cheerful, half-frozen faces coming into the hastily-erected wooden shacks and warming their hands against the portable stoves. Among those elderly men and women who were so important a part of the Civilian Defense, social differences were completely wiped out. Instead, there was an easy camaraderie which had moved Magda deeply.

They were both engrossed in their own thoughts when Magda broke the long silence.

"Chappie, do me a favor? I check the casualty lists daily, which is pretty ghoulish, but I can't go any further than that. Could you find out for me if Archie is back? Perhaps at home?" The words came out with difficulty.

"Can do," Chapin said, devoid of expression.

"I suppose you think I'm a weak fool."

"I try to not make personal judgments."

"Oh, don't be so exasperating. Go ahead and tell me that it's time I learned."

"I don't think you need to have anyone tell you anything. I'm sure you've thought of everything there is to think."

"How righteous you are," she said sharply, and was immediately contrite. "I'm sorry, Chappie. It's just that every time he goes, I'm afraid he'll never come back. At times I feel I've grown old and dry and weary, except where Archie is concerned. Only then do I become young and hopeful—too easily wounded and too easily elated. I want to end it, because we hurt each other; but I *don't* want to end it, because it makes me feel alive. Do you mind my talking?"

330

"If it helps you," his voice answered, noncommittal. "Give me another cigarette, will you?"

"Sometimes I wish—I don't know what's got into me, talking so much about myself and my feelings. Perhaps it's because of all I've seen in the last few days. Now, I'll play turnabout, and listen to your troubles."

"Sorry, Magda, I can't oblige you—I've never needed a confessor."

"No, I suppose not. You're very self-sufficient. I used to be. I've become so terribly fond of you, Chappie. You're such a good friend."

"Have over with it, will you?"

Magda winced, surprised. He sounded curt and angry. "I'm sorry, Chapin," she said, thinking she knew what bothered him.

"Sorry? Why? About what?" He was incongruously startled.

"You know. I've become such a chatterbox about myself. I won't indulge again, I promise. In fact I'm a bit embarrassed."

"No need. I offered you a shoulder, didn't I?" He forgave her with the old twinkle in his eyes and a trace of a smile, and it was all she needed to feel comfortable again and reassured.

When they arrived at Hatter's Castle, she invited him up for a drink, but he hesitated.

"I thought perhaps a hot toddy, and I have some good biscuits I've been saving. Besides, I have something to talk to you about. Not about myself, something rather important."

With a fire crackling in the grate and the hot drinks warming their hands, she began. "It's Waldemar."

"What? You've heard from him?"

"No. Nothing like that. You know that one of the inflexible rules in the department is not to talk about our work to anyone, not even to a member of the team. Only to our immediate superiors."

"It's a good rule, Magda, don't break it," he warned.

"I think it's important that I do—with you. I've been thinking about it since before Dunkirk, when I first caught on to it. I've never had occasion to talk to my superior. The courier brings me my assignments in a sealed envelope, and I return them the same way."

"You mustn't tell me anything, Magda. I might have to report it. If it concerns me, it will come to me from the proper sources."

Chapin had suddenly become Mr. Desmond, Senior Officer of British Intelligence.

"You're making it very difficult for me, Chappie. I'm not betraying anything confidential—it's just because you know the entire story about Waldemar, and it will make sense to you where it might not to anyone else. Please, Chapin. This should be checked more thoroughly than would seem necessary."

"Well, get on with it, then."

"My work is mostly censoring letters from prisoners of war or foreign residents. In a stack of them, I came across a couple that I am certain are from Waldemar. It was the word "Zorro" which first alerted me. It appeared in a simple letter in German, to a friend, saying how well he was treated here and that he'd been to see the old movie, *The Mark of Zorro*, with Douglas Fairbanks. The writer chatted on about this and that and said that he was using his free time to study the history of England. All very innocent—except that Zorro was the line of horses Waldemar bred, and Zorro Historian was one of his best. I can just see Waldemar enjoying the joke. I won't describe the way I checked it out, except to tell you that Historian was the key word of the code message. It translated: 'Contacts are well established, be prepared for the program to commence shortly as previously planned.'"

"Clever work, Magda. We are well aware of everything Waldemar has been doing and he is under our close observation since he arrived. Now, let me think this out for a minute."

Magda saw Chapin separate himself in intense concentration. He placed his elbows on the table, pressed his fingers against his brow, and sat absolutely still for a few minutes. She could almost hear facts clicking into order. When he looked up, Magda wondered how she had ever considered him nondescript—but as rapidly as the look of strong intelligence and intense power had come, it vanished, leaving behind the comfortably ordinary face Chapin showed to the world.

"The first thing to take into consideration is that Waldemar would not be here under our surveillance were it not for you. Without your special knowledge of him, this particular letter would not have been decoded. This message is not of particular importance, but your specialized knowledge of the man could be useful. On the other hand, you are almost too closely associated and thus may have a prejudiced point of view, which could be a serious handicap. We have found through experience that the more objective a counter-spy is, the more likely we are to get the results we seek.

"Point two is strictly a selfish one from my viewpoint. I very carefully put you outside of my department because another one of our rules is to have no firm friendships within the same department. I'm giving you a choice —I think you deserve one. If you want to follow up on Waldemar, you will be placed directly in my department and we will have to disassociate ourselves from each other. But, your special knowledge could be fed to someone else and leave you to develop your talents and grow in importance to us." He dropped his professorial air and grinned. "Well, which do you choose? I must admit I would feel rather forlorn if we had to give up our evenings together. What's the verdict?"

"You," she said without any hesitation, and then flushed. "I mean that I don't want to lose your friendship but also that you're right. I'd always see more in Waldemar's actions than was really there. I despise that man and I fear him."

They smiled happily at each other and drank a toast to their friendship. Chapin gave her detailed instructions on how to proceed with regard to Waldemar.

"It seems that his personality profile is never to rely on any one person or one way of doing things. His unpredictability makes him even more dangerous. Be careful. Well, my dear, I must be leaving."

He kissed her lightly and left the apartment.

Magda waited every evening, hoping to receive a call from Archie. When it did come she was quite distracted, trying to construct a code which couldn't be broken. She answered the phone impatiently, and heard Archie's voice.

"Maggie! I've an eight-hour leave. I'm coming over."

"Darling! I've been going crazy with worry. Have you eaten? All I have are eggs. I think the bakery is still open. I'll run down and get French bread, and I'll make a salad. Oh, good, I have a can of mushrooms."

Archie laughed. "Silly goose! I'm coming to see you, not to eat. Though I can always stand some good grub after what I've been getting. See you in about half an hour."

"Oh, yes!"

He was safe, and Magda was able to give her attention fully to her work once more.

Germany's attack on France lasted barely six weeks before France was crushed. It was fortunate for England that Germany had decided to mop up France before attacking England—for, after Dunkirk, Great Britain was helpless militarily. Those six weeks of grace gave them a chance to build up their depleted air force, to overhaul their navy. Factories hummed day and night, turning out equipment to replace what had been left behind in Europe.

In all this activity, Magda thrived. Her life had become meaningful and complete. Such free time as she had from her job and the Nurses' Auxilliary she spent with Chapin, trying to arrange her time off with the occasional days Chapin could take from his work. These they usually spent in the country, where Chapin had a cottage.

It was some twenty-five miles from London and yet it was a different world, where for a few hours they could put the war behind them. They walked in the rain and strolled down country lanes on sunny days. They talked when they needed to, and were silent when saying nothing felt right. They renewed themselves from the devastation of the war by watching nature continue its cycle: little creatures burrowed, undisturbed; birds nestled; and flowers dared to bloom. For Magda, Chapin became her English William, dependable friend, good companion. And Chapin—he was as always, friendly, discreet, and unfortunately for him, her confidant.

On June 25, 1941, France capitulated. Only then did the Germans turn their full attention to England. The six weeks' respite for Britain was over and the Luftwaffe went into action. The bombs fell on England in waves, and their main target was London. Perhaps it was, as Churchill proclaimed, England's finest hour, for instead of succumbing to the massive attacks, the people rallied as never before. It would take more than wrecked buildings or waves of bombs to shake British confidence in their country or in themselves. The tide started to reverse a little as England's armaments were built up. The newspaper headlines read proudly that, in one day, two thousand German planes had flown over London like a black cloud of destruction, and that the RAF had shot down over two hundred of them.

Magda walked with dignity amidst the ruined buildings, her eyes gleaming with pride for the heroism of her countrymen. She stepped over newly-fallen rubble in streets full of shattered glass, the air still filled with clouds of dust and the sound of fury still echoing in the air. The spirit of courage was contagious as she and her Nurses' Auxilliary attended the wounded and the dying, working along with the clean-up crews, ignoring the possibility of another wave of destruction from above.

Like all Londoners, Magda soon became accustomed to the shrill warning signal that the bombings were about to begin. At first, everyone rushed to the shelters; soon, many were taking it all in their stride, accepting the enemy planes as a commonplace event.

The same good fellowship and courage spread to the bomb shelters. Shortages, deprivations, and danger threatened everyone equally. The first time Magda went down into a shelter she saw, to her amazement, the kinship which thrived in those dark and musty cellars. The Cockney, with his sharp wit, was as proud as the monocled baronet, and high-born ladies sat huddled next to charwomen. In the democracy of death there were no social distinctions. Magda found, in this community of people brought together by circumstance, that the manacles which had handcuffed her to her father's obsession were finally unlocked and discarded. She felt gloriously free—not a half-caste, not a MacDougall, not a Chen, but proudly one of the British fraternity. At last, her school motto *In uno omnia juncta* made sense to her: In one are we joined.

In August, Magda received a letter from Tasha. She

and Barry were being evacuated. Barry was to be stationed in San Francisco—possibly permanently. Authorities had instructed all foreign civilians to leave Hong Kong, and all British wives and children had been sent to Australia for their safety. Newly-made bachelor-husbands were fighting the edict, demanding their wives back. In fact, Tasha wrote, there was far more in the local newspapers about this marital revolution than about the war itself. Everyone not involved took it as a huge joke, but the husbands were genuinely up in arms.

Tasha couldn't believe that she was actually leaving China, perhaps never to return . . .

A letter from William arrived at the same time. The tri-partite treaty Japan had signed with Germany and Italy, he wrote, finally told the world what he and Magda had known for a long time. William was sending his family to Chungking, out of the Japanese war zone. Lotus had many relatives there. She did not want to leave him but it was difficult enough for him to work ostensibly with the Japanese without the worry of Lotus or the children being hurt in the crossfire. He was filled with repugnance, but each man had his duty. Magda thought it odd to receive such a letter from William—he was usually so reticent about himself—but she understood that the war had brought his deep-felt emotions to the surface.

The war dragged on, but Magda was too busy to notice the passage of time. She liked working with the others in her department, and she enjoyed Chapin's company thoroughly and knew he enjoyed hers. He was wise, attentive, and she had learned to appreciate his droll sense of humor. More than that, he knew her well, and understood her almost more than she did herself. Had it not been for the interruptions of Archie's visits, she would have been fully content.

Whenever Archie called, Chapin stepped aside tactfully so that Magda wouldn't have to make embarrassing explanations. There were times when making the explanations to herself became difficult, and she was forced to persuade herself that Archie was facing death with every mission, that it was her duty to be there when he wanted her. Duty! The very use of the word shocked her. What was happening to the undying love to which they had committed themselves?

Archie was changing so rapidly that she barely knew him. The gentle man, tender in his passion for her, had almost disappeared.

In the beginning, he told her of his early missions and of how sick he had been when the first shell was dropped. They had been given maps of cities and towns which had been suspected of harboring munitions plants. They bombed a little village suspected of having a disguised plant; when he flew his plane low for the hit, he saw a little boy dash out of the cottage as the bomb fell, and then there was nothing at all. His eyes filled when he repeated the story to Magda.

But the war toughened him, changed his personality. Magda wondered if the war changed all men so drastically and wondered if there was still the same sensitive man under the uncaring armor.

Archie had developed a plan of action for his free time: he spent his short leaves with her, longer leaves, which stretched for a few days or a weekend, were spent in the country with Jennie and the children. He came back from them feeling refreshed, looking happy and well, speaking frequently of his family and their pleasant life in the country. He seemed unconcerned how the comparison would affect Magda. When he came to her directly from the fighting, he was worn out, depressed and tired, needing her physically, in order to assuage the horrors of war.

Magda never reproached him by word or sign. She had made herself that vow—to keep their love untarnished and tender, without reservations, without criticisms, but her doubts grew with each of Archie's visits.

Britain had already experienced two years of devastating war when the Japanese struck Pearl Harbor on December 7, 1941, and the United States entered the conflict.

The following day, Hong Kong was invaded. The Japanese came not by sea, but by air, followed by masses of troops who had been lying in wait. The big cannons which British military experts had so confidently placed in key positions on the hills were never even fired. It took the

337

Japanese eighteen days to take the "impregnable fortress" of Hong Kong, leaving behind havoc and bloody death.

William wrote from Shanghai for the last time:

My little Lotus and our children are dead. My poor Lotus! She never wanted to leave me but I insisted for her safety. My heart weeps—I cannot believe I shall never again see her or my children. I have adopted your half-brother as my son. We are safe for the time being because the Japanese, with whom I deal, believe I care only for my personal fortune. I know I can serve my country better by joining my people. I must leave here or go mad.

The Americans who did not heed the warnings are in internment camps, as are the British who still believed in treaties and friendship pacts, closing their eyes to impending disaster. They can only blame themselves.

The Portuguese are about the only people here still unaffected by the Japanese invasion of Shanghai—they are neutral in this war. The Germans, as we predicted, are in a position of strength.

For some time now, college students and professors have been leaving Shanghai for the interior. China is vast. Somewhere in the far recesses of China we will rebuild our country. I do not know when you will hear from me again, for where I go the mail will be uncertain.

My dear cousin Magda, you who are so very close to me, I pray to Buddha that only good will come to you, and that your soul be made clear, and bright and invincible. Ever your true cousin, William.

Following Pearl Harbor, the British were jubilant to welcome the United States into the Allies, which consisted of Great Britain, her commonwealth, and the underground fighters in all of the countries which had already been invaded. It gave a spirit of new life to the people who had survived thus far through sheer indomitability. The year 1942 began with a feeling of renewed and replenished confidence.

Magda was busier than ever; each moment of her time was fully accounted for in some needed effort. But Archie's behavior became more and more wearing. He had put a

338

stamp of ownership on her and she was finding it increasingly difficult to tolerate his easy acceptance of two homes and two wives—one recognized by the world, the other in the shadows. Most annoying, though, was his assumption that what she did was not of great importance, that she was expected to drop whatever she was doing as soon as he called and meet him without delay.

It took all her self-control at these times not to counter his demands with sharp retorts. Magda tried to excuse him. After all, he had no idea what kind of work she was doing, however—she did not dare consider her feelings too deeply. She told herself that everything worthwhile was fragile, and must be preserved—that their love was beautiful and she didn't intend to destroy it.

She hadn't seen him for over a month when he called her office one day and said that he was on his way over to see her.

"But, Archie, I can't possibly leave now. I'm in the middle of an important assignment," she reasoned patiently.

"Oh, come on. It can't be all that important. Look, Magda," he said, his voice aggrieved. "I only have an eight-hour pass. I called you first of all. I didn't even call home, and all you can say is that you're working."

"But, Archie, we're all working for England in our own ways. I can't just get up and leave. My hours aren't my own, and my work can't just be neglected. It would look very suspicious, and you wouldn't want that, would you?" She knew that suggesting discovery would cool him off. It always did.

"No. I suppose not. Not after all our efforts to be so careful. How soon can you get away?"

"Why don't you go over and take a shower and a nap? I'll try to make it in a couple of hours. And I'll get something for dinner. I don't suppose you have any coupons?" she asked wistfully.

"No, I turn them all over to Jennie."

Magda arrived at the apartment, having spent most of her week's ration coupons in order to get him a decent meal. She felt guilty for having been sharp with him—and even more so for her thoughts.

He was lying on the bed, sleeping heavily. He was tired and gaunt, and he needed a shave. She started dinner on her two-burner stove, and soon the odor of spices filled the room as she prepared Hungarian goulash. As soon as the food started simmering, she undressed to take a shower and found Archie sitting up, scanning her lustfully. For the first time with Archie, she felt embarrassed and debased by her nudity.

"God! But you're gorgeous! I'll never get my fill of looking at you. Come here."

"No, Archie," she said, quickly putting on a robe. "I'm tired and sticky and I'm going to take a shower. I hope you left me some hot water."

She tried to speak nonchalantly, but she was uncomfortably aware of his staring.

"Come here," he demanded, his voice thick. She shook her head and went determinedly to the bathroom, but Archie rose and seized her, kissing her hungrily. He pulled off her robe and carried her forcibly to the bed.

"Stop it, Archie. Stop it!" She struggled with him fiercely but he paid no more heed to her struggles than to her words. This time there was no electricity for her, no rapture, no pleasure: only an unfamiliar repugnance, a feeling of wanting to draw herself in, to hold her breath until it was all over and done with. Her muscles were taut as she resisted him but he was too wrapped up in his own desires to pay any attention to hers.

Finally it was done, and he lay back, satiated. Like a rhythm, beating with her pulse, the same thought kept pounding, over and over. This can't be happening. This is Archie. This can't be happening.

Then the refrain stopped, and the words came sharp and clear in her mind. You've been lying to yourself long enough, Magda. Face the truth: Archie has no love for you, nor do you for him. All that's left is lust, and all you've been doing is trying to keep alive a dream that's long since dead.

"You don't know the dreams I have of you," Archie was murmuring. "Sometimes when I'm miles in the air, the clouds are like a soft pillow, and I see you on the pillows with me, just as distinctly as I can see you now. I think I know every wonderful inch of your body. It's almost real up in the clouds, imagining I'm with you."

Magda had no such dreams. She felt only limp and soiled.

"Pull yourself together, old girl," she spoke to herself. "You're just tired and annoyed. This is Archie, the man you love." But after that voice came another: "Don't be a bloody fool. How long can you keep on deceiving yourself? What sort of love is this, anyway, without tenderness, without companionship?" Magda sat unmoving, alone with her thoughts.

"Umm, that food smells good. You're a great cook, Magda. I wish Jennie could learn to cook decently. Everything *she* makes tastes as though it had been boiled for hours—without seasoning. Mother has tried to teach her —she's willing enough, but her talents just don't lie in that direction. Why don't you take a shower while I set the table? I'm so hungry I could eat a cow. Nothing like a good romp to whet the appetite, eh?"

Archie went to the stove and lifted the lid covering the stew. "Hey, I haven't seen that much meat in a long time. You must have used all your rations on me. I'm really a very lucky fellow—a beautiful lady in bed and a good cook to boot."

Was he always that insensitive? Magda thought, listening to him objectively for the first time in months.

She scrubbed herself violently as though trying to wash away her sudden revulsion, not only for Archie but for herself. He had become just a man who fully enjoyed his sensuality; he fornicated with zest and made no pretenses. But she, how she despised herself, despised her delusions of a romantic love which had not existed for a long time. The revelation of the sham, finally admitting it to herself —how long had she deliberately been blind?

The hot water trickled away and a thin stream of iciness chilled her flesh. She stepped out of the shower and rubbed herself raw, punishing herself, yet still making excuses for him.

"Oh, no," she scolded herself finally. "Don't go that route again. It's finished. This terrible evening will be over soon. Let it die decently, but don't act the self-sacrificer any longer."

Archie chatted away during the meal, all of the tensions

341

gone from him. He told her a story about Daphne, his youngest daughter. When had he started to bring his family into her life? They had made a pact to keep their lives separate.

"Go and lie down, Archie," Magda urged. "You'll need all the rest you can get before you leave. I'll clean up."

"No way," he grinned. "I can sleep in the barracks. That's not what I came here for."

She did not struggle when he reached for her. It was useless.

There was no haste this time. He enjoyed her, caressed her body, cupped her breasts and kissed them. He cradled her and stroked her stomach and her thighs. He played with her as though she were a toy, and then, when his passions were fully aroused, he took her.

"You're wonderful," he said when it was over. "What a body you have—there are times I'm afraid I'll crush it." With his arms around her, and his hands on her breasts, he fell asleep, murmuring, "Wake me up in an hour. I'm due back."

Magda lay there. She wanted to take his hands off her, remove herself from his clutches. But she remained where she was, still and motionless, waiting for it to end.

The hour passed and she awakened him. He blinked his eyes open as though he didn't quite know where he was. Then he smiled at her lazily.

"Hello, my sweet Maggie," he whispered. With a big yawn, he drew himself up. "Time to go."

He jumped out of bed and went to the bathroom, took a quick shower, and dressed.

"Next time in I'll be going to the farm," he said, coming from the bedroom. "I think I'm due for a whole weekend. I'll call when I can." He gave her a quick squeeze and opened the front door.

It was as though he had finally said the secret words to release all her restrained fury and resentment which had been stored up for years. She was tired of taking the blame—he had been the one who shattered what should have been a lasting love. She had been blind, but he had carelessly tossed their love away as if it were of no importance. Magda felt as though he had stripped and humiliated her publicly—showing their "love" to be nothing more than a sordid affair.

"You forgot something," Magda said very quietly.

Archie looked around.

"I don't think so."

"You forgot to put the fiver on the dresser."

"Oh, are you short of cash? I think I have some," he said as he put his hands in his pockets; then a puzzled look crossed his face. "What did you mean?"

"I'm not too sure of the current rate but it's customary, I believe, to pay for favors."

"What the hell are you talking about? I don't like this kind of joking."

"I'm not joking. If you're going to treat me as though this is an assignation, then go all the way with it. Your delightful godfather enjoyed calling me a whore and the daughter of a whore. Why he thought he had that right, I'll never understand. But that's how you're treating me, as your private little piece to take when you're in the mood and to leave when you're done."

"Great Scott! You're not after me to marry you again, are you? I thought we fully understood each other, that there's no way I can divorce Jennie for you."

"Then you'll be pleased to know that I don't want to marry you."

"Then what is this all about?"

Magda put on her robe and belted it tightly. "It's not a matter of marriage; and, I'm sorry, really sorry to say that it's no longer a matter of love. I only realized it tonight when you tore the last tattered veil from my eyes. You come in here like a wild man whenever you feel like it. Tonight you took me by force and now you're off, fed and satisfied. There is no tenderness, no companionship, no closeness of any kind. We don't go anywhere because you might be seen by someone who knows you—or else there's no time. I wasn't seduced tonight, I was *raped!*"

"That's nonsense. You enjoy it as much as I do. We seduced each other. Dammit, we love each other."

"I don't know what sort of love you're talking about, Archie. We had it once but it's over. I tried desperately to keep up the myth, until the truth became so glaring that I could no longer hide from it."

Archie re-entered the room and closed the door behind

him. He moved toward her, but she put up a hand and shook her head.

"I'm not talking about whose fault it is—a person can only feel what's there. It's all finished, dead and cold. It should have been a long time ago."

"But I always call you whenever I can. You know what the situation is. We agreed. I thought we were in love. Is there someone else, like that Chapin Desmond?"

She looked at him steadily without saying a word and finally, abashed, his eyes fell.

"I don't know what makes me say these things, Maggie. You know I don't mean it. I don't understand what you're bringing up. Look, I won't tell Jennie about the next leave and we'll spend it together, maybe go away somewhere. It'll be like old times again, we'll have fun. All right with you?"

She shook her head. "No, Archie, it's more than the amount of time we spend together. It's everything. If you don't understand, I can't explain. You disrupt my life. I want peace and quiet, and I don't want you coming here any more. Go back to your Jennie, be the true husband to her that you've always wanted to be. Be a full-time father to your daughters, and be the kind of son to your mother you wish you were—truthful and loyal. It's long past time we turned away from each other."

"I've hurt you badly, haven't I, Maggie?" he looked at her with concern in his eyes, the old Archie brought back to life. "I'm so sorry, dear."

At this sign of tenderness, her eyes filled with unbidden tears. He came to her and brushed them away with his fingers, kissing her gently.

"So dreadfully sorry, so thoughtless. I've been an awful brute. Can you forgive me? It won't happen again."

"There won't be a next time," she insisted, pushing him away.

"You're not serious. You know you don't mean it. I think you feel you have to argue with yourself every once in a while, but you know that you're my real life. It's all empty, otherwise. What will I do up in the skies if I can't imagine you there—and our next time together? You mustn't do this to me; you know I love you, Magda. I need you."

"It's no good, Archie."

344

"But you said yourself you'd do anything to be with me."

"Archie, I've *done* everything to be with you. For too long. Yes, I felt that way once, but it has to be reciprocated, and it hasn't been—not for ages. I'm only sorry we didn't end it while it was still sweet and lovely and memorable. Let's not talk about it any more, it only prolongs the agony. Archie, please go."

"Magda?"

"Please, please go. I won't discuss it. I can't!"

"I can't stand it, I just can't stand it. I can't stand knowing what I've become. I can't stand what I've done to you, and to Jennie and to the girls." He gulped and choked, and tears came into his eyes. Magda sat on the edge of the bed with his head on her lap. She murmured over him and patted him as she would a child, while he sobbed hard, dry sobs, heartbreaking, agonizing sounds which tore Magda apart.

Then he stumbled away to the bathroom to wash his face. After a few minutes he came out, bashful and utterly vulnerable as he tried to grin. "Certainly made a complete ass of myself. I've got to rush or they'll think I've run off. We'll work something out, dearest Maggie. I'll call you next time in."

Without waiting for an answer he rushed out.

Magda shook her head. He hadn't understood a thing she'd said.

"I won't be here," she called after him.

CHAPTER TWENTY-FIVE

◄◄◄◄◄◄◄◄◄◄◄◄◄◄◄◄◄◄◄◄◄◄◄◄◄

CHAPIN DESMOND DROVE Magda to the nearest American air force base, which was situated about an hour's drive from London. He spent the entire time trying to persuade her that she should not leave England, but it was to no avail.

"Oh, Chappie, let it be. It's the only way I can give my poor unborn child a fair chance. I had the lawyer draw up that document I asked you about. Are you positive you don't mind being named as trustee to my estate?"

"I'd do a great deal more if it would give you peace of mind."

"You know it does. At least I'll know that my child will have your concern—that's very important to me. My lawyer arranged it so the money remains entirely in my hands until I decide otherwise. I thought you'd be more comfortable with it that way."

"You'd better name an alternate trustee, just in case something happens to me," Chapin said drily.

It had taken Magda a great deal of soul-searching to finally decide to go to the United States. To leave England, her work, and, not least of all, Chapin, was a sacrifice of real proportion. But she had considered all of the possibilities and felt it was the only choice.

Chapin, after trying to change her mind, reluctantly did everything he could to ease her departure. He managed to transfer her to the American Secret Service, arranging, he hoped, that she'd be stationed in San Francisco, and getting her a flight on the daily cargo plane which left from the nearby base.

Chapin drove up to the padlocked gate and showed his credentials to a tall, lanky American with the two stripes of a corporal on his sleeve. The airman examined the passes, opened the gate, made a sharp salute, and directed them to a wooden building nearby.

There, the officer in charge examined Magda's papers scrupulously and stamped and returned them.

"All in order," he said quickly. "You can wait in the shed or park by those other cars. Take-off's in about half an hour." Rather shyly, he looked at Magda and offered, "Too bad about your husband, ma'am. Tough break. I hope you'll be happy in the States."

For a moment Magda looked puzzled, then remembered. "Thank you, captain. You're very kind. I must learn to live with it. As so many—" Her voice broke, not with grief but with disgust at the role she was forced to play.

"You're very brave, ma'am."

Chapin drove over to the parking area, where they sat silently, looking out at the grey, dreary afternoon. It was too foggy to see anything but the dim shapes of planes and a few flickering lights; even the sound of the engine being revved for take-off was muffled.

"I feel like such a hypocrite," Magda burst out.

"Nonsense! What is your name?" he quizzed her.

"Mrs. Joseph Bentley."

"How long have you been married?"

"Three months. We hardly knew each other, but he was due to go on another mission and we decided impulsively that it was the thing to do. That night was the last time I ever saw him."

"Be very sure of the facts, Magda. You can't afford the slightest hesitation or you'll put the whole department in a spot. They'll disown all knowledge of you if you're found out. That's part of the agreement, so be careful."

He lit a cigarette for her and one for himself, and they smoked in silence.

"Joseph was a real person, wasn't he? You've never told me."

"If you must mention him, call him Joe. I thought it best for you not to think of him as real. No need to dramatize him, you know. He was a person all right, poor guy. Quiet lad, a loner. Orphan. Not even his barracks mates knew him well enough to remember him. He left no mark in his life except to give you a name. Fortuitous, that."

"For my unborn child, at least. I wish I could do something for him. I have a lot of money, you know. Could I, Chappie? Set up some sort of memorial fund for widows and orphans or something?"

"I think not. The less attention we draw to him, the better."

"I keep wondering why the department went along with it. Did you put yourself out on a limb, Chappie?"

He ignored the second part of her question.

"I suppose you'd better know. Waldemar has escaped. Disappeared into thin air. I don't even know whether he's in England any more. I think I outsmarted myself when I took you off his mail—dereliction of duty on my part for personal reasons. At any rate, Sir Nigel Lewisholm's body was found a few days ago. Appears to be an accident, but it has all the earmarks of suicide."

"No! That poor man. I wonder what agony Waldemar put him through first."

"He must have found out what Waldemar was doing," Chapin mused.

"Knowing Waldemar, he probably taunted him about it when he knew he couldn't get any more help from him and blackmailed him by threatening to disclose his help in trapping the Jews still in Europe. It's Shanghai all over again," Magda cried out bitterly. "I don't have the words to tell you the kind of devil he is. He should be stamped out of existence. Even the earth he is buried in will grow poisonous nettles!"

"Watch out for him, Magda. He could be very dangerous to you," Chapin warned.

She shuddered and took his hand. "You've been so kind to me, Chappie. I'm going to miss you more than I can say. How can I ever thank you?"

"By changing your mind and staying here," he replied without an instant's hesitation. "Marry me, Maggie. We could make it work, you know. Have a good life together, as good as anyone can expect."

"I couldn't do that to you, Chappie. You're too good to take second place in anyone's life."

"Dammit, Magda! Refuse me if you must, but don't do it to do me a favor. As the Americans say, I know the score."

"You really force a person to wipe away all pretext and tell the plain, unvarnished truth."

"It's easier to take. I've never enjoyed the Alphonse and Gaston act, or long goodbyes, or self-sacrificing persons, most especially, I think, the last. You're not a self-sacrificer at heart, and neither am I. I asked you to marry me because I want to, not from any misguided notion of selflessness. If you don't want me, I'd rather you said so. You make me feel that, if I did something a little differently, your answer might be yes. And don't tell me I'm too good to be used because, if I am, I'm asking for it. I'd have spoken up much sooner but I knew you were too in love with Archie to consider anyone else. I was prepared to wait patiently until you got over him. I always hoped you would."

"I thought your feelings had changed when I told you I was carrying Archie's child."

"Not at all, except to damn him for his carelessness. Actually, it's all quite splendid if you'd let it be. I think I'd make rather a good father. Magda, we like each other, and that's a solid basis for marriage, or partnership, or call it what you will. The thought of being your husband makes me very happy."

"Chapin, my dear, it wouldn't work. I don't think I've ever met a man I could lean on as I lean on you; and it would be wonderful to have that." She sighed. "I'm so terribly fond of you, too. I think one of the reasons I'm so comfortable and relaxed with you is because you're not really in love with me. Somehow I create havoc in the lives of the people who care for me. I'm really happiest left to myself, with a few very good friends. We have that in common, I think. That's what attracts you to me, isn't it, unless I talk your ear off, as I'm doing now?"

"You've rationalized everything so neatly, Magda, except that your first premise is incorrect. You see, for one thing, I'm not, as you say, merely fond of you. I care a great deal for you. I'm not the romantic type, and I don't know how to make speeches of love. I—well—you could say, or rather, I could say that I've been sort of in love with you since Hong Kong days. And it's grown, my dear, it's grown very much. When Archie was around, I knew it was useless to compete. It's not that I'm lacking in fight, but it would have been like jousting with a dream. There was no way of fighting that, so I stuck around, waiting for the right moment, hoping the day would come when you'd see him for what he was. My dear, I must speak now—you'll be leaving in a short time and I'll have lost my chance with you. Don't waste any more of your life grieving for Archie."

"Grieving for Archie?" she echoed his words in a sort of wonderment.

"Listen to me. One day you'll be able to put this all behind you. It would give me infinite joy to help you do this. I wouldn't expect you to love me as you did Archie —I know it wouldn't be like that for us. Nor do I want to live in a world he made. Let us build our own kingdom. I'm a very patient man, Magda. I could wait until you were ready, in your own good time, if and when you felt you could be my bride. I'm saying this very badly and, I'm afraid, rather stupidly. I want you in all the ways a man wants a woman, but if it were only a marriage of convenience, as it is occasionally called, it would still make me extraordinarily happy—to have you as my dear and close companion and be father and protector of your child. In time, I swear to you, Archie would be forgotten."

Magda eyed him steadily. Then, she opened the door and got out of the car. The cold, damp wind whipped her coat around her knees and she gave a little shiver as a blast of cold air suddenly rushed up her legs. Chapin joined her and she stood close to him for warmth. He put his arms around her and lifted her face to him.

"What's the matter, Magda? Did I say the wrong thing?"

"Everything is wrong. I'm not pining for Archie. He died for me three months ago. There's a void where he was, a blank spot with no feeling at all. Not even a dried bouquet to press into a book of memories. But a living child. What residue of love is left in me will go to that child. I want it to know a different kind of love, one that is free from obligation. Love will be a gift, not a bribe, nor a demand. Not something compounded of greed, not something to bargain with, but a sweetness to be shared.

"Maybe love can happen more than once to a man and a woman, but not to me again. I won't allow it. Before you told me that Archie was missing in action, he was out of my life. I'm sorry for the people he left behind, but I'm not among them. I want you to understand that."

Magda looked up at him, her great oval eyes, dark pools in her pale face open to him at last. There was nothing hidden in their depths. "I'm going to miss you dreadfully, but it would never work. I don't want you to love me except as a friend. I'm a jinx, Chappie. People who love me end up dead or miserable. You're a strong man, perhaps the only strong man I've ever known, except my cousin William. I used to go to him when I was in trouble and he always knew what to say. Will you be my cousin? Be my friend? My dear, dear friend, but not my lover?"

She shivered, and he drew her closer to him.

"It's all right, Magda, dear. It's all right." He kissed her lightly on the forehead.

"When I was a girl, I swore never to become entangled in my emotions. Sometimes I wish I were still that girl, aloof from the world and safe from hurt. But I forgot my vow and fell in love—not once but *twice* with the same man. It was the same love, but inflamed to an even higher degree. Love can be Heaven and Hell all at once, you know. Perhaps I would have refused him if I had known the consequences, the guilt, the anguish and misery. But I needed him to love me, and no risk seemed too great." Her shoulders shook as sobs overcame her.

"Hush! Hush, my dearest. It'll be all right, I promise."

He took her clenched fists, opened them gently and kissed them. "Such a passionate outburst from such a sensible one!"

Magda laughed a little shakily, then looked at him seriously. "I'm truly fond of you, Chappie. I hate to think of your being hurt. You have my devoted friendship for whatever it's worth."

"Perhaps that'll be enough for us. I'm ready to settle for it, together. It's better than loneliness."

She shook her head.

"That says it all, then," he said as he patted her hand. "If you ever change your mind, I'll be waiting. Now, don't say anything foolish like I'll meet a nice girl. I've already met a lot of nice girls in my life. Just know I'll be here, Magda; in fact, a cable will bring me to wherever you are." He forced a grin. "Now, I'll be expecting reports from you, long and newsy ones. Frequently. We'll use that tricky code you worked out."

"It's funny when I think about it. Before I ever got into this work, I used to use codes. There was something about them that intrigued me. William and I used to correspond in Chinese code, of all things, when I was at school in Switzerland. There must be something secretive about my nature," she finished weakly.

"Look after yourself, my dearest. I don't want you to walk around afraid, always looking over your shoulder, but, in the off-chance you see or hear anything about Waldemar, don't take it on yourself. Cable me immediately—let me take proper action. He's a devious man."

The signal for departure sounded, and they walked slowly toward the plane. At the steps, they shook hands rather awkwardly. Then he opened his arms wide and she walked into them. He hugged her with all his strength.

"I'm going to miss you most awfully," she whispered and kissed him full on the mouth for the first time. She felt so safe and secure with him, so protected and cherished.

"Me too, most awfully," he murmured, kissing her again.

You fool, she thought, weakening at the last moment. Why not stay? She tore herself away from him, and ran up the stairs into the plane without glancing back.

Chapin watched the door of the plane close after her. She did not turn around and wave—that was not her style. Had he mentioned to her that he didn't like long farewells? This one time he didn't want the farewell to come to an end.

"You poor fool," he told himself. "You knew it was never any good. You waited too long for Archie to fade out, before saying anything. That bloody bastard—too selfish to take proper precautions and now he's left her with a baby. God, if he wasn't missing, I'd make him wish he was!"

There was already a deep void in Chapin's life and she had not been gone five minutes.

Perhaps, he thought, he could find some excuse to go to San Francisco, pick up where they left off—good friends enjoying each other's company. Maybe this time it would lead to something more. But even as the thought came to him, he damned himself for a fool. Chappie knew only one thing: there had never been anyone for him before he met Magda and there would never be anyone else again. He'd just have to learn to live with it.

A wisp of sunshine broke through the leaden sky.

They'll have good flying weather, he thought, looking up as a streak of sunlight turned the muddy path into a strip of sparkling topaz. He turned up his coat collar and strode toward his car.

The United States had been at war less than six months and heavy precautions against any threat of invasion were in effect.

Everything was secret, and everyone was warned not to talk. The simplest procedures were tangled in red tape. Confusion reigned, as departments made their own rules on top of existing rules. All foreigners were suspect, except the British.

Airships, filled with troops, supplies, advisors, and every kind of important personnel, were flown to Britain. Many remained there, especially newsmen. Everyone who could tried to get a free trip on the transport planes.

The whole country was geared up for war. The military was given priority "A" on all trains, and even on commercial airlines within the continental United States. A passenger could no longer be sure of his travel plans, no matter how long before he had made reservations.

Trains loaded with troops were sent to the West Coast, while trains loaded with troops passed them going east. Men were shifted at random: those with sea experience were drafted to the infantry, and vice versa. At first, volunteers to serve had made up endless lines—now even longer lines passed through the draftboards.

It was Magda's good fortune, when she landed in Washington to clear her credentials, that there was someone from the British Embassy to ease her way through the red tape and speed her on to San Francisco.

Blessed Chappie, she thought. I owe him so much. I may have been a fool to leave him. It seemed she always made the difficult, the unnatural choices, but she believed that in the end she would have hurt him. It seemed preordained.

But she knew one thing: this unexpected child must have a chance in a new country. A natural way of life, on an equal footing with the children of many nationalities, all assimilated into little Americans, without divided loyalties. To grow up, and not be different, or outstanding in any way—just to have the chance of a normal life that she had missed.

353

The night before she left for San Francisco she wrote to Chapin:

To his Lordship, Chapin of Desmond: June 14, 1942
Dear Lordship:

I have been asked to write to you by a commoner who wishes to remain nameless. She is unaccustomed to writing to lords and ladies. She says you deceived her. Fie on you. All is known and will be made public, unless you send her one British penny on a chain, in which case she will keep your secret. Yours, etc. Anonymous.

Chappie, dear, what fun knowing a lord—and what a long list of names you have, grandmother. I understand your brother Peregrine is a duke (makes me think of a falcon—do you have one on your coat of arms?) I shall have to study Burke's Peerage.

General Massey let the cat out of the bag. What a perfect old dear he is, and what a difference from Sir Alfred, yet they're the same generation: one grown mellow and the other sour. I don't believe he bought the Bentley story for a moment; he had a wicked gleam in his eye and I'm sure he thinks you're the father of the unborn one. You cad! He did everything but wink, paid me outrageous compliments and invited me to dine with him and Lady Iona (lords and ladies cropping up everywhere!) During our conversation I told him I was half-Chinese, and he didn't blink an eyelash. It made me feel so free and confident. What a fool I've been! It was Sir Alfred who first made me feel worthy of contempt, though I admit my father helped unintentionally. Poor man—he loved me so much and wanted the best for me, but in his own mind he was convinced that it was shameful, and Sir Alfred put on the finishing touches. Well, pish-tosh to him. What jolly good fun it would have been to confront him as Lady Desmond. He's such a snob. He's only a baronet for his services to the country, whereas I understand your family dates back hundreds of years.

I shall be leaving Washington very soon—tomorrow, I hope. The way has been smoothed for me, so much that I felt quite like royalty myself. You are so good to me, there's no beginning or end to it. It makes me feel so lucky to have your devotion.

I have no idea where I'll be living in San Francisco.

I understand the natives there take umbrage at anyone calling it 'Frisco' so I am practicing. Write to me poste restante at present. I'm sure I could always use Tasha's address, but I think I shall rent a post-office box. You know I like my privacy.

Gratefully and affectionately yours,
Magda

>>>>>>>>>>>>>>>>>>>>>>>>>>>>>>>>>>>>>>>

PART SIX

San Francisco

1942–1944

>>>>>>>>>>>>>>>>>>>>>>>>>>>>>>>>>>>>>>>

CHAPTER TWENTY-SIX

<<<<<<<<<<<<<<<<<<<<<<<<<<<<<<<<

THE HOUSING MAN at the British Embassy in Washington had managed to obtain reservations for Magda at the St. Francis Hotel in San Francisco. As soon as she unpacked, she telephoned Tasha to be sure she was at home, and then mischievously hung up. She couldn't resist surprising her.

Tasha was watering the garden in her front yard when the cab drew up. She gaped at Magda in disbelief and then rushed up to embrace her. They went inside, both laughing and talking at the same time, and entered a cheerfully decorated living room which ran the length of the house.

Tasha proudly took Magda on an inspection tour through the two bedrooms, the fully-equipped kitchen, which was still a marvel to her, down the stairs to a paneled playroom. Then, as though saving the best for the last, she led her to a glassed-in porch which jutted out over a little backyard. It looked as though it were part of the garden itself. An aviary full of singing canaries filled one wall and the picture window was fringed with hanging plants. Gaily covered rattan furniture made the room welcoming and airy.

"This is my favorite place in all the house. Do you like it, Magda? At any rate, you can see there's plenty of room for you, and I won't hear of your staying in a hotel. Besides," she added triumphantly, "the house is partially paid for with your money, so it's partially yours."

Magda smiled but made no answer.

After a quiet dinner, when all their talking and reminiscing was done, Magda told Tasha that she was expecting a baby in six months.

"Archie's, of course. Why couldn't he have had the decency to leave you alone to find a good life for yourself?" Tasha stood up, her face flushed with the determination to say what had been on her mind so long.

"Tasha, Archie is missing in action."

"Oh, dear! How dreadful I've been!"

"I didn't mean it that way. I just felt you should know. I really didn't know that you disliked Archie so much. Tell me something: why is it that you could say exactly what you think of him, no matter how bad, but as soon as you think he's dead, you feel guilty and apologetic? Death doesn't change the truth about people."

Magda lit a cigarette and leaned back in her chair, gazing thoughtfully into the darkness. She took a few puffs, then stamped out her cigarette and said abruptly. "And another thing, my name is now Mrs. Joseph Bentley. Joseph was killed in action three months ago."

Tasha looked at her, stunned, but Magda's face was closed. Every instinct in her urged her to confide in Tasha, but she had promised Chapin complete secrecy, and she could not break that promise—it was only his influence which had made her trip to the States possible.

Shortly after Magda's arrival, she went to the Chinatown branch of the telephone company, and requested the help of the supervisor, Mrs. Rose Lee, a Chinese-American, for assistance in locating one Chen Sheng-fong, who was not listed.

"I don't know how I can help you in that case." It sounded strange to Magda to hear this completely Oriental-looking woman speaking in uninflected American English.

"It's important that I locate him, Mrs. Lee. He's very old, and I made a promise to see if he's in good health and circumstances."

"Well, stop back in tomorrow and I'll make some inquiries for you," she said.

The following day Magda returned, and Mrs. Lee sent her to a small office where an elderly man was surrounded by reams of ledgers in Chinese. Once again, she gave the information, and further details going back to the third and fourth generations of the family.

"Chen is a very common name," the wispy man grumbled as he checked over his records. "Ha!" he said finally and victoriously, with a craggy smile on the wrinkled map of his face. "He lives with his grandson, Peter Chen. Here is the telephone number."

"Give me the address, too, please."

"No can do. He may not want to see you. You have the telephone number, you call first."

"May I offer you a contribution for your work?"

"Can always use the money. Plenty of work to keep the records of the families. The young people are not so much interested."

Magda handed him a five-dollar bill, which was immediately tucked into his capacious sleeve.

A woman answered the phone. Once again, Magda told of her mission and asked if the old man were alive and well, saying that she would very much like to visit him.

"Well, I don't know," the woman said with reservation. "He's almost senile. Give me your number and I'll ask my husband when he comes home. He'll be back about six."

"I'll call back myself, if you don't mind."

Peter Chen answered the phone the next time Magda called. Yes, his wife had explained the situation to him. He couldn't see that it would be of any value to visit the old man—he was practically blind and didn't hear too well, either. He, Peter, would consider that the courtesy from his far-off relative had been received.

Magda couldn't understand why she had become so obstinate about seeing her relatives. At first, it had been a fleeting idea on her part, to test her feelings for her Chinese ancestry and whether she were willing to be open about it. The Chens were certainly not eager to make her acquaintance. Perhaps the Chinese here were as suspicious of their white neighbors as in Shanghai.

"I hate to sound so persistent," she went on, firmly, "but I did promise William that I would, and I feel obligated. If it isn't too late, I'd like to come now. I promise I won't stay long."

"You will be welcome, Mrs. Bentley." Finally the customary Chinese courtesy conquered his reluctance, and he gave her the address.

The Chens lived on California Street in a large apartment with many small rooms. Mrs. Chen, Estelle, was a slim, sharp-looking woman, her face carefully made up. Peter was a middle-aged man with a definite resemblance to William, but grown stout and soft with good living.

The dining room adjoined the living room and both were filled with people. One boy was hunched over the dining-room table doing his homework, while two smaller children were playing a quiet game of checkers on the floor in the corner. Mr. and Mrs. Chen had been lingering over their coffee; near them in a large armchair, a shriveled old man was huddled in front of a radio going full blast.

Magda introduced herself as a close friend of their cousin William and again begged their pardon for her intrusion. The Chens looked at her curiously but welcomed her politely.

"The old gentleman likes to listen to the radio, but he doesn't understand a thing that's being said," Estelle explained, bringing Magda over to the bearded figure. He sat with his mouth slightly open, blinking myopically at regular intervals. His thin, bloodless skin looked like crushed parchment; in its heavy folds, the only signs of life were his eyes.

Peter went to him and shook him gently, shouting in Chinese: "Old father, you have a guest!"

He repeated it three times and finally turned off the set and looked apologetically at Magda. She stepped forward and bowed formally to the grandfather, saying a few words of Chinese greeting to him. The Chens looked at her in surprise, and some signs of intelligence crossed the old man's rheumy eyes as she continued to talk. He wiped his face with a clean handkerchief, and, making a feeble attempt to bow back, replied in a quavering voice.

Magda pulled up a stool near him and for several minutes talked to him gently. A wide smile crossed his face, showing toothless gums. It seemed impossible for a face to have so many wrinkles.

"Shu-ming—ha! Ha! He lives still?" he asked suddenly in a loud voice.

"No, grandfather, you outlive him, but his grandson Wen Chu lives in his stead. He is married and has three children." Suddenly, in saying so, Magda felt the full shock of the annihilation of William's entire family.

The old man went into long, broken reminiscences,

361

his face more animated than it had been in some time. Then, in the middle of a sentence, his head started to nod and he fell fast asleep. Impulsively, Magda kissed him on the forehead.

"What a dear old man. I am grateful you permitted me to talk to him. I wish I could tell William, but I have no idea where he is. I know he would be pleased."

"You speak Chinese remarkably well for a foreigner," Peter commented.

"I was born in Shanghai," Magda replied cautiously.

"We meet many people who have lived in China, and most of them can say a few words of Chinese, mostly swear-words they picked up from the coolies. They think it affirms their superiority—that they had not bothered to learn the language."

Magda could see the change in their attitude since she had spoken with the old man. All at once, she wanted very much to be accepted by them, accepted as one of their own, to join the family clan, to be more than a foreigner come to pay her respects.

"He appears to be too old to be your grandfather, cousin," she said to Peter in Chinese.

"Don't talk Chinese," Estelle said impatiently. "I don't understand it too well, and you speak too fast."

"Cousin?" Peter repeated, raising his eyebrows. He motioned his wife to be quiet; annoyed, she went into the kitchen to bring out some hot tea.

"I don't understand. Unless things have changed a great deal in China, the term you use is a form of address among intimate friends and relatives. You know Chinese too well to misuse the language. I am a little bewildered."

"Perhaps I am overbold to use it with you, whom I have just met, but as William is my cousin, so too are you."

He looked at her steadily, examining her. "I do not understand your purpose, but if this is a joke, it is in extremely bad taste," he said sternly.

"My mother was Chen Mei-ling. William's father's father was my mother's uncle by the marriage of her mother into the Chen family. My father was Angus Mac-Dougall, of Scotland."

"Extraordinary! I wouldn't have believed it. Welcome to my home, cousin," He bowed again as though being introduced for the first time, and she responded in the same manner. She felt wonderfully light-hearted.

"Is this privileged information, or may others be told?"

"There is no reason why not, except that the curiosity it creates I find distasteful, and many questions will be asked which could be awkward. Of course, your wife must know. I'm sure she will be discreet. Peter, I hope you understand my position."

"Yes. It must raise many problems for you." He turned to the children and addressed them in English. "Children, please leave the room. I have important things to discuss with your mother." He sighed a little as they left obediently. "They have no desire to learn Chinese. They have so much homework of their own to do, but, more than that, they want to be like Americans, not Chinese. I send them to schools to learn Chinese, but it's an upward struggle.

"Estelle," he called out. "Bring that special wine—we have an occasion to celebrate. Let us drink to a new-found cousin from distant shores!"

"What's going on?" Estelle demanded, bringing in a tray.

Peter told her with many flourishes and her eyes opened wide. When he was through she was over-whelmed.

"You poor child, what you must have gone through! You must consider our house your own." She went to Magda and embraced her with emotion. "Poor child," she repeated, and Magda looked at her in wonderment. This stranger was the only person who had ever understood. She felt a strange new warmth flow through her and kissed Estelle on the cheek.

A letter arrived for Magda from Chapin:

So you have found out my dread secret. If that infor-mation makes you change your mind, I'm sorry that I didn't dangle it in front of you sooner. We could still con-front Sir Alfred, if you wish. In fact, how would you like to be presented at court? I am happy that you've begun to live with the idea of being part-Chinese. If you ever change your mind about us, I'll blazon it in headlines. In fact, we'll make having Chinese blood a thing of glamour, and everyone who doesn't have any will start hunting up records to prove otherwise. If I weren't so busy I'd try to wangle some important job in the States which could only be performed by yours truly. I long to see you again, in any role you wish. Life has become unbearingly lonely without you. Is this the way to melt your heart? On the other hand, I don't think that's the way to win you at all. Yes, I want to be your husband, or your companion, but not because of sympathy. You've taken that road before, if I'm not mistaken, and it's not for me.

You sounded so cheerful in your letter, I believe your self-prescribed cure was the best thing for you, in which case I cannot regret your leaving, as long as you promise to return. Take good care of yourself.

Always yours devotedly,

Chappie

Magda's letter to Chappie crossed in the mail.

I don't know exactly what is happening to me. It's as though I were undergoing a series of operations. Each time I begin with reservations, but each one frees me of an ache I have been carrying for a long time. I feel a great inner satisfaction. It is strange that it should be happening to me now, when, for the first time in my life I feel truly British, loving my country and loyal to it. I cannot quite understand myself.

Except for you, Chappie dear, I feel my past fading away so absolutely that it might never have existed. I may come out of this a totally different person, one you won't recognize: open, placid, quite unlike the old Magda.

My big problem is deciding where to live. I thought of buying a house—fortunately, I have no financial problems. It is difficult to remember that once I thought the pursuit of money the most exciting thing in life. Today I am grateful to that Magda for being so successful and efficient in using the money where it might do the most good. She was a smart girl, if I do say so, but she was missing so much of life.

Dearest Chappie, you are never far from my thoughts,

Magda

CHAPTER TWENTY-SEVEN

◄◄◄◄◄◄◄◄◄◄◄◄◄◄◄◄◄◄◄◄◄◄◄◄◄◄◄◄◄◄◄

St. Mary's Hospital, San Francisco
November 2, 1942

Chappie dear:

My baby was born today. I have not been allowed to see her yet, but I lie here feeling remarkably well, my mind clear and my heart at peace. Here it is clear and sunny outside, and I know where you are the weather will be downcast and cold to the bone. But, unaccountably, my thoughts drift to London and to you, and I miss you very much. I am taking the liberty of borrowing one of your many names for my little girl. I am naming her Pauline Josepha Bentley. Josepha is for the poor man who died so young and had so little—at least his name will be passed on. And you, my dear Chappie, will you be my daughter's godfather? I want her to have all the things I didn't, like a religion and god-parents and a real place in the world. I want Tasha to be her godmother, but she has no religious background, either. Tell me, what should I do? I am embarrassed by my ignorance.

There is some sort of intestinal flu in the nursery, and unless one is nursing, the babies are not brought to the mothers. My obstetrician advised me not to nurse the baby—he says I'm anemic, and that it would be better for me to rest and gain my strength. The nurse has just come in, so I'll close now.

Cable from Chapin Desmond to Mrs. J. Bentley:

Am honored and delighted stop kiss Pauline for me stop am a member of Church of England but can act in any church affiliation stop if Tasha has no preference the Episcopal Church is closely allied stop would you like me to make arrangements for baptism stop no trou-

ble have a bishop cousin with contacts in the States stop
wish I could be there stop all love to mother and child
signed Chapin Desmond.

Tasha and Barry went to the hospital as her closest
"relatives" and were taken to the glass window to view the
baby. Tasha started to laugh and cry a little hysterically
when she reported to the baby's mother.

"Oh, Magda! She's a proper little Red MacDougall.
Your father would have been so pleased," and then she
broke down and cried tears of joy and wonder.

To Chapin, January, 1943:

Dearest Chappie, how ever can I thank you enough?
The ceremony went off beautifully, thanks to you. The
minister was kind and thoughtful and I wasn't a bit embarrassed. Little Pauline wears the chain with your coat
of arms every day. I had it shortened so that she can't
grab it and swallow it. I'll lengthen it as she grows up.
So the falcon is truly your coat of arms—*In Omnia
Paratus*—ready for all things; it's a brave motto, and
you really personify it, certainly for me. The war effort
here has intensified and the people are eager to do everything they can to help. Rationing has started in earnest;
and already, I'm sorry to say, there is a blackmarket for
gas coupons and tires. Automobiles are almost impossible
to purchase without priority, and I'm delighted that I
bought mine before the restrictions became so tight. I
still miss London, not that I miss the bombs falling; but
I do miss the closeness, of feeling united with my countrymen.

As you can see from the address, I'm still living with
the Winters. They insisted that they not only had room
for me, but that Tasha needed me because Barry is away
so much. They both pleaded with me and made me feel it
would be selfish to refuse.

They've both fallen madly in love with Pauline. I think
they are frustrated parents. For some reason Tasha hasn't
been able to conceive, though I tell her it's early yet.
Barry seizes every opportunity when he's home to play
with the baby; he delights in feeding her and she clings to
him tightly when he puts her on his shoulder to be burped.

We all hold our breath until the baby lets hers out, and then we cheer, which makes her laugh and laugh. During the day, Tasha's delightful garden room has been made into her nursey; at night she has her crib in my room, the downstairs playroom, which is away from the rest of the house. She's really such a beautiful child, Chappie. I wish you could see her. She has large hazel eyes, which still can't decide whether they are blue or gray or green; sometimes they look golden. Her hair is a riot of red-gold ringlets, and her complexion is peaches and cream. Do I sound like a besotted mother?

Magda watched the child with increasing wonder, as she grew up with such a happy disposition that she won everybody's hearts. Tasha called her "Jolly Polly" and hugged and squeezed her while the baby squealed for joy and demanded more. Polly responded to the affection as a flower worships the morning sun.

Magda marveled how such a joyous little baby, who gave and received love so freely, came to be born of two such frustrated people as Archie and herself? Archie! How long ago it seemed they had been together, been in love—the great love of her life, the love which was going to endure forever . . .

For the sake of the child, she promised herself, I must erase those memories from my mind and my heart. Archie was gone from her forever. Whether she lived or died, she was free of him, need never think of him again. And then, suddenly, for the third time in her life. Magda was convulsed with tears as though every drop of blood, every nerve and muscle and bone in her body were buffeted by emotions, raging and twisting in all directions. She came out of it weak and shaken, but the storm washed away her past and made it possible for her to begin a new life.

The baby's first word was predictably "Ma-ma." Polly said it to Tasha when she was six months old; Tasha lifted her high and hugged her, her eyes wet with tears of pleasure, and then she looked at Magda guiltily as though she had stolen something precious.

Amused, Magda had reassured her. "Don't feel badly, Tasha—to her you are as much a mother as I am, maybe more. I have no gift with children. Who knows? Maybe my maternal instincts can't compare with yours. I only look at her and wonder that I gave her birth."

Tasha brought the baby over to Magda, and the plump, warm little arms tightened around Magda's neck. Polly bestowed a wet warm kiss on her cheek, and Magda felt for the first time stirrings of the exquisite pain and delight of mother love.

Magda wrote to Chapin:

Your goddaughter has given me renewed life. Ever since her birth I've been waiting to feel a cataclysmic love for her, but it didn't happen. She was so sweet, and I enjoyed looking at her. I enjoyed doing the things mothers do with their babies, but she never really belonged to me nor I to her. I started to believe that I was an unnatural woman, that my ability to love at all had been forever destroyed. I felt like an outcast. I told no one, not even you. But today it happened. Today little Polly put her arms around me and called me "Mama-ga." A door was unlocked, and I felt a gushing of warmth and life. Dear, dear Chappie, do I bore you with my outpourings? You who know me so well, you are my confidant, my guardian, and my friend. In return for all the grief I have poured on you, I want you to share my happiness. It must be a miracle—my soul has been returned to me!

Little Polly now had a middle-aged Chinese woman as her nurse. Magda had gone to Estelle and asked her to recommend someone, and Violet Wing was the answer. She was a jewel in every way; not only did Tasha feel at home with her, but Violet liked to help around the house as well as to take care of the baby. A cot was placed in the baby's nursey so that Violet could spend the night if they wanted her to.

Magda visited the Chens frequently and felt very much at home there. She and Estelle had become firm friends, and Magda thought nothing of it when she was invited to the Chens for dinner one evening. But when Magda arrived she was greeted by a feeling of suppressed excitement. Everyone had expressions of great expectation on their faces, especially Estelle and Peter. The excitement was contagious, and it spread to Magda.

"All right, what is it?" she entreated them.

Like a chorus they answered, "You have a letter from cousin William!"

Magda sank into a chair, weak and speechless. Peter handed her a small flat square of paper, folded over so many times it looked like a thin pad. Magda's hand shook as she picked it up; she had worried about William for so long.

Carefully, she opened up the folded sheet so as not to rip the thin onionskin paper which had been rubbed down by wear and was frayed at the edges. Peter explained that he had managed to get a courier to China to try to locate William, and, if possible, get a message from him. This note had been disguised as a pad under the heel lining in one of the courier's shoes. Finally, it was spread open on the table in front of Magda.

All watched anxiously as she started to read the tiny Chinese characters which filled the page. She looked puzzled at first, then a smile broke through her bafflement.

"It's in code," she told her audience. "It's one William and I made up long ago. I shall have to rely on my memory. You'll excuse me if I leave right after dinner, I've got to go to my office where I have got better facilities. Peter, how can I thank you, and Estelle—" Sudden tears flooded her eyes as she whispered rather incoherently. "It's so wonderful to have a family . . . I never had one."

In her office, Magda worked carefully. She fixed the paper firmly on her scanner and placed a strong light over it. Much of it was illegible, having been rubbed off in transit.

I am well, but I cannot say the same for our country, over-ridden as it is with the Japanese. No Machu fist ever pressed so hard as the boot which now treads upon us . . . our leaders occasionally forget their private wars for power and join against the common enemy. The puppet governments the Japanese have set up are cause for bitter jest and cries of "death to the traitors." My adopted son and I made our escape to the southeast . . . several American air-bases and I am appointed liaison officer because of my knowledge of English. I do not consider these Americans the saviors of my country. They are fighting not to save China but only as a military tactic for themselves as they . . . in Europe. Our general is to my mind too friendly with them and will owe them too great a debt. Once again we will be exploited by the foreigner when the war ends as it must inevitably . . .

Just before we left Shanghai your stepfather was put to death by the Blue Society—the fool—Mei-ling is inconsolable; by some strange quirk, this was the man she loved.

Life is a shadow without my Lotus and my children. I do not burn joss sticks for them, for the fire within me to avenge their wanton deaths burns enduringly. Ah, my bright cousin Magda, what service you could render China . . . could I persuade you to forfeit your life of ease—even your life itself for such a cause?

Can it be possible that two bloodthirsty countries have the entire world in their grip? Is there no sanity left on this earth?

My ears echo the thunder of guns, my eyes grow weary of dead, swollen bodies. My soul is tired. Death would be almost a relief. But as long as I have mind and body, they belong to China.

Tell my cousin Peter, that as Elder Brother of the Chens, I delegate to him the responsibility of looking. after our cousin, Magda.

Bow to our venerable ancestor for me and. . . .

Your cousin,
Wen Chu

There was little conversation following the reading of the letter to the Chens the next day. It was as though some of the agony of China had seeped into the room.

Peter took her aside before she left and told her that if she wished to reply, he might be able to help her. She was starting to realize that under his affable exterior, Peter was a man of consequence. Through her growing familiarity with Chinese circles, Magda learned that there were forces within forces in San Francisco's Chinatown. Now she knew that there could be communication to those on the Chinese mainland by secret couriers and, most surprisingly, that her cousin Peter was a key figure in their activities.

At the Winters, Magda tried to cover up the despondency which William's letter had produced, and Tasha, usually so perceptive, was too full of excitement and preparations for the big day approaching—Polly's first birthday—to notice any sign of her friend's disquiet.

Chapin sent a brightly-wrapped package containing an antique musicbox. When the key was turned, two groups of children danced toward each other, their hands reaching up to pick imaginary nuts from a tree in the center—to the tune of "Here we go gathering nuts in May, nuts in May . . ." It was a sweet and charming present, and Polly chortled with delight when it played.

A letter was enclosed with the package. In it, Chapin wrote:

Magda, my dearest,

I have tried not to plead with you on my own behalf. I know you had enough to think about, and above all else, needed time to recover from a difficult situation. Is it dreaming on my part, or wishful thinking, that detects a different note in your letters? Would it be unfair to ask you if your attitude toward me has changed? For me, there is only one person: there will never be another. In that hope I ask you again if you will marry me.

I think I shall not ask you again after this, but you will know that I shall always be here. I am not wealthy despite the title which accompanies my name, but I don't think money has ever been a concern to you. My brother Peregrine owns the family estate, and his heir, if he ever marries and has one, will have a lean time of it as taxes will swallow what little remains. From my mother, I inherited a very decrepit place in Scotland which is falling apart, and a small income. Thus, you see I have little to offer you but my love and devotion and protection. That, and my promise that I shall be a good father to little Pauline, whom I already consider my own.

It would mean coming back to war-torn England, which is not much of an inducement, but my life is here, as yours will be if you say yes.

Tell me, Magda, will I be welcome in your life? There

is an important conference which will be held early next year in Washington, D.C. I believe I can get myself invited. Would you take a few days off and meet me there, so that we can get re-acquainted? (Not that I need to!) Give me my Christmas present early, and write, "Yes." I would be happy if this answer could apply to the whole question, but I will accept it for now to mean, "Yes, I will be there." Cable me that one word and give life to a lonely heart . . .

There was no need for Magda to think long. She went directly to the telegraph office and sent the message:

Yes stop Pauline and I send you our love signed Magda.

That night, when she went in to give a last hug and kiss to her daughter, she played the musicbox, to Polly's delight, and whispered, "Who knows, little one, this could be from your new papa." As she heard the words fall from her lips they sounded unreal—but somehow right.

To Chapin, she wrote:

I am full of humility that you feel so much for me. Chapin, if there is anything in the world I want, it is for this to happen. We will know, won't we, when we see each other. There is no one in the world, and I mean both living and dead, with whom I would sooner spend the rest of my life than with you, in whatever circumstances. But only if I can give you a whole woman, capable of the love I wish so desperately to give you. I would be ashamed to give you any less, and I would not want you to accept less than all. Let me know the time of the conference so that I can prepare the office for my departure. Thank heavens for Tasha and Violet; I know I can leave my daugher in good hands.

How I would love to bring her with me, but I think this must be our time alone, to meet and know each other again, and be sure beyond any doubt that marriage is right for us.

Yours, Magda

CHAPTER TWENTY-EIGHT

CHAPIN'S PLANS OF meeting Magda in Washington suffered one postponement after another. This delay resulted in their increased anticipation of being together and stimulated their hopes and dreams for the future. They had been apart for over two years, and in that period, Magda found her affection for Chapin had developed into a very real and mature love.

In the face of her impatience over the delayed meeting, she threw herself into her work and also did some extracurricular work in the evenings, secure in the knowledge that Polly was well looked after. Not only had Violet become a live-in member of the household, but Tasha rarely left the house at night. Barry was being primed for a top spot in Hawaii and Tasha never knew when he'd come home.

One of Magda's major interests became the organizations helping with the resettlement of Jews who managed to escape from Europe; thus, it was with more than casual interest that she read of a lecture to be held at Temple Emmanuel, which would deal with ways and means of aiding these people. She had always made substantial contributions, not only in memory of Max but through her own deep concern. But recently she had felt a need to involve herself more fully—giving money wasn't enough.

This talk sounded like something of particular interest. But it was her evening to work for the women's auxiliary at the hospital. She called to see if she could work the earlier shift. That arranged, she phoned Tasha to say she wouldn't be home for dinner, that she'd grab a bite at the hospital. When she was through at the hospital there was neither time to eat nor change. Magda grabbed her coat, threw it over her volunteer's uniform, and drove to Temple Emmanuel at Masonic and California.

The parking lot was crowded when she arrived, and she was forced to park about a block away. She followed a couple to the building where the lecture would take place, and chose a seat near the back, with easy access to the exit if she decided to leave early so she could slip out without disturbing anyone.

The chairman pounded his gavel, cleared his throat, and began to make a short introductory speech about the speaker and his aims.

". . . And now, ladies and gentlemen, I want to introduce you to a man who will speak to you from personal experience. He travels through the occupied countries of Europe with the credentials of a German businessman, and has been successful in furthering the escape of many of our suffering brothers and sisters. This man always travels with two friends whom he laughingly calls his bodyguards, though it is no joke. His life has been in danger many times. At the end of his talk he will answer all of your questions except personal ones. Who knows when one word misspoken could mean the death of many? Our committee has inspected documentary proof of his courageous actions, which have proved, to our satisfaction, that this man is a true hero. We vouch for him one hundred percent."

Then he paused, and announced the guest.

"Ladies and gentlemen—our speaker for the evening, a man who has put aside all personal ambition to save our people."

The thunderous applause drowned out his name. The audience stood up in tribute to this courageous man, Magda among them, thrilling to the thought of his personal sacrifice and dedication. What an extraordinary satisfaction, Magda thought, to be so devoted to a worthwhile and fulfilling cause.

A sturdily built man of middle height walked onto the stage, followed closely by two men. His hair was very black and worn a little long by American standards; he had a full moustache; his complexion was swarthy, his features heavy, and he wore pince-nez, the gold center clipped so tightly as to make a permanent crease on the bridge of his nose.

Everyone remained standing and applauding as he strode to the center of the stage, waiting for the ovation to cease. The man stood comfortably at ease, accepting the applause as his right. Magda stared as a hideous knowledge struggled unspoken in her mind. There was something horribly familiar about the man's walk, his stance, his cockiness, his complete self-assurance. His eyes, keen and penetrating eyes even behind the glasses, roved over his audience, and, in passing, met Magda's.

There was an instant of electricity in the mutual recognition. Magda was frozen. Her heart seemed to stop beating. The name Waldemar formed on her lips. For what seemed to be an eternity she was unable to move; then her reflexes flashed a warning to her: Run!

She slipped through the audience to the exit, but not before she saw Waldemar turning to his bodyguards. She was out the door and running. She seemed to herself to be moving in slow motion. Her heart was beating rapidly, choking her. The car seemed miles away. At last she stumbled in. Like an automaton, she did all the right things, and the car moved forward.

In the rear-view mirror she saw the two men leap into a dark-red car, but everything seemed hazy. She could not be sure of anything. The streets were dark—the overhead lights had been shielded so as not to be seen from the air. Dimmers were enforced on automobiles, even traffic lights were hooded, and neon signs were prohibited. Magda felt smothered in a blanket of terror, but somehow she managed to drive.

She found herself on Divisidero, heading toward Sloat Boulevard where they lived. Suddenly, her survival instincts were awakened. Not home. Not to Tasha and the baby. Away from them. Heavy traffic was what she needed to lose herself in, to confuse her pursuers. They could do nothing where there were so many people. She must try to get to a phone long enough to call the authorities. But what could she tell them—her personal fears? Time enough for that later. Get away first. She turned a sharp left at Golden Gate Avenue, and drove furiously to Market Street; only then she remembered there was no left turn. She continued on to Mission Street—that was almost as good. She peered at her rear-view mirror and saw a car behind her—the light was too dim to see its color.

On Mission Street, she found herself in a steady stream of traffic with cars in front of her and cars behind. She heaved a sigh of relief. For a moment she felt safe, until she saw a red car pull itself out of the traffic lane and squeeze in behind her. Horns honked. Damn the drivers, why had they made room for it? She screamed inside helplessly.

She was hemmed in—she could make no move. In the dim light she saw she was in the lane of traffic getting on the Bay Bridge. Once on it there was no way to turn. She hardly knew Oakland—she had to lose them somehow. Magda looked at her gas gauge. She was going to need gas—she should have bought some this morning, but there had been no dire need and her gas coupons were nearly gone.

If she could get far enough ahead, she could stop at the gas station at the other end of the bridge. Perhaps her pursuers would drive right by. They wouldn't think she'd be so foolhardy as to stop. Then, she could phone for help—and there'd be people around, at least. The traffic ahead moved at a steady pace, but there was a truck in front blocking her view. She moved quickly out of her lane and dashed ahead, almost causing a collision. Car windows opened and people shouted, "Damnfool woman driver!" And worse.

She raced ahead, almost hoping that she would be arrested. At least the red car was not directly behind her any more. The service station was so dimly lit she did not dare take the chance of stopping—it was probably closed. Where to now? She had to keep to busy streets; one false turn and she'd be on the road to the mountains. Her gas would run out and she would be helpless, completely at the mercy of her pursuers—but they had no word for "mercy" in their vocabulary.

Magda saw a sign with an arrow pointing to Lake Merritt. There were many hotels there, and she headed that way. The traffic had lightened considerably, and she drove quickly, looking not ahead of her, but staring into her rear-view mirror. She'd lost them. But before she could feel a moment's relief there they were again: in the red car, swerving in and out of traffic. She saw a man lean out of the passenger side, and her eyes seemed to have developed magnified vision. She could clearly see that he was holding something—or was she imagining it?

This was the end. They were going to kill her. She knew that she posed a serious threat to Waldemar—that he had to get rid of her.

Where were the traffic cops? If only she could hear that blessed siren—and if only an officer would stop and arrest her.

Magda saw a dart of fire. The man was shooting at her! It couldn't be happening but it was, right here in the United States. Why should she be surprised? She had read about things like this happening every day. There would be nothing to point to Waldemar. He'd get clear away, and it would be all over for her and the people he was deceiving.

He was so clever, so dangerous. He could talk his way out of anything—the way he had talked himself into the confidence of good Englishmen, even when they were at war. How had he escaped from England? Someone must have helped him, another poor fool blackmailed into aiding the enemy.

Why was she wasting her precious concentration on the past . . . she *had* to escape. Above all else, she had to keep Polly and the Winters out of danger. Perhaps she should have exposed him at the meeting. Too late to think of that now, she mused. Besides, it wouldn't have worked; he'd have turned the tables on her before she had a word out; he was probably doing that now. Waldemar would do anything—he had no scruples at all. If she got out of this alive, should she get in touch with the authorities? That would be the best solution—not her department, though. They would take too long to take any action.

Barry's? Same thing—again, it would take interviews and checking out her story. She'd have to get clearance first—by that time Waldemar would have disappeared. That mustn't happen.

If only Chapin were here, she thought. Waldemar had to be eliminated—he was a danger to everyone.

Magda's mind jumped from one plan to another. She finally realized she was racing at top speed, and driving around Lake Merritt now; she hadn't realized it was so large. The red car was no longer in view. She had lost them.

The car was starting to make noises, and the gas gauge was almost down to empty. She'd heard that there was always another gallon left for emergencies. Everything was so dark. There were apartment houses all around, but the blackout curtains made them look dark and foreboding, unoccupied by people.

Magda knew she had to find a hotel soon, preferably one with an underground garage so the men who hunted her would not recognize her car parked outside. She dared not hope they would give up the search. She was afraid to turn into any of the side roads; with her luck it would turn out to be a dead end. How long could she keep circling around the lake?

There was that car again—coming into view—

This was it, then. Waldemar wins.

Then, flashing in the sky like a sign from Heaven, a neon sign flickered the word Hotel, on and off. She headed that way with a final burst of speed.

She parked in the basement and dashed up the stairs, too nervous to wait for the elevator. She entered the lobby from the garage entrance and approached the desk. A night clerk looked up sleepily. There was a room available for one night only, he said. She was very tired, she told the clerk, too tired to drive any farther. She had no luggage but said she would pay for the room in advance, and she was given a room key.

Magda went upstairs, still not believing that she had reached shelter. She double-locked the door, put a chair under the doorknob and stumbled into the room.

Her mouth was dry and tasted sour; her breath came in short gasps, her hands shook, and her pulse beat like a sledge hammer. She sank onto the bed but immediately sprang up again. She drank some water from the carafe. She rinsed her face.

Magda told herself to slow down; this was no time to be demoralized by fear. The first thing to do was to order something to eat and perhaps a drink to calm herself. She called room service and placed an order for sandwiches, coffee, a whiskey and soda, and, as an afterthought, a pack of cigarettes.

Fortunately she had plenty of money with her, in the

anticipation of making a contribution to aid the refugees
—to Waldemar! She smiled bitterly at the irony. He was
still hungry for money, but most important of all, he was
still playing the same game—getting names and addresses
from anxious families. They would be as eager to give
him the information as the Jews in Shanghai had been.
It was the same operation on a grander scale. But this
time there was more involved—much, much more. She
could see the whole plan as though she had read the
script: someone gives information to the trusted bene-
factor, then with that information he blackmails the
victim to supply more, to incriminate others—a vicious
circle. Poor creatures, believing they were helping others
to freedom, and ending up by dragging their friends down
with them, forced into the depths of betrayal. How much
mental torture could a person take?

Enough with dwelling on the terrible possibilities! She
had to start thinking coldly and logically, as though un-
ravelling a code—had to get her mind off the dangers
Waldemar represented. It was time to plan her next move.

The waiter knocked, and Magda removed the chair and
opened the door cautiously. There was no one behind
him, so she let him in and quickly closed the door. As
soon as he put the tray down, he went to close the blackout curtains which she had left open when she checked
outside.

"Don't you know there's a war on?" he demanded
sternly. "This light could signal a Japanese bomber."

She looked so guilty that he consoled her. "You're not
the only one. Some idiot forgot to turn off the neon sign
outside and the air-raid warden really gave him what-
for."

"I'm sorry," Magda said meekly.

"That's all right," he replied good-naturedly, pock-
eting the generous tip Magda left in addition to the bill.
"Just leave the tray outside when you're through. We're
short-handed tonight."

Once again she double-locked the door and placed the
chair under the knob. She took a deep breath, and drank
the whiskey and soda in small sips to settle herself. She
put everything out of her mind while she ate the food in
front of her. Then, with deliberation, she lit a cigarette

379

and set her mind to work, carefully considering all the facts and possible moves with which she was faced.

Her fear was replaced with hatred for Waldemar, which over the years had lain dormant, but was now rekindled into a steady flame, demanding reprisal. Max's death and much more had to be avenged, and Magda intended not to be a sitting target.

Time sped by unnoticed as she concentrated. Then, with her mind made up, she walked to the telephone. Magda knew what she had to do and was ready to take the first painful steps. She called the Winter house, hoping Barry would answer the phone. She knew that he was home, because Tasha had told her so when she called on her way to the hospital. Was it only a few hours ago? It seemed days had passed. Tasha answered the phone, and they had a short conversation. Magda forced her voice to sound normal as she apologized for not calling earlier to say she was spending the night with the Chens. Then she asked for Barry, to give him a message she had for him from the office.

"Oh, darn! I bet he's got to go out somewhere, just when we're all cozy. We'll soon be strangers at this rate. Okay, I'll call him. I've got to run now, I think I hear Polly. Good night."

"Magda?" came Barry's deep voice, sounding very irritated. "Smitty has no right sending me messages by anyone. He knows better than that."

"That was just an excuse to get you on the phone. Listen, Barry, please don't repeat anything I say. I don't want Tasha to worry. I need to talk to you privately; then you can use your own judgment about what to tell her."

"Look here, Magda—" he broke in.

"Listen carefully. I'm in deep, deep trouble. Can you come? I'm at the Lakeside Hotel in Oakland, near Lake Merritt. I don't know the exact address. Room 713. Just come straight up."

"Can you tell me more?"

"When you get here. There's not only danger to me but for Tasha and Polly, and you, too. Please hurry."

"I'm on my way." He hung up, cursing Magda for spoiling his evening at home.

"I'm going out, honey," he called out to Tasha. "I don't know when I'll be back, so don't wait up. I have to leave you all alone. Now, you be sure to lock all the doors and windows. Hear?"

Tasha came and hugged him. "Okay, you old fuss-budget. Don't worry about me, just you look after yourself. Hear?" she mimicked.

He kissed her. She was unutterably dear to him at that moment. Whatever Magda's problem was, it couldn't be permitted to touch his family. He got into his car and drove off, stopping at a phone booth to call an unlisted number.

"Smitty? Barry here. I've got to go on a mission. Could be nothing. Assign a man to keep guard on my house tonight." Then, as an afterthought, he said, "Better have someone watch Lakeside Hotel in Oakland, but don't be obvious. If anyone leaves with a red-headed woman, have them stopped on some pretext."

"Well?" he said, rather belligerently, as Magda opened the door when she was sure of his identity. She locked the door behind her and replaced the chair before she faced him.

"Barry, you know me well enough to know that I don't act hysterically. Can you take me on faith, without further information? You know I wouldn't call you unless I was desperate. Just get me out of this hotel safely and I won't bother you again."

"Let's put it this way, Magda. I don't put it beyond you to be devious, and I don't know what you're up to. I know you're clever and I know you're capable, but I'll tell you right off that I won't go out on a limb for you unless I know a great deal more than I do—which, at present, is nothing. First of all, is national security involved?"

"It could be," she answered very softly. "There's a dangerous man behind this, and he's probably found out where I am by now. There's not much time. Of course I didn't register under my own name. But they'll have my license number. There'll be reinforcements soon—I'm surprised they're not here already It seemed to take forever to make up my mind what to do."

"You're not making any sense. Are you sure you're all right? You're talking in riddles."

Magda took a deep breath, trying to control herself.

"It's all so clear in my mind, but every nerve in my body is quivering. Let me ask you first: did you see a red car parked in front of the hotel when you came in?"

"I noticed a car with two men in it parked very close by. It's too dark to distinguish colors."

"They've been following me from San Francisco. I was sure they'd caught up. I kept seeing flashes of the car all the way here. Once, I was sure I heard a shot. And I saw a dart of fire. I thought, at first, that I could lose them in the bridge traffic, but the driver is more experienced in following someone than I am at evasive maneuvers. Will you look out the window and see if it's still there?" She moved to the door and switched off the overhead light.

"Yes. They're there all right, but if you want my help you'll have to tell me what this is all about," he demanded, still puzzled.

"It's really better if you know nothing—better for all of you. This is something I must settle by myself, and I don't want anyone to get hurt. I don't want the authorities to interfere at this time—there would be too much machinery to put in operation, too much proof I can't provide, too many loopholes, and too many impressionable people who can be taken in by an extremely clever man who has made it his business to gain the full confidence of the people he deals with."

She paced the room, nervously lighting a cigarette. Barry had never seen her so restless, so uncontrolled. Even though she tried to keep a tight hold on herself, he could feel the emanations of an animal that knows it is being hunted.

"Tell you what I'll do," he said, more kindly. "If I don't think it's pertinent to the country, but your own private affair, I'll keep it under my hat."

Magda looked at Barry wearily. She sat down as though the life had been knocked out of her. Then, with a great effort, she drew herself up and addressed him slowly, as though each word pained her.

"There are two reasons why I asked you here, Barry. One was to help me get out of here without anyone seeing us, but the main reason was to ask you to adopt Polly." She held her hand up to stop his protest and swallowed hard before she could continue, her voice breaking a little.

"Will you adopt her, my sweet happy Polly who doesn't know anything about traitors, or fear, or unkindness. Will you? I shall give her up completely to you. I even want the name Bentley removed from her birth certificate. Let her be Pauline Winters and never let her see me again."

In spite of herself, Magda choked on the words, and it took several seconds before she could continue.

"Take Polly, and take the position in Hawaii. That's part of it—for you to leave here immediately, so that you can't be followed. Put your house up for sale; I'll buy it at the going price through an intermediary. I'll make a contract with you that you can have it back at the same price any time you want it. I just don't want your name on the property, or mine.

"I'm asking a lot of you, I know, but it is the only way to keep Polly and Tasha safe. Every possible connection between us must be erased—no trace of me to lead to you. Maybe I'm exaggerating the danger, but I'd sooner take too many precautions than too few.

"They're both so vulnerable now. Polly thinks of both of us as her mother; she'll soon forget me. And Tasha dotes on the child. I think you love her, too. You wouldn't want either of them to be a pawn in some terrible game of blackmail. I'm so afraid of this man and what he can do. I never really knew what fear was until tonight. It was all so sudden and unexpected—all I could think of was to run away."

Suddenly, she started to tremble, and Barry put his arms around her.

"It's okay, Magda, take it easy. Of course we'll take Polly. We both love her, and we do want a child. We'd love to adopt her. But for your own sake, are you sure it's necessary? We could just keep Polly for a few months for you," he suggested.

"Will you take the transfer to Hawaii? It's really important for you to leave without delay."

"I don't have a choice any more. They've been on my tail for months, and I can't hold them off much longer. You don't argue with the government. I could be on my way tomorrow if necessary, but I hate to tell Tasha."

"Will you be allowed to take them with you?" Magda asked urgently.

"Sure. It's a long-term assignment. Family allowed. We can keep Polly for as long as you like."

"Oh, Barry! You're so good." Once again came the gulping sob, and her eyes looked red from the effort she made not to cry.

"But it's no good that way," she went on. "I would like to think it could be, but it's no good." She started to speak in jerky little sentences, the words forced from her, explaining more to herself than to Barry.

"I thought my ability to love had been destroyed, then that little baby—my baby—put her arms around me and my heart started to beat again. I never knew it could be like that. I didn't know I had any maternal instincts. I thought I was dried out, an empty vessel, a machine with a mind and body but no soul."

Barry saw a new woman in this Magda, a person for whom he felt real sympathy. This broken woman—she who had always seemed so self-sufficient. He wanted to comfort her, and he needed to ask many questions, but he felt the best thing he could do was to let her get it out of her system.

There was silence for a few moments.

"No. It won't do," she said suddenly and firmly. "There is only one way. Half-measures don't work for me. I must get out of her life completely. I'll always be a jinx and a problem. I have to get out of all your lives. I've brought nothing but grief to those who love me. Will you adopt her legally, bindingly and immediately?" she pleaded.

"If you're sure, it will be our great happiness to do so."

"Can you do it secretly? Can you do it without my being present? Can you do it simply with a letter of intent? I mustn't see her again, or Tasha. Never, oh, never ever again—my happy, laughing, little Jolly Polly!" Magda covered her face with her hands, and almost immediately looked up. "I'm sorry, Barry. I didn't intend to put you through this."

"I don't know the answers to your questions yet, but I'll damn well find out in a hurry." Barry spoke gruffly and then waited a moment. He continued gently, "Look here, Magda, you've got to tell me why . . ."

"I will, Barry, but let's get out of here first, please. Get me out of here without those men seeing or following us. But—I just thought—I can't leave with you. It would be a dead giveaway."

"Now, Magda, you forget we have our strengths too. You're overestimating this man, and underestimating us. I've had this place under surveillance since you called."

"What are you going to do? You must give me time," she clutched his arm desperately.

"Don't worry; go into the bathroom and freshen up. I have a phone call to make."

She gave him a little grin. "Don't worry. I don't want to know your code name."

He waited until the door was closed and dialed a number.

"Cougar here." He received the confirmation response and went on. "I need two cars, one with a classified license, right away. A driver in one and two men in the other. The car with the single driver to hold back, the other will pick up two men in a red car parked outside the Lakeside Hotel off Lake Merritt, Oakland. They are to say they are special police who have been notified that a suspicious car is hanging around. Take them away for interrogation. I want to know everything about the ownership of the car. Take prints while you're about it, too. If you find nothing suspicious about them, let them go tomorrow, late afternoon. As soon as they are taken away, let driver two park and come up to room 713 and pick me up. On the double. By the way, if anyone tries to stop you, take them in, too. Got it? This is important. Step on it. Cancel present surveillance."

"Okay, Magda, it's all settled. Now, no more delaying tactics. Give." He sat down on the bed and waited.

"I'll tell you this much," Magda said slowly, weighing each word. "I recognized a man tonight, and he recognized me. I'm a real threat to him. If he learns my present name, and where I live, he has to kill me—it's his only safety. If he finds out I have a child, he won't kill me; instead, he'll use her to threaten me into doing anything he wants. If he finds out where I work he'll force me to get him secret information. And if he knows about you, he can get at you through Tasha."

"And what makes you think we'll stand idly by while he does all these things?"

"Because I know him, Barry, and how he works. He not only threatens, he acts; and sometimes he acts without prior threats—just to make his point."

"If you really believe all this, then you're very foolish not to get in touch with the proper authorities. You don't have much confidence in us, do you? I must insist we turn this over to the department immediately."

"Don't you understand? I know these things but I can't give you proof of anything. Don't you think he's covered himself? If you arrest him, what will it gain us? He's involved in something big. Don't you see all the reasons I have to act alone in this? I know him and how his mind works. I'll get some proof—and then it will be a different story. But in order to do this, I must wipe out all trace of myself and my closest friends"

She paused in her pacing back and forth across the room.

"I just thought of something. Those men surely checked your car when you entered the hotel. They're trained observers, they can check up on your license plates," she worried aloud.

"I came in a taxi," he replied quickly.

"How smart of you."

"Basic training, or shall we say, native intelligence. Why would you be in Oakland unless you thought someone was following you? In which case, if I came to see you, it would tie us together and they could check me out. *Voilà!* Don't take the car."

Magda gave him a wan smile. "In that case, they've got my license number and can follow up on that. Their leader is very clever."

"It's too late for him to get any information about that tonight, and I'll get to work on it first thing tomorrow morning. You see, we have our ways. There is one thing I must know. Does Tasha know this man? Is it someone from Shanghai or Hong Kong?"

"I hoped you wouldn't ask me that. I don't want Tasha to live always afraid of shadows."

"You may have known Tasha all your life, but evidently you don't know that my girl's got nerves of steel, and more courage than most of the men I know," Barry said proudly.

"You don't have to tell me about her," Magda answered. "I just don't want to put my burden on her. I think we won't have to worry too much about the future if the present is taken care of. I need time."

She lit a cigarette but this time her hands were steady. The flame on the match did not shake and there were no tears. Her nervousness seemed, instead, to have descended on Barry.

"Hey, now, Magda! Don't do anything rash and get yourself in a jam you can't handle. How about that fellow, Chapin Desmond? British Secret Service must be as interested in the fellow as we are. Maybe they know something for certain about him."

"It's crossed my mind," Magda admitted.

"I have grave doubts about your not informing the department about your experience tonight. This is the wrong way to handle it."

"What is there to tell, really? That I thought I recognized someone tonight from my lurid past? That I believed two men chased me? If you believe me, you must believe I can't provide proof of anything. Just think of it this way —if I hadn't told you anything, you'd know nothing."

"I'm not convinced. It's too deceptive. I'm making you no promises, Magda. I'll have to consider this seriously. And talking about license plates: one of the men must have gone into the garage, and if he didn't recognize your car, which is unlikely, all he'd have to do was to feel the heat on the hood. He could take your name and address from the registration slip on the steering wheel. Well, that settles that. I'm afraid you have no choice. We must go official and report this immediately. I can stop anyone from touching you now, but they'll have your name and address. I can't stop further repercussions without the department."

For a moment, Magda looked at him blankly, her mind already immersed in further plans. Then, his words penetrated.

"Oh, that?" she asked as she reached into her handbag, and brought out her registration card enclosed in its plastic cover.

Barry looked at her and shook his head. "It's a good

387

thing for society that you're not a criminal. What made you think of taking it?"

She shrugged. "I suppose my mind was so full of *not* leading them to your house that I was particularly aware of names and addresses. This was right in front of me, so I unstrapped it. Barry, it's been so long—I can't understand why your people haven't come yet!"

"It's not been that long since you called me; it only seems long," he comforted.

Time passed slowly. Even Barry caught Magda's agitation, and, turning off the light again, peeked several more times at the car still parked out front. A feeling of foreboding was present—as if there were a third person in the room. Magda was positive that Waldemar had not been idle all this time; he would not permit *anything* to jeopardize his plans. As soon as he knew where she was—and he had to know by this time—he'd force the desk clerk to bring him up. And he'd shoot two as well as one.

"Barry, you're right. Tasha must be warned. Tell her the name is Waldemar."

"Waldemar? Never heard of him," Barry replied with a quizzical glance at her.

"She has. He was my husband's Nazi cousin who came to Shanghai and made our lives miserable. My husband was a Jew."

"I get the picture." Barry's face was grim.

"There's another thing to tell you if you're going to adopt Polly. My mother is Chinese."

"So, that's it. I knew there was some mystery somewhere. Well, if Polly grows up looking like you, she's got nothing to worry about, has she?"

"I pray to all the gods, real and unreal, that she doesn't," Magda cried out suddenly. "Above all else, I want her life to be uncomplicated. If I knew how to pray, I'd ask that she could lead her life like all the others around her. I'm even a little sorry she has red hair. From the very beginning, my life would have been different but for the simple fact of the color of my hair."

"You're talking in riddles, Magda. What has red hair to do with this? Not that yours isn't fantastic."

"I'm talking way too much, Barry. I never intended to give you all this information. I wanted you to know nothing, for your own protection, except that Waldemar is dangerous—more so than ever—and that you should take no chances and not be fooled."

They heard soft steps outside the door and both tensed. Barry stood flat against the side of the door, one hand raised in a chopping position. Magda stood behind him. Both of them were prepared for anything.

There was a soft knock on the door.

"Who's there?"

"A good friend from the cat family."

"Which one?"

"Jaguar."

Barry smiled and opened the door.

CHAPTER TWENTY-NINE

WALDEMAR FACED THE audience in the Temple hall. The sight of Magda had shocked him but his reactions were instant. He sent his aides after her at the moment of recognition. His order was simple—"eliminate her and get away or keep her under cover until I come." She was a threat to the careful network of evil he had established throughout the United States, not only his plans for extorting substantial sums of money—millions from the large Jewish population—but, even more important, his plans for gleaning information, for instigating sabotage, and for creating distrust and fear.

Waldemar smiled sardonically at the idea of fleecing the friends and relatives of victims. It was a satisfying arrangement. He hated this decadent country where Jews held so many positions of importance. It wouldn't be that way when the Fuehrer was victorious over this vast and rich land.

There was only one man Waldemar respected besides himself. He had laughed, early on, at the little man with the funny moustache and hysterical voice, but he had come face to face with him once, and everything had changed. Waldemar had no use for omens, but his cynicism about most beliefs and traditions had given away to a solemn faith in his leader. To him, Adolf Hitler was a glowing figure in the grey mass of humanity—a man who was marked by Fate to lead the world, a great new world, where obsolete and tarnished myths would be erased forever, where the old and sick and maimed and marred—the unproductive—would be eliminated. The world was a jungle where only the fittest and ablest survived. He, Waldemar, was one of them, and, when the day came, he would be recognized as such and stand next to his leader—marked, himself, as a man of destiny.

At first it had shamed him to pretend that he was his weak and spineless cousin, Max—that half-Jew who had had the audacity to consider himself a German. The only thing he had ever envied in his cousin was his blond good looks. By some strange twist, Max always looked more the Aryan, Waldemar more the Jew. It had turned out to be useful, but Waldemar's gorge rose at having to share the company of these insolent Americans who thought themselves equal to everyone. They were a different breed from the frightened refugees in Shanghai. But their turn would come.

He and his aides were already kindling a flame of undercover anti-Semitism, which, Waldemar was positive, existed in most people, beneath only a thin layer of tolerance. The Jews throughout history had been scapegoats and would once again serve that purpose before they were eradicated forever from the face of the globe. Yet this time, Waldemar gloated, they would not die simply in gas chambers—they would be consumed by universal hatred which he, Waldemar von Zoller, and his fanatic cohorts, intended to fan into a fiery conflagration. It had started in Germany and would spread throughout all the countries of the world.

These people may have been hard-headed in business, but they were sentimental fools where their suffering brothers were concerned, naive and credulous, like Nigel Lewisholm. Waldemar gloated inwardly at the memory. It had been like training a puppy to obey by means of reward and punishment. Nigel had learned soon enough to obey without question. It had been laughable to see the face of the philanthropist change to one of stunned bewilderment, and then horror, when he was faced with his acts of betrayal toward the very people he had sought to aid.

From the podium, Waldemar beamed down on the gathering.

"You may have noticed that a few moments ago I sent my aides out." He spoke quietly; it made people concentrate better when they had to strain to listen. "You in the back may have noticed a red-headed woman leave in a hurry. I recognized her immediately as she did me.

"We have met before. She is a member of the most anti-Semitic division of the Nazi Party, planted here in the United States to destroy the work of my colleagues and me. It is essential for all of us that she be found and brought to me personally. Your laws are vulnerable in their complexity, and even though you are now at war, it is still easy for a war criminal to escape. However, there are people who know how to proceed in cases like this, where undercover work is essential."

The audience was hushed, brought as it was, face to face with the drama of war in all its ugly reality.

"We have had among us a seasoned spy. Is there anyone of you who noticed her particularly?"

People called out details. She drove a blue coupe, possibly a Dodge . . . she wore a nurse's uniform, but it could have been a waitress' or hairdresser's. It was a meager offering.

"It is very important that she be located," he went on. "She can possibly ruin the underground routes that I and others have built so patiently over the years. I know her well. She is very clever and will likely try to reverse the situation, claiming that I am the spy." Waldemar smiled grimly.

"I have encountered her before when she and her group almost ruined my plans. Listen well. She has brilliant red hair, fair skin, and eyes that are almost black. She speaks with a clipped English accent. Let me warn you—do not discuss my work with anyone if you care for the safety of your brothers and sisters now in jeopardy."

A man put up his hand.

"You said," he stammered nervously, feeling himself the focus of all eyes, "that we should bring this woman to you by force if necessary. Well—that's against the law. It's kidnapping." He mopped his forehead but continued doggedly. "Why all the secrecy? Tell the authorities; they'll know how to proceed."

All heads turned to Waldemar.

"I see," he said softly. "It is too bad no one explained to me about breaking the laws of the different countries I have entered—about false passports, false names, bribing officers. Do you suggest I tell the authorities everything I do? My plans, my routes, the people I set out to bring over? Do you think it would be wise?"

Then he related stories of horror perpetrated on his "fellow" Jews—of escapes foiled by treachery. He cited true stories—true enough, except that the roles were reversed. His listeners were mesmerized. It entertained Waldemar to speak of actual happenings, painting the brutality and terror, the humiliations and the complete subjugation of Jewish prisoners.

Waldemar was a seasoned speaker; he knew well how to play on his listeners' emotions, and he enjoyed his power. He stimulated their desire to help, he prodded them into assuming more responsibility; he placated them and milked their sympathy, exhorting them with the clear implication that if there were a choice, service to their fellow men should come before duty to country.

The collection began. He stood there—belligerent, forceful, frightening—watching their expressions. There were those who were torn in their loyalties, but in whom doubt had been instilled; there were those who drew themselves in, determined not to involve themselves further. Many were annoyed and some were definitely suspicious. Lastly, there were those who felt an intense motivation. It was the last group that interested Waldemar. They would become his pawns.

The officials of the Jewish Protection League for the Refugees met with Waldemar in their office and turned over to him the proceeds of the collection, which were double their highest expectations. At the same time, they were so swayed by Waldemar's speech that

392

money seemed inconsequential in comparison to the higher sacrifice.

Waldemar took a cursory look at the total, amused that Magda's presence had inadvertently been to his financial advantage. He signed a receipt and nonchalantly stuffed the donations into a briefcase, purposely leaving it open.

It had been well over an hour since the incident had occurred, and Waldemar expected to hear from his men at any moment.

"I would like you to wait for me; I may need your help. I am not familiar with the city."

He explained to them that, naturally, all the talks which had been scheduled for the general public would have to be canceled until the woman was caught; that in future they would meet only in the private homes of those who were known to be completely dedicated; and that word would be spread only to those passionately, uncompromisingly interested in the saving of lives.

"During World War I, German Jews received medals for extreme heroism and patriotism," he went on. "I, myself, was awarded a medal by Kaiser Wilhelm. I was a German first, a Jew second, honored in a country which now despises me. I learned where to place my loyalties."

He looked around—Waldemar, the great actor—pausing for effect.

"There are times," he said confidentially, "I would like to unshackle myself from the ignominy of being connected with a race of losers. Maybe we can change that."

They were all quiet. Several left the room, but three remained, uncomfortable at the seeming desertion of the others.

"Well, now we know where our loyalties lie, don't we?" Waldemar jeered. He did, indeed. It wouldn't take him long to implicate them in his schemes.

The phone rang. Waldemar picked it up on the first ring. He listened more than he spoke, and then he gave some orders in German, spoken far too rapidly for the men to understand, however close it may have been to

Yiddish. The sound of that language made them feel uneasy. It was difficult to believe that this German-speaking man was one of them—he was too overbearing too arrogant—there were times he seemed to talk down to them, but quickly they smothered their faint misgivings. This man came highly referred to them by their companion league in England, and his credentials were unassailable.

Waldemar hung up the phone and turned to them triumphantly.

"She is in the Lakeside Hotel in Oakland. My men were close enough behind her to follow her car. They looked at the hotel register and found she had checked in as Mrs. Aimee McPherson."

He saw the amused looks on their faces and frowned. Laughing at others was his prerogative. He looked at them questioningly, and they told him who Aimee McPherson was. He smiled, a chilling smile.

"So. She plays games with us. You see how sure she is of herself. That should tell you she has an organization behind her. An evangelist, indeed. An evangelist of death. Now, listen. My men are guarding the exit to see that no one comes for her. We must hurry over there to see she doesn't escape our little trap. Is there anyone among you who has anything to do with, or knows someone who is connected with the Lakeside Hotel? We must keep her from escaping, but it would be better if we could confront her ourselves without involving outside help." Waldemar looked at the three men.

One of them nudged the president of the committee, but he angrily shook off the man's hand. Waldemar saw the interplay.

"Well?"

The third man spoke up. "Irving's brother-in-law is a director of the Lake Merritt Hotel Organization."

Waldemar stared Irving down coldly. "There is no one forcing you to remain with us. It is your choice."

Irving flushed. "In my opinion, I may do what I choose, but I have no right to involve others." He turned to his companion. "In future, you will not speak for me, understand? Why don't you tell him about your relative who works for—" He stopped suddenly.

They are already in my hands, Waldemar exulted. Aloud, he said, "Well?"

"I'll call him," Irving said reluctantly. He dialed a number. "Rae? I'd like to talk to Harry. He's napping? Listen, this is very important, please wake him. If he's angry, I'll take the responsibility—you'll get the brunt, anyway? Hello, Harry? No time for that—this is serious." Irving related the situation. "You can help us, Harry, the woman is registered at the Lakeside Hotel in Oakland—that's one of your group, isn't it? I thought so. Look, we just need to see her alone before she does something harmful." Irving looked at Waldemar questioningly, then nodded. "All we want is the number of her room. She is registered as Aimee McPherson . . . No, I'm not being funny . . . Maybe you could alert the hotel detective to keep a watch out . . . He's gone to work in a munitions plant? . . . What sort of hotel system are you running? Okay, okay—hold your horses . . . No, of course not, no rough stuff, you know me better . . . No, the hotel will not be involved, I guarantee you—will that suit you? You don't want any part . . . Harry, remember Sam Schwartz? Hamburg? You remember? On my word of honor, no harm will come to the woman. Though from what I understand she is high on the list of the criminals who are working against us."

Irving held the phone for a long time, listening to a harangue on the other end, shaking his head and nodding.

"No—I swear to you, not in the hotel. Just have someone keep an eye on her room. Okay, call me up as soon as you know her room number. Harry, don't wait. This is crucial."

A few moments later, the phone rang and Irving dashed to answer it.

"Room 713. Okay You won't regret this, I promise you."

In the commotion of leaving, no one saw Waldemar slip a syringe from the open briefcase into his pocket before asking Irving to lock the case in a safe place.

Waldemar's suspicions that all was not well were instantly aroused when he saw the empty car and no sign of his men. A feeling of foreboding and rage churned inside him. Magda must be dealt with.

They rode the elevator to the seventh floor. An elderly man sat outside her door, looking sleepy and bored. He stood up when they arrived and stretched his arms.

"Who are you?" Irving demanded.

"I'm the night watchman. They told me downstairs to see no one gets out of this room."

"How long have you been here?"

"Just checked in ten minutes ago. No one has been in or out."

He was dismissed by the prearranged password Harry had concocted for the occasion. Waldemar very quietly opened the door with a skeleton key. He had not wanted the desk to know more than necessary.

The lock clicked. He opened it, and they all rushed in, finding the room empty. Waldemar stood aside as the others went through the hopeless task of searching the closet, the bathroom, and the space under the bed. The kind of exhilaration they had felt at the beginning of the chase was completely faded.

They avoided looking at each other; they felt utterly ludicrous. They turned to Waldemar awkwardly, but were not prepared for the blaze of fury in his eyes. It took him several minutes to control himself enough to speak evenly.

"Now, do you believe me? She's been whisked away and my men have disappeared. There must be another spy in our group, and we will find out who it is. No one is above suspicion." He spoke malevolently. One of the men started to back out of the room but Waldemar's cold voice stopped him. "We are in this together," he said with an icy glance.

They went through the motions, asking questions of the desk clerk and the waiter, though Waldemar knew it was a useless exercise. But it would have looked suspicious to the others if it had not been done. This was the second time Magda had slipped through his fingers —but not for long, he promised himself.

He knew his men would not have left their mission under threat of death—they feared him more. Who had helped Magda? He knew she was shrewd, but shrewd enough to fool him . . . ? No! Impossible! He growled like a thwarted animal, then quickly changed it to a cough as the others stared at him in bewilderment.

He lowered his eyes in deep thought—she couldn't have left too long ago—and flipped through his memory like a card index, recalling every car they had passed on the highway since leaving San Francisco.

CHAPTER THIRTY

◄◄◄◄◄◄◄◄◄◄◄◄◄◄◄◄◄◄◄◄◄

THEY WERE WELL away from the hotel when Magda thought she saw a glimpse of Waldemar in a car that raced by them. She shuddered violently next to Barry, and he looked at her anxiously.

"Just a case of delayed jitters," she smiled weakly. It would not do to tell Barry. He'd probably send someone back, and it would warn Waldemar.

"Could you have been alarmed unnecessarily?" Barry asked. But then he saw that his effort to lighten the situation was the wrong thing to do.

"Drop me off at the Stewart Hotel on Geary. From this moment on, I'm cutting all ties with you. It's too dangerous."

"It's not necessary, Magda, you're—"

"Please, Barry."

"I'm through arguing with you. Just don't check in under the name of Aimee Semple McPherson, okay? Why on earth did you?"

She laughed, a very small laugh. "There's no logical explanation. I just needed a name and hers popped into my mind. Don't worry, at the Stewart. I'll register as respectable Mrs. Joseph Bentley. It's fortunate I have some money with me. I'll pay in advance."

"You're sure you'll be okay?"

"As much as I can be until this nightmare is over, Barry," she spoke hesitantly. "You will keep in touch with Chapin, won't you? He's Polly's godfather. You won't take that away from him, will you?"

"Of course not," he said gruffly.

She stopped him from coming in with her at the hotel.

"Okay. Have it your way. I'll check with you in the morning."

"Barry, I haven't the words to tell you how grateful I am to you for coming to my aid tonight. And for everything else," she added.

"It's all right, Magda." He felt a wave of something like pity. "Look, kid, you take care, eh? If you're sure, I'll be on my way." She nodded to him, and he was off.

Tasha was half asleep when she heard Barry's key in the lock. She jumped out of bed to greet him, all warm and sleepy, rubbing her eyes like a child. He hugged her tightly.

"Mmm, nice," purred Tasha, brushing her cheek against his.

"Wake up, honey. Really wake up. I've got something to tell you. We're off to Hawaii, maybe tomorrow. I'm sorry but I don't have any choice any more."

"You've always thought I cared more about the house than I do," Tasha answered from the kitchen, where she was making some coffee. "Of course I love it, but wherever you are is my real home. Goodness, this will be tough on Magda. I hate to awaken Estelle, but I'd better tell Magda right now. Hey, do you think she'd like to rent the house? That would be a great solution."

"I doubt it. I've already talked to Magda about our leaving, and she asked me if we would take Polly for a few months. She's in the middle of some very private work, and doesn't dare take the responsibility of the baby herself."

"How perfectly marvelous!" Tasha ran into the living room and planted a big kiss on his forehead. "Magda's changed so much since she had little Polly. I've never seen her so happy and contented. I don't know how she can bear to leave her, even for a day. She's a remarkable person."

"Yes, she is."

"I don't think you used to like her much."

"You're very perceptive, Kitten. Come here and I'll make you purr for me."

Finally, laughing, she struggled away. "Beloved of my heart, I'm happy to know you love me but a little more of that and you'll squeeze the life out of me." Her eyes sparkled with green lights.

"What about the house, Kitten, shall we sell it?"

"Do we have to decide in a hurry?"

He nodded.

"Then, yes, I think so, if it's up to me. Otherwise I'll be worried about my little garden and what damage different people will do to it. This way, there'll be no thinking that this is my house anymore."

"You're sure?"

"Positive."

"We'll probably be leaving tomorrow."

"I'll have to tell the office. They're going to *love* having me leave without giving notice." She giggled, "This is one time I get to say, 'Don't you know there's a war on?' Did Magda tell you what to do about her things?"

"She said she'll get in touch with Violet and let her know."

"Well, I'd better start getting the packing organized. I like doing things suddenly—it's exciting."

Tasha asked no more questions. She knew that both Barry and Magda worked in different branches of the same service, and that she could not always account for their actions. If she thought it odd that a cryptologist was being sent on a mission, she didn't voice it.

At six o'clock the following morning, Magda checked out of the Stewart and went to her office. It seemed to her that weeks had passed, not just twelve hours, since she had left it. She proceeded to clean out all of her personal possessions.

Regardless of what her department might think of her departure, she intended to go underground without wasting any time. She wrote to Mr. Norris, her superior, that she had not taken even a day off since her arrival, two years ago, except to have her child, and that suddenly she felt she was cracking up, that even the thought of facing anyone to apply for a vacation was more than she felt able to do.

"So I am going AWOL, as they say in the Army, though I hope you will not consider it that serious a breach. I shall return as soon as I am able, if you will still want me . . ."

Then came the most difficult task of all, writing a letter to Chapin Desmond, cutting away from herself all that she held dear. It was the only way she could do the job ahead of her.

She was shocked to find it was after eight when she finished. The other employees would soon be coming in. She addressed her letter and put it in the diplomatic pouch in the head office which she and a very few others were privileged to use. Even though the mail was supposed to go through uncensored, she had used the code that she and Chapin had devised for emergencies.

A small shop on Geary Street was being swept out for the morning opening, and she persuaded the clerk to sell her a scarf before regular opening hours. Once she wrapped it around her blazing hair, she felt safer. Now she had to find a suitable hotel. She was certain that Waldemar was already sending out men to look for her. She fastened her coat to hide the uniform she was still wearing.

She walked to Post Street. It was mostly apartment houses, but a little further toward Sutter and Leavenworth, she saw a small sign: Cartwright Hotel. A janitor was washing the floor, and a sleepy-eyed girl was nodding over a book at a reception desk in the tiny lobby.

Yes, they had a vacancy. Magda registered under the name of Pearl Young. She paid a week in advance and had begun a long involved explanation about not having luggage when she noticed the girl, completely uninterested, was holding out a key.

"Room 203, to the right of the elevator," she said, and went back to her book.

Magda started to say something about going out to get some breakfast and clamped her mouth shut. She had to stop making unnecessary explanations. It wasn't like her.

She noticed a drugstore on the corner, and she went in to make some necessary purchases. Suddenly, she discovered she was enormously hungry, but she disciplined herself: "Breakfast after."

Magda shook the bottle of hair dye vigorously. She looked at herself in the mirror—for the last time a Red

MacDougall, her father's pride. She faltered for a minute and then applied the brush swiftly to the roots. Half an hour later she combed the dye through her hair. Another half hour, and the job would be complete. She refused to look in the mirror again. She had never had much vanity—just enough to know that her hair was extraordinary and to enjoy the way it caught every glint of the sun. That red hair! All the extravagant words of admiration for her beauty had been for her hair, she was certain. Without it, she was ordinary looking, which was what she wanted now. Her hair had literally made her road through life what it was. Her father had thought she was fortunate to look so European—cousin William had thought the reverse.

She combed the viscous stuff through her hair. It had a strange and repelling smell, one she would never forget. Finally, the time was up and she rinsed it out in the shower, watching the soapy water stream down her body in black rivulets. When the water ran clear, she stepped out of the shower and rubbed her head until it smarted. It didn't even feel like her hair. Without looking at herself, she combed her hair forward from the crown and cut bangs by feel, long heavy bangs covering her eyebrows. She dressed, and only then did she look at the stranger in the mirror.

"Well, well! Hello, Pearl, you're not so bad looking after all. In fact, quite impartially, I'd say you were quite stunning—but we'll have to change all that, won't we?"

Her eyes seemed larger and more brilliantly black, her features even more delicate and finely delineated. She had worn black wigs before, but this was different—she felt different inside.

Pleased at her forethought, she took out the new makeup she'd purchased. She began to apply dark foundation and matte powder to dull her skin; then dark lipstick drawn heavily over the contour of her lips, black eyebrow pencil to elongate the slant of her eyes, and, as a final touch, she put on a pair of lightly-tinted blue sunglasses. That does it, she thought. Now for the right clothes.

Magda stepped out of the hotel with confidence, looking at her reflection in the shop windows she passed. She would have to change her walk. She had been trained by enough Intelligence departments to know the points of seeing through disguises. The walk, the stance, the movements, the ears, little habits you were unaware of, and names. Never to use your own initials—hence, Pearl Young. Young was good—it could be Chinese or Occidental. Was Pearl a little too much?

Speech—that shouldn't be difficult for her. She had deliberately used an American accent that morning, but it wasn't enough. She'd have to pick up the slightly sing-song speech Eurasian girls had—except that this was America, not Shanghai. She'd have to do some listening.

She would give herself two days to perfect her speech pattern and practice her walk—no longer, or Waldemar would be leaving San Francisco for other areas of the country and she would lose his trail. She was positive he'd stay here for at least some time. He would not easily give up the chase for her.

Money was next on her list. She wrote out a check for five hundred dollars and cashed it in a nearby bank, not her own. After a short wait, it was honored. She'd have to do something about money. She would need a great deal.

At his office, Barry informed his superior that he was ready to leave for Hawaii, the sooner the better.

"You're damned right you're ready. I've given you enough time. There's a transport leaving in twenty-four hours. I'll put you and your family down for it."

"I'll be packed and ready to go. Draw up the papers to include my wife, Natasha, and little Pauline."

"You're a close-mouthed devil, aren't you? Didn't know you had a kid."

Barry looked at his superior thoughtfully, wondering if it was necessary to say anything.

"It's this way—we're taking care of her, she's not our child. We've had her since she was born, about a year and a half ago, and we're working on adoption. She's a real cute little monkey." Proudly, he took a photograph out of his wallet.

"Spoken like a doting father. You shouldn't have any

trouble if you have her birth certificate and parents' permission. This a picture of your wife and baby? Good-looking family you have, Winters. Almost makes me wish I weren't a bachelor, but not quite. Just a minute. If you're all ready to leave, I think I can get you on a transport leaving at sixteen hundred hours. Better get it while I can. Hold on, let's check." He dialed a number and listened. "It's set. You, your wife and the kid, minimum luggage. Come back at one for your final papers and instructions. If I'm not here—good luck."

The two men shook hands and Barry left.

On Market Street her stomach began to rumble hungrily, and Magda entered a drugstore. Probably panic, she decided. Aside from a normal disquiet, Magda felt a strangely heady excitement blended with fear. She was completely on her own, in a real life-or-death situation.

She called Barry at his office. He was out, and she'd have to try him again. Then, against her stern admonitions to herself, she dialed her own number, half-hoping Tasha wouldn't be home, but wanting desperately to talk to her best friend. She knew what she had done, but the physical fact of calling Tasha suddenly made her realize, as nothing else had, the consequences of her actions—she was cutting herself off from all she had ever known. It was too much, she thought nervously—there had to be another way. But she knew that there wasn't. Fear for everyone she loved would haunt her all her life, if she lived—and, if she didn't, what would happen to them? She knew Waldemar's vindictiveness.

She heard the phone ring several times, and she almost hung up. She was choking, she couldn't talk. Then she heard Tasha's voice and put aside her qualms. There was so much she had to tell Tasha, but above all else she wanted to hear her little baby's voice once more so that it would ring in her ears for the rest of her days. It would do no harm this last time.

"Tasha, this is Magda."

"I'm so glad! I'd have felt awful not to talk to you again, before we left, but Barry told me not to call you at the office. We're leaving at four this afternoon; you can imagine the things that still have to be done. I'm expecting Bekins Van & Storage at any minute. We decided to put the house up for sale.

"I hate to leave you in the lurch like this, Magda, but what can I do? My dear, don't worry about Polly. You know how much we both love her. I'll promise to look after her until you're ready to take her back. I'm just so happy to have her, even a few months."

So Barry hadn't told her about the adoption. Was he doing that as insurance, in case she changed her mind? He was more sensitive than she'd thought. Maybe he was wise to let it go until they were settled on the island. It made no difference to her, though; there would be no going back.

Tasha was still talking. Wise Tasha, who hid her sharp intelligence under endless chatter. How much did she guess?

"What shall I do with your things, Mag?" she asked, finally.

"That's one of the reasons I called. Cut off all the labels and names in all my clothes, and have Violet take them down to the Bundles for Britain." She gave Tasha detailed instructions, trying to think of anything which would help wipe out all traces of her existence. "Have you got all that?"

"Weird instructions, but clear. You have my promise. Magda?"

"What?"

"Oh, nothing." Tasha's voice trembled.

"You are a dope, but a very dear one. I'll try to keep in touch with you, but don't worry if I don't. Listen to me carefully, this is very serious. I don't think it's likely, but if anyone should come to you with a message from me, don't believe it. If anyone mentions my name as a reference, don't believe it, either. Should I need to get in touch with you, I'll do it personally, or through Barry. I don't mean to act so mysterious, but there's a lot at stake here. Okay?"

"Okay. Don't worry, Magda. I'm not an absolute idiot. Barry didn't tell me much, but what he didn't, I think I can guess."

"Keep it to yourself if you have."

"You take care now," Tasha's voice choked a bit.

"Do you think you could get our Polly to gurgle for me?"

"I can give it a good try."

A moment later Magda heard the high sweet voice of the little girl talking her usual nonsense. Then she heard Polly say distinctly, "Ma-ma-ga, Ma-ma-ga," with a trill of delighted laughter.

"Did you hear her all right?" Tasha's voice broke through the child's gurgling. Magda held the phone to her ear while Polly kept on repeating "Ma-ma-ga" with screams of joy. Suddenly Magda felt a pain so bitter, so strangling, it seemed a foretaste of death. Her mind was filled with a long silent scream of anguish which shattered. Slowly, she hung up the phone, struggling to hold back the tears.

Magda needed desperately to get in touch with Barry before he left. She called his office again and again.

"Your obsession for secrecy defeats its own purpose," Barry said curtly when she finally reached him. "I had no way to contact you and so many things to do. I've had to waste valuable time. You could at least have left a message at the hotel for me."

"Don't scold, Barry," she sighed. "I'm sure you're right. I'm sorry to have given you unnecessary trouble. Is this phone secure?"

"So you're still at it? Okay. I understand. Give me a number and I'll call you from outside. You know you're being ridiculous; this is headquarters."

In five minutes the phone in the public booth rang.

"Very well, Mrs. Aimee Semple McPherson, is this cloak-and-dagger enough for you?" Barry said good-naturedly. The sound of her tired, spiritless voice had made him realize the strain she was under.

"Barry, however foolish you may think I'm being, I have to do things my way until I feel more secure. I'm going underground—out of sight and almost out of hearing. I intend to be successful in this—more than my own life depends on it.

"I know, perhaps better than anyone else, how this man thinks. It's not anything I can share with or explain to others. It's more an instinct, and that is why I must start by working alone. But when I began to figure out my plan, I realized I would need some official backup from time to time, not to mention some classified information. I need a contact I can trust and who will trust me and act upon my information."

"You're asking a hell of a lot for giving me nothing. By the way, I intended to tell you earlier. I have reconsidered my agreement to keep quiet for a while. I fully believe that this is a matter for security, and my country has to come before your plans, whatever they may be. I took an oath when I entered the service, and I didn't do it lightly."

"You do what you must, Barry. I appreciate your position. All I ask is that your department delay action on the information—which is incomplete, anyway. If your people start asking questions, they'll alert Waldemar and his network, which I am certain exists. I have written to London, in fact, to Chapin, asking for clearance to divulge what we know. In fact, I asked him to contact your department chief personally, if he could. It would carry more authority coming from him. You see, I, too, am under oath. Anyway, it will clear me of any deception. The OSS, hopefully, will acknowledge my requests for action when I am ready to give them whatever I find out."

"Now you're being smart. I'll repeat what you said to the right man and try to persuade him. You see, I do believe you. Call me at this number in half an hour, and I'll see what I can do."

When Magda called him back a short while later, he was very businesslike and told her that the department head had agreed to give her time, unless the incidents of the previous night were repeated.

"I put myself on the line for you, so you'd better come up with something substantial. Your code name is Vixen!" Magda stifled a laugh. "I hope you will be as sly as the word suggests. The response will be Brer Rabbit if the contact is made in California. This number you are calling is a classified one. Should you make the call to Washington, D.C., or to New York, add the abbreviations of the state. Do you understand? Your contact in these places will be called Plutarch and he will give you another number to call. Then you will say: 'The official time on the tenth meridian is 2:19 A.M.'

The response will be, 'Not on your old tin hat. The time is the day before yesterday.'

"Can you remember all that? No notes. And don't let me hear hysterical laughter from you. It's no joke."

"If it were, I could enjoy it more. Barry, I called Tasha today. It was a weakness I couldn't resist. I needed a moment of sanity. There is one last thing I wish you'd do. I'll have someone deliver my car keys to you, if you'll arrange to have my car hauled away to a garage to repaint and sell, with new license plates, of course. Let the money go to the Salvation Army. Have you instructed your real estate agent to sell the house yet?"

"Yes, I have."

"Barry," she paused. "I told Tasha nothing, except to be careful. I think she's guessed. You evidently haven't told her much of anything yet. Tasha is not a gossip, and she'll never talk about me unless you ask. If I can, I'll keep in touch with you. If not, send the adoption papers to Chapin Desmond. He'll see that I get them. That will eliminate any possibility of their being intercepted, okay?"

"You're even worse than the government. Magda, don't take any unnecessary risks."

"I won't, I promise. There's too much at stake."

Suddenly the whole proposition looked very bleak. What had made her think that she, and she alone, could outwit Waldemar? Waldemar, with his unlimited resources of people and money, his knowledge and his experience. Who was she to think she could succeed where British Intelligence had failed? Who knew how many people he had already killed in his terrible crusade and she, Magda MacDougall, thought she could fool him!

Nevertheless, Magda knew, had always known, that a confrontation between them was inevitable. There was still time for her to make a final decision. If she were going to doubt herself and worry about her chances of success, she had better give up now and let the proper authorities take over. If not, then she should start fresh and be of stout heart, like the heroine of the tales Angus used to regale her with: a long-ago namesake, an

407

Amazonian figure with long tawny tresses, who girded her skirts and led her clan into battle. Magda smiled a little sadly; she wished her role were as straightforward.

Still wearing her uniform covered by her coat, Magda wandered by a few of the Chinese dress shops on Grant Avenue. She made up her mind, entered, and forced herself to ask a disdainful salesgirl to let her try on one of the modern-type cheongsams in which they specialized.

The girl reluctantly took her into a booth, resigned that her customer was wasting her time. Magda chose a close-fitting, black sleeveless gown with jadelike studs in the fastening frogs. It was slit on the sides and showed a lot of leg.

The salesgirl became excited by the enormous difference in her timid and dowdy customer and took her in hand. She insisted that Magda put on a pair of sandals which were little more than webbed straps on stilt heels, some dangling earrings, a touch of green eye-shadow and bright lipstick from the makeup counter, and finally a beaded handbag. She was finally ready to show Magda the transformation in front of a tall mirror.

"My goodness!" she breathed. "I bet you could even get a job as a cocktail waitress at Ernie Kann's cocktail lounge, if you wanted. The best people go there. You could make a mint." Magda stifled a smile and thanked her for all her help.

The first step in her plan was to make herself absolutely unrecognizable, and to this end it was essential to change her speech patterns to match her appearance. Magda listened to the voices and chatter around her, analyzing and remembering the sounds—higher pitched than her own speech, with the slight cadence of singsong still in the language, but staccato and chopped off. It wouldn't be too difficult, she thought, focusing all of her attention on it.

She felt hysterical laughter rising inside her when she left the shop, rather awkwardly tottering on her very high heels. She wouldn't have to worry about learning a new walk, the shoes were doing it for her. She found that in order to retain any kind of balance, she had to sway her hips—so, that was the way it was done. She had often wondered.

Cocktail waitress in twelve hours! What good would this outfit do her? It wasn't really what she'd had in mind. Well, at least she was getting accustomed to being Chinese and to having a new personality. That was a plus. Besides, she had to admit it was a bit of fun, just as when she used to wear a wig and dress Chinese-style in order to meet William in Shanghai. Oh, William, she thought, I wish you were here to advise me what to do. You could see right through to the objective. Well, she knew the objective, but she would have liked the advantage of his clear, sensible thinking, the elimination of nonessentials, the getting down to basics. Except that he didn't sound like that any more. His letters from China were increasingly bewildered, not at all like the William she knew—as though he was losing his faith in China's leaders.

Come back to earth, Magda, she chastised herself. This is no time to get lost in memories, on a street in the city.

She took a taxi to the hotel and walked in, swaying a little with her extremely tight dress and high heels. For the first time, the receptionist really looked at her when she asked for her key.

"Hey! I didn't know you were a Chink, sorry, I mean Chinese."

"Sometimes I go one way, sometimes the other," Magda said casually.

"I don't know," the receptionist said doubtfully. "I don't know if you're allowed here. We usually don't take Chinese. We got restrictions. I've got to check with the boss."

"Check all you want," Magda belligerently placed her hands on her hips. "I've paid for a week, and I'm going to stay for a week."

"Look, lady, I couldn't care less one way or the other, but I got to call, see?"

"How would you like to have all my secret Tong friends come around here making trouble? Hmm? Tell you what I'll do; here's a ten to forget you saw me. I'll be gone in a couple of days. How about it, huh?"

The girl looked hungrily at the ten-dollar bill.

409

"Uh, I don't know. Well, okay." She took the bill, quickly slipping it into her pocket. "Stay out of the lobby though, will you? You don't want me to lose my job?"

"You tell them that it was either let me stay or give me back my week's rent and get plenty of trouble besides!"

The receptionist was surprised to hear a wave of laughter as Magda rode up in the elevator.

Now for the supreme test. Estelle. If she could pass with Estelle, she could pass with anyone. She called and arranged to meet Estelle in the ladies' lounge of the White House department store the following day at noon.

Magda was already in the lounge when Estelle sailed in on the dot of twelve. She glanced quickly at Magda and sat down, impatiently checking her watch. Estelle disliked tardiness. Noon meant twelve o'clock sharp.

Magda swayed to the mirror, arranged her hair and put on fresh lipstick. She sat down again, crossing her legs, then said in her new Chinese-American, slightly-accented voice: "Don't you hate to wait for people?"

Estelle looked disapprovingly at the overdressed, over-madeup Chinese girl sitting opposite her. She was not a type Estelle admired.

"It's a nuisance, all right," she said shortly. She tried to cover her irritation when the girl walked over to her and asked for the time.

"It's twelve-fifteen, and I've half a mind to leave."

"How about having some lunch with me first?" Magda asked in her natural voice and started to laugh.

Estelle showed no astonishment but regarded her coldly. "I believe you have mistaken the date. This is not Halloween. If this is a joke, I don't think it's funny. But, since neither of us are practical jokers, I assume this is your idea of a disguise. Well, it works to the extent that you are not recognizable, but I'm not too sure I want to be seen having lunch with a Chinese floozie, or a very good imitation of one. If it suits your purpose to be whistled at and be noticed, then you've succeeded."

Magda's good humor plummeted. "I thought I'd mix with people in Chinatown and get lost among them," she explained, embarrassed by Estelle's obvious disapproval.

"I thought that having spent all my life so far being European, I'd go the other route."

Estelle's disapproval became even more pronounced. "Being Chinese is not a game. We who are fully Chinese are proud of being so. It is hardly complimentary to us when you change from well-to-do, educated, British to Chinese—and opt for the lowest social level. Is that the best you can do, or is your white snobbery showing itself? You can only get the feeling of being Chinese when you are proud of it. But *you* think of it only as a means of hiding."

"Estelle! What are you saying? You know you are deliberately misjudging my motives. Look, I really need a friend."

"I'm not so sure I want to be your friend. To be truthful, I don't even know if I want you in my house. It would set the neighbors talking, and they do enough of that with my red-headed friend coming to see the Chens so often."

Magda was aghast. "Do they really do that?"

"Don't worry," Estelle said, more kindly, when she saw the real anxiety in Magda's eyes. "When it comes to outside questioning, we all 'no understand English.' "

"If I've been thoughtless, I'm sorry, Estelle. In my wildest imagination I never thought you'd think I was insulting you. I'll tell you as much as I can." Briefly, she outlined the situation. "I'm desperate, Estelle. Help me."

Somewhat mollified, Estelle replied. "Go and wash your face, and take off that junk jewelry. Let's get something less spectacular for you to wear. First of all, do you particularly need to look Chinese?"

"Not at all. I want only to escape recognition—certainly not to draw more attention to myself."

"You're either very innocent or very naive," Estelle remarked drily. "The way to do that is to be as nondescript as possible, not to flaunt yourself as a sex symbol, Chinese style. All Chinese women have to face the fact that there are geisha girls, singsong girls, bar girls, dance hall girls—but we don't exactly invite them to our homes."

"I never knew you to be so touchy about anything before."

"There's a lot about me you don't know," Estelle said

cryptically. "Come on, then, if we're going to do something about you!"

Having failed in one change of character, Magda put herself in Estelle's capable hands with relief and appreciation, first for her honesty and shrewdness, and, more importantly, for not asking any questions.

The young woman who left the department store with Estelle later was a quiet, neat, rather dull-looking woman of no particular nationality. The bangs were still there, but thin and scraggly rather than full; the hair had been lightened from jet black to a rusty dark brown. She wore a greyish-beige dress which was draped over a shapeless body. That, to Magda, was the worst of all. The flat-type bra she now wore not only pressed in her breasts, but seemed to inhibit her breathing. She wore sensible flat shoes which lowered her height substantially, and she carried a large imitation-alligator purse. She was the image of a dependable, efficient office-worker who spent her weekends at home—undeserving of a second look.

At Estelle's suggestion, they went to an optician relative of hers, who provided a pair of bifocals, heavily magnified in the reading section and with plain glass for the rest. He was dubious, but Estelle waved his objections aside. When they left she told Magda to get accustomed to looking through the plain glass, unless she saw someone observing her too closely, and then to give them the benefit of the magnified part.

"They'll distort your eyes and make them look like an owl's; of course you'll be blinded yourself, at the time."

"You should be a movie director." Magda was both intrigued and uncomfortable.

"I've been told that I wasn't making full use of my potential," Estelle answered smugly. "Let's say you're my project now. Seriously, Magda, Peter and I are one hundred percent behind you. I know how he feels. You've told me enough so I know this is more than just a personal vendetta. This is for the country, too. You should know this. We are proud of our race, with much more reason than any other people. We have good reasons for feeling superior. But remember, also: though we are Chinese in origin, we are Americans first. If you accomplish your mission, it will be for the good of our country, not only

412

for the Jews, who seem to be uncharacteristically gullible in this matter. But, I don't know—if my family were directly involved, I guess I'd shut my eyes, too. Well, what's next?"

"I need a lawyer I can trust to make out a power of attorney for himself, so he can sell some securities for me."

"No problem. My brother-in-law is a lawyer. He's terrific. You know, I'm not pleased with your name, Pearl. It sticks out a bit. Somehow, I don't think the kind of mother you'd have would have chosen Pearl. More likely something like Betty or Nancy. I kind of like Nancy myself. Nancy Young—it sounds right," she giggled. "Right now you even look like someone called Nancy Young."

"That's great. We've done it, Estelle, the whole thing. Now all I have to do is to get to work. You're really something!"

"I know," Estelle said modestly.

And thus Nancy Young was born.

CHAPTER THIRTY-ONE
◄◄◄◄◄◄◄◄◄◄◄◄◄◄◄◄◄◄◄◄◄◄◄◄◄◄◄

In March, 1944, Chapin received a letter from Magda, giving him all the details of what had happened and an outline of her future plans. The letter was coolly impersonal, written in their private code, but with no message for him.

He reread the letter several times, his sense of personal loss and pain growing with every reading. Recently, her letters had been so happy and encouraging. They came from a Magda freed at last from emotional stress and self-doubt—the Magda he had always known existed, a Magda proud and victorious, rising above the shadow under which she had lived.

In the last year, the changing tone of her letters had

encouraged Chapin to hope that he and Magda might eventually be married, might join their lives together forever. But suddenly the dream seemed to be slipping through his fingers.

Heightened wartime measures had failed in one particularly important instance for them—had failed to keep Waldemar von Zoller under close scrutiny. Once again, he was menacing Magda's life, as though the mathematics of coincidence had forced a confrontation between them.

In his imagination, Chapin pictured Magda's slight figure in a death struggle with Waldemar—he, heavily armed and guarded, with an army ready to jump at his bidding.

"More truth than imagination," he muttered. "Let's see what I can do to even the odds."

Chapin had risen to the post of second-in-command in British Security, gained it by merit, not influence. Lord Chapin Paul St. Hugh Desmond kept a low profile and used his title only when strict formality insisted. But, on occasions when it served a purpose, he had no compunction about making full use of his connections and influence. This was strictly such an occasion.

After all, he thought, British Intelligence has some responsibility in the von Zoller affair. Even though he felt heartsick at the risk Magda was taking, Chapin was confident that she had the intelligence, persistence, and courage to bring her quarry down. Too much courage, unfortunately. Perhaps he had always feared that she would try to tackle Waldemar alone. Now she was caught in the quicksands of his machinations. She needed massive help, and Chapin set the wheels in motion.

There was a flurry of coded cables from London headquarters to Washington headquarters. Washington concurred and orders were relayed to San Francisco. The result was that within three days of her disappearance, everything related to "Mrs. Joseph Bentley, Christian name—Magda," was withdrawn from the employee records in the bureau where she had worked. All inquiries as to her whereabouts were put on ice. It was as though she had never existed. On the other hand, the green light would be given automatically to any requests from code name Vixen. Barry's former chief in San Francisco had more or less dismissed the case as one of hysterical imagination. After all, his department had already received its full quota of unfounded rumors about suspected spies.

"Humph!" he grunted, and alerted Brer Fox to the importance of possible calls from Vixen. He gave orders that all such information regarding requests or call for assistance be relayed directly to him.

Magda left the Cartwright Hotel. It had become dangerous now that the receptionist knew her as a person, and not merely as "Room 203." Renting an apartment was next to impossible except through government agencies, and that way was too time-consuming. She did, however, manage to obtain a room and bath, with a separate entrance, in a private residence on Franklin near MacAlister, and Nancy Young soon became a shadowy figure, easily ignored.

She was consumed with the necessity to act immediately, even though her good common sense advised her not to rush into anything. Magda was convinced that Waldemar was not acting alone, but headed a widespread organization. It was no longer enough to expose him; his whole operation had to be smashed or her crusade would be worthless.

Impulsiveness was not part of her nature, but this time she had to force herself to plan her movements carefully. As her scheme grew more complex, she realized that she would have to appeal to the department for some aid.

She hadn't wanted to seek assistance from headquarters so soon, but she knew she would need to travel extensively. Airplane and train travel were at best unpredictable. Most of all, she missed the easy and immediately available transportation of a car, but she no longer had a driver's license, either. Magda called the secret telephone number Barry had given her.

"This is Vixen."

"Brer Fox."

They went through their coded ritual, suppressing the urge to laugh at their exchange, responding to the gravity of the situation.

"Vixen, call this number."

She dialed the number given. The voice on the other end was authoritative.

"Go ahead, Vixen, speak up."

"I need transportation and a driver's license for a Nancy Young, 5'7", dark hair, eyes, complexion, approximately 106 pounds. She requires priority on planes and trains, but nothing official which might point to any connection with the government, just in case the wallet is searched or she is captured."

"What does Nancy Young want? A tattoo?" the voice answered testily. "Contact through sources in an hour. Conversation ended."

Magda was astounded and pleased to have her requests taken so seriously. She called back in an hour.

"Tell Nancy to proceed to Trader Jack's on Van Ness. She is to be there tomorrow morning at ten-thirty sharp. Her brother, Arnold Young, has bought a car for her and will meet her there. Her brother will give her a driver's license, which she will sign. The driver's license is adequate identification. Code number on it is given to those entitled to travel priority. If she needs passport for any purpose, call again and give reason for same."

"Yes, sir."

"Conversation ended."

Magda felt her mind reeling. This was above and beyond all of her expectations. It was as though someone were pulling strings for her. At the thought, her eyes gleamed with sudden knowledge. Chappie, of course. All the way from England. Chappie! Her heart gave an unexpected lurch. Dear, wonderful Chappie.

The thought of him behind her efforts gave her flagging confidence a lift and encouraged a belief in her ability to trap Waldemar. So many times recently she had thought she must indeed be mad to think that she could out-maneuver him. And then the enduring cold flame of her hatred had burned the doubts away. That flame had lain dormant for several years, but the sight of him had ignited it once more. In everything she did, even in the few moments of relaxation, Waldemar was ever-present —an obsession which had taken precedence over love, over life itself.

The operation she had planned was slow in developing.

There was so much preparatory work to be done. One thing she knew for certain: Waldemar had proved to her that his own self-preservation was his highest priority.

Germany had been at war for over four years and was feeling the pressures of the United States' participation. Germany needed to sow discord in the country, to break down morale, to create division; it also needed vast sums of money. This was Waldemar's favorite kind of intrigue. Magda tried to put herself in Waldemar's place—how would he act? The answer was simple. Pit the victims against themselves. Milk the Jews. It was an age-old game played through centuries of victimization, but this time it had to be played with different rules. In the United States, it would have to be done covertly. Seeing this much, Magda pursued the idea further and realized that Waldemar's web could reach many possible sources of sabotage. She shuddered at the opportunities presented for it in this large country. She also knew that there were limits to the amount of information she could uncover. All she could do was to poke around the edges and try to find enough proof to make her case against him.

A courteous exchange of greetings went from the leader of San Francisco's most prestigious secret society to other Chinese societies in four major U.S. cities. The heads of these Tongs included Chinese business and political leaders, heads of charitable organizations, and underground bosses. Magda doubted that any one of them would have the resources of Dzu Bing Lok, but, if she could convince them to cooperate, their accumulation of information could be significant.

After considerable research, she had picked Los Angeles, Chicago, New York, and Washington, D.C., as likely operation points for Waldemar. Then, gambling that she was correct in her estimation of him, she had opened a small office in a dingy neighborhood in each of the four cities.

Peter Chen, as head of the imaginatively titled Gracious Goddess of Mercy Aid Society, wrote letters introducing Nancy Young as an honored worker for the good of the country. He asked the recipients for their good offices on her behalf, saying "I vouch for her honesty

417

and loyalty to both the United States and our beloved China."

Armed with the letters, she visited these men of power who frequently hid their importance behind insignificant fronts. She met them singly and she met them in groups. She knew that even the bitterest of enemies and competitors could work together, at least temporarily, given a common foe.

Nancy Young was an object of little curiosity to them —just a plain, unglamorous woman whom they were asked to befriend. They assumed that she was the middleman, a small link in some greater network. They were condescending to her because of her impure blood, but, on the whole, they tolerated her. The Chinese had so long a history of assimilation that, as long as she accepted her position in the world as a secondary, inferior person, they ignored her background.

In spite of the letter from their honored brother in San Francisco, they demanded to see some further proof. Magda had received permission to divulge to them Waldemar's close involvement with the Japanese in Shanghai, and she gave them some inkling of his overall plan for the United States. She showed them some sections of William's letters to prove that she was loyal, and interested in the affairs of China. Her own motivation was obvious as she displayed the death notice of her husband, who had been killed by a German Nazi. The article had become so frayed by now that the names were almost indecipherable.

But what gave them the impetus to act was not her personal story, though they could well understand the need to avenge her husband's murder. Instead, it was the German alliance with Japan. It was an accepted fact that Waldemar had worked hand-in-glove with the Japanese before there was even a treaty between the two countries. Add to that the fact that they felt a dual loyalty. Their new country, the United States, was also at war against Japan, and what weakened one would hurt the other.

These men had been carefully chosen by Peter and were on their honor not to discuss the situation. Their word was their bond, but it was strengthened by the implication that this operation might have been instigated by some branch of the government. No money was asked of them, and there was no risk of any sort of repercussion. It would give them great satisfaction to put obstacles in the path of the enemy.

One by one, each leader agreed to help in acquiring and sending to Nancy Young's office the type of information required. Whereupon she humbly told them that her organization, though poor, was prepared to pay a small reward for each item of interest. They nodded. It was suitable. As a person, this unpretentious woman meant nothing to them. But as the unlikely front for a major organization, she was acceptable.

The word went out to laundries, restaurants, banks, loan companies, waiters, servants, office clerks, small shop owners, businessmen, salespeople, to report all information, however trivial, regarding: new Jewish residents; new visitors to residents' homes; connections between new and old residents; sudden misfortunes; money inexplicably changing hands; meetings in homes which were not customary. They were also asked to watch for any gatherings which were not of the usual sort, or strangers meeting in groups, in fact, all information which seemed to indicate something out of the ordinary was going on.

The underlings to whom the message was addressed were at first unwilling to obey. Some were fearful of getting into trouble; others thought the items too insignificant to report—concerned that they might be thought foolish. But at the urging of the powerful secret societies to which they all belonged, a trickle of miscellaneous information drifted in. Much of it was worthless, but many dollar bills changed hands. The word spread to the underpaid, lowest levels of laborers, that money was offered—one did not have to be able to write or speak English, just to go and report what was seen, so long as there was something to tell.

Slowly, carefully, Magda gathered a nucleus of assistants to sift and collate the information.

Leaders of the Jewish communities in the four selected cities then received calls asking for private interviews on a matter of grave importance. The caller was usually a colorless young woman who introduced

419

herself as Miss Nancy Young. Her purpose was to tell them about a group of Nazi spies who impersonated Jews who had either escaped from Europe themselves or planned the escape of others. They were convincing in their roles and their credentials and papers were either authentic or so well-forged as to be undetectable.

Before she continued, stated Miss Young, she had to have the listener's assurance that the conversation remain totally confidential.

"Please do not believe me or accept my identification or credentials without checking—they could be as false as the ones I describe. I ask only that you call the head of the local FBI, or Washington, if you prefer, and insist on speaking to the chief of the identification department. Just give them my name and driver's license number."

She waited patiently while the call was made. The answer was always satisfactory. She frequently received curious glances at the improbability of a woman like herself being involved in such a high-level situation. But she, the individual, was soon forgotten as she told, in a monotone, the appalling stories of what had happened to the refugees in Shanghai. She told them of an Englishman of good faith who had been taken in, who had assisted one man into England, and who had unwittingly betrayed his own people.

"This is now going on in the United States," she said simply, and she described Waldemar as she had last seen him.

"But he is not alone—there are many of them. It is no good to remove one branch of this poisonous tree—the whole of it and its roots and its seed must be destroyed."

She had no intention of prying into anyone's personal affairs she told them, but in order to pursue these imposters she had to have information on any approach made by those who wished to give talks about Jewish relief, and where such meetings were held.

"Even if they are people known to you personally," she went on, "we promise that there will be no repercussions for members of the community. Many men of great intelligence and insight have been duped. We can see the bigger picture, but we need names to put on the faces, and addresses to pinpoint the action. The information you can give us is vital. Please don't be misguided by qualms

420

about getting anyone in trouble, nor about whose names you give us, or the places of potential meetings—the longer you delay, the more people will be destroyed."

She gave each person she spoke to the address of her office in that city and the telephone number and a parting caution that it was important to show no suspicions and to give no warnings which might alert the German agents.

Then she left as unobtrusively as she had arrived.

Ripples of disaster and stories of suicides came to her attention from different parts of the country.

Irving Katz in San Francisco was one of the tragedies. He had been a prominent member of the Jewish community and the *San Francisco Examiner* printed a long obituary on him, including an interview with a close friend who implied that Katz had been withdrawing large unaccounted for sums of money. Lately, said his friend, he had become wholly unpredictable.

"He was one of the most active members of the Temple and extremely active on behalf of the Jewish Relief from the atrocities in Nazi-held Europe, very personally involved. Then, suddenly, he had withdrawn from all activities, but shortly afterward he became sporadically active once again. Usually a man of robust health, he had lately become thin and drawn, almost gaunt."

Magda, who received the information from her sources in San Francisco, sent a copy of the article about the death of Irving Katz, who "took his life while of unsound mind" to each of the persons she had spoken to, with a typed addendum:

"A victim of the pseudo-Jewish infiltrator, and a typical example of the operation: appeal, use, implicate, blackmail, and destroy."

It was extraordinarily effective.

Magda worked tirelessly, flying from one city to another, using her lucid mind and talent for analysis and organization. She existed for this work alone. The qualities which had made her a successful investor and an outstanding cryptologist were the same that helped her in decoding Waldemar's pattern.

Pictures started to form slowly, like tiny pieces of a jigsaw puzzle coming together. Though some areas were blank, the shape was apparent. She relayed information to Brer Fox on the West Coast and Plutarch in the East, always warning them not to play their hands too soon but to gather more information on the leads she gave them.

It was slow, grueling work, but the outline of the German operation was frightening in its scope and power.

A wave of vandalism spread through the country. The news was kept under tight censorship, but enough leaked out to make people suspicious of their neighbors. Wild rumors flourished, instigated by the perpetrators of the violence.

Americans who, by age or physical handicaps, were prevented from fighting for their country, were lured into joining secret groups, induced by their very patriotism to work on what they thought were important missions for their country. Their participation always ended in some disaster. Minor ones mostly, but their proliferation throughout the country posed a major hazard to the war effort. In terms of human values, it left a bewildered and frightened people, crushed by their unwitting acts of betrayal and subject to the pressure of blackmail.

The massive Nazi underground movement was apparently untouched by any of the government ploys to halt their activities, but U.S. Intelligence, alerted initially by Operation Vixen, was putting together its own network to counterattack, which had supplied them with a great deal of damning evidence. Preparations were underway for an overall crackdown on this insidious movement that was designed to undermine public confidence by turning all ethnic and minority groups against each other through the use of propaganda. There was some pressure on Operation Vixen to work more closely with the department, but its spokesman, the quiet Miss Young, faded into deeper obscurity, and the operation was permitted to function as it had been.

From London, Chapin started a letter to Magda:

"It is, as you suggest, first an appeal to the most dedicated, the most fanatic of patriots—to get them involved . . ." He broke off.

"Why the devil am I writing to her, when I should be

422

over there with her?" Chapin demanded of himself. And he tore up the letter.

From what he knew from his own sources, the case on which Magda was working was coming to a close. He considered every angle and decided it was justified that he go to Washington to be in on the kill. He damned himself for letting the Waldemar affair spiral out of his control; he damned himself for permitting Magda to go underground and put herself in extreme danger; but, most of all, he damned himself for not having gone to the States when he had first proposed it. Magda had been eager and ready then.

"Hindsight is a waste of time," he decided, and he made arrangements to leave London. He sent word to Magda to meet him in Washington and hopped a ride on a transport plane that night.

To Chapin's great disappointment, Magda's secretary, a nondescript woman named Nancy Young, came in Magda's stead.

She gave all the proper signals, all the proper answers, but he was not interested in espionage at that moment. He wanted to see Magda. He was more disappointed than he thought himself capable of being and made no attempt to keep his anger from showing.

"You've given me all the right responses, but they can be easily duplicated by a professional agent. How do I know you are really Nancy Young, or that Nancy Young is really a friend of Magda's? You may have forced information from her, for all I know," he growled, not believing a word he was saying.

"Mrs. Bentley thought you might feel that way, sir, so she told me to say this: 'A vixen is a female fox, shrewder and more deadly.' " That had been one of their jokes.

Chapin looked at the woman, unreasonably wanting to hurt her for Magda's intransigence. Her eyes behind the bifocals were enlarged to a startling degree. He turned away in disgust as she mouthed the words in a monotone.

"Very well," he said curtly. "Give her this letter. It's private." He waved his dismissal.

"Mrs. Bentley told me to say, as soon as I was convinced you were really Chapin Desmond, that she was

423

delighted you came in person because the roundup—I'm sure she said 'roundup'—would take place soon, and she wanted you to direct it personally. She asks you to stay for a week, because it will take place sometime during that time. If you are here, she says she knows she can leave it entirely up to you."

"Did she also tell you why she hasn't the courtesy to give me the message personally, if it is that important to her? You may tell Mrs. Bentley that I am honored by her trust. But surely she knows, or should know, that I am a guest in this country and could no more take the lead than an American could direct proceedings in Britain. You may also tell her that I am extremely angry and hurt that she could not arrange to see me. Tell her that it's been too long, and I am very tired— Of course, you will tell her none of that rot. Forget everything I've said."

He shook his head as though to clear it. "I must be batty," he muttered to himself. Then, in a firm voice, he said. "You will tell Mrs. Bentley to go through the usual channels. She must remember that this is their country, and that I trust she will act accordingly."

"Yes, sir. I am not to give her the more personal messages?" the woman asked in a voice so low he could barely hear her.

"Correct. That's all." He stood up to dismiss her.

Miss Young stood up awkwardly—a little shakily. "She— I mean—"

"Yes? Well? What is it?" he asked irritably.

"There is one final thing Mrs. Bentley asked me to do. I hope you won't mind, sir, but she asked me to do this for her."

She went over, put her arms around him, and kissed him. Her mouth was unexpectedly full and soft. Chapin found himself, unconsciously, responding with hungry passion. His arms tightened around her and their lips clung together. Her body seemed to melt in his arms. The woman slowly pulled herself away. Her glasses slipped, and for a fleeting moment Chapin saw a pair of huge dark eyes, luminous, strangely familiar. Quickly, she pushed her glasses back on, almost fearfully.

The woman stepped backward, and her voice faltered as she said: "She also told me to tell you it is the only way." With that, she ran out of the room with amazing speed and grace.

Chapin was still shaken by his own extraordinary reaction. He could only stare after her. "What on earth had got into Magda to—My God! That was Magda herself you bloody idiot! How could I have been so blind?" He sprang from the seat into which he had fallen in his surprise, and went racing down the hall. A guard stopped him.

"Did you see—?" Chapin started to shout.

"Did I see whom, sir?"

"That woman who passed—?" His voice broke.

"Is there anything wrong, sir?" the guard asked stiffly.

"Sorry, officer. Something she said—it's all right. I remember now—quite . . ." He let the sentence die away, and returned to the office. "That was an asinine thing to do," he said to himself. "I almost succeeded in making her a suspect."

He shook his head again, and a soft look came into his eyes. So she couldn't deny coming down even if it endangered her cover and her disguise! He still savored the soft lips pressing hard against his. His instincts were better than his eyes. But why? What did she mean? He had to find her immediately.

9 A.M. June 16th, 1944:

"This is Vixen."

"Plutarch."

"The official time on the tenth meridian is 2:19 A.M."

"Not on your tin hat. The time is the day before yesterday."

"Very well, Vixen, what is it?"

"I wanted to make certain again about the time."

"All set for fourteen hundred hours on the dot. The other cities are synchronized timewise. We all hit at once." The voice made no attempt to hide his tenseness.

"Vixen?"

"Yes, Plutarch?"

"Good work."

"Thank you."

10 A.M.:

Now for her final moves. Once again, she went

through all the same arguments. Seeing Chapin again had almost weakened her resolve. She added up all the pros and cons and it came out the same. It had to happen the way she had planned it—as if it were preordained.

10:30 A.M.:

Nancy Young had been working for Waldemar for three weeks, placed in his office by the man who was sponsoring his latest schedule of talks. She entered through the front door quietly, hoping not to disturb him.

Since arranging to work for Waldemar, she had gotten a set of dentures which fitted over her own teeth perfectly. The false upper teeth protruded enough to change the contour of her face completely. Waldemar was far too perceptive for her to take any risks.

Waldemar came out into the hallway as she entered. He looked extremely upset, as though something was making him nervous. She had never seen him like this before.

"What the hell are you doing here? I thought I told you not to come in today. Go home," he ordered.

"Mr. Blumenthal particularly wanted the accounts today, sir." She didn't have to pretend; she was quailing under the ruthless tyranny that was his stock in trade.

"Mr. Blumenthal and his accounts are expendable . . . Mr. Blumenthal . . . well, don't stand there like a useless object, get on with them and don't bother me."

Those damn Jews and their accounts. That swine would soon see what he could do with his accounts. Waldemar's lips stretched in a thin smile.

Something seemed to prickle his spine with the threat of danger. He had felt it all day, and he trusted his instincts. They had served him well in the past. There was something in the air. He sniffed it, as though he could smell a tangible, acrid stench.

His two bodyguards lumbered in from their posts to show their vigilance; one entered from a room facing the front of the house, one from the rear. Waldemar snarled for them to get back to their stations. "Or," he asked with heavy sarcasm, "do you think I cannot protect myself from this nondescript woman?"

She could see them cower in the face of Waldemar's

ferocity and they returned to their posts. They were better off keeping out of his way today.

Nancy Young went to her small office with its adjoining door to Waldemar's. She set her bag carefully within reach, took off her gloves and placed them on top of it, then went about her preparations. For the several weeks she had worked for Waldemar, she had made a practice of brewing fresh coffee and bringing a cup laced with brandy to each of the guards, along with a fresh doughnut or a piece of coffee cake. So humbly and quietly did she bring her offerings every morning that it didn't elicit so much as a grunt from the men, who, endearingly, had nicknamed her "Buck Tooth."

She brought a tray to each man this morning with a thick slice of apple strudel, made especially with a rich filling and studded heavily with nuts. She waited until she saw them starting to devour the cake, then returned to her office to fetch the coffee urn to freshen their cups. If Waldemar saw her, he paid no attention to the familiar routine. She slipped back into the rear room, carefully closing the door behind her. Her eyes gleamed behind her glasses. The guard had been completely knocked out, his mouth agape, his eyes closed, a piece of the strudel still held in one hand. She hoped it wasn't an overdose; she wanted him up and about before the trap was sprung.

She removed the coffee cup and the cake and closed the door behind her, her heart pounding so hard that she felt her ears pop. Then, drawing a slow breath, she went to the front room and repeated the procedure with the other guard, who likewise had fallen into a heavy sleep.

The whole action took less than five minutes.

She returned to her office and spent a few minutes washing the cups and putting everything neatly away. It could have been done later, but she needed the few minutes to steady her nerves.

Suddenly, she stiffened and turned around. Waldemar was watching her from the doorway between their offices—his eyes glazed, not really focusing. She shuddered. It was as though he had antennae searching the air, picking up the unknown—something was troubling him and his nostrils flared, like those of an animal scenting danger.

"Did you want something, sir?" She peered at him

427

questioningly through her bifocals. She kept her voice calm but was frightened to the point of fainting. She knew his incalculably rapid reactions.

"No! No! Hurry up. You are a nuisance. Get done and get out."

"Yes, sir."

She waited until he reached his office through the open door. She heard his chair creak as he sat down heavily.

Now! Now, Magda! Now! The flame within her sparked and rose high. The time had come.

She put on her gloves, opened the purse, and took out a handkerchief, leaving the bag open. She had not yet removed her hat. She entered Waldemar's office. He was sitting, alert, at his desk, drumming his fingers on it. He was staring into space as if straining for a message he could not quite understand.

He started as she spoke, and his look of concentration deserted him.

"If you don't mind, sir. I think I shall do as you wish and leave now."

"Don't bother me. Do as you want," he growled. He looked at her. *Gott in Himmel!* What an unappetizing piece! If that swine Blumenthal insisted on shoving someone on him to do the damned accounts, he could at least have provided him with some . . .

The woman removed her glasses and something from her mouth and drew a gun from her handbag. He watched her, unbelieving, when he saw the gun. The danger he had smelled all day was suddenly a reality. His eyes narrowed, his lips stretched in a snarling grin, showing his teeth like the teeth of a menacing wolverine at bay. A strange animal sound gurgled in his throat.

Magda could almost see his muscles readying to leap at her. She raised her hand steadily and took careful aim.

Don't wait, she warned herself. Don't wait, she screamed inwardly. Fire now. But there was still one satisfaction she had to have, or it would all be meaningless.

"Remember Magda," she said, but even before she could get the words out, the look of stunned recognition crossed his face. He mouthed "Magda" as though it was choking him and started forward, his eyes blazing with satanic fury.

Magda hesitated no longer—but with steady hand took

aim and pulled the trigger. She felt the sharp recoil, and through it, she could almost feel the contact of bullet tearing through bone. He was still moving. She fired again.

She watched, mesmerized, as the neat black holes appeared miraculously in the center of his forehead. She saw blood gush out, saw his body leap in a final spasmodic jump, his hands clawing out to reach her, as though he could not permit defeat by death itself. For a moment, the frightening thought reached her brain that he really was invincible. She fired again, and, even as she did so, she saw the body slump back, half in the chair, half over the desk.

She watched him for a moment without breathing. She as motionless in life as he was in death. The hatred which had motivated her for so long still smoldered, still burned. It was physical. Total. Consuming. And it was over. Over. She could feel it slowly subside and flicker before it died.

Magda gave a deep sigh as though releasing her breath after an eternity.

Carefully, she laid the gun down.

No need to make the police waste time searching for the weapon. She had bought it some time ago in a pawnshop when she knew what she had to do. She could not even remember in which city. It didn't matter; the number had been filed off a long time ago by someone other than herself.

She walked slowly to the fallen body.

"That was for Max." She recited each word as though delivering a eulogy. "That was the way it happened with him, wasn't it?" she continued conversationally. "Only you leaped up and jumped him. Some might call it self-defense, but you had destroyed him long before. What was it Max wrote? 'There would be so many to congratulate him for doing the deed.' I finished it for him. There is no one to grieve for you, Waldemar, only feelings of joy at your death."

She had wondered how she would feel about taking a human life. Would she be suffused with guilt? Would she shake and shiver in the aftermath? Would she weep perhaps? Or be shocked at what she had done?

Magda studied her reactions curiously and objectively. All she felt was great satisfaction and relief that it was over. If anything, she felt purged. The world would be a better place with that mad animal dead. She did not try to justify her actions by saying she did not trust the slow machinery of the law. She had always known, from the very beginning, so long ago, that the final blow had to come from her. For that, she had forfeited her last chance for contentment and happiness, her child, and perhaps even her life.

She felt no tremor of remorse, though—only satisfaction that she had not wavered.

She had covered her movements well. Only the drugging of the bodyguard could point to her; however, the man who had supplied the knock-out drops knew his business. He told her that they would be groggy, but conscious in approximately three hours. That left plenty of time for them to discover the dead body. If they were not fools, they would run away—not only from being arrested by the authorities for murder, but, even more terrifying, from being found guilty by their own people of extreme negligence.

If not . . . Magda shrugged. It was the risk she took. She was prepared to face whatever happened.

The time had not come to fully gauge the price.

>>>>>>>>>>>>>>>>>>>>>>>>>>>>>>>>>>>>>>

EPILOGUE

London

1945

>>>>>>>>>>>>>>>>>>>>>>>>>>>>>>>>>>>>>>

CHAPTER THIRTY-TWO

<<<<<<<<<<<<<<<<<<<<<<<<<<<<<<<

CHAPIN WAS TOLD of Waldemar's murder on the day it occurred. No one was aware that, under his imperturbable facade, his blood was chilled with a sense of foreboding.

The department was jubilant over their successful rout of the massive spy ring. Operation Vixen went into limbo, and Nancy Young disappeared along with it.

For several days, Chapin searched for the quiet little secretary. Many recalled her vaguely, but no one had known her well and they had difficulty remembering anything definite about her.

Chapin's questions had to be understated since he didn't want to bring her to the attention of the curious. But he wanted desperately to see her; to tell her that nothing mattered and that he would stand by her.

Chapin wanted to go to San Francisco. He felt his search would have to start from there to have any validity. He wanted to see Peter and Estelle Chen, of whom Magda had written many times—maybe they could help him. All this he wanted to do, but primarily, he wanted to take Magda back to England with him. He wanted to tell her that he would retire to his estate in Scotland as soon as possible, so that there would be no conflict of loyalties; that he would protect her; and that he would be a loving father to Pauline.

But he met with failure, and, heavy-hearted, Chapin returned home alone and lonely, even more so for the brief moment of hope he had known. He had no doubt though, that Magda had been responsible for Waldemar's death.

Chapin had been an important public servant for too many years to ignore his duty. Too much was happening in the war zone for Chapin to delay his departure any longer. The war in Europe waged fiercely on. The tides were turning for the Allies. Germany lost North Africa. Mussolini was deposed. Russia had routed the Germans from their land and was now taking the offensive. In England the damaging blitz was reversed, and Germany felt the full brunt as the RAF and the Army Air Force filled the skies in reprisal.

For months, Chapin continued to write to Magda, using addresses that had worked before, but mostly the post-office box in San Francisco. His letters were not returned. He received no answers, but at least he preserved a forlorn hope that she was reading her mail and knew how he felt. He understood her pride and knew that she would never come back to him if she thought she'd be a burden.

He picked up his routine and once again submerged himself in his job, but nothing lessened the emptiness in his life. In time, he knew, the void would shrink. In time, perhaps, the memory of Magda would fade; but that he regretted. He preferred the pain of loss and the chaos of his emotions to the man he had been—a man whose needs had been satisfied only by the challenges of his work and who had become more self-contained, more impervious to human relations, as the years had rolled on.

Before meeting Magda, he had never known his capacity to love, nor that any love could become so important that he would willingly sacrifice his career for its sake.

He questioned himself reluctantly. How long would that have lasted before regret for his lost career set in? He had no answer—no way of knowing. And now it seemed academic, anyway.

Every weekend, when he was free to do so, he escaped to his cottage in the country, where he had spent so many delightful days with Magda. Each time that he stopped at the post office in Chelsea to check his private mailbox, his pulse quickened. There was always the dim hope that something from Magda would be there. He refused to believe she would cut all ties with him so completely; yet, she had done no less with her own daughter. He had learned that what she promised, she invariably did.

Chapin's mind was very much on Magda on the cold, wet afternoon of January 14, 1945. Things on the war front were hectic. Chapin was now officially the head of M-17, and privy to sessions among the top military brass. He had been alerted to the plans being made for a massive invasion of France, and the war's end seemed less distant than ever.

His department was humming. The responsibility was heavy and the work load staggering. It was almost a pleasure to turn to his own personal ache, the deeply rooted ache which seemed to have become part of him, but was never so intense as when he neared the post office. He kept repeating "Let there be something from her—just a word—please let there be something," as if it were a prayer.

He drew out his accumulated mail. In the midst of it, there was an unusually thick envelope, a large sealed one, almost a package. With his heart pounding, he separated it from the pile and, sure enough, it was addressed to him in Magda's script—as exquisite and clear-cut as he remembered it.

Chapin sailed out of the post office in a state of immeasurable relief and drove to his cottage. His caretaker had, as always, lit a fire in the grate before leaving. There was a hot meal warming in the oven—but food was far from Chapin's mind. It took every ounce of self-discipline to resist the impulse to tear open the envelope. He swallowed his anticipation as he followed his usual routine, took a hot bath and dressed in comfortable slacks and smoking-jacket. A tray of assorted liquors had been placed by his easy chair in front of the fireplace. He sat down and poured a drink, now relishing each moment of postponement, the better to savor the fact that the letter was from Magda herself, the better to hear her voice in every word she wrote.

He filled his pipe very carefully with his special blend of tobacco, and only then, after it drew to his satisfaction, did he pry open the seals without breaking them. Carefully he opened the envelope without tearing it and withdrew the contents.

434

There were several envelopes enclosed, and man
pages of close writing to him. Ignoring his disappoint
ment that it was not all for him, he started to read:

Chapin:
How do I begin? Are there any adequate words? Deep
in my veins, in my heart, my nerves, in the recesses of
my mind, you are alive in me and are part of me, and
you always will be. But this I do know; that we must
tread different paths. I have agonized over this, as I
read and reread your letters, which I had delivered to
me, hoping somehow it would turn out differently. You
must try to understand—may already have understood,
perhaps—that my road and yours can never meet again.
The neat thread of your life is forever in England, and
the scrambled skein of mine must unravel itself in so
many other places.

Chapin put down the letter with a sense of deep anguish—but not surprise—the knowledge confirmed, at
last, that the tiny ray of hope was being snuffed out. He
stared blankly into the fire, and a deep resolution filled
him—he would not permit the hope to be extinguished so
easily. He read on:

I took the law into my own hands, and you, my dearest,
are a man of the law, a very dedicated man of the law
—it is part of you. I made my choice many months ago,
forswearing all else. Only once did I weaken, when I
went to see you in Washington. It was foolish and rash of
me—but it was one moment I could not deny myself.

"I was the fool, the bloody fool who let you go," he
muttered under his breath, so stirred he could hardly read
on.

I do not wish to say anything to explain my action; if I
had the chance to do it again, I would.

Chapin scanned the next page rapidly, but some
phrases and words caught his eye.

. . . he did not kill in anger or hunger, even as a rabid

435

imal does . . . he enjoyed destroying a person first . . .
here can be nothing so terrible as living in a state of
sustained fear . . .

Unexpectedly shocked out of his usual composure,
Chapin found himself gripped by a mindless fury. As if
from a distance, he saw his hands clench, his knuckles
whiten, and something inside exploded: a desperate need
for personal vengeance against Waldemar—that man—
what he had done to Magda, and through her, to Chapin
—even in death, his evil genius was destroying their hopes.

Chapin shuddered. Get a grip on yourself, old man,
he prodded himself. This isn't doing any good, he
thought sadly. His pipe had gone out, and he relit it with
fingers still shaking from his explosion of impotent rage.
He poured himself a stiff drink and gulped it down. Ah,
Magda, Magda! I, too, could have killed him. Once again,
he picked up her letter.

I will say no more on the subject lest my hard-won
tranquility be destroyed. Chappie, dear, it is lovely here.
I am in a retreat high up in the hills. I cannot tell you
where it is. Only a few are permitted here as guests. I
was recommended and accepted and was asked no questions. It is a private place, totally secluded. The hills bear
a thick carpet of trees, and, beyond them, in the far distance, the snow-capped mountains blend into the clouds
above.

Here, I am at harmony with the elements. It is a place
to cleanse oneself spiritually and physically. I came here
in a state of mental exhaustion. For weeks I denied myself all thought, until my mind was at last clear of the
cobwebs of worry, sorrow, misgivings, and hatred. Three
times a day, in front of my door, someone places a covered bowl of plain rice and vegetables and a pot of tea.
I've walked daily until my body ached and sat in steam
rooms until I was weak. The day finally came when I
awoke in the morning and felt renewed, with the sense of
quiet order around me.

I saw the workers in the groves of fruit trees and
in the greenhouses and the gardens. Some work as laborers, some are skilled technicians. If I approach them,
they are courteous, but few words are spoken.

There is a little temple here for those who wish to pray, but, other than that, it is a refuge for those who seek another way of life. I feel no need for words of prayer. The glory of Nature sows a seed, and whatever blooms is too complicated and too perfect to be an accident.

It pleases me to watch the people at their work, especially the botanists who are experimenting with grafting. I see them make incisions and fit branches of different fruit trees on the mother tree. It is amazing to think that on one tree there will be peaches and apricots and loquats, all taking their nourishment from the same roots.

Sometimes I daydream. I see a seed of heather being blown by a careless wind from the cold north of the West, and by accident landing in the warm south of the East, and, there, being pollinated with the bamboo. An exotic mixture—the tall, flexible bamboo, which serves man with its edible root, its useful trunk, and the branches above. The bamboo tree does not fight the wind, but sways with it, flexing as it changes direction. It remains alive while sturdier trees split in the storm and die.

Can you imagine it mated to the indomitable heather, which grows low in the heaths of Scotland! Every year the heather pushes its tender head stubbornly through drifts of snow and sleet, mindless of the harshness of earth and weather. With its feathery lavenders and spicy perfume, it softens the bleakness of the endless moors. It is a strange combination, the silvery green of the leafy bamboo and the rich pastels of the heather.

To the tangled roots of my own tree of life was grafted a branch of wild English rose—my Polly. Surely the flexibility of the bamboo and the fierce determination of the heather, added to the delicacy and perfume of the rose, must bring forth a flower of such essence as was never before conceived. In my dream, I see a vast tree of life to which branches from all over the world are grafted —all nourished from the same roots, all borne by the mother tree.

When one thinks of the winds of chance which have seeded the world for eons, one knows there is no such thing as a pure race. If it existed, it would be a poor and meager thing, thin-blooded, drawing constantly from its wn sap, never enriching its bloodlines with new vibrant forces.

Today, as I am now, I wonder at the grief I suffered, at the intolerance I encountered. How futile it all seems. If we could *truly* trace back the bloodlines through the millenia, what would we find? Certainly Asiatics invaded the plains of Europe. Surely the Occidental invaded the far purlieus of the East, and we all know that, at the height of their power, the people of the Middle East brought in, for their pleasures, beautiful women from all over the world.

I stand, today, in my own image, not the half-and-half my poor father despaired of, but as one person, myself, responsible only to myself, and not to any one culture. Chapin, when I knew I was bearing a child, my only wish—no, it was more than a wish—a vow—that my child should not endure the agonies of my twin heritage. I wanted to smother her origins. But, today, I want her to know of her rich descent.

I have now reached the business portion of this long, long letter. It feels so good to be writing to you again, even if it's for the last time. I have no wish to hurry, for, while I write, you sit across from me. I am talking to you, and I can see the quizzical look on your face. How wordy I have become!

I think I know where you are as you read this letter. Are you not at your cottage, where we spent so many days? You are sitting in front of the fire, I know. Give it a good raking, Chappie, it's cold and dreary outside. There is a drink of whiskey on the table beside you. Take a good swallow, for I am about to place a burden on you. I hope you will not find it too great. The trusteeship we discussed before I left England has been activated, and you are now, as of this date, in full control of my estate, to be paid a salary to cover the expenses of a clerk and whatever other expenses are entailed. (Please don't mind this; the lawyer insisted.)

Instructions as to the handling and disposal of my estate are all detailed and enclosed in a separate envelope as is a list of my securities amounting variously . . .

Chapin's eyes widened as he glanced at the sums of

money involved. He turned the pages impatiently. could all be left for later.

Far more important to me than the management of my money is the knowledge that, as trustee, you will be in contact with your goddaughter.

If I never see you again, my dearest love, I shall have the satisfaction of knowing that Polly is in your life, that she will share in some small part the richness of your mind, your loyalty, and your love. I know that Tasha and Barry will be loving parents to her—she could have no better—but it is with you I share her, not with them. When the war ends—I think it must be soon—and your time is more your own, please do try to see her occasionally. I enclose a letter to the Winters asking them, when Polly is older (and, of course, if you desire it) that she pay a yearly visit to England, so that she may know the country I learned to cherish . . .

You know I'll find a way. Of that you may be certain, Magda. There'll be no trouble, Chapin promised her across the miles.

I think I should clarify the annual deposits I requested you to make to my Swiss bank account. I opened it in the dark days of Shanghai—information as to the code number and name is enclosed in another envelope. It is known only to you and to me, and to my Swiss friends who arranged it for me in the first place. My account there is fairly healthy, but I do not know what my needs will be in the future, and I must provide for the unknown. I have not removed any substantial sums from the bank in recent months, because money can be the simplest way to trace someone, and I choose not to have my whereabouts known.

I beg you not to try to find me. I know too well your capabilities, dear heart, so all I can do is to plead with you. I shall disappear. Should I live and be free to communicate, I shall do so through Otto Aberzant of Lucerne and Geneva. He is a friend of mine from the past, when I was a lonely child in Switzerland. I used to visit the Bourse whenever possible; it was the only place where I felt on familiar ground. Otto befriended me. His son

439

cripple and the most gentle and brilliant person I
w. I have sent them full copies of all my instructions
you, to be opened by them only in the event of your
eath. (My heart screams even as I write those words.)

I hope the war will be over soon, and when time per-
mits, that you visit them. I am sure you will enjoy knowing them, and any word from me (which I must repeat is
most unlikely) will come through them.

And that, my love, about covers it.

The one last and important charge I make to you, over
and above all else, is to see that Polly receives the enclosed, sealed letter in her eighteenth year, from your own
hand, when she is young enough to receive ideas and old
enough to understand; but you will know her well enough
to be able to judge her maturity. (How I wish I could
materialize then. Might it be possible? Give her a kiss
from me, wherever I am.) It would give me such great
happiness if I knew you were with her when she reads it.
I want her to know that I did not give her away idly. I
want her to know what I intend to do in these interven-
ing years. Above all, I want her to take pride in her heritage, and the vibrant bloodlines which enrich and mingle
in her.

And to you, my dearest Chappie, I leave the regret
of our unconsummated love. I learned to love you in a
way I had never known; to respect and honor you, my
most trusted friend, and gradually to know that friendship alone was not all I wanted to share with you.

You stand tall before me, taller than the tallest tree in
this land of trees. Frequently, the thought of what life
with you and Polly could be has dimmed out even the
vision of my purpose; blotted out even the snow-capped
mountains which grace the world around me. But they are
just dreams, and I have become strong enough at last to
erase the what-might-have-been from my life.

Tomorrow, I leave this place. With me, I take the
golden penny you sent me, and which I value above all I
possess. It is the only thing of the past I shall carry with
me into the future, except for the good memories. I see no
reason to discard them—they carry their own riches and
their own seeds—for from the seeds of yesterday, the
bright promise of today is born.

Chapin closed his eyes for a moment, his head throbbing with vehement denials. He had loved her too long, too silently, too patiently.

As I write these words, I feel you are here with me. Each time I think of you, and there will be many, it won't be with regret for what might have been, but with undying joy and gratitude that you thought me worthy of your tenderness.

So, here I am, Chappie, ready to write *finis* to one book of my life and prepared to open the first page of another.

I know where my road leads, but whether I will arrive there, who can say? The way is difficult. Of this I am certain.

I hope you find a companion in your life—I shall envy her—but keep aside for me one small, warm place in your heart, where, in moments of loneliness in the years ahead, I may curl up knowing the warmth and solace of your love. My greatest treasure. Always . . .

Magda

Bestsellers from BALLANTINE